THE DIVIDE

THE DIVIDE

A Novel

Morgan Richter

Alfred A. Knopf
New York
2024

THIS IS A BORZOI BOOK
PUBLISHED BY ALFRED A. KNOPF

www.aaknopf.com

Library of Congress Cataloging-in-Publication Data
Name: Richter, Morgan, author.
Title: The divide : a novel / Morgan Richter.
Description: New York : Alfred A. Knopf, 2024.
Identifiers: LCCN 2023031560 (print) | LCCN 2023031561 (ebook) |
ISBN 9780593685679 (hardcover) | ISBN 9780593685686 (ebook)
Subjects: LCGFT: Novels. | Detective and mystery fiction.
Classification: LCC PS3618.I3637 D58 2024 (print) |
LCC PS3618.I3637 (ebook) | DDC 813/.6—dc23/eng/20230731
LC record available at https://lccn.loc.gov/2023031560
LC ebook record available at https://lccn.loc.gov/2023031561

Jacket photograph by Sammy Salgado Jr.
Jacket design by Mark Abrams

Manufactured in the United States of America
First Edition

To Mom, Dad, and Ingrid

THE DIVIDE

CHAPTER 1

Some Kind of Actress

The first Tuesday of November, it hit ninety-six degrees. The woman in the silk racer-back sundress in front of me in line at the Shell station on Fairfax that morning told the weary, sweaty kid working the register that it was okay, even good, because it was a dry heat. That it would cool off at night, that we're lucky to live in Los Angeles instead of someplace that has to deal with snow and ice for Thanksgiving. I don't know who that woman was, but I know her home has air conditioning.

My clinic was stuffy and stifling and, I was aware, a little smelly. The blue nylon carpet hadn't looked new at the start of my lease six years ago, and while I ran a handheld carpet sweeper over the floor each morning, it'd been three years, maybe four, since I'd rented a professional steamer to deep-clean all the accumulated grime and stink away. As the small room heated up, the sour funk grew more pungent. It smelled like failed hopes, or the unventilated fitness center in an airport hotel geared toward business travelers on a budget. If I'd had any clients scheduled for the afternoon, I'd have lighted some incense to cover it up.

No one was scheduled. I sat at my little table, my tarot deck resting on the white plastic surface, hoping for walk-ins while trying to ignore the smell.

The woman who entered my clinic looked like the type who'd have strong opinions about the odor. She stood in the doorway and stared at me with what looked like surprised annoyance, as though she'd arrived home to find a despised ex-lover sitting in her living room.

"Hello," I called out to her, smiling and professionally pleasant. "Care for a reading?" I gestured at the tarot deck.

She stared at me a moment longer, then closed the door behind her and stepped into the room. She glanced around the clinic. She looked first at the three-foot plastic statue of Kali I kept in the corner. It had been dark brown when I'd picked it up at a yard sale, but I'd spray-painted it copper, and from a few feet away it looked like it could be made of hammered metal. It was surrounded by clean white pillar candles. Those had come from the 99 Cents Only store; the glass holders had been emblazoned with shrink-wrapped images of the Virgin of Guadalupe and Olaf from *Frozen*, but I'd sliced off the shrink-wrap with a razor, and now, arranged in a cluster, they looked tasteful, like I'd paid seventeen bucks apiece for them at the kind of store that sold hand-woven yoga mats and water bottles made of marble.

When she spoke at last, her tone was just a hair shy of hostile. "I don't have an appointment."

"I can squeeze you in," I said. "What can I help you with?"

She pulled out the chair opposite me and sat. Her skin was deep brown, and it glowed like she'd just come from an afternoon at a spa. She kept her hair in glossy box braids pulled back and secured at the nape of her neck in a twist. She wore a well-cut navy suit, not expensive but not cheap, over a button-down shirt the color of fresh cream. She folded her hands on the clean white plastic tabletop and leaned forward slightly. She locked her eyes with mine. "My mother passed on six months ago. I'd like to see how she's doing."

I was shaking my head before she'd finished her sentence. "Sorry. I don't talk to the dead."

"Don't, or can't?"

"It's not a service I offer. Is there anything else I can do for you?"

"I thought all you people talked to spirits." It was antagonistic. After a pause, the woman smiled. She smiled like she'd learned the basics from observing people, but had never understood there was more to it than just the coordinated movement of a group of facial muscles. It didn't touch her eyes.

"Some do. It's not in my particular bag of tricks." I tried to look serene and composed, though I was sweating too much. My indigo linen tunic, selected off the Goodwill racks because I thought it looked like the kind of shirt someone effortlessly chic and in possession of a lot of disposable income would wear, clung to the wet space between my breasts. I shifted in my chair and tried to discreetly pull the fabric away from my body.

"I'm an intuitive counselor. Think of me as a life coach, one who can give you insights into your past, present, and future." It sounded smooth and well-rehearsed. A variation on that speech was on the homepage of my business website, for which I paid $12.98 per month in hosting fees.

The woman nodded. "Okay, I get that, I want that," she said. "What do you charge to tell me about myself?"

"For an initial half-hour consultation, that's fifty dollars. Beyond that, it depends. Every client's needs are different."

She stared at me again, and I felt an almost visceral contempt radiating from her. Some people can't stand psychics, though I didn't see that too often with my clients; by the time someone walked into my clinic, their mind was at least open to the possibility we aren't all total frauds.

This woman, though. She knew I was a fraud, which made

it interesting when she placed her pebbled leather shoulder bag on her lap, removed her billfold, and counted out two crisp twenty-dollar bills and a pair of fives, which she placed on the table between us.

I didn't touch it. "You can pay me afterward at the register. There will be sales tax, too." In truth, I was generally happy to skip the tax and pocket the cash, but warning bells were telling me to tread carefully.

Because this woman was a cop. She didn't look like a cop, but she had the body language of one, that aggressive yet hyper-wary confidence that characterized every police officer I've ever encountered. Not that my experience was extensive; I'd never run into any legal trouble, probably because I'd flown beneath all possible radars. Psychics do get arrested sometimes, but usually that's because someone's been cheated in an egregious way, their life savings drained, their bank accounts closed, their property deeds signed over.

I hadn't taken anyone's life savings, just small nibbles of their cash. Nothing anyone didn't have to spare, and I always gave clients good value for their money. Good enough, at least.

I thought about turning the woman away by telling her I didn't like her aura, but that might not be enough to get her out of my hair, and besides, I was curious. "What do you want to know about yourself?"

"Whatever you can tell me. You're the psychic. Tell me who I am. Tell me what I came here for." The corner of her mouth pulled in a faint sarcastic quirk.

"You got it." I reached my hand across the table. She hesitated, then extended hers, palm up. I took it lightly and examined it. Her skin was cool and dry to the touch. By comparison, my hand was a sweaty, meaty paw.

There were certain trappings of the psychic trade I avoided. No crystal balls, no astrology, absolutely no chats with spirits. I tried to exist in a nebulous zone between clinical and New-Agey, aiming for a clientele of upwardly mobile women who were too pragmatic to *really* believe in the occult, but who, as they liked to tell their friends over glasses of sulfite-free wine, kept their minds open to all possibilities.

Palm reading existed on the border of acceptability. Early on, when I'd started this endeavor, I'd checked out a bunch of dusty books on palmistry from the library and had been unconvinced by all of them. But clients expected me to look at their hands, so I'd trained myself to go through the motions.

I raised my eyes and met the woman's stare. "Your mother is very much alive. You were setting a trap for me, because you love your mother and feel protective of her, and if I'd claimed to be in contact with her spirit, it would have validated your belief that I'm a fraud."

Her face was immobile. You'd swear I hadn't spoken at all. I continued.

"As for who you are, you consider yourself a star in your field. You're arrogant about your abilities and your accomplishments, but you have reason to be. Your coworkers don't like you much, but you don't lose sleep over that, because you don't like them either. You don't fit in; you're smarter than them. You dress better than them. Your worldview is uncompromising, but with reason, because you see the worst of humanity on a daily basis. The spirit realm doesn't exist for you. Under usual circumstances, you'd never bother with someone like me, but today you're here in your professional capacity with the LAPD." I released her palm and sat back. "Will that do?"

"You messed it up at the end," she said. She seemed calm and unruffled, but I'd felt the tingle of wary excitement coming through her hand as I'd told her about herself. "Los Angeles County Sheriff's Department. Other than that, good guesses. Though maybe you had reason to suspect a visit from the police."

"Can't say I did. The psychic realm is hazy as to why you're here."

She reached into her suit coat, extracted a wallet, opened it, and held it out to me. I stared at her badge and license. Detective Toni Moreau.

"Nice to meet you, Detective Moreau," I said. "I'm Jenny St. John. Maybe you knew that already."

She didn't acknowledge me. "How long have you been in the psychic business?"

"If you're asking how long I've been a psychic? Since birth. If you're asking how long I've been making a living from it, six years."

"Before that, you were some kind of actress." It wasn't a question.

"Some kind, yeah. A long time ago. Twenty-five years ago, I starred in an independent film. That's my only credit."

"*The Divide*," Moreau said.

My brows raised. "Right, *The Divide*, exactly. You've seen it?"

I felt a twinge of disappointment when Moreau shook her head. I shrugged. "That's no surprise, I guess. You're just about the first person I've met who has even heard of it. It never made it into theaters. A couple months before it was supposed to be released, the production company went bankrupt and shelved it."

"The director got pretty famous later on though, didn't he?" Moreau's tone was very dry.

"Yeah. It was Serge Grumet's first film." I blinked. "Oh! Are you here about Serge?"

She nodded. "I'm investigating his murder. You heard about that?"

"I read about it online yesterday," I said. I'd gone blank upon seeing the headline on a news site, my brain unable to make sense of the words on the screen, and then I'd spent the afternoon feeling bewildered and adrift, like I was no longer certain who or where I was. "He was a cool guy, and I feel crappy that someone shot him. Why are you asking me, though? I haven't seen him for more than two decades. If you're going back through all of his known acquaintances, I can tell you right now you've gone too far."

"Did you know his ex-wife?"

"He was unmarried when we did that film together. I don't know anything about his life now."

"His ex-wife has disappeared. She hasn't been seen since Sunday, the night Grumet was shot at his home in Malibu." Moreau stared at me, her expression unreadable, and the mild electric buzz of warning I'd felt since she walked through my door exploded into a full-on sizzle of danger. "Genevieve Santos. She's a painter. Pretty famous in the art world. You absolutely certain you don't know her?"

"I don't know current artists," I said. "And like I said earlier, I've been out of touch with Serge for years. I wouldn't know how to get in contact with him if I wanted to."

"Try the astral plane. Isn't that where the spirits live?"

I stared at her. "Seriously, though," I said. "I don't know why you'd expect me to know anything about Serge's death, or his wife."

"Ex-wife." The correction was automatic; Detective Moreau obviously prized accuracy. "Something you should see."

She took out her phone from her purse, tapped on the screen, and passed it to me. I found myself looking at a *Los Angeles Times* piece on Serge's murder. "What am I looking for? You want me to read the whole thing?"

"Just the part I scrolled to. Read it out loud."

I read. "Early on, Santos dabbled in acting, with a starring role in Grumet's directorial debut, the little-seen experimental feature *The Divide*. Their paths crossed again a few years later when he visited a gallery featuring her works, and romance soon followed."

I looked up from the phone. "They got that wrong," I said. "She wasn't in *The Divide*, unless she was a background extra or something. There were only, like, eight people in the cast, and unless she changed her name, she wasn't one of us."

"She did change her name." Moreau almost sounded amused. "From Jenny St. John to Genevieve Santos."

My brain tried its best to track what she was saying. "I'm Jenny St. John," I said.

She took her phone and scrolled some more, then wordlessly passed it back.

I found myself looking at the professional photo of Genevieve Santos that accompanied the article. She was seated on a backless stool in front of a gigantic canvas featuring what was presumably one of her own paintings. It was dramatic and abstract; I thought I could make out a cityscape lurking beneath the dark swirls of paint, spectral fragments of buildings jabbing up at an ominous sky.

Genevieve Santos wore a baggy sleeveless moss-colored jumpsuit, her pale hands clasped together in her lap. Her hair was long and hung in tangled waves on either side of her face. It looked dark brown in the photo; I'm a sunshine blonde after monthly maintenance, but my roots are the color of sandy dirt.

Her face, though. Her face was mine. I felt that shock of recognition you get upon coming across a photo of yourself you didn't know existed. Her eyebrows were thinner and darker than mine, but her eyes, her small nose, her jutting chin, her thin lips, which were curved in a smile that showed no teeth . . . all of that was mine. I always flashed my teeth when I smiled, but it took a long time to train myself to do that, because when I was younger I wanted to disguise my slight overbite. Santos smiled like someone who was still hiding her overbite.

A moment of dizzy confusion, and the spell broke. "That's not me," I said. I felt a surge of relief I couldn't quite explain, like the photo of Genevieve Santos had knocked me out of my usual orbit, and now I was sliding back into my correct place in the universe.

"Sure looks like you," Moreau said. She sounded light, even flippant, and yet I was aware of a new intensity. "And she was in that movie you said you were in."

"No, she wasn't." It was sharp; Moreau's eyebrows twitched up at my tone before her face settled back into implacability. "This article got that wrong, or she lied about it. I was in that film. I can prove it . . ."

I trailed off. I *could* prove it, surely, though at the moment I didn't know how. I'd been close to my small cluster of costars at the time, Ronnie and Annika and Dave, and we'd stayed in loose contact for a bit, but now, I had no idea how to track them down. Annika was on some Hulu series, but I'd lost her phone number years ago. I didn't have any photos from the production, no stolen props or wardrobe, no tangible evidence I had spent the happiest eight weeks of my life on the set of *The Divide*, taking what I'd hoped and expected would be the first big step in a long and successful film career.

"Are you Genevieve Santos?"

The directness of the question caught me by surprise. "Obviously not."

"It's not obvious at all." Moreau settled back in her chair. "Santos is on the run. Or in any case, she disappeared the night her ex was found dead. We got a call this morning from a client of yours. She'd read about Santos being in that film, and she confirmed that photo of Santos as being a photo of a psychic she sometimes visited, a psychic who'd once mentioned she'd starred in that very same film. So that led all of us down at the LASD to suspect Genevieve Santos leads a separate life as a low-rent psychic named Jenny St. John."

"But she doesn't," I said. It sounded feeble. "That's not me. That's an entirely different person."

Moreau stared at me for a long, long time. It was impossible to tell what she was thinking, but I had a faint hope that she realized, upon saying it out loud, how absolutely crazy this sounded. "Let's start with some identification," she said at last.

I got up from the table. She looked wary at that and stood as well. She followed me as I opened the door leading into the clinic's small back room to get my purse. She'd unbuttoned her suit coat at some point, and one of her hands hovered near the waistband of her pants. The idea that she thought I might grab a weapon sent a spike of shaky adrenaline through me.

She stood in the doorway. She looked around the space while I retrieved my wallet from my purse. I could see her noting the open door leading to a grubby bathroom with a toilet and an industrial sink, the yellow laminate countertop where I kept a coffeepot and a mini fridge, the mattress on the floor, the ragged stack of banker's boxes holding my books and possessions next to the back door leading to the alley, the cheap plastic rolling rack of hanging clothes. "You living here?" she asked.

"It's temporary. I got evicted from my apartment during the pandemic," I said.

"During? It was against state law to evict anyone for nonpayment of rent."

"It's cute that you think that slowed landlords down. They weren't supposed to, but I wasn't in a position to fight it. I moved out. It's been easier just to stay here." "Easier" in the sense that I didn't have other options; my income level was too low to pass a background check for another apartment.

"This is a commercial building. Seems like living here would be in violation of your lease."

I turned to look at her, then decided she was making an observation, not a veiled threat. I didn't answer. I extracted my driver's license from my billfold and handed it to her.

She scrutinized it closely, then set it down on the countertop and photographed it with her phone, front and back. "Jenny's not short for Jennifer?" She handed it back to me. "Or Genevieve?"

"Nope. I thought Jenny St. John sounded like a better stage name than Jennifer St. John. I had it legally changed years ago."

"What's your birth name?"

"Sheila Bunn."

Both eyebrows raised. "Sheila?"

"Sheila. Bunn with two *n*'s. Is it any wonder I changed it?"

"Where do you come from, Sheila Bunn?"

"Hayes, Iowa. Seventy miles from Sioux City. But I've lived here for a long time."

"So has Genevieve Santos." Again, Moreau sounded dryly amused. At least one of us was getting some entertainment out of the situation. "And nothing you've said yet proves you're not the same person."

"Fingerprints?" I said. I waggled my license in the air. "The DMV has my thumbprint on file. You could compare it to Genevieve Santos's prints, and it would show I'm a different person. That would do it, right?"

"DNA is more accurate. We can take a sample at headquarters," Moreau said. "If you're not Santos, we can get you cleared by the end of the day."

"You said Malibu, right?" I asked. "Do I have to go all that way? Can't I just give you a lock of hair right now or spit into a cup or whatever?"

"I don't work in Malibu. Homicide is in Monterey Park." Moreau sounded distracted, like she was mulling something over. "But we could clear this up fast. Genevieve Santos was diagnosed with breast cancer in late September. She's been undergoing treatment." She met my eyes, unflinching.

I didn't get it at first, and then it hit me. "She's had surgery?"

"Partial mastectomy last month. She hasn't had the reconstruction yet."

It hung in the air. I cleared my throat. "So . . . you want me to flash you?"

"Absolutely not." Moreau sounded annoyed, and I realized irritation was her reaction to finding herself on uncertain ground. "But Santos would have fresh scars. If you're not her, you wouldn't."

"This is unquestionably the least sexy way anyone has ever asked to see my tits," I said. "And there's actually been some stiff competition for that honor."

"I'm not asking to see your tits," Moreau said. The annoyance was thicker now. "I'm just saying . . ." She trailed off, ending the sentence in a tense shrug.

I closed the door leading into the clinic, because this would look weird if any prospective customers decided to pop in just then, and, without stopping to think about it, lifted the hem of the linen tunic up to my chin. Because it was such a miserably sweaty day, I hadn't bothered with a bra. "Is this proof?

Moreau fell silent, standing motionless a few steps away. "I didn't ask you to do that," she said at last.

"I know. I just want to get this over with." I lowered my shirt and smoothed it out. I could feel my cheeks burning. "I had some work done on those a long time ago. After I made *The Divide*, a casting director suggested better tits might help me get roles, which turned out to be absolute crap advice, by the way. But in any case, it's clear I haven't had a recent mastectomy, right?"

"Yeah." Moreau looked me in the eye. "You're not Genevieve Santos."

"That's what I've been saying."

"Then we're done here for now." She was trying to hide it, but she'd been embarrassed by the request she hadn't quite made of me, and embarrassed by my acquiescence to it. It humanized her somewhat. "Thank you for your time."

She didn't say anything else until I'd walked her to the clinic door. She paused on the sidewalk, the afternoon sun reflecting off her braids like a halo. "It doesn't prove you were the one in that film. It seems to be widely accepted as fact that Santos and Grumet first met on the set while it was being made."

"I was in that film," I said. It sounded feeble and defensive, probably because I was feeling both feeble and defensive. "Look into it some more and you'll see. I don't know why she told people it was her, but it was me."

Moreau gave me a look that, for once, wasn't filled entirely with cold contempt. "Thanks for your cooperation," she said, and left.

CHAPTER 2

Inoffensive Prettiness

Once Moreau was gone, I closed the clinic, which consisted of locking the front door and turning off the lights before retreating to the stuffy, windowless back room. I sat on the mattress and drew my knees up close to my body, arms wrapped around my legs, chin on my kneecaps, and thought.

When I'd read the news about Serge's murder, I'd been transported back twenty-five years to a post-audition dinner at Spago, during which Serge had told me all about *The Divide* over salmon pizza and too much wine. He talked at length about the lead role, the schizophrenic Diane, who slid through parallel universes like a cormorant diving into the sea. The role hadn't been mine then, not quite yet.

He was living in New York and staying at the Chateau Marmont. After dinner, we'd driven into the hills. He'd seemed sober at the wheel of his rental car, but I'd seen how much he'd had to drink; young and stupid, I'd felt too wary of disrupting the germinating rapport between us to suggest he shouldn't drive. What if he thought I was a nag, what if that gave him an excuse to cast that other actress at the callback, the blonde with the tiny pink mouth and the long, center-parted hair?

He hadn't cast her. He'd cast me, and maybe that's because we'd parked somewhere on Mulholland and hiked a short distance down the hill to find the perfect spot to sit on the dusty earth and look at the glittering city skyline, and I'd ended up with leaves in my hair and scratches on my back and a pretty good hunch I had the part.

I'd been good in the film, inexperienced as I was; Serge coaxed a tricky, believable performance out of me, and my instincts for how to play Diane were generally on the right track. It wasn't my fault the production company went bankrupt, scuttling the planned theatrical release. The film slithered onto the racks at video rental stores a few years later, after Serge's third feature made him a rising star. And at some point between then and now, Serge's ex-wife had decided the role of Diane had been hers, not mine.

Did Serge know? Of course he did. He had to know. Didn't he? From the photo Detective Moreau had shown me, Genevieve and I looked alike, but he would have known. Maybe it was a private joke between them: Genevieve Santos looked enough like an obscure actress who'd worked briefly with her husband to claim her sole film credit as her own.

I looked up Genevieve Santos on my phone. Her Wikipedia page didn't list her date of birth, but after piecing together a timeline of her career, I figured she was in her early forties, like me. Born to wealthy expats in Bruges and raised in White Plains, she'd flaunted the expectations of her chilly and repressive family by skipping college and moving to Manhattan to become an artist. Which, apparently, had worked out pretty well for her.

I felt a pang in my chest, some aching combination of envy and regret. Maybe if I'd made other, better choices, Genevieve's success could have been mine. My high school art teacher, Ms. Rooney, had been certain I had a once-in-a-lifetime gift for painting. She'd helped me assemble a portfolio of my best works for my application to the Pratt Institute; she'd gone with me to our school's tiny career center, where we'd looked up information on scholarships and grants in big bound volumes.

Rooney saw more promise in me than Pratt had. For a long time after receiving the rejection letter, I'd been angry with her for filling me with false hopes. I abandoned my long-held dream of living a glamorous life as a struggling artist in New York, and I turned my attention to the other coast. In Los Angeles, I figured, my success wouldn't hinge upon genius, only upon my inoffensive prettiness and my ability to recite dialogue without stumbling over my words. Now, with that inoffensive prettiness ebbing away as I sank into middle age, any chance of success was in the past.

The rising temperatures inside my clinic were beginning to feel oppressive, so I headed down the block to a wellness café with robust air conditioning to cool down for a bit. The prices were ridiculous and everything on the menu tasted like moss, but it was convenient, and one of the baristas was an occasional client of mine. The only client, in fact, with whom I'd recently discussed my short-lived film career.

The interior of the café was stark white and minimalist, as sterile as a doctor's office, featuring a smattering of tiny round tables paired with tall metal stools. There were no other customers; from behind the high counter, Tish looked up with a reflexive welcoming smile as I entered. The smile froze on her face as she recognized me. "Oh, hey," she said at last.

"Hi, Tish," I said. "You called the police and told them I might be that missing artist, huh?"

Tish still looked frozen, like a video someone had forgotten to unpause. "They told me it would be anonymous," she said at last.

"It was. Your name wasn't mentioned. I just knew," I said. I tapped my temple. "Psychic abilities, you know. Anyway, I wanted to tell you it's all a mix-up. I just talked to the police and straightened it out. That artist, Serge Grumet's ex-wife, is a completely different person. She just happens to look a whole lot like me."

"Ah." The alarm faded from Tish's body language as it sank in that she probably wasn't chatting with a fugitive/possible murderer. "So you weren't really in that movie?"

I felt a flare of irritation. "No, that was me. I don't know where the confusion started, but I'm the one who starred in *The Divide*. Not her."

"Oh, okay. Sorry if I got you in trouble with the cops."

"Don't sweat it. It's useful to know there's someone out there pretending to be me." I glanced up at the menu printed in elaborate multicolor cursive on the chalkboard above the counter: lattes made from matcha and beets and turmeric, coffee laced with CBD and adaptogens, a million different herbal tea blends designed to boost brainpower or relieve anxiety or soothe an overtaxed immune system. "What's the coldest thing on your menu?"

Tish looked uncertain. "People seem to like the iced almond mocha, I guess?"

"I'll take it." Tish rang it up—nine dollars, which I didn't really have to spare, but it was almost worth it for the chance to hang out in blissfully chilly air—and set about scooping brown powder from a glass jar into a cocktail shaker filled with ice and cold brew. She shook it vigorously, raising her voice to be heard over the clatter of ice. "I tried watching your movie. I found an old copy on YouTube."

"Yeah? What did you think of it?"

Tish shook her head. She dumped the contents of the shaker into a plastic cup, added a paper straw, and passed it across to me. "The story was confusing, all those parallel universes. But I thought you were really pretty when you were young."

When you were young. "Thanks," I said. I sipped my drink. It was gritty and sticky sweet and tasted, not unpleasantly, like a combination of maple syrup and freshly dug soil.

"How's the mocha?" Tish asked.

"Cold, which is really all I'm looking for. I'm not sure I'm getting much almond flavor."

"It's nut-free. And chocolate-free, actually; it's made from powdered chaga mushrooms. They taste like chocolate-covered almonds." Tish shrugged at my skeptical expression. "I mean, sort of."

I sat down at one of the tiny high tables, determined to savor the welcome respite from the heat until I'd consumed every last drop of liquid mushrooms. Tish came out from around the counter and hovered nearby. "Hey . . . if you're not busy right now, could I get a quick reading? I've got an audition today at four o'clock."

"Sure. You want me to grab my tarot deck?"

She shook her head. "No, I don't need the full workup. Could you just give me some idea how it's going to go? If I don't have a chance of getting the part, I don't want to waste my time."

"Twenty bucks." I gestured across the table. "Grab a chair."

Tish dumped out the contents of her tip jar and counted the bills into a small pile. "I only have seventeen. I can throw in one of our collagen scones? They promote skin health."

"Sure, why not?" These days, my skin could use any boost it could get. I waited while Tish scooped the scone, a dense brown hockey puck covered in hemp seeds, into a little paper sleeve and handed it to me along with the pile of bills. She sat across from me; I extended both my hands, palms up. She placed hers on mine.

Is this a good place to point out I'm not really a psychic? To the best of my personal knowledge, legitimate psychics don't exist. Even so, my clinic was, in a way, a family business: my mom's sister Connie opened up a fortune-telling shop in Sioux City over forty years ago, which she operates to this day, and which has always been a modest success. Because she radiates firm yet kind-hearted common sense, her clients willingly accept her claims that her solid, practical advice comes directly from the spirit world.

Unlike me, Aunt Connie isn't a fraud. Not a deliberate one, at least. She wholly believes in her precognition and her ability to read minds, both of which she says have been part of her since birth. I can understand how it happened; I was certain I was psychic as a child. I believed it well into my teens, in fact. I was good at talking to people, good at reading body language, good at sensing when someone was keeping secrets, good at figuring out what I could say to make them open up. Good at making people feel like I understood them better than anyone else in the world. I wanted, very badly, to believe this was a special and exclusive gift bestowed upon me from another realm.

Moving to Los Angeles, though, made me realize I'd been kidding myself. I'd go on auditions, dozens of ego-deflating cattle calls, clutching my cut-rate headshots while standing in a hallway crowded with willowy twentysomethings with flawless bone structure, many of whom looked a lot like me and many of whom were much prettier than me, all of us desperately angling for the same ten-second appearance in a yogurt commercial or whatever. After going through that time after time after time, after repeatedly failing to find any way to stand out from the pack, it became impossible to maintain a belief that there was anything special about me, psychically or otherwise. The spirit realm hadn't blessed me with an otherworldly ability; if it had, surely I would have been able to use that gift to my advantage in Hollywood.

I stared into Tish's eyes and tried to radiate a deeply focused intensity. "Just relax and think about your audition. What's it for?"

"It's the lead in a horror film. The budget's really low, but it sounds cool. The audition is at this casting office in Studio City; I'm carpooling over there after my shift with two other girls from my agency."

Ah. I remembered when my agent started sending me on

the same auditions as a bunch of his other clients, all young women about my own age who were experiencing a similar inability to gain any traction in the industry. He'd dropped me as a client shortly thereafter. "What's the role?"

"It's a period piece, set in Victorian England. I'd be playing the daughter of a duke. Her new stepmother has her committed to a haunted asylum."

The description made me think of pale, wraithlike girls with tangled locks and flowing white nightgowns. Tish was tiny and curvy with a ton of short reddish curls and a billion freckles. Her voice was high-pitched and endearingly squeaky; she was as cute as a ladybug, and if she ever navigated her way into a role that capitalized on her strengths, she could go on to have a robust career. But a tragic Victorian heroine trapped in a haunted asylum didn't seem like that role.

"So am I going to get the part?" Tish asked. She asked it wryly, like she was mostly joking, but I could hear the hint of genuine longing under her words.

I shook my head slowly. "Not this one."

She hid her disappointment well. She withdrew her hands from mine and straightened up in her chair. "I didn't think I would," she said. "It didn't really sound right for me. I shouldn't bother going, should I?"

"No, you should absolutely go. Do the best job you can. You're not going to get this specific role, no, but I sense all kinds of interesting possibilities branching off from this point." I leaned across the table, keeping my eyes fixed on hers. I took her hands again in both of mine and gripped them. "If you go to this audition, something great will come into your life at some point in the future. But you have to keep your eyes open for it."

A glimmer of hope crossed Tish's freckled face. Her brow creased. "So what do I do?"

"Watch for the opportunity. Strike up as many conversations as you can. Not just with the casting director; be chatty and friendly to everyone—the receptionist, the assistants, your fellow auditioners, everyone. You've got a fun, bubbly personality, and someone you talk to today is going to remember that personality at a moment when it will be of great benefit to you, but you'll have to lay the groundwork."

"Do you promise? That something good will come from this audition?"

I shook my head, but it wasn't quite a denial. "The potential is there, that's all I can tell you. I see the universe starting to open up, ready to send you some wonderful gifts. But whether or not you receive those gifts is entirely up to you."

Tish nodded as I spoke. "Okay. Okay, I see. That makes sense."

"The universe has faith in you, Tish. Try not to let it down." I released her hands. I scooped up the pile of bills and the scone and stuffed both in my purse, then got to my feet. "Thanks for the mushroom stuff."

I was almost at the door before Tish spoke again. "It's really uncool that someone else is taking credit for your role."

I paused in the doorway. "Yeah, honestly, I'm not thrilled about that."

"That movie is your big thing, right? Your best accomplishment. If someone took that from me, I'd want to find out how it happened."

I came close to snapping at Tish that *of course* I wanted to find out how it happened, that my brain had been consumed with the idea ever since Moreau had shown me the *Los Angeles Times* article, that I felt a burning, primal urge to track down the missing Genevieve Santos and expose her to the world as a con artist and a thief for stealing something so precious to me. But none of this was Tish's problem, and I was better off controlling my anger until I could unleash it on the appropriate target. So instead I just smiled at her, as nicely as I could manage. "You and me both," I said, before venturing out again into the dazzling heat of Beverly Boulevard.

CHAPTER 3

That Dumb-Ass Movie

Some of Genevieve Santos's works were currently on display at a Beverly Hills gallery called Lally, which turned out to be a flat-roofed brick storefront nestled between a sleek Italian trattoria and a jewelry store featuring a display of opal pendants the size of robin eggs. I drove past the gallery slowly, noted that valet parking was twenty-eight dollars, and almost drove directly back to my clinic. Instead, I found a spot on a residential street about seven blocks away.

I'd paired the blue linen tunic with skinny white pants and my old Bottega Veneta strappy sandals, which I'd bought almost twenty years ago. The women of Beverly Hills had keen and judgmental eyes for footwear, but the sandals might be old enough now to register as vintage instead of outdated. They were designed for admiring, not walking, and the wire-like straps had reduced my feet to ground chuck by the time I reached the gallery.

I looked enough like Genevieve Santos, fugitive at large, that I didn't want to cause any confusion at a display of her art, so I donned a disposable face mask on the sidewalk before entering. It was flu season, and there'd been rumbles about the possible emergence of another vaccine-resistant virus strain, so I doubted I'd be scrutinized for the choice.

The glass double doors had chunky bronze handles that were too thick to wrap my hand all the way around. I pulled one open with some effort and was hit by a blast of air conditioning, brutally cold and welcome.

The gallery was a single large room, airy and white, with high ceilings. The walls were lined with Genevieve Santos's oil paintings, most of which were done on a grandiose scale. Soft white recessed lights bathed the art in a glow that made it look sacred.

About twenty people milled around the room, arranged in couples or trios, admiring the art. The reception desk near the front was unoccupied, but as soon as I let the door fall closed behind me, an unsmiling young woman with huge green cat eyes stepped forward and brandished a wafer-thin acrylic tray bearing flutes of champagne at me. Mask on, I accepted a glass with a nod of thanks and moved into the gallery to get a closer look at Genevieve's artwork.

Despite my teenage pretensions, I would never claim to understand art, but sometimes it triggers an emotional response in me, a tremor in the belly that tells me to stop and look closely. Here in the gallery, I felt that response. Maybe it was simply the scale of the works, the way they soared up the white walls to the ceiling, grabbing attention with their sheer size.

I hadn't picked up a paintbrush since moving to Los Angeles. Whenever I thought of my past artistic aspirations, it was with a sense of embarrassment that I'd ever been so full of myself as to think I could be an artist. Genevieve's paintings, big and expressive and filled with amorphous shapes that my mind immediately tried to resolve into logical patterns, made it clear how little I knew about art. At the same time, though, some long-dormant part of me twitched with the stirrings of life, reminding me that I'd once considered art vital.

I found the painting from the photo of Genevieve Detective Moreau had shown me. There, I'd thought it was an abstract city skyline. Standing in front of it, though . . . I had the impression of a field as seen from the perspective of a child, or of someone crouched low to the ground, head tilted back, surrounded by tall stalks. Corn, maybe, left unharvested too late in the season, withered and dying. A threatening dark sky, thunderclouds overhead, a storm waiting to strike. If I concentrated, I thought I detected a whiff of something clean and electric in the air. Ozone, the scent of gathering lightning.

I'd forgotten all about the punishing heat just outside the gallery. Now, staring at Genevieve's painting, I felt chilled, like the air conditioning had been cranked up several notches. The sweat that had collected between my shoulder blades slid down my spine in an icy trickle and pooled in the small of my back. If I hadn't been holding the champagne flute, I might've wrapped my arms around myself for warmth.

"It's impressive, isn't it?" I hadn't noticed the small blond woman until she was at my shoulder. She smiled at me and nodded at the painting. "This one might be my favorite of Gena's works."

"It's very striking," I said through my mask. I looked at the slim printed card affixed to the wall near the base of the painting to see the title. *The Divide*. I felt a tiny, weird thrill. "When I looked at a photo of it, I saw buildings, but here in person . . . It's a field, isn't it?"

The blonde tilted her head back and scrutinized the painting. "I see skyscrapers, but we all take different impressions away from it. I knew Gena in New York, years ago, and I like to imagine this is the city she and I both knew when we were young and silly. Did you grow up near fields?"

"Iowa. This reminds me of the cornfields of my childhood."

She smiled again. She came up to just above my shoulder, even in her slingback pumps. She was about my age; the skin around her eyes pulled in the corners when she smiled. She wore a gauzy blush wrap dress with puffy shoulders, like something a fairy princess would wear; her honey-colored hair fell in soft waves past her shoulders. She extended a hand to me, nails painted a pearly soft pink. "Antoinette Lally."

I shook it. "Jenny." I stopped myself from saying my full name. She'd just said she'd known Genevieve for years, and there was a chance the name "Jenny St. John" would be familiar to her. "Is this gallery yours?"

"It is. Are you a collector?"

"I'm not. I'm just here to look. I'm sorry," I said.

"Of course. You're more than welcome. It gives me great pleasure to expose the world to Gena's works." She glanced around the gallery. "Though I suppose many are drawn here by the recent news." Shadows cast by the recessed lighting turned the lines at the corners of her mouth into dark gashes, and all of a sudden she looked older and more somber.

"In a way, that's why I'm here," I said. I cleared my throat, which seemed dry and thick. The champagne in my hand was still untouched, but I hadn't dared lower my mask to take a sip. "I was questioned by the police this morning about . . . about the news. Apparently I bear a strong enough resemblance to the missing artist—Genevieve Santos—that someone thought I might be her in disguise."

Antoinette stared at me blankly. I thought my mask might have made my words unintelligible. Finally, she spoke: "Show me, please."

With my free hand, I unhooked the mask from one ear and let it dangle. She gazed at my face, her soft blue eyes wide and unblinking.

"Yes, I see. You have Gena's features. Gena is a beautiful woman, so I hope you consider that a compliment." She smiled. "You move differently than she does, and you speak differently. Even so, the similarity is striking. You and Gena aren't related?"

"Not at all, not as far as I know. All my family is in the Midwest. I read that Genevieve—Gena—grew up somewhere in New York, I think? White Plains?" I hooked the mask back around my ear, covering my face again.

"Yes, that's what she has said." Antoinette looked bemused, filled with skeptical affection. "When I first met Gena, more than twenty years ago, she told me other stories. She grew up in Seville, she grew up in New Orleans, she grew up in Dubai. These days, her biography consistently says White Plains. It might even be the truth."

So Gena was a liar. That wasn't exactly breaking news; the entire reason I was here was because Gena had lied about *The Divide*. "So she *could* be from Iowa, like me. Maybe she's my fourth cousin or something."

"It could be. Maybe someday you'll have the chance to ask her that yourself." Antoinette smiled. "Gena and I met in SoHo. I was a receptionist at a gallery. She was a struggling artist, one of thousands. No formal training, though it seemed like she'd been painting all her life. She was living with a collective of artists in a gloomy warehouse in the Bowery; I never knew whether they were renting or squatting. She'd come into the gallery and bother me. I had no power, none at all, but to her I was a gatekeeper, a barrier between her ambitions and her future success. She wore me down; I showed her work to my superiors, and they warned me never to do that again. I'd overstepped my boundaries."

She took a sip of her champagne. "But Gena and I became good friends anyway. Eventually another gallery took her on. Years later, when I finally branched out on my own, I displayed her works in my gallery. When I moved here, Gena followed."

"I'm sorry she's missing," I said. It sounded inadequate. "You were close?"

"*Are* close," Antoinette said. The hazy wistfulness sharpened into something direct and clear. "Gena is alive, and she's no murderer. She's too . . ." She seemed to consider her next words. "I was going to say 'gentle,' though that's not exactly right. There's nothing soft about Gena, but murder isn't in her bones. Even in the middle of her divorce, when she had good reason to hate Serge, she would never do him any harm."

I found myself trusting her quiet, soft belief in the innocence of her longtime friend. I almost asked her what she thought had happened to Genevieve, but that would be an overstep. I didn't know Genevieve; I'd known Serge only briefly.

Though there was a time, long ago, when I could have sworn I'd known Serge very well.

The noise of the crowd increased incrementally, as though someone had turned the knob on a sound system up a single notch, raising the volume from a muted hush to a low murmur. Antoinette glanced toward the front of the gallery. "Excuse me," she said, patting me once on the arm before heading toward the door. I looked over at the new arrival whose appearance had generated a buzz of conversation and instantly recognized Boots Pontifex.

Elizabeth Pontifex—Boots to friends and fans and strangers alike—had been instantly recognizable for maybe thirty years, long before her Oscar win for that Josephine Baker biopic, long before her acclaimed performance as a weary alcoholic public defender on a buzzy HBO series, long before she'd parlayed her stardom into a lucrative gig as an influencer/entrepreneur upon the arrival of middle age. She'd founded Eternality, a freakishly popular online store with a complementary smattering of brick-and-mortar shops devoted to products designed to counteract the ravages of age: skin care, makeup, supplements, clothing, fitness gear.

I returned my attention to Genevieve's artwork. I wandered about the gallery, looking at various pieces, reading the descriptions on the placards at the bases of each. My champagne was still in my hand, neglected because I hadn't wanted to remove the mask. I really wanted a drink, so I let the mask dangle from one ear while I sipped. I made a full circuit of the gallery, then returned to *The Divide*.

That smell again. Ozone.

A fragment of a memory from my teen years, back when I was on the cusp of adulthood. A stormy summer night. A life-changing decision had just been made, and maybe it had been the wrong one, maybe I should have picked differently. I was soaking wet and miserable, lying on my back in the cornfield, head pounding, my vision blurred by rain and blood . . .

A hand closed around my upper arm and gave it a quick squeeze, yanking me back to the present. A female voice, low and husky, addressed me: "Gena?"

I turned to face the new arrival. My first thought was that the chemists and dermatologists who developed Eternality's skin-care line must know their business, because up close, Boots was flawless. Her skin had the texture of petals and seemed entirely free of pores; her hair fell in a smooth golden-brown flood down her back. Her eyes, expertly lined in a glossy shade of violet that matched her satin sheath dress, were wide with astonishment.

"What are you doing here?" she asked. "We've all been worried sick about you."

It took me a moment to connect my brain to my mouth. "I'm not who you think I am," I said at last.

Boots stared at me. Her face was very close to mine. She seemed frozen; I'd swear she wasn't breathing.

She swallowed, and something in her face relaxed. She released my arm, her face still inches from mine.

"Wow. You're not, are you?" She raised a hand, and she seemed like she was going to take hold of my chin, maybe move it from side to side to look at me from all angles. She thought better of that and lowered her hand. "But you look . . . Who are you?"

"My name's Jenny St. John. I just found out today that I look a lot like Genevieve Santos, which is why I came here. I'm sorry I confused you." I pulled the mask back up over my mouth and nose and hooked it around my other ear. "I was wearing the mask to avoid this. I'm sorry."

"No, take it off. Please."

I obeyed. Boots scrutinized my face. Finally, she shook her head, eyes still very wide.

"Wow," she said again. "Are you related to Gena? A sister or something?"

"No, no chance of that. It's just a coincidence."

"Jenny St. John." Boots said the name slowly, drawing out each syllable. "That's the name Gena used early in her career. That dumb-ass movie she was in."

I let that slide. *The Divide* hadn't been a dumb-ass movie, but it wasn't the time to argue about it. "No, that was me," I said. "Did she tell people it was her?"

Boots stared at me. When she spoke, she sounded incredulous. "When she was married to Serge, they had a huge poster for that film on the wall of their den. That was how she and Serge met."

"I don't know how they met, but it wasn't while filming *The Divide*," I said. It came out harsh, even angry; Boots widened her eyes in surprise at my tone. I paused to compose myself before speaking again. It was a struggle to sound calm.

"A detective talked to me this morning because she'd heard I was the actress from *The Divide*, and she thought there was a chance I was Genevieve in disguise. I don't know why Genevieve told people she was in the film. I don't know whether Serge believed her; I'd say it was impossible, because I worked pretty closely with him, and while Genevieve and I apparently look a great deal alike, we are not the same person."

Boots's expression went blank, and then she barked out a laugh, loud enough that gallery visitors turned around to look at us. She got herself under control.

"Oh my god," she said. She smiled, wide and dazzling. "That little liar. I'd say I can't believe it, but of course I can."

I felt an almost shameful rush of relief at being believed. "Do I really seem that much like her? I know there's a physical resemblance, but do I act like her, or sound like her?"

Boots thought it over. "No. Not really. As soon as you spoke,

I knew you weren't her. If Gena were a skilled actor, sure, she could adjust her speech patterns and shift her body language to mimic yours. You're an actor, you could do it, right? But talking to you right now, I don't feel like I'm having a conversation with Gena."

"Why would Gena claim she was in my film?" I asked.

Boots snorted. "Because she thought it was cool, I guess. Because probably someone once assumed she was you, and she ran with it. I'm sure she found it flattering to be mistaken for a movie star." Boots looked at me closely. "I'm surprised she got away with it for so long. You've been in other projects, right?"

I shook my head. "That's my only credit. I got cast shortly after I first moved to Los Angeles, and then it didn't get a theatrical release, and my agent dropped me. I went on a bunch of auditions, but . . ." I shrugged.

"The film industry's tough. It takes a long time to get results. You've got to hang in there if you want to be successful."

I tried not to feel rankled by the condescension inherent in Boots's words. Nobody ever thought it was easy to score paid acting gigs, but often people who'd struggled their way to a secure spot in the industry believed it was a meritocracy, that all it took was the right mixture of time, talent, and determination, that luck played a minimal part. "I hung in there for a while, then decided it wasn't in my cards. These days, I'm an intuitive counselor. Like a psychic life coach. I run a clinic on Beverly near the Grove."

Boots's eyebrows rose. She had great eyebrows, thick yet immaculately groomed. "You must know Della DeLaurenti, then. I consulted with her before I set up my business, and she helped free me of some fears that had been holding me back. I owe much of my current career to her."

"Sure. Our paths haven't crossed much, but I know of her, of course." When I'd first opened my clinic, I'd tried to model myself after DeLaurenti. I'd read her books, had watched her videos, had briefly considered paying four hundred and fifty dollars for her online seminar before deciding that was madness. My sense of Della DeLaurenti's business model was that she did, with great success, exactly what I tried to do: she told her customers, who were mostly wealthy and well-educated women of a certain age, positive and affirming lies about themselves in the guise of giving them psychic insights, then served as a cheerleader for all their endeavors. It surprised me a bit that Boots, who struck me as nobody's fool, was taken in by DeLaurenti's racket, but I'd met plenty of smart women who took comfort in the idea of otherworldly forces championing their successes. Boots's anti-aging empire shared some territory with the wellness industry, and wellness, I'd noticed, often drifted into the realms of mystical healing that encompassed tarot cards and chakras and crystals, all the areas covered by intuitive counselors like myself.

Boots looked at me with what seemed like genuine interest. "Good for you," she said. "It's smart that you were able to pivot to a second act when your film career didn't work out. I admire that spirit."

Only a rich person would think it was somehow a choice to make such a pivot. "Thank you," I said.

She examined my face in silence, brow furrowed in concentration. She glanced around the gallery, then returned her attention to me. "Look, I just dropped by to see how Antoinette was holding up. She's been friends with Gena even longer than I have, and this has got to be hard on her. But I'm done here, so do you want to grab a drink or something?"

If I still believed in my psychic ability, I would have said it was tingling at the back of my head, alerting me to the presence of ulterior motives. But there was nothing otherworldly about my suspicions; I was simply good enough at understanding human behavior to realize everything Boots did was calculated. She had a strategic brain and a mercenary streak; she would have needed both to maintain her high level of success in the entertainment industry for so many years, and then to pivot to a second act, to use her lingo, as soon as maintaining that level was no longer feasible due to the onset of middle age.

So Boots wanted something from me. That was fine; I wanted something too. I wanted to get back what her good friend Gena had taken from me, and Boots might be able to help me. “That sounds great,” I said.

CHAPTER 4

Extremely Online

We ended up at the trattoria beside the gallery. It had a garden patio underneath a wrought iron trellis covered in grapevines, but the heat was still oppressive, so we sat indoors, in the chilly dark, at a small corner table in the bar area. Our tabletop was a small disk of black marble, not much larger than a dinner plate, with a little gold doll hand sticking out from each side; I had no clue what they were for until Boots hung her purse from one. She drank Scotch, something she'd ordered by name from a bottle that the bartender had needed to stand on her tiptoes to pull down from a high shelf. I was optimistic Boots would be picking up the tab, since she'd suggested this tête-à-tête, but I was far from certain of that, so I just asked for a glass of the house white.

Boots nodded at my glass when our server placed it in front of me. "Drink up," she said. "Hope you don't mind me saying it, but you look like you could use it."

The wine tasted of smooth oak, cold and clean. "I could, in fact," I said. "Today has been a *lot*. First, I get visited by the police on suspicion of murdering someone I haven't seen in over twenty years, and then I find out I have a doppelgänger. A rather famous doppelgänger, in fact. I'm a little overwhelmed, honestly."

Boots seemed to consider this, sipping her Scotch, her fantastic eyebrows pulled together in deep thought. "I don't know that I'd call Gena famous," she said at last. "If you know the art world, there's a decent chance you know Gena, but it's not as though she's a household name."

"Unlike you," I said, then regretted it. I sounded like a sycophant.

Boots took the compliment in stride. She nodded. "Unlike me, sure. But Gena and I, we got along from the start, even though she had every right to hate my guts. You know this story?"

"The first time I'd ever heard of Gena was when I read about Serge's murder," I said.

"Okay, well." She shrugged. "I know the basic facts of this don't make me look great, but you seem mature enough to realize that sometimes things aren't as big of a deal as outsiders might think. I met Serge at a Golden Globes party, and we clicked right from the beginning. He'd been married to Gena for five years at the time."

She sipped her Scotch. She slid her gaze up over the rim of her glass to look at me, trying to gauge my reaction. "I'm not making excuses here, but it's not as though Serge and Gena had any great passion together. It was . . . well, Serge was a cool guy. You knew him; you must know what he was like. He could talk about anything, and so can I. We had a connection."

Her gaze became dreamy, and then she shook her head, snapping herself back to the present. "Gena and I hit it off, too. We became close. Sure, when she found out about me and Serge, she wasn't thrilled, and she stopped answering my calls for a while, but she didn't hold a grudge for long. I still consider her one of my best friends."

"And you and Serge?" I asked.

Another shrug. "That ended after the divorce. I think he assumed he and I would get married, but that didn't fit with my plans."

I drank my wine. At a nearby table, a pair of well-maintained and very tan women kept shooting covert glances over at Boots between bites of their orzo salads and Mediterranean flatbreads. Their glances included me, too, as they tried to figure out if I was anyone they should know. I ignored them with some effort and focused my attention on Boots. "What do you think happened to Gena?"

"I think she split," Boots said. "She was at Serge's home the night he was killed. She was supposed to be there, at least; that's where she told her boyfriend she was going. What I think is that she saw whatever happened to him and got scared, and she's in hiding now. She'll come out when his killer is arrested. Hopefully that's soon. You know she's in the middle of medical treatment? Breast cancer. She had the surgery last month, and she's due to start radiation soon. She's got biweekly doctor appointments that she shouldn't be missing."

"Why was she at Serge's home? They've been divorced for years, right?"

"They're still friends. Or friendly, at least. She and Serge were working on some kind of project together. I don't know the details." Boots made a dismissive gesture with her hand, and just from that motion, I knew she was lying, that she knew all about whatever the project was, but wanted to give me the impression it was no big deal. I filed that away for future consideration. "In any case, she returned to her own home late that night. There's a security camera on her front gate, and it recorded her arrival. She parked in her garage as usual, and she left her phone and purse inside the house near her front door, and no one ever saw her again. The car is still in the garage, but nobody's seen Gena."

"It was definitely her?" I asked. "She's visible on the camera? It couldn't be anyone else driving her car?"

"It could. Which is scary." Boots's mouth was drawn in a thin line. "Gena's Porsche has privacy glass. MMP saw the footage when the cops came to the house to investigate, and he couldn't tell if it was Gena behind the wheel. And the front gate and the garage open automatically to anyone driving that car, so . . . who knows?"

Taking the missed medical appointments into consideration, Boots's theory about Gena hiding because she witnessed a murder seemed improbable. If Gena had been driving her own car, it meant she'd killed Serge and had gone on the run. If someone else had been driving, it meant they had murdered Gena along with Serge and were covering their tracks. If there was a third possibility in there, I couldn't see it; it was overwhelmingly likely Gena was a killer or Gena was dead. "Who's MMP?" I asked.

"Gena's boyfriend." The corner of Boots's mouth pulled up. "Are you Extremely Online?" She made finger quotes in the air. "If you are, you know who that is: Matthew Mark Park. MMP. It's what everyone calls him." She smiled benevolently. "Kids today. They're weird. But he's a cool guy."

I shook my head. "I've never heard of him."

"Good for you. I spend too much time watching kids who are thirty years younger than me making an epic fuck-ton of money doing nothing on YouTube or TikTok or wherever, and MMP—Matthew Mark Park—certainly qualifies. He's a singer, or an actor, or a mixture of both, but he started making these DIY handyman videos, and he became really famous for them. He'd take apart a toilet and demonstrate how to fix it, and millions of viewers were *riveted*. Anyway, he moved in with Gena a few years ago."

A song was playing quietly in the trattoria, something I remembered dancing to when I was in my teens, and Boots shimmied her toned shoulders to the beat, a purely reflexive gesture. "MMP doesn't remember Gena coming up to bed that night. Sunday, I guess it was. He says he's a sound sleeper, and

Gena usually gets up much earlier than he does, so it's possible she was in and out without him knowing it."

I took another drink of my wine. "If Gena didn't take her car or purse, where could she go? That seems ominous, doesn't it?"

"Yeah." Boots's mouth pulled into a grim line. She was already done with her Scotch; she caught the eye of the bartender and waggled the glass in the air. "I don't have an explanation for it. I hope she's somewhere safe."

"Do you have any guesses about what happened to Serge?" I asked.

She nodded emphatically. "Yes. I do. It was Malis."

"Meliss? Melissa?"

"Malis. M-A-L-I-S. Malis Sao. Serge's second wife. She's a sculptor from Cambodia. Her sculptures are political. I'm not entirely sure how a sculpture of a blobby shape can have a political meaning, but that's what Malis says, and the major art critics seem to agree with her, so what do I know? Fine art isn't my forte." Our server set down Boots's second drink; she gave him a quick nod of thanks and flashed him a megawatt smile before returning her attention to me.

"To be fair to Malis, she's nice enough, but the spouse is always the primary suspect in a murder, with good reason, right? As far as I know, she inherits everything from Serge, and he has millions. The studios gave him points for his movies, which made him buckets. And according to pretty much everyone, Serge slept around, particularly with all those pretty young actresses starring in his films. Gena says Malis never seemed bothered by that, but if I were in her shoes? I'd be bothered."

Boots leaned back in her chair and examined me. The Scotch seemed to be working its magic on her; her face had softened a bit, had become less focused. "She's got an alibi, says she was working in her studio downtown, and I guess there's evidence to support that. But alibis can be faked."

"Or she could have hired someone to kill Serge," I said. Boots nodded at that.

"Exactly. I've been thinking along those lines. Serge and Malis have some ex-con living in the guesthouse on their Malibu property. An old friend of Serge's. From what I've heard, he's not considered a suspect, but someone like that might know someone. Maybe he put Malis in touch with a hit man. Or she could have hired someone online. The dark web. I don't know."

I finished my wine and set my empty glass on the table. If Boots wasn't picking up the tab, my budget didn't extend to a second round. "I hope the police figure out who killed him," I said. "I liked Serge. He was a good guy."

We fell into silence. It felt a little strained. Boots might have been embarrassed about pouring out her soul to a stranger in a bar, but it felt more like she was thinking something over, trying to come to a decision.

"Are you really a psychic?" she asked. "Can you tell me things about myself, just by looking at me? Tell me something that you wouldn't be able to find online."

I inhaled once, then plunged in. I'd learned early on that it was better not to think too much before giving someone a psychic reading, to just pop off with the first thought that came into my head. "You are crazy worried about Gena, and yet you don't want to let it show," I said. "What you told me about thinking she's in hiding, you don't believe that. You know she's not a murderer, and you know she's not the type to run and hide, and the only explanation that makes sense to you is that she's dead. Nobody's really saying that, not the police or anyone else, because they're looking at Gena as a possible suspect, but you've been thinking about it a lot, and you think someone, probably Serge's wife, must have killed her."

Boots exhaled, long and slow, and I realized she'd been holding her breath the whole time I'd been talking. "Yes," she said. She nodded and kept nodding while she was speaking, like it was a reaction she had no ability to control. "Yes, damn it, that's it exactly. I think Malis killed Gena at the same time she killed Serge. Malis is quiet, but she's smart as hell, and she's got a lot going on beneath the surface. If she planned a murder, she'd do it right. She'd set up an ironclad alibi, and she'd make the police go off in all kinds of wrong directions, like thinking Gena is the culprit."

She took another drink of her Scotch to stabilize herself. She was brimming over with electric energy, some coiled tension that was releasing itself inside her. She looked especially beautiful at the moment, focused and magnetic, her eyes very wide. "I don't know what she did with Gena's body, but you should see their house, it's in Malibu on the cliffs, right above the water. Malis is a small woman, but she could drag a body out to the edge of the property and roll it over the side. The waves are wild; Gena would be swept out to sea, and no one would ever find her."

"What do you want from me?" I asked. I sounded composed, though some of Boots's manic energy spilled over to me. My heart beat a bit faster than it should. There was a request coming, something Boots had been thinking over ever since meeting me in Antoinette's gallery, some favor she wanted to ask . . .

"Can you find out who killed Serge? Can you find out what happened to Gena?" she asked. "If I introduce you to Malis, would you know from talking to her if she did it?"

Tricky. Very, very tricky. Because no, of course I wouldn't know. Boots spoke to fill the silence, her words rushed.

"I asked Della if she could do it, but she's spending the month leading a spiritual wellness retreat in Baja. I'd pay you for your time, of course, whatever your hourly rate is. I could take you around to meet Malis, and a bunch of Serge's friends as well, maybe Gena's too, and you could talk to them and tell me what you think happened to Serge and Gena. Everyone would be fascinated to meet you, since you look so much like her."

I could just about see that working. Since my very existence would uncover Gena's big lie that she'd starred in *The Divide*, my presence would create a disruption. Interesting things tended to be revealed in disruptions. Somebody in Serge's inner circle, such as his current wife, might very well have a reason to be afraid of disruptions. And there was something immensely satisfying about the idea of exposing Gena as a fraud in a public manner while setting the record straight on that film.

Maybe I could crack the case open, using my brain and my instincts if not my (nonexistent) psychic abilities. Maybe the disruption I caused would unearth some clue that would help Detective Moreau arrest the murderer. Maybe I'd get a bit of media attention, and maybe Boots would switch her allegiance to me instead of to Della DeLaurenti. Maybe I'd become the hot new celebrity-endorsed intuitive counselor.

Maybe I'd make a fool of myself, get the cops mad at me, expose myself as a fraud.

That last part seemed the most likely, but even still, surely Boots would pay me for my time. And I was curious about Gena, my doppelgänger, who had stolen my film career, the one thing in my life in which I took unqualified pride.

"Of course," I said. I was impressed by how calm I sounded. "I think that's a great idea. I can't promise I'd know anything instantly, though; that's not the way psychic ability works."

Boots nodded, like what I had said made perfect sense. "Of course, you'd need time to get to know people. Della's the same way. The more time she spends with someone, the more deeply she understands them. But I'm very curious what your initial impressions would be."

I came close to backing out right there. Not just because I was afraid of making an ass of myself with wildly incorrect guesses, but because I'd be blatantly scamming Boots. I'd made peace, more or less, with doing phony psychic readings in my clinic, because telling people nice things about themselves in exchange for small amounts of cash isn't the worst crime in the world. Letting Boots think I could use extrasensory perception to find a murderer seemed dirtier, more nakedly dishonest.

I could rationalize it to myself, though. If I talked to Serge and Gena's friends, the spirit world wouldn't reach out and point a magic finger at the guilty party, no. But in the six years since starting my psychic business, I'd learned to trust my instincts, and I thought I might be able to find Serge's killer even without any paranormal aid. Psychics are investigators by nature, what with the carefully penetrative questions we must ask our subjects before we can give them the right answers to their questions, and Serge's murder might be a mystery I could solve.

On a fundamental level, I wanted to accept Boots's offer because it was a chance to regain some lost ground. When I'd first read about Serge's murder, I'd been overcome by a surprisingly intense wave of grief. I was upset about Serge, of course, but more than that, I'd mourned the final loss of my dream of someday recapturing that unrestrained happiness and sense of purpose I'd felt on the set of *The Divide*. By inserting myself into the remnants of Serge's life and solving the final mystery of his existence, I could at least carve out a small legacy: Jenny St. John, Serge Grumet's first leading lady, rose up from the ashes of obscurity and captured his killer.

Boots drained her drink. "Let me text MMP and see if he's home. I'll take you by Gena's to meet him. Malis and I aren't close, so I can't just drop in on her without a good reason, but MMP might be able to give us one."

She got out her phone and began to text, fingers flying over the screen. She paused, and her phone chirped back at her almost immediately.

She glanced at the screen. "He says it's cool for us to come over." She tilted her phone at me so I could see the thumbs-up emoji MMP had sent in reply to her message. "You want to follow me? The house is in Silver Lake."

She held her credit card in the air between two slim fingers and waggled it at our server, shaking her head once when I made a half-hearted offer to pick up the tab myself. This was moving fast, too fast for me to consider it too closely, which was probably for the best. If I stopped to think, I'd probably realize this was a ruinously bad idea, and I'd back out of it. If I backed out now, I'd never get the chance to ask Gena why she'd taken credit for *The Divide*. Right now, that seemed like an even more compelling reason to go along with Boots's plan than getting the chance to investigate Serge's murder: Serge might have been the one to hand me my sole great accomplishment, but Gena was the one who had swiped it from me.

CHAPTER 5

Eight-Figure Deal

Genevieve Santos lived on a winding drive that snaked through Silver Lake, continuously approaching yet never coming within view of the shimmering blue reservoir at the heart of the neighborhood. A sliding iron gate separated the house from the street; Boots, driving a silver SUV in front of me, rolled down her window and reached out one impossibly long arm to press a button on a call box that rose up from the ground on a slender iron stalk. The gate slid open, and we drove through and parked in the half-circle courtyard in front of the house, my tiny clunker dwarfed by Boots's behemoth of a vehicle. Another car was already parked there, a shiny Mini Cooper the color of sea glass.

The house was a chunky two-story box, painted a deep slate blue and trimmed in gray. The unpaved courtyard was blanketed with loose flat sea pebbles, the kind that would be perfect for skipping across water; they shifted around under my heeled sandals, which had failed to grow more comfortable as the day went on.

Before we reached the front door, it flew open, and I got my first glimpse of Matthew Mark Park.

A dizzy rush of blood to my head, euphoric, like I'd just done a bump of coke on a crowded nightclub floor. Matthew Mark Park was an updated composite of all my teen celebrity crushes, all thick spiky hair and smooth, clear skin stretched over a framework of perfectly placed bones. He was beautiful, not handsome, and his face was untouched by age or worry. He grinned at Boots, radiating youth and good cheer. His teeth gleamed.

"Hey, Boots!" he said. "I'm glad you stopped by. I've been thinking of you. How are you holding up?"

"I'm good, or as good as I can be, under the circumstances. How are you?"

He tilted his head from side to side in an expression of ambivalence. "Don't know. On edge, I guess. Every time my phone buzzes, I start to panic that it might be news about Gena." He glanced at me and favored me with that grin. "Hi. I'm MMP."

"Nice to meet you, MMP. I'm Jenny." "MMP" did not roll off the tongue.

He opened his mouth to say something, and then he saw me, really saw me. All animation drained from him, and his large eyes widened. "Oh, wow," he said at last.

Boots stepped forward and placed a hand on his wrist. Her nails were painted a deep matte violet tipped with liquid gold. "She's not Gena," she said. "She's not even related. Though she's got a weird connection to Gena that we wanted to talk to you about. That's why we stopped by."

"Oh, okay." He hadn't taken his eyes from my face. "Come in. Kira's here." He stepped aside to usher us into the home. Boots kicked off her sandals by the door, so I crouched down and unbuckled my own designer death traps, and we padded barefoot into the foyer.

Air conditioning blasted. Ceramic tiles, placed in an alternating pattern of indigo and peacock, felt cold and smooth under my feet. MMP was barefoot as well, his legs lean and muscular beneath his baggy white shorts. His loose blue tank top slid off of one well-defined shoulder as he glanced back at me. "I don't mean to stare, but . . . oh, man, you look just like her. Did you know her?"

"We've never met," I said. "A detective talked to me today. She thought I might be Gena in disguise."

MMP's eyes grew huge again, but he didn't say anything. He led us into the living room. A midcentury sofa and matching love seat in weathered navy leather framed two sides of a low coffee table made of dark wood with brass accents, all of it arranged on a pale Persian rug, its pattern faded to shadows. On top of the table rested an arrangement of white anemones in a hammered bronze bowl.

Someone rose from the sofa as we approached. At first I thought she was a teen, but then I realized she was in early adulthood, probably right around MMP's age. Everything about her seemed young, thrillingly and painfully young, and still in the process of developing. Huge eyes, golden skin, tiny pert nose, straight black hair pulled loosely back in a pink silk scarf. She smoothed out the skirt of her sundress, which was printed with white batik elephants, and smiled at us. "Hi," she said. Her eyes were pink, like she'd just stopped crying moments ago.

"Boots, you know Kira? Kira, this is Jenny. She's . . . she's not Gena," MMP said, a tone of helplessness creeping into his voice.

Kira smiled at me, polite yet distracted. "Nice to meet you," she said. It was automatic. She seemed neither surprised at nor interested in my resemblance to Gena.

"Hi, Kira. Good to see you again." Boots sat down on the sofa and motioned for Kira to take a seat beside her. "Everything okay?"

"Kira got some bad news about the film today, so I'm helping her sort her way through it." MMP gestured for me to take the love seat. A quintet of open bottles of soju in candy flavors rested on the table, lined up in a precise row: watermelon, grapefruit, yuzu, pineapple, green grape. They'd been drinking out of small hexagonal glasses. Also on the table was an abundance of open packages of Korean snack foods; I spotted shrimp-flavored crackers, honey-butter potato chips, and small rolled cakes filled with bananas and strawberry jam.

"Serge's film?" Boots asked. "Has it been canceled?"

Kira nodded. "I think so, yes. Officially, they're still looking for a new director to step in. But my agent called today and told me to be prepared for the worst. We'd barely started filming, so the studio thinks it'd be easiest to scrap it, instead of searching for someone who could fulfill Serge's vision."

"Ugh. I'm sorry, Kira," Boots said. She looked over at me. "Kira's starring in Serge's latest—well, last—film."

"It's my first lead role." Kira's eyes glittered with fresh tears. She kept her eyes wide and tilted her head back a bit, and the tears didn't fall. "I know losing it isn't the most important thing in the world, especially after what happened to Serge, but I'm worried I'll never get another chance like this again."

MMP procured a clean pair of hexagonal glasses from a sideboard that matched the coffee table and splashed soju in them from bottles grabbed seemingly at random: watermelon for me, pineapple for Boots. He plopped down on the love seat beside me, and I caught a whiff of his aftershave, something herbal and complex and strangely intoxicating. "You'll have lots more chances," he told Kira. "Tons and tons of chances. You're super talented, and you're so beautiful, everyone's going to want to work with you."

"You really think so?" Kira discreetly swatted away a tear with the side of a small hand.

"Definitely," MMP said. Boots and I murmured our assent, though I had my private doubts. Kira *was* beautiful, absolutely, but even assuming MMP was right in his assessment of her talent, that combination might not be enough. I didn't know the precise odds, but it seemed like getting cast as the lead of a film while still a relatively unknown actor was about as likely as getting struck by lightning. Having it happen twice would be close to impossible.

I should know. Bizarrely enough, I'd been struck by lightning, literally, back when I was a teenager in Iowa, while I was being stupid and reckless during a thunderstorm, and it had been the most traumatic experience of my young life, one that had made me feel chilled in the gallery when the sight of Gena's painting had reignited old memories. And then I'd been cast as the lead in *The Divide* as a complete unknown, but that giddy stroke of beginner's luck had proved impossible to replicate.

Kira gave a little laugh. It came out a bit strained, but she was trying, poor girl. "Thank you for cheering me up." She rose to her feet. "I should go. It was good seeing you, Boots, and it was very nice meeting you." She nodded at me.

"You should stay until you feel better," MMP said. He rose and took her hands in both of his, looking into her eyes. "I don't want you leaving while you're upset."

Boots frowned, her gaze locked on their clasped hands. She glanced up and noticed me observing her, then shot me a friendly smile. She sat up straighter on the sofa and sipped her pineapple soju, her expression benign and calm.

Kira detangled her hands from MMP's. "You're very kind. But I feel much better now, thank you." She picked up a tiny crossbody purse and slung it over her shoulder.

"I'll text you," MMP said. He leaned in to press his cheek against Kira's, their skin barely touching before he moved back. I wasn't looking directly at Boots, but out of the corner of my eye, I could sense her sitting ramrod straight, spine filled with tension.

After walking Kira to the door and seeing her off, MMP once again flopped down beside me. He refilled all our glasses from a bottle picked at random. Green grape mingled with the traces of watermelon still in my glass, the taste powerfully artificial yet pleasant, like the fruit punch served at a child's birthday party. "Boots, you wanted to talk to me about something?"

"So here's the thing," Boots said. She leaned forward on the sofa, placing her hands on her bare knees. "Here's how Jenny comes into this. You know that film Gena was in?"

"*The Divide.* Sure. It's great. Gena made me watch it, and I was blown away. She was an amazing actress."

"Okay, so that wasn't Gena. It was Jenny." Boots nodded at me. "Gena and Jenny just happen to look alike, and their names are kind of similar, so for whatever reason, Gena has been letting everyone think that's her in the film."

MMP blinked twice in surprise. He had very dramatic eyes, huge and rimmed with long, dark lashes, and blinking in an exaggerated manner heightened his resemblance to an anime character, which was probably exactly why he did it. "But . . ." He turned and looked at me, his face open and questioning. He looked back at Boots. "I don't get it. Serge would know who was in his film, wouldn't he?"

"Yeah, you'd think so." Boots sounded tired, like she was already exhausted by the topic. "We're not sure what Serge's deal was, whether he knew his wife wasn't the same actress who'd starred in his film years before they got married, or if Gena fooled him, too. I really don't have a guess."

MMP looked back at me. "That can't be right," he said. "I sat on this couch with Gena and watched that film on her laptop, and she told me all about filming it. That was her movie."

"It wasn't," I said. It was an effort to keep from sounding bitter and resentful. "I don't know how I can prove it to you, but that was me."

"There's another interesting angle to all this," Boots said. She gestured toward me, the gold tips of her nails glinting in the low light of the room. "Jenny is a psychic."

The two blinks came again, perfectly timed for maximum dramatic effect. He raised his eyebrows until they disappeared beneath his long spiky bangs. The visible skin of his forehead remained crease-free despite the exaggerated gesture; even though he couldn't be more than twenty-four, twenty-five at the most, he was probably already using injectables to fend off the coming ravages of time. "I'm sorry?"

"I'm an intuitive counselor. I operate a clinic near the Grove," I said. I cleared my throat. "I give psychic career advice."

"She has a genuine gift. I met her just today, and she did a quick reading of me, and it felt like she'd known me forever," Boots said. "I thought we could use her abilities to find out who killed Serge, and to find Gena."

MMP lowered his brows. He nodded. "Okay, I see. Cool deal." Maybe he calmly accepted that I was psychic, maybe he was being polite, maybe some combination of both. "How would you do that?"

It was directed at me, and I had no answer, since Boots hadn't let me in on her plan. Boots jumped in. "Could you throw a party here? Sometime this week would be best. Not like a party-party; I don't think anyone is in the mood to celebrate. It'd be a gathering of people who know and love Gena and Serge, as a way to remember Serge and demonstrate our support for Gena. Could you do that? It'd be small, maybe eight or ten people."

"I . . . guess?" MMP looked uncertain. "But . . . look, the police haven't said I'm a suspect, and I honestly don't think I am. I didn't really know Serge, much less have any reason to want him dead, but the fact remains that my girlfriend is missing. I don't want to do anything that would make it look like I'm not taking Gena's absence seriously, and a party seems unserious, you know?"

"I get that, I really do," Boots said. "But we'd make sure it seemed sincere, not callous or exploitative."

"You think someone at this party could be the person who killed Serge?" MMP asked. He drained his glass in a single swallow, looked around to see if either Boots or I needed more soju, saw we were doing fine, and refilled his glass.

"I do, yes. Hard truth, the killer is probably someone close to him." Boots fished a shrimp cracker out of the bag on the table and sniffed it curiously before popping it into her mouth. She crunched and swallowed. "This wasn't a home invasion. Serge opened the door willingly to greet his murderer."

"Yeah, but . . ." MMP looked distressed. "He was shot in the doorway, right? I don't see how that rules out a random attack. Someone knocks on the door, Serge answers it, and he gets shot."

"I hope that's the case," Boots said. "But it's far more likely Serge was killed by someone close to him. Like his wife."

"Malis? You think Malis killed him?"

"It'd make sense, wouldn't it?"

"You'd know better than I would. I've met Malis like twice, and she's always seemed okay to me." MMP refilled his glass again. He drank soju like he was trying to quench a deep thirst. "Here's the thing, though: if I throw a party, Malis won't come. She wasn't all that close to Gena, she doesn't really know me, and from what I've heard from Gena, she's not social under the best of circumstances."

"I bet you could talk her into it, though. You're very persuasive, MMP. Thirty million devoted social media followers can't be wrong."

"Closer to forty million, actually," he said. He shook his head. "No. I want to help, but I don't see it happening. If you want Malis to show up to a party, it'll have to be hosted by someone else. Try one of her friends. Or maybe someone who could make her think it would be in her best interests to show up. Maybe Linus."

"Linus?" I asked. I'd been sitting back, sipping my soju in silence while trying to decide whether Boots's plan was disastrous or brilliant. I'd read enough Agatha Christie to enjoy the idea of assembling a room full of suspects at a social gathering in the hopes of unveiling the identity of the killer at the climax of the evening. But I was not at all confident I could ferret out Serge's killer via an evening of insightful conversation. The stakes for making a bad guess in the course of a routine psychic reading were pretty low: I might lose a regular client, or feel shamed into giving someone their money back. I'd face more serious repercussions for misidentifying an innocent party as a murderer. At best, I might embarrass myself badly in front of Boots and her influential friends.

At worst . . . I'd have to look into California's laws regarding both slander and fraud, but I could see myself slapped with a lawsuit by someone wealthy and powerful, if I didn't watch my step.

"Linus Halpern. He manages fine artists, Gena and Malis included," Boots said. "He doesn't handle the sale of their individual works, per se; that's usually something gallerists like Antoinette do. But he organizes collaborations with brands, finds sponsors, maybe lines up sales to big commercial clients. If a corporation is looking to commission some artwork for their courtyard or lobby, Linus can set them up with one of his artists."

Linus Halpern . . . "Linus has known Serge for a long time, right? Since before Serge was famous?" Both Boots and MMP turned their heads to look at me. They looked impressed; I shook my head to dispel whatever they were thinking. "That's not a psychic vision. I knew Linus when we made *The Divide*. He was credited as one of the producers, but I got the impression he was just a college friend who had loaned Serge a bunch of his own money. If I'm thinking of the same guy."

"That's probably him. I know he and Serge go way back." Boots thought about it. "Going through Linus might be smart. He'd want to find Serge's killer as much as we do. And I bet he's going nuts about Gena being gone."

"Are he and Gena close?" I asked.

"Sure, of course. They've worked together for years. But Gena is also a huge source of income for Linus. Especially with the Elliott Thwaite collab."

I'd visited the Elliott Thwaite boutique in Beverly Hills once, a high-ceilinged marble palace on Rodeo. I'd been lured in by the simple, clean, universally flattering lines of the dresses that adorned the silver mannequins in the window display; I'd backed out quietly once I spotted a handbag that cost more than my total income for the past year. "Gena does fashion design, too?"

"Sort of," MMP said. "She wrapped up a huge contract with Elliott Thwaite right before she disappeared. Her designs will be on handbags, scarves, coats, you name it. It's an eight-figure deal, this whole collection. She'd been working on it solidly for the past six months."

Eight figures. All my life I'd heard that working artists generally made peanuts.

"I'll talk to Linus, see if we can work something out." Boots got to her feet. "Hey, is it okay if I give Jenny a tour of the studio? I want to show her Gena's work."

MMP rose as well. "Oh, yeah, of course. All the Thwaite designs were handed over last week, so there's no problem with the insurance people now. I haven't been in there since . . . well, it's not like I went there much anyway. But yeah, go ahead. Hang on a sec."

He rummaged in the pockets of his baggy shorts and extracted his phone. His thumbs flew over the surface, texting with a speed and ease I envied. "I sent you the code. Don't try the door without it; the alarm will go off if you touch the handle before you hear the lock click, and then the security company has to come over to check it out. That's a big reason why I don't go in there; the alarm terrifies me." He grinned.

"Thanks." Boots shouldered her purse. "We'll leave from the studio, so we'll say goodbye to you here. Thanks for letting us stop by."

"Oh, my pleasure. It's good to see you." MMP took Boots's hand in both of his and leaned in to quickly press his cheek against hers. He took mine as well and repeated the gesture. His cheek was soft, no hint of stubble. He still smelled good. "Really nice meeting you, Jenny."

"You too," I said. "Though I'm sorry about the circumstances."

"Yeah." MMP exhaled. "It's just . . . I'm going crazy, seriously crazy with Gena gone. It's good having company. Keeps me from falling to pieces."

"I'll text you after I've talked to Linus," Boots said. She gestured to me. "This way. We'll go through the back of the house."

We left MMP on the sofa, drinking soju like it was Kool-Aid and looking very, very young and overwhelmed.

CHAPTER 6

Charm School Graduate

On the back patio, Boots and I sat on teak chairs topped with thick blue cushions and slipped on the shoes we'd retrieved from the entryway. Night had fallen, and beyond the border of Gena's backyard, which was marked off with an iron fence too low to obstruct the city view, the downtown skyline glittered.

Boots glanced over at my feet. "Nice. Vintage?" she asked.

"Yep."

"I had a couple pairs of those maybe twenty years ago. Cute as all hell, but deadly on the feet."

Gena's house and its neighbors on the twisting drive were built along the slope of a hill; from the patio, I could glance directly onto the roof of the home bordering hers to the south, while the plot of land immediately to the north was undeveloped, too steep for easy construction. A retaining wall made of dark concrete blocks ran along the north border of Gena's backyard, reinforcing the side of the hill and shielding her home from the threat of earthquakes and mudslides.

On the far edge of the property, flush against the retaining wall, stood a single-story cottage painted in the same color scheme as the main building. The door didn't match the cottage; it was steel, with a chunky industrial handle and a keypad embedded in the jamb. I tried to peek through the closest window, but it was covered with some kind of privacy film; my own reflection stared back at me.

Boots took out her phone and checked the text MMP had just sent her. "When Gena agreed to the deal with Elliott Thwaite, Linus made her install a new security system at the client's request. Insurance reasons. Her designs were the property of the client, and they wanted to make sure there were no leaks. She wouldn't even let me in here while she was working on them."

She typed a series of numbers into the keypad, referring frequently to the screen of her phone. I heard an audible click as the magnetic lock released, and a red light on the keypad switched to green.

She opened the door. I was hit by the smell of my high school art classroom, the rotting-pine aroma of oil paint and turpentine. A young woman looked up from her perch on a rickety wooden stool and glanced at us from beneath a mass of tangled curls, then returned her attention to the canvas on an easel in front of her. "Get out. I'm working," she said.

"Brynna." Boots sounded unnaturally chipper. "MMP didn't mention you were here."

"He didn't mention *you* were here." Brynna stared at her canvas, paintbrush held up near her ear. It looked at first like she was wearing a single glove, and then I realized the hand gripping the paintbrush was almost entirely covered with paint, multiple shades of green layered on top of one another. I caught a glimpse of her work in progress, something with ominous dark shapes framed against a darker sky. I couldn't tell what the painting would eventually evolve into, but it had some quality that drew my attention, something similar to what I'd felt in Antoinette's gallery while looking at Gena's work. "What do you want?"

"Just touring the space," Boots said. "Jenny, this is Brynna. Brynna, Jenny."

"Nice to meet you," I said.

Brynna still didn't look at us. "You're not supposed to be in here."

It pained me to admit it, because her personality seemed overwhelmingly crappy, but she was beautiful. Bushy eyebrows, a long straight nose, a wild amount of thick brown hair that stuck out in a tangled cloud. She looked like a feral goddess who lived in the wilderness and dined on raw hearts ripped from the chests of wolves. Large splatters of paint stained her terry-cloth romper. Her bare legs were streaked with greens and blues.

"We'll just be a second," Boots said cheerfully.

I followed Boots deeper into the studio, which was only a single room, unfinished and unfurnished. Stacks of canvases lined the walls, haphazard piles of what was probably Gena's art, or maybe Brynna's, since it seemed like she belonged here somehow.

A few canvases were on display, including one large piece hanging on the far wall. I walked over to examine it. It depicted a blobby white figure, frail and almost featureless, crouching down, long translucent arms wrapped around her head and body to shield herself. She was surrounded by gigantic angry slashes of charcoal and black that formed savage apparitions. They were attacking the girl, beating her to a pulp, tearing her apart.

I'd only been in one violent fight in my life, back when I was a very stupid teenager. I'd done something shitty, and I'd probably deserved the beating I'd taken, though that hadn't made it come as any less of a shock when it happened, that split-second when friendly faces turned dark and blotchy with wrath. Staring at Gena's painting, I felt that moment, felt the sudden concussive pain of a bottle smashing into fragments against the side of my head. I smelled my sweat, acrid with terror; I felt the rain pouring down on me where I lay in a ball on the wet earth of the cornfield, bewildered and helpless. I heard the torrent of abuse shouted at me, hysterical young voices calling me a slut, a sneak, a traitor. I felt my sheer horror at the brutality of the attack, combined with the sick, guilty knowledge that I'd earned every kick, every blow, every curse . . .

"She's good, isn't she?" Boots stood at my elbow and cocked her head toward the painting. "I think a lot of contemporary artists are ridiculously overrated, but Gena's stuff makes me feel things. I look at this painting, and I think I'm somewhere else. Does that make sense?"

"Yeah. It does." I swallowed hard, my throat thick and parched. I was back in the studio, dry and safe, an accelerated heartbeat the only lingering evidence of my unscheduled trip to the past. The blobby figure in the painting, the girl, she was hiding something, a secret no one else should know, and all of a sudden, I didn't want Boots at my side, because maybe if she stared at the painting for too long, she'd be able to look beyond the girl and see that secret too.

"What the fuck," Brynna said. She stood at my side. When I first looked at her, I could have sworn I saw fear in her expression, but it evolved swiftly into rage, her skin turning purple and blotchy. I thought for a moment she was furious with me for looking at the painting, but her next words cleared up the reason for her sudden burst of emotion. "Who are you?"

"She's no relation to Gena. They just look alike," Boots said. "I brought her over to meet MMP, and I thought she'd be interested in seeing Gena's work."

Brynna scowled at me, like she was angry I had the audacity to physically resemble Gena. "Then take her to the gallery. I'm working here."

"We'll be out of your hair in a minute," Boots said with a bright smile. She took me on a leisurely tour of the small studio, keeping up a lively flood of chatter, showing off various paintings, regaling me with anecdotes about Gena's creative process.

I got the sense Boots was dragging out our visit for the sole purpose of pissing Brynna off, which was something I could support. When we left at last, Boots called out a friendly goodbye; Brynna responded with a raised middle finger, her attention fixed on her canvas.

I didn't speak until we were on the redwood deck, far enough from the cottage that I thought there was little chance of being overheard. "Who was the charm school graduate?"

"Brynna is Gena's protégée. Adorable, isn't she?" Boots wrinkled her nose. "She's the daughter of some big executive at Warner. Classic spoiled rich kid; I have to remind myself, very firmly, that she's just young and stupid and full of herself, like we all were at that age, and she'll probably grow up someday. There's a lot of buzz about her artwork right now, she placed in some big competition last year, so Gena has taken her under her wing. God knows why."

I trailed Boots along a narrow path of flat stones that ran beside the garage to the courtyard where we had parked. "Her painting looked pretty good," I said.

Boots glanced at me. "Yeah? I can't stand her stuff. I think she copies Gena's style as best she can and assumes that's enough to make her famous." Her mouth tightened. "I'm surprised MMP still lets her use the studio space while Gena's gone."

I looked around the courtyard. I saw Boots's SUV and my junky old car, and that was it; Kira must have driven off in the Mini. "Does Brynna park in the garage?"

Boots glanced around. "No room. Gena's car is still there, and MMP's has got to be in there as well. He bought himself a Maserati over the summer, and he's still in the phase where he's terrified of getting that first scratch, so he keeps it tucked inside as much as possible. Brynna probably took a car service here, or got dropped off by a friend. Why?"

"Just curious." I stared at the garage, which was attached to the house. From what Boots had told me earlier, I knew

Gena—or someone driving Gena's car—drove through the gate the night of Serge's murder, parked in the garage, left her purse and phone in the house, and disappeared.

But how? I sorted through the possibilities, my thoughts branching out in multiple directions. If Gena, or whoever it was, had left through the front gate, either in a car or on foot, the security camera would have picked it up. Having seen Gena's backyard, I knew it would be tricky for anyone to leave the property that way. They'd have to scale the retaining wall to climb up the hill, or they'd have to risk a steep drop over the back fence to go down the hill, or they'd have to climb over the fence of the neighboring property and exit through their backyard. None of those would be impossible, but none seemed easy.

So where did Gena go?

I found myself consumed with the urge to find the answer. Not because Boots was paying me to find her friend, and not because I wanted to force Gena to admit she'd stolen credit for my accomplishment, but simply because I needed to know. My favorite part of being a psychic—okay, yes, a fraudulent psychic—was getting the chance to solve puzzles. I loved digging beneath the surface of a client's request and unearthing answers to the questions they hadn't quite dared to put into words. I loved talking to people, thinking about them, figuring out what made them tick. I loved analyzing situations and behaviors, searching for anomalies and discovering logical explanations. I loved all of that, and I was good at it. Given enough time and freedom to snoop around and ask questions, I figured I could find Serge's killer, and I could find Gena.

"What'd you think of MMP?" Boots asked, breaking through my thoughts.

"He seemed great. Kira, too."

She was quiet for a long time. When the question came, it sounded casual, as though she was just making conversation, like she couldn't care less about the answer. "Are they sleeping together?"

"Kira and MMP? Yeah, they are," I said. "From the look of it, I think they're in love."

She inhaled. "Are you sure? Like . . . psychically sure?"

"Yeah." It didn't require a psychic to pick up on the small clues, the way MMP looked protectively at Kira, her shy glances at him, the way his fingers had stroked hers when he clasped her hands in his.

"Damn it." Boots seemed wounded. "With Gena missing, you'd think he'd have the sense . . ." She gave me a tense smile. "Kids are stupid, right?"

I was quiet. Then: "How long have you been sleeping with him?"

"What are you talking about?"

I didn't reply. She inhaled, held it, huffed it out in a powerful burst of air. When she spoke, she sounded calm. "My own dumb fault for hanging out with a psychic."

She walked over to the driver's side of her SUV. I followed her. There was little chance of MMP or Brynna overhearing our conversation, but I shared her desire to be cautious. She spoke in a low tone; I had to lean in to catch all her words.

"It happened, okay? I stopped by, Gena was out, MMP invited me in for drinks. He'd just hit thirty million subscribers and was in a celebratory mood, and that mood spilled over to me," Boots said.

I didn't answer. I probably looked disapproving, because Boots laughed at my expression. It sounded forced; her grin was a wobbly imitation of her world-famous smile. "I know. Believe me, I know. I turned fifty last year, not that anyone needs to remind me of that. He's half my age, literally. Going to bed with him wasn't my proudest accomplishment, but what can I say, it was nice. I was feeling my age, and he made me feel young again. It meant something to both of us, but it didn't mean the world, if you know what I mean."

"Did Gena know about it?"

"Maybe. I don't know. MMP might've felt obligated to tell

her. I don't think she would have cared." Boots tilted her head back and looked up. The sky glowed a neon azure, the color of a nightclub ceiling. "That's a lie. She would have cared, especially after what happened between me and Serge, but that was an entirely different set of circumstances. What I mean is, it wouldn't have destroyed our friendship. You know?"

"Yeah. I know." I thought I probably did. Friendships were complex; friendships could withstand a great deal of crappy behavior.

There was a moment of silence, and then Boots said slowly, as though the words were being pulled out of her, "You look so damn much like her. You really do. Are you sure there's no connection?"

"Like I'm her long-lost twin sister?" I shook my head. "No."

"Okay, but is it possible? Could your mom have had twins and not told you?"

"Absolutely not." It was curt. I smiled to soften it. "It's just a coincidence."

"Okay." Boots opened her car door, then turned back to face me. "I don't want to sound mushy, but it's nice having you around. It makes me feel like she's not really gone."

I found myself at a loss for words. Guilt always makes me flush, and I could feel my face growing hot. Boots was drawn to me because I reminded her of her missing friend, and I was milking her fondness for Gena for my own financial gain. It came to me suddenly that Boots was lonely, that her level of fame forced her to keep her inner circle small, and thus the loss of Gena had created a void that she hoped I could fill, at least temporarily.

Or maybe I had Boots all wrong. Maybe she knew more about Gena's disappearance than she was letting on. She'd slept with both Gena's former husband and her current boyfriend. The husband was dead, and Gena was missing, and I only had Boots's word for it that her actions hadn't made waves throughout this little cluster of friends and lovers.

Boots's world-famous face looked open and genuine. I examined her, trying to decide whether she was hiding anything from me, but came up empty. If I were really psychic, maybe I would have been able to glean some kind of preternatural insights into Boots's emotional state, her feelings of guilt or anger or satisfaction or grief, to give me some indication as to whether she knew more than she was saying about what had happened to Serge and Gena. But I wasn't psychic, and all I could read from Boots was a mild weariness, an impression that she had reached the end of a long day, and now she just wanted to say goodbye and part ways. And so that's what we did.

CHAPTER 7

Maserati Money

The next morning was an ordeal. The rituals of my daily existence—the stuffy clinic, the funky smell, the endless wait for drop-in customers who almost certainly would never materialize—felt unbearably mundane in the wake of my unsettling but exhilarating foray into Boots's glamorous world. I wanted to dive right into my investigation. I wanted to dazzle Boots by uncovering the true story behind Serge's murder and Gena's disappearance. I wanted to make some cash, gain some powerful friends, level up to a higher playing field. I wanted to find out more, much more, about Gena, the doppelgänger who'd been leading a comfortable, privileged life, a life so much more satisfying than my own.

But there was nothing much I could do at the moment, not until I heard back from Boots. As the afternoon dragged on, as I sat at my table and silently wished for clients, I took out my phone and conducted some research into Gena and her circle of friends. This mostly involved watching a bunch of MMP's short, cheerful videos, the ones that had shot him to internet fame. He did home repairs, showing viewers how to replace a faucet cartridge to stop a drip, or how to swap out a broken outlet without getting electrocuted. The hook was that he wasn't an expert at any of this and in fact was downright incompetent, in a way that was mostly charming instead of obnoxious; he'd fumble his way through the process, consulting manuals on his phone for guidance while grimacing at the camera and laughing at his many screwups.

I watched him take apart a table lamp and repair a broken switch. The lamp looked expensive, with a heavy gold base shaped like a series of intricate knots; if it was Gena's, I hoped she was okay with MMP reducing her possessions to their component parts.

On the wall behind MMP, just a glimpse in the corner of the screen, I spotted a familiar movie poster, my anguished face on an epic scale. It was framed in gold and hung in a place of honor against a deep blue wall. For a film Gena had never been in, she sure felt a sense of pride about it.

Seeing that poster pissed me off. Gena had no business displaying it in her home. She didn't need *The Divide*. She already had everything I lacked: widespread acclaim, financial stability, close friends who were boldfaced names. She was my exact physical double, as mind-boggling as I found that concept, and yet when I considered her formidable achievements, I felt like a weak, watery copy. My only accomplishment in life was *The Divide*, and everyone believed that was hers as well.

It occurred to me that I might hate Gena, at least a little.

I read a profile of MMP on some website that tracked the goings-on of prominent social media influencers. He was twenty-five; he'd been famous for a few years and had been kicking around the fringes of the public eye for ten. Born in Los Angeles, he moved to South Korea with his parents when he was twelve. At fifteen, he signed with a management company and began training to become a pop idol; he withdrew from school so he could devote himself to endless days of dancing, singing, and media training, all as a part of an up-and-coming boy band called Fantazzy. The name made me think of strip clubs, but the group itself, online footage reassured me, was determinedly wholesome. MMP, as he was already known by then, was one of seven clear-skinned teens dressed in thick-soled sneakers and sequin-covered hockey jerseys who sang up-tempo anthems while flawlessly executing tricky choreography.

By the time MMP was eighteen, Fantazzy was no more, having failed to differentiate itself in South Korea's idol-glutted market. He'd moved to Los Angeles to pursue an acting career and eventually hooked up with Gena; they'd been together for three years, which made them the equivalent of an old married couple by Los Angeles standards. Reading between the lines, it seemed like he'd been out of work, wholly reliant on Gena's largesse until his videos had taken off in a big way, earning him hundreds of thousands of dollars in ad revenue. Maserati money. Life was looking pretty sunny for MMP these days, apart from the great glaring problem of Gena's absence.

Could he be a killer? Based on my initial impression, I thought it was unlikely. Still, he couldn't be ruled out, not yet. I reminded myself that I didn't know him well enough to tell whether that outer shell of sweet-natured amiability hid any darker impulses.

I set my phone down and looked up as the door opened. A young woman dressed for the heat in cutoff jean shorts and a sleeveless white T-shirt glanced around my clinic nervously before her gaze settled on me. "Hi. Are you Jenny? I'm Lily. Tish sent me here."

"Hi, Lily. Are you here for a reading?" It was nice of Tish to throw some business my way. The nine-dollar mushroom mocha had been a good investment.

At my gesture, Lily sank into the chair opposite me. She was extremely tall and coltish, with a chiseled face and glossy dark hair, and I knew without her having to mention it that she was an actress. "I need help, or advice. Tish and I have the same agent. We went on an audition together yesterday, and . . . Tish got cast." She shrugged. "I didn't."

"The horror film? Tish got the lead?" Huh. Apparently I'd missed the mark about not picturing her as a fragile Victorian heroine. Whoops.

Lily shook her head. "Right when we arrived at the casting office, we were getting our parking validated, and she started joking around with this random guy in the lobby. He mentioned how his Irish mother had red hair like hers, so she told him all about her class trip to Dublin her senior year, and she did this goofy Irish accent, and . . . yeah, he turned out to be the director. There's a part in the script for an Irish maid who gets murdered by a ghost, and he gave it to her right there. She didn't even have to read for it." She sounded impressed and envious, in roughly equal amounts. "She told me during the ride home that she'd asked you how the audition would go, and you'd said that would happen. So . . . could you do the same thing for me? Tell me what I should be doing?"

Hot damn. I was good at this. I mean, technically I hadn't predicted any of that would happen, but it sounded like Tish had glossed over the specifics in her explanation to Lily, which was lucky for me. "What do you want to know?"

"I've been in Los Angeles for a year." She folded her hands together on the table in front of her and leaned forward, intense. "I've been trying really, really hard. I've gone on so many auditions, and I'm getting nowhere. My parents pay my rent, but Mom says if I don't start supporting myself by the end of the year, I'll have to move back home to Tucson." Her upper lip twitched, as though living with her parents was equivalent to a stint in the federal pen. "So what do I do? What am I doing wrong? How do I get a film career?"

I refrained from telling Lily that I'd spent half my life pondering those very same questions. "It sounds like you could benefit from a tarot reading. That's fifty dollars."

"Absolutely, yeah." Lily flicked her hair back out of her eyes and sat up very straight in her chair. "Just tell me what I should be doing, please. I'm desperate."

I passed the tarot deck to Lily and instructed her to shuffle it while mentally projecting her hopes and fears about her current existential crisis out into the spirit realm, then took it back from her and began to lay out cards in a precise arrangement. Tarot readings were my comfort zone as a fake psychic, thanks to the nebulous, slippery, and boundlessly interpretable meanings I could extract from the cards. It was impossible to trap me in a lie; everyone hears exactly what they want to hear from a tarot reading.

While I was deeply immersed in persuading Lily that the universe wanted her to start searching for a stable desk job at one of the studios, a job that would reassure her parents and make her financially independent while still keeping her close to the heart of the film industry, my phone buzzed on the table. Lily's eyes widened as she saw Boots's name flash across the lock screen. "Oh my god," she said. "You know Boots Pontifex?"

"I'm sorry, I need to take this," I said.

"Yeah, of course, go ahead," Lily said. She sounded dazed.

Boots was in a chipper mood. "Short notice, I know, but I just talked to Linus, and when I told him about you, he asked me to bring you over. Are you free this afternoon?"

"Sure." My schedule would be clear for the rest of the day, unless Tish happened to send over more discouraged auditioners. "Did Linus remember me?"

"He did. But he always assumed you and Gena were the same person, and now he's very curious, and probably a little confused. If we're going to get him on board, it'd be a good idea to satisfy his curiosity."

"You bet. When and where?"

"His office is in Century City. I can pick you up; it'll simplify things if we arrive together. Where are you?"

"At my clinic," I said. I gave her the address.

"I must have passed your place a billion times," Boots said. "I'll be there in an hour."

I replaced the phone on the table. Lily's eyes were still too wide. "That was really Boots Pontifex?"

"I'm helping her with a project," I said.

"Wow," Lily said. "She's amazing. I would kill for a career like hers." She was impressed by Boots, and impressed by me for working with Boots, and this gave me a little stab of self-importance. If word spread that celebrities relied on my psychic guidance, maybe I could become the next Della DeLaurenti. Failing that, maybe I could at least slow down my current descent into poverty and squalor.

Boots texted me from the curb, long after Lily had been sent on her way with a head full of practical career advice disguised as missives from an unearthly realm. I hit the lights, locked up, and climbed into her SUV.

Boots wore a fluttery crepe dress in a swirling taupe-and-cream pattern, paired with dangling gold earrings shaped like giraffes. She shot me a grin before she nosed her vehicle into traffic. She flipped it south to Olympic and headed west in the direction of Century City.

"So you told Linus about me?" I asked.

She nodded. "He's excited to see you. I think I short-circuited his brain when I told him that wasn't Gena in Serge's film."

"Was he still close to Serge? Do you think he'd know whether Serge knew Gena wasn't in *The Divide*?"

"I have no idea. Does it matter?"

"It does, yeah. I'm proud of that film. It bugs me to think Serge might not have realized Gena wasn't me. It's a confusing situation, and I don't like it."

"I can see where that would be annoying, sure." Boots's tone was brisk yet kind. "But do you want some advice? After all this time, you might want to let it go. You quit acting, and no one saw that film anyway."

It was a little blunt, but I couldn't say it wasn't true. Still,

I wanted to argue the point, to make Boots understand how important *The Divide* had been to me. How hard I'd worked to get every aspect of my performance right, how optimistic I'd been that I was heading toward an impressive career. How, whenever I lay awake at night on my lumpy mattress in the stuffy back room of my clinic, consumed with regret about the past and dread about the future, I could soothe myself by remembering *The Divide:* I'd starred in that film, and even though no one had seen it, I'd been extraordinary.

But Boots and I weren't at the stage of our acquaintance where I could expect her to care about any of that, so I kept quiet and just stared out the window at the passing scenery.

Linus's offices were in one of the Century City skyscrapers. Boots pulled into the parking garage and handed the SUV off to a black-vested valet, and then we visited the security desk in the main lobby. A beefy man in a tight black suit beamed at Boots, a flash of happy recognition in his wide bearded face, and directed us to the elevators without checking to see if we had an appointment.

Linus's company had a suite on a high floor. A receptionist with cherry-red hair cut in a blunt pageboy smiled up at us. "He's not on a call, so you can go right in." She pointed a slim finger down the hall to the right.

"Perfect, thanks." Boots headed into the hall, with me at her elbow. She paused in the open doorway of the first office we passed and rapped her knuckles on the jamb. "Hey."

Linus Halpern looked up from his computer, and I felt a spike of immediate recognition. Yeah, I'd known that guy. He'd hung out on the set of *The Divide* a few times, sitting beside Serge, leaning over and talking to him between takes. We'd gone to dinner one night after shooting had ended early, him and Serge and me and a couple of others associated with the production. It had been a good evening, fueled with multiple rounds of strong drinks; Linus had talked a lot about Patagonia, having just come back from a long summer spent backpacking through the Andes. I'd gone home with Serge after dinner, leaving my car parked in a lot somewhere on Sunset. He'd driven me there to pick it up in the early hours of the morning so we could arrive on the set separately, and if anyone noticed I showed up in the same clothes I wore the night before, no one pointed it out.

Then a handful of years later, Serge had married a woman who looked exactly like me, who was evidently quite willing to let everyone assume she and I were the same person. Did he know the truth? When he and Gena reminisced about old times, when they lay in bed together, did he know she wasn't me, or had she fooled him, the same way she'd apparently fooled everyone else in her life?

And if someone who'd never met me could replace me that easily, didn't that suggest there was nothing all that memorable about me?

"Boots! Good to see you!" Linus rose from his desk, smiling at her, and then he turned to look at me. His expression didn't change, but I could tell the instant he processed my appearance. For a moment it seemed as though he'd turned to stone, his smile fixed on his face. He didn't swallow or blink.

And then the spell was broken, and the smile deepened. "Holy hell. Boots, you weren't kidding, were you?"

He extended a hand to me. "Hi. Linus Halpern."

"Hi, Linus. Jenny St. John. We've met." I shook his hand. His grip was firm though not overly aggressive. His eyes were fixed on my face.

"Yes, we certainly have, haven't we?" He grinned. He had a nice grin. The corners of his eyes wrinkled, like grinning was usual for him.

He was holding up well. He was tan and fit, with curly dark hair and a pronounced widow's peak. He looked like he still went backpacking through Patagonia or cycling through Andalusia whenever his schedule allowed. He wore a navy tailored three-piece suit with a blue-and-pink-striped tie over a blindingly white shirt. His office had a great view of neighboring Beverly Hills, and it was expensively appointed, with a curved executive desk made of shiny red wood and a chesterfield sofa in buttery-soft black leather, which rested under an oversized painting hanging high on the wall. The painting, which depicted stylized lions in an African savanna, was probably the work of one of Linus's clients, though not Gena; I was good at detecting her style by now.

"Take a seat. Can I get you anything? Coffee, kombucha? There's wine, too, if it's not too early for you."

Boots and I arranged ourselves in chairs in front of his desk; Linus waited until we were comfortable before he sat. "We're good, thank you. We know you're busy, so we just wanted to quickly swing by," Boots said.

"I'm so glad you did. This is fascinating." Linus looked at me again and beamed. He seemed shocked yet delighted. "Jenny St. John. Wow. You're going to have to excuse me; my mind is officially blown."

"It's good to see you, Linus," I said, realizing I meant it. "It must be strange for you. I take it you had no doubt that Gena was . . . that Gena was me?"

"None at all. Not a single doubt. Isn't that weird? I've known Gena for fifteen years. I've been her manager for ten. I've dined at her home. We've shared a hotel suite in Miami during Art Basel. I never had any clue she wasn't that cute girl who'd been in Serge's first film."

"In your defense, we only met, what, three or four times? And that was more than twenty years ago," I said.

"Yeah, but even still, I'm embarrassed I was so confused." He beamed at me. "You and Gena have to be sisters, right? Or cousins?"

"No, no relation at all, unless it's very distant. It's just one of those things."

"Wow." Linus shook his head. "Wow. Jenny St. John. *The*

Divide, man. That was another lifetime ago. Remember when Serge made you guys film all night in the Bradbury Building? I stopped by the set in the morning to see how everyone was holding up, and you were so exhausted you could barely string a sentence together."

I laughed at the memory. By the time filming finally wrapped for the day, I'd needed to cling to my costar Ronnie between takes to stay on my feet. "Good times, yeah. But it wasn't the Bradbury, it was the lobby of the Biltmore. Serge had wanted to film at the Bradbury because of his love of *Blade Runner*, but renting it would have blown the budget, remember?"

Linus nodded, his eyes locked with mine. "Ah, that's right. Of course. I'd forgotten."

He hadn't forgotten. He'd been testing me. Well, I couldn't blame him for that. In his position, I might very well suspect I was an interloper who'd weaseled my way into Gena's life for unknown yet certainly nefarious purposes. To Linus, that probably seemed easier to believe than Gena, his client and friend, deliberately deceiving him for so many years.

He smiled at me again, bright and amiable. "What have you been up to? Boots told me you're a psychic?"

"Yeah, I'm an intuitive counselor." I cleared my throat. "I'm doing well. I got out of acting a long time ago. But I find it so weird that Gena would pretend to be me. Do you think Serge knew?"

"He'd have to, wouldn't he? He'd absolutely have to. There's no way he'd be fooled." Linus shifted in his chair. "I mean, you and Serge . . . You two were dating, right?"

I was looking at Linus, but I could sense Boots turning her head to stare at me. My face felt warm. "Just for a microsecond. But offhand, yeah, I'd say he should've known we were two different women."

"Yeah, I should say so." Linus shook his head. "Crazy. Absolutely crazy."

Boots leaned forward in her chair. "Thing is, as soon as I met Jenny and found out she was a psychic, I had this idea that she might be able to help us. Help us find Gena, I mean."

Linus was quiet for a moment, like he was having trouble following Boots's train of thought. "Find Gena. You mean . . . find her psychically?"

"Sure. At least she could find out what happened to her. So I had this idea of hosting a dinner party," Boots said. "We'd invite a few of Gena's friends, Serge's, too. I'd like to have it at your place, if you're game for it. Jenny could chat with the guests and use her abilities to sense if Serge's murderer is among them."

Linus stared at us, unblinking. It was impossible to tell what he thought of the idea, which, when Boots said it out loud like that, sounded profoundly stupid and bad. "You think that would work?"

He was asking me, not Boots. I went with a shady version of honesty. "I don't know," I said. "I think I'd be able to detect something if I found myself talking with Serge's killer. But it's not as though there's a yes or no switch in my head that gives me answers. It's more like I receive vague impressions that become clearer over time."

"Okay, I see. But I don't know how . . ." Linus stared straight ahead at some indeterminate point between me and Boots, maybe looking at the lions, maybe seeing nothing at all. His gaze went fuzzy, and then it sharpened, and he looked at Boots. "You're setting a trap for someone specific, right? You think you know who it is."

"Maybe," Boots said. "Isn't it obvious?"

"Not to me." Linus sounded firm yet cheerful.

Boots raised her eyebrows and looked at him, her expression expectant. Linus slumped back in his chair and groaned. "Oh, god, don't say Malis. Please don't say you think Malis did it."

"Sorry. But is it really so unthinkable that she could be a murderer?"

"I think anyone could be a murderer, under the right—or

wrong, I guess—circumstances," Linus said. "Physically? Sure, it's possible. From a deeply selfish perspective, though, I'm already in deep shit because of the circumstances surrounding Gena. I can't handle the thought of another client being in trouble with the law right now. So just for my own sanity, I will not consider the idea of Malis being a ruthless killer."

"What kind of shit are you in?" Boots asked. "The Thwaite deal is all over, isn't it?"

"Sure. Gena's side is done. She handed off her designs to me, and they're amazing, of course. The client is thrilled. But the circumstances of her absence make things extremely complicated."

"Does it kill the deal?"

"Not necessarily, but it could." Linus folded his hands together and rested his chin on them, elbows on his desk. "Gena received half the payment up front, with the other half pending upon final approval of the designs. If Gena had been found dead along with Serge, that second payment would go to whomever inherits her estate. I don't know who that would be; I can't imagine it's the young boyfriend. Her family, maybe."

"She doesn't have a family," Boots said. "Or at least she's not close to them. I get the impression she's estranged."

"Ah, okay." Linus shrugged. "I don't know how to talk about this without sounding like an asshole, and that's not my intention, so I want to make it clear that my hope is that Gena will be found alive and well. With that said . . ." He exhaled. "Gena's contract with Elliott Thwaite has a morality clause. That's pretty standard. If it turns out Gena killed Serge—and of course she didn't, before you say anything, I know damn well she didn't—the contract is voided, and that big advance gets returned to the client, and that includes my commission. Elliott Thwaite is an old and prestigious fashion house, and they won't want the scandal of working with a murderer to poison their brand. So we're in a holding pattern until we find out where Gena is, and until we find out who killed Serge."

"If Gena turns up dead . . ." Boots let it hang in the air.

"If it turns out Gena has been murdered along with Serge, and I can't stress enough how much I don't want that to be the case, Elliott Thwaite will consider the terms of the contract fulfilled, and the collection will be released as scheduled. From a cynical and frankly gross standpoint, it will probably be very good for their sales, because the final work of a dead artist always becomes a hot commodity. People are ghouls. If there's an announcement that Gena is dead, Antoinette will find her gallery depleted of art, because collectors will buy it up before funeral arrangements have been finalized."

Linus spread his hands as if to indicate an acceptance of the art world's strong mercenary bent. "But none of that really matters right now. Finding Gena and finding out who killed Serge are the obvious priorities right now. I do understand that, of course."

"Even if it turns out to be Malis?"

"If Malis killed Serge—which, for the record, I think is so unlikely as to be impossible—of course I want her caught. Whoever did it, I want them arrested, client or not. More importantly right now, I want to find out what happened to Gena." He grinned, shedding his somber mood like he was removing his suit coat and tie at the end of a long day. "So let's throw a party."

His sudden acquiescence surprised me. Linus was too well-mannered to show open skepticism about my psychic abilities, but he almost certainly knew I was a fraud. Nothing about him suggested he was the type to believe in otherworldly powers.

But Linus was fascinated by me, I realized in a flash, and fascinated that Gena had been able to deceive him for so many years, and even though he undoubtedly thought the psychic realm was bullshit, he wanted to put me right in the path of Serge and Gena's friends, because he figured something interesting might happen when they were faced with Gena's doppelgänger.

Smart man, Linus. He was almost certainly correct in his suspicion: something interesting *would* happen, and I'd be smack in the center of it. For a moment, I felt queasy. This dinner party could be risky for me, if I wasn't able to work miracles. I resisted a sudden urge to speak up and put a stop to Boots's scheme before irreversible events were set in motion. I had to remind myself firmly that I could handle this, that as long as I kept cool and alert, I could come out ahead, even if miracles turned out to be in short supply.

He glanced at his computer screen, clicking his mouse and frowning. "How's this Friday, at my place? Seven o'clock?"

"Perfect. You want to do the inviting? We'll keep the guest list small. You, us, Malis. We'll round it out with MMP, Antoinette, and Brynna," Boots said.

Linus looked surprised. "You want Brynna there?"

"It's not really a question of *wanting* so much. But she's one of your clients, and she's got ties to Gena, and it would look suspicious to Malis if she was invited and not Brynna."

"Yeah, I understand that, but look, Brynna is sometimes . . ." Linus tilted his head back, trying to access the far reaches of his brain to come up with a suitable euphemism. "Well, she's difficult. Don't get me wrong, she's a good kid at heart. But in social situations, she tends to act out a bit. It's kinder for everyone to leave her out."

"There's another reason we might want her there," Boots said crisply. I could sense she was annoyed at being stonewalled by Linus, even on such a small thing. Boots was very much accustomed to getting her own way. "This could all be about Gena, not Serge. Brynna's attachment to Gena seems unhealthy to me. You said Brynna was difficult; she's not my client, so I'll go ahead and call her a brat. If we're rounding up people who might have wanted to hurt Gena or Serge, she needs to be there."

Linus looked like he wanted to argue the point, and then he relaxed and nodded. "I'll start texting," he said. He picked up a slim gold pen and jotted names down on a memo pad. "Malis, Antoinette, Brynna. You want to ask MMP yourself? It'd seem more natural coming from you. I barely know the kid."

"That would be perfect. I'll make sure MMP is there." Boots rose to her feet, picking up her purse. I followed her lead. "You'll call me if there are any problems?"

"Sure, of course. Otherwise I'll see you then." Linus rose as well. "Jenny, it's really good to reconnect with you, though I'm sorry it's under these sad, weird circumstances. I'll see you both Friday?"

"Friday." I smiled. "Nice to see you too, Linus. We should have done this years ago." We should have. Linus and I had lived in the same city all this time; I should have called his office at any point during that time and asked to meet for drinks. It would have been easy. Stupid of me never to have bothered.

As I hoisted my purse over my shoulder, I found myself clenching the strap, both hands balled into tight fists like I wanted to punch someone. Myself, probably. If I'd made more of an effort to keep in touch with everyone I'd known—fleetingly yet with surprising intensity—all those years ago on the set of *The Divide*, then Gena never would have been able to casually steal my sole claim to fame.

I'd written to Serge once, maybe twenty years ago, contacting him via an email address I'd found online because I didn't have a current phone number for him. I'd kept it light and cheerful, just a quick congratulations for his recent successes and a casual suggestion that we should grab a drink to catch up on old times. It had gone unanswered, and I'd tried my best not to take it personally. The email address might have been a bad one, or he might have had an overzealous assistant screening his messages.

But it had left me feeling shy about attempting to contact Serge in other ways, so I'd stopped trying. I'm not a masochist; rejection never feels good. If I'd only been a little tougher and more tenacious, though, maybe I wouldn't have ended up as such a disappointment.

My examination of my failings consumed me during the elevator ride back down. I didn't realize Boots had been talking to me until she jabbed me lightly with her elbow to get my attention. I looked up. "Sorry, what?"

"I said, you should have told me you'd dated Serge. We could have compared notes." She grinned, then nudged me again. "You look miserable, like your puppy ran away or something. What's up?"

"Nothing," I said. I cleared my throat. "Sorry. It was talking to Linus about *The Divide*. I think I just got a little lost in the past."

"I get that." Boots tilted her head back and looked at the ceiling of the elevator. She smiled, relaxed yet wistful. "Sometimes I think about all those films I made long ago, back when I was young and hot, and it seems like that was the greatest time of my life, like it'll never be as good as that again." She straightened up and looked at me, her gaze direct and serious. "But there's no point in getting too wrapped up in nostalgia. If you don't mind my saying so, it'd be healthier for you to move beyond that film."

It echoed what she'd said during the ride over, and though she meant it kindly, the sentiment still pricked at my skin like a million invisible needles. I wanted to explain to Boots exactly how important *The Divide* had been to me—how I'd felt a deep bond with my role the first time I'd read the screenplay, how I'd arrived on the set each day filled with a sense of joyous purpose, how shattered I'd been when the promised theatrical release had been scrapped—but it would sound gooey and sentimental and painfully naïve if I tried to put any of that into words. So I just smiled at her and nodded, not trusting myself to speak.

CHAPTER 8

Golden Mile

Boots and I arrived separately at Linus's party, which was good from the perspective that I'd be able to leave whenever I wanted, and bad from the perspective that Boots was my passport into Gena's social circle. If Boots said I was okay, of course I was. Untethered to Boots, I was an interloper.

Linus lived in an art deco high-rise with an accordion-pleated front, dainty balconies made of bronze and glass tucked into the pleats. The building was painted a pale icy green like the flesh of a honeydew melon. It was part of the Wilshire Corridor, the series of tall residential buildings bridging Beverly Hills and Westwood; years ago, I'd overheard someone refer to the area as the Golden Mile, but that seemed like a term only used by real estate brokers. All the parking at Linus's building was handled by valets; I told a young woman in a red vest who I was there to see, and she nodded once, smiled, took my keys, and drove my clunker down a steep driveway into the bowels of the building.

Inside the lobby, which featured soft chairs in champagne-colored velvet surrounded by tropical plants in chunky bronze urns, I told the security guard I was there for Linus Halpern. He checked my ID against a list on his tablet and walked me to the elevator, then used his card key to summon it and press the button for the twelfth floor.

Linus greeted me in the doorway. "Jenny! I'm glad you could make it. You look great." Barefoot on the bamboo floors, he wore a thin gray V-neck sweater and loose-fitting black pants. When he placed his hands on my shoulders and kissed me on each cheek, I caught a whiff of something soapy and fresh, some high-end cologne manufacturer's interpretation of the scent of mountain air.

"Thank you for inviting me," I said, which was probably a little silly, because this had all been Boots's idea. I handed him the bottle of wine I'd brought. I'd spent too much money on it, but I wanted to make the right impression.

Linus took it without even glancing at the label. Damn it, I should have saved my cash and picked up a cheap bottle at Trader Joe's instead. I tried to smile at him, blithe and carefree, like worries about money were the farthest thing from my mind, but my facial muscles felt as stiff as hard rubber.

He ushered me inside. "Fantastic. Thank you so much. Let me get you something to drink. Red wine okay? Have you met Brynna?"

"Red wine would be perfect. Thank you." Rats. The only guest there was Brynna. "Hi, Brynna. Nice to see you again."

Brynna had cleaned away the paint smears, though her lustrous hair was still an unbrushed catastrophe. She probably knew it looked great that way, witchy and chaotic, the ends ragged and snarled. Her eyes narrowed over the rim of her balloon goblet. "I'm not talking to you. You're a liar."

"Could be." I kept my tone cheerful. Linus had moved into the open kitchen to fix my drink. There was no way he hadn't heard Brynna, but he didn't turn around or react. I flopped down on the sofa beside her. It was covered in ivory suede, and if anyone splashed wine on it, it would probably cost hundreds to get out the stain. "But you don't know me well enough to know for sure."

Brynna propped her feet against the edge of the coffee table, her knees bent. The soles of her feet, visible beneath her dusty Birkenstocks, were dirty, though her toes were freshly pedicured in a glossy mushroom shade. "Linus says you're a psychic. Psychics are liars by definition."

"That's one way to look at it," I said. "Why should that bother you? We live in Los Angeles. It's not like there's a shortage of liars here."

"I just think it's super convenient that nobody's ever heard of you, and then you pop up out of nowhere as soon as Gena disappears." Brynna's eyes narrowed. "What's your scam? Because I know you've got something going on that you're not telling anyone."

Linus hovered behind the couch, an outstretched balloon goblet in his hand and a smile tinged with desperation fixed on his face. I accepted the goblet and smiled my thanks, grateful I didn't have to come up with an answer to Brynna's question. I turned back to Brynna. "Are you working on anything interesting these days?"

Swerving the conversation into polite chitchat had the desired outcome. Brynna stared at me, and then the eyes narrowed again. "I said I'm not talking to you."

"Got it. Message received." I glanced back at Linus, who had retreated again to the safety of the kitchen and was moving something around in the refrigerator. "Linus, is there anything I can help you with?"

A phone chirped. Linus picked it up from the kitchen counter and glanced at the screen. "Malis is here," he said. He sounded relieved. "Jenny, can you bring down the rest of the goblets? They're on this middle shelf."

He poured a glass of wine and headed for the door while I rose to busy myself in the kitchen. It gave me a chance to think about Brynna.

Could I picture Brynna as a murderer? I tried to set aside my natural distaste for her and think about it dispassionately. I could only give it a firm maybe. Brynna was unpleasant and confrontational, and if she learned something disturbing about her mentor, maybe she was capable of unleashing violence against her, and against Serge by proxy.

But what could Gena have done to make Brynna turn against her? Gena wasn't above indulging in a little shady behavior, as indicated by the tall tales she'd told Antoinette about her background, to say nothing of her willingness to assume ownership of my screen career. Maybe that dishonesty extended into other areas of Gena's life. Maybe she'd stolen credit for one of Brynna's paintings, or sabotaged some promising opportunity behind Brynna's back, and maybe Brynna had uncovered her deceit, and maybe she'd responded with violence.

Linus greeted Malis at the door, handing her the wine and exchanging remarks about the bizarrely hot November weather. Malis was petite, with long black hair shot through with strands of gray that made her appear a bit dusty. Her small form was swaddled in voluminous folds of olive-green jersey, which culminated in an uneven hem that hit just below her knees.

Linus touched her shoulder and guided her over to me. "Malis, you haven't met Jenny yet, have you? Malis, this is Jenny St. John. Jenny, this is Malis Sao. She's a sculptor," he added.

Linus had been startled to see me in person in his office. Malis, though, was disrupted to her core at the sight of me. Her eyes went very wide, and her face drained of all color, leaving her skin grayish and sickly. She looked unwell, and I felt guilty about the entire plan for this evening. If Malis wasn't a killer, she was a grieving widow, and my sudden intrusion into her life as the incarnation of her murdered husband's missing ex-wife was thoughtless and cruel. The silence dragged on as my mind spun in circles, trying to think of some appropriate words of apology, and then Malis smiled. It was tentative, yet it seemed genuine.

"I'm sorry. I'm being rude. Linus had briefed me on what to expect, but seeing you in person . . . I'm sure you're tired of hearing it, but you really do look like Gena." Malis extended a hand. She looked to be my age, maybe a bit older, which I found strangely reassuring. After my initial attempt to get back in touch with Serge had been met with silence, I hadn't gone to any particular effort to keep tabs on him, but every once in a while I'd run across references to his personal life on celebrity gossip sites, mostly consisting of semi-tawdry accounts of his affairs with the young and beautiful stars of his high-performing films. It had made me feel shabby to realize I'd been one of many, that this was Serge's well-documented modus operandi, that he apparently boinked his leading ladies and forgot about them as soon as the production had wrapped. All that aside, though, Serge had twice married age-appropriate women who had achieved substantial successes in a field outside the entertainment industry. Maybe that mitigated his louche behavior, at least somewhat.

It'd be nice to think so. Because as much as I'd liked Serge at the time, as much as I still felt warmly toward him, as fantastic and life shaping an experience as filming *The Divide* had been, every once in a while I found it hard to shake off the nagging suspicion that maybe Serge was a bit of a sleazeball.

"I'm sorry about your husband," I said. "I don't know if Linus has told you that I knew Serge, years ago. I'm horrified by what happened to him."

"Thank you." Malis touched my wrist. "Do you want to go to the balcony? Linus has such a spectacular view that I try to see it every time I'm here."

I followed her. Linus's balcony was tiny. We sat on bronze folding chairs and looked at the view of the Hollywood Hills in front of us. Somewhere far to the west was the ocean, with Malibu, where Malis lived and where her husband had met a brutal end, to the north.

Malis arranged the folds of her outfit around her and raised her goblet. “To Serge,” she said, tilting her glass toward mine without quite touching it. Linus had nice stemware, as thin as a daydream and shimmering with a rainbow trace of iridescence. I had the feeling it could crack if I placed my lips against the rim too forcefully.

“To Serge.” We sipped in silence.

“Linus tells me you’re a psychic,” she said at last.

“That’s right,” I said.

She nodded. “And you think you can find who killed my husband.”

“Did Linus tell you that?”

“No. But I assume that’s why we’re all here.” She looked bemused. “When Linus invited me to this gathering and explained about you, I drew the logical conclusion. I suppose it was Boots’s idea? Her faith in the psychic realm is, I’m afraid, much higher than mine.” She took another sip of her wine and gave me a sidelong glance while still facing the million-dollar view. “I thought at first that you were attempting something dishonest. A con of some kind. Perhaps you thought you could trade on your resemblance to Gena to extort money out of Boots.”

She turned her head to face me. “Meeting you in person, though, that idea seems less likely. I consider myself a decent judge of character, and you seem relatively benign.”

Malis appeared very calm and unruffled, but I could feel my heartbeat speed up. It’s never good to be called a scammer, no matter how diplomatic the phrasing. I’d viewed Gena as a con artist since learning how she stole credit for *The Divide*, but none of her friends or professional associates seemed to consider that act especially despicable, or even noteworthy. From their perspective, I was the potentially shady one, and it’s not as though they didn’t have a point: Malis’s initial assumption about my motives wasn’t exactly accurate, but it wasn’t exactly wrong, either. “I don’t really know why I’m here,” I said at last. “I want to help, if I can.”

"I want to know who murdered my husband. I doubt you'll be the one to figure it out. But if you are, I'll be grateful." Malis glanced at me. She seemed so composed that it came as a shock to realize her husband had been dead for less than a week. "I suppose I'm a logical suspect. I have a financial motive; the majority of Serge's estate goes to me. But I'm under minimal suspicion. I was working in my studio downtown, thirty miles from Malibu. I was seen on a security camera entering the parking garage in the early afternoon, then leaving at around three in the morning. When I arrived home and found"—she hesitated, her voice wavering, but she swallowed once and steadied herself—"and found Serge, he'd already been dead for a few hours. The police confirmed that."

"From what I can tell, it doesn't sound like Serge had many enemies. Nobody obvious, at least."

"People generally liked Serge," Malis said. "Women, especially. And Serge liked women right back." Her expression was wry. "But that was his nature; we all accepted it. There were people in his life I didn't trust. But my suspicions might be poisoned by my personal feelings, and I have no business pointing fingers at someone simply because I don't like her very much."

Her. "You don't mean Gena, do you?"

She shook her head. "Gena had no reason to want Serge dead. Their marriage exploded, but that was a long time ago, and Serge considered her a close friend. She reached out to him for support when she received her cancer diagnosis; he drove her to appointments with her oncologist when her boyfriend was unavailable. And they'd been working together on a documentary, did you know about that? That's what Gena was doing at our house the night . . . the night it happened."

The project. Boots's dismissive attitude toward it, her subtle attempt at redirection. "Was the documentary about Gena? Her art?"

"Not quite like that. Gena was directing it; Serge was advising her. She'd never worked with video, so he was guiding her through the process." She frowned. "I don't know what the documentary was about. Something to do with the art world, I believe, about how it becomes entangled so closely with commerce that it sustains damage along the way, becoming corrupted from its original intent."

"Gena might have felt that was happening with her own art," I said. "The collaboration with Elliott Thwaite, right? Her artwork would be forever linked to a big luxury brand."

Malis nodded at me, and I got the sense she was pleased I'd brought that up. "She was happy about the Thwaite deal. But she was a thoughtful person, so of course she had questions as to whether she'd made the right decision accepting that contract."

"Probably all artists of note worry about that sort of thing, don't they? Selling out?" I asked.

"Speaking from my experiences as an artist of some note, I haven't had to worry about selling out." Malis smiled, wider and more genuine than before. "I could say I'd resist an eight-figure offer from a luxury brand to license my sculptures, and I'd mean it, but I've never faced that temptation. Nor do I imagine I ever will. What I do isn't as user-friendly as Gena's work. That sounds like I'm slighting her art, but I assure you I'm not; Gena is brilliant."

"Do you like Gena? Do you consider her a friend?"

"She's my husband's ex-wife. Our relationship is complicated, but I like Gena well enough. Why do you ask?"

"I'm looking for a way to understand her." Malis nodded, like I'd answered her question to her satisfaction, but I found myself continuing, my words coming out faster and faster, almost like I was compelled to explain further. "I've never met Gena, and yet she took something valuable from me, and I'm trying to figure out what kind of person she is. I need to understand why she would do that to me."

"Took something?" Malis's brow wrinkled. "Do you mean credit for Serge's film?"

"That role was mine." It came out much more snappish than

I'd intended, almost hostile. Desperation tastes like sour milk; it's a taste I knew well. "Maybe it's petty, but I can't stop thinking about it. When I saw it printed in the *LA Times* that she'd starred in *The Divide*, it felt like she'd broken into my home and robbed me. Did Serge ever talk to you about *The Divide*? Did he know Gena wasn't me?"

"I don't know." Malis mulled it over. "He talked about that film in a general way, of course. And we'd meet with Gena socially; we'd have her over for dinner, or we'd see her at events. They'd talk about their marriage, but never, to my recollection, specifically about *The Divide*. But I might not remember. For as long as I've known Gena, I've assumed that film was how she and Serge originally met." She examined me. "That part bothers you as well, doesn't it? Not just that Gena took credit for your achievement, but that Serge might not have realized it."

"It was a long time ago," I said. To compensate for my earlier outburst, I tried my best to sound nonchalant, but Malis looked sympathetic, like she could guess what I was thinking. That I was shaken to my core at the possibility that Serge had met and married Gena—had fallen in love with her, had lived with her, had cheated on her, had divorced her—without ever realizing she and I were entirely different people.

"Were you and Serge lovers?"

"'Lovers' might be too grand. What we had was nice, but it didn't last any longer than principal photography." I cleared my throat. "Still, though. It would surprise me very much under those circumstances if he couldn't tell that Gena wasn't me."

Through the open sliding balcony door, the volume inside Linus's apartment had increased, suggesting more dinner guests had arrived. Malis glanced over her shoulder. "Shall we rejoin the group?"

I trailed her back into the condo. MMP had just arrived, and he'd brought Kira along with him. They looked beautiful and casual—MMP in board shorts and a loose T-shirt with an inscrutable logo scribbled across it, Kira in a halter-neck romper—and they looked like a couple. They stood close together; three of MMP's fingers touched Kira's wrist.

Resplendent in a red silk caftan, Boots addressed them, exasperation in her voice. "I know you're just being foolish, not destructive, Matthew, but you should give some thought to appearances."

"What's wrong with this?" MMP said. He seemed as open and guileless as ever. "Kira's a friend, and she's been going through some things, and I thought a night out might do her some good. Maybe I should have asked if it was okay to bring her. If it's a problem, we can go."

"It's no problem at all. Kira, we're delighted to have you." That was Linus. He beamed at both of them, flashing his nice teeth, radiating laid-back SoCal hospitality. "The more the merrier."

Boots gave Kira a distracted smile. "No offense to you, Kira; I'm happy to see you. But you both should know better than this."

"Better than what?" MMP sounded . . . not quite annoyed, but maybe something heading in that direction.

"Your girlfriend is missing. She could be dead. Going around in public with another woman sends a bad message."

"MMP and I are just friends." Kira's soft voice sounded shaky.

"That's not what Jenny said," Boots said.

Well, damn. That wasn't a direction I wanted this evening to take. I expected anger from MMP and Kira, and that anger would be fully warranted.

What happened next reminded me that I don't understand today's young people, not at all. MMP stared at me, a perfect rim of white visible around the irises of his eyes. It took him a while to get his thoughts together enough to speak. "Whoa. You really are psychic, aren't you?"

"We're sorry," Kira said. "We're very sorry. But it wasn't . . . It's not . . . We just like each other a lot, that's all."

"Gena and I have an open relationship. You know that, Boots," MMP said. Boots's brow furrowed as she realized the weaponized intent behind his words.

"We'll leave now. We didn't mean to make things awkward." Kira set her wineglass down on the coffee table. "Linus, we're sorry. We're ruining your party."

"Nonsense. The best dinner parties always contain a healthy dose of drama." Linus sounded hearty and relaxed. He'd been genuinely entertained by the confrontation, I realized. He had a quick brain on him, and it seemed likely he knew or had guessed that Boots had a horse in the race entirely unrelated to her desire to defend her missing friend. "Stay, both of you. I insist."

His phone buzzed, and he glanced at the screen. "Antoinette's here. That's the whole group. Anyone need more wine? As soon as she's settled, we can dine."

CHAPTER 9

Dinner Party, Continued

Antoinette wore a royal-blue satin dress with padded shoulders and a narrow skirt slit up the side, which made her look like a character on a nighttime soap opera. My mother loved those while I was growing up. She'd take careful note of the fashions, which were difficult to replicate just by scavenging the racks at the big mall in Sioux City, but she did her best; her wardrobe was packed with boxy statement blazers in bold colors and shiny dresses with plunging necklines and pleated peplums.

"I'm so sorry. I had a client arrive at the gallery to take ownership of a painting just as I was closing," Antoinette said. "And then the traffic . . ." She let it trail off. People never spoke in specifics about the traffic in Los Angeles; there was no need. Traffic was simply invoked as a general concept, and everyone let their personal experiences shape their understanding of what was meant.

She kissed Linus on the cheek, then looked at the rest of us. "Hello. I'm sorry if I've held up dinner."

"You're right on time. Do you know everyone?" Linus asked.

"Of course." Antoinette crossed over to Malis and took her

hands in both of hers. "Malis, it's good to see you. I've been meaning to write to you. I sent flowers to your home."

"Thank you. They were lovely." Malis brought up Antoinette's hands, clasped them, and released them.

Antoinette nodded, her soft blue eyes very solemn, then looked around the room. Her glance fell on me. Her face went still, and then she smiled, warm and gentle. "It's Jenny, isn't it?"

"That's right. Jenny St. John. It's nice to see you again."

"And you as well." She studied my face. "It still seems so remarkable. Even your names are similar. Jenny St. John, Genevieve Santos."

"That's a coincidence. I changed my name a long time ago."

"So did Gena," Antoinette said. "She told me that once; I don't know what her birth name was." She leaned forward and touched my hair. "She colored her hair darker. When we first met, hers was a very light brown."

Also known as dishwater blond. That was the way my mother, a golden-haired siren, always described my hair color. She'd dig through my mane with the sharp point of a painted fingernail, lifting a few strands and clucking in disappointment. "You ended up with your father's hair," she'd say, her tone hovering in some nebulous territory between disappointed and smug. I'd filed that away for future reference: my father, whoever he was, was a dishwater blond.

Antoinette tapped me on the arm. "Come with me. I could use some wine."

I followed her to the open kitchen, where Linus shifted a lidded copper Mauviel pan to another burner before pouring wine for Antoinette and topping off my glass. Antoinette motioned for me to follow her to a corner of the living room.

"I wanted to tell you, I saw that film with Gena," she said. "*The Divide.* This was years ago, in a seedy art house theater in Alphabet City. We'd been sitting in Tompkins Square at night, sharing a bottle of wine and hoping no police officers would come around to hassle us. It was cold, so we wandered to the theater, half drunk, and bought two-dollar tickets to whatever second-run film happened to be showing. We stumbled inside, and there was Gena on the screen."

I hadn't known the film had played in any theaters at all. "Except it wasn't Gena."

"No. But I had no idea of that at the time." She smiled. "I assumed she guided us to the theater to surprise me. Afterward, Gena told me she'd visited Los Angeles, and she'd been approached on the street by this director, this Serge Grumet, and he told her she was the most mesmerizing creature he'd ever seen, and he offered her the lead in his film. I accepted this as the truth, because quite plainly, it *was* Gena on the screen. Or so I thought."

I could picture that sequence of events. I'd told brainless lies before, usually while under the bravado-boosting influence of alcohol—I had hazy but mortifying decades-old memories of telling a handful of new acquaintances in a bar that I was romantically attached to Robert Downey Jr.—and as soon as Gena got a good reaction from her lie, she would have deemed it worthwhile to continue telling it. Jenny St. John, the actress, had disappeared from public view and was unlikely to resurface and cause complications.

If Gena had been able to see into the future, she might have reconsidered that decision.

Antoinette raised her goblet closer to the light and swirled her wine, watching as legs formed on the interior of the iridescent glass. "I introduced them, Gena and Serge. Though at the time, of course, I assumed I was reuniting a pair of old friends."

"This was in New York?" I asked.

"After I moved to Los Angeles. I had a gallery, a small one, just a storefront in Little Tokyo. Serge was scouting locations for a film. He saw Gena's artwork and complimented it, and I mentioned he was already acquainted with the artist. He asked to be put in touch with Gena." She contemplated her wine. "Soon they were seeing each other regularly. She moved into his home—he'd just bought that house in Malibu, right on the water—and a year later they were married."

Antoinette looked like she was about to say something further, but Linus approached us, wineglass in hand, to tell us dinner was ready, so we let him direct us to our seats.

Linus had prepared scallops atop coiled bundles of squid-ink angel hair. Conversation stilled as we dug into our plates. Brynna picked the scallops off her dish and deposited them in a small pile on the table. Linus smiled at her.

"Sorry, Brynna. I thought you said you ate seafood."

"Not scallops. Scallop dredging destroys reefs," she said.

"These are diver caught. Ethical harvesting. It should be fine," Linus said.

"You don't know that for sure," Brynna said. "That's what they say, but corporations lie."

Brynna's comment was met with silence. She looked around the table at each of us in turn. "What? They do, you know. You can't blindly accept everything they tell you."

"I don't think any of us do, really," Linus said. He seemed nonchalant, as though after years of dealing with clients like Brynna, he could navigate prickly conversational minefields on autopilot. "Of course corporations lie. Everyone lies. But at a certain level it becomes impossible to tell who's lying and who's not, and I like to eat scallops. So I try to be a conscientious consumer as much as I reasonably can and hope for the best."

Brynna stabbed a pile of inky black angel hair and twisted it around her fork, then set the pasta-wrapped fork down on her plate without raising it to her mouth. She gave the plate a small push away from her.

Stuck to Brynna's right, Malis smiled at her. "What have you been working on lately, Brynna?"

I'd asked Brynna the same question earlier, and she'd bitten my head off. It seemed Brynna had more respect for Malis, because she only shrugged, indifferent but not hostile. "I shouldn't talk about it. Linus has something big in the works for me. Don't you, Linus?"

I thought a trace of mild pique flickered over Linus's face, but he smoothed it out so deftly I might have imagined it. "I can't talk about deals that might or might not be in progress."

"It's not 'in progress.' It's a done deal, or close to it." Brynna looked around the table. "Elliott Thwaite wants to license my designs."

Antoinette looked startled. "Gena's contract? Is that what you mean?"

"It can't be Gena's anymore. There's too much negative publicity surrounding her."

"This is premature." Linus was calm but firm. "The deal with Gena is still very much in place, and it will remain so unless extraordinary circumstances arise."

"Did you tell Brynna she'd get the deal if Elliott Thwaite voids the contract, Linus?" Boots's tone was friendly, but the corner of her mouth twitched with irritation.

"I did not. This is getting blown out of proportion." Linus might have been defending a mildly controversial opinion about a TV show. He looked bemused by the situation developing at his dinner table. "There are contingencies for everything in this business. Everyone in this room knows that. Cancellation of Gena's contract is very unlikely to happen, but I'd be naïve to say it's not a possibility."

He seemed relaxed. It had to be an act. He was on the brink of losing a huge deal for one of his clients, a client who might be dead or might be a murderer. I supposed I could see why Linus might have floated Brynna as a possible replacement to the suits at Elliott Thwaite to salvage the deal.

No. On second thought, I didn't think I could see that. Brynna was too young and too unknown. What I *could* see was Brynna assuming she'd be the natural replacement for her mentor and bringing up the idea to Linus, who wouldn't want to risk offending his mercurial client by shutting that nonsense down immediately. So he'd let the idea hover in the air like a cloud of flatulence, and he was probably regretting it now that Brynna had aired the stink in front of everyone.

"I'm surprised you'd consider a partnership with the fashion industry, Brynna," Malis said. "If you object to scallop dredging, the ethical tangles of the fashion world should be anathema to you."

Brynna shrugged, disdainful. "You're thinking of fast fashion. The mass-produced stuff that raises carbon emissions and ends up in landfills. The stuff tacky people wear." I didn't imagine the glance she shot across the table at me.

"The luxury brands are complicit, too." Malis hadn't raised her voice, but her dark eyes sparked with a sudden emotion. Anger, maybe, or even simple amusement at putting Brynna on the spot. "Elliott Thwaite very specifically. Serge and I watched a BBC documentary last year that detailed all the ethical scrutiny they've been under, particularly in regard to their fur and leather goods. Mistreatment of animals, mistreatment of workers, sweatshop conditions, labor violations, and a catastrophic environmental impact stemming from their production methods. To me, they seem insupportable."

"But you thought it was okay for Gena to accept their money?" Brynna asked. "Just not me?"

"I didn't think it was okay. Neither did Serge. Gena had qualms about it as well. Serge and Gena had many discussions about whether she should sign that contract. But Gena is her own woman and can make her own decisions. As can you," Malis said. She carefully sliced into her scallop and popped a dainty bite in her mouth. She chewed and swallowed. "It goes to what Linus said earlier, about trying to be conscientious consumers as much as we reasonably can. Compromises are made along the way. I don't buy luxury goods. I do eat scallops. Some may judge me for that, and that's fair."

Linus cleared his throat. "For what it's worth, I shared Gena's concerns at first. We discussed this extensively," he said. "I arranged a meeting with the Elliott Thwaite representatives, and they did an excellent job of showing us all the changes they've made to their production standards since that BBC documentary aired. They're trying to make it right. Gena was convinced of their good intentions, and so was I."

"Right. So you're all making a fuss over nothing," Brynna said. She slumped back in her chair.

I glanced over at Linus, who still radiated carefree bonhomie. He caught my stare and, without moving another facial muscle, winked at me, so fast and smooth that I almost missed it.

Linus served us individual bombes glacées for dessert, molded in lacy chocolate shells with layers of cherry and pistachio ice cream separated by thin almond cookies, served in a heavy sauce thick with dark chocolate and rum. I doubted Linus had made them himself, but when we all cooed over our plates, he accepted our praise with sincere thanks. This made me think that, hell, maybe he *had* made them, maybe in addition to being a whiz as a manager Linus had some serious chops as a chef. Then I realized he was simply too slick to confess to a weakness without need. He never explicitly took credit for making the bombes; he simply failed to contradict our assumptions.

Following some after-dinner chitchat over healthy pours of warm Armagnac served in delicate tulip glasses, everyone began to trickle out. Brynna had been the first to leave, followed by Antoinette and Malis. Kira and MMP held hands in the doorway as they said their farewells to Linus. Boots took me by the arm and leaned close to my ear. "So?"

It wasn't hard to understand what she meant. "I have some thoughts," I said, which was true, but I wasn't exactly sure what they were yet. "I'll call you."

She squeezed my arm in a conspiratorial manner and left, which meant I was the only guest remaining. I considered trailing Boots out the door, but Linus didn't seem in any hurry for me to leave, and I thought this might be a good opportunity to talk to him alone, so I helped him clear the plates. His dining table was a perfect rectangle of onyx, the smooth surface marked with splashes of wine, smears of pesto and chocolate, and Brynna's pile of uneaten scallops. "You need help with the dishes?" I asked.

"If you wouldn't mind, that would be great. Otherwise my temptation is to go to bed and hope the magical dishes fairy takes care of them overnight." Linus smiled at me. "Thanks, Jenny."

He stumbled over my name just a bit, because he'd meant to call me Gena. "That was an interesting party," I said. "Thanks so much for going to the trouble."

"Sure, no problem. I enjoy hosting." Linus rinsed off the dishes in the sink and loaded them in the dishwasher. I set about wrapping up leftovers and stashing them in his fridge, which was almost bare apart from a few bottles of white wine and champagne on the bottom shelf and an open carton of oat milk stuck in the door. While tossing Brynna's scallops in the trash, I'd spotted the discarded delivery wrappings of a much-heralded Italian restaurant in nearby Westwood, which explained where our elegantly prepared meal had come from. "What'd you think?"

He was asking the same question as Boots. "I don't know. It's difficult to envision anyone in this group as a murderer."

"I'm not a psychic, but that's my feeling, too." Linus dried off an oversized china serving platter and replaced it on the highest shelf in a cupboard. "I think the answer to this, when we find it, is going to come out of left field. It's going to turn out to be a crazy person who knocked on the door at random, or one of Serge's online trolls who decided to take one of his films too seriously, or something along those lines."

"It could be," I said. "Hey, it's none of my business, obviously, but it sounds like steps are being taken with the Elliott Thwaite people to consider an alternate plan, in case the situation with Gena takes a bad turn?"

"Oh, Brynna. I wish she'd just kept that to herself." Linus winced. "I can't talk about it, of course. I think it'll turn out okay, but it would be simpler all around if we had an answer to this whole messy business soon. Brynna's such a talented artist, but she's not Gena. She doesn't have Gena's reputation—there's no way she could yet, she's still just a kid—and while I have no doubt she'd do a good job on the Thwaite project, I'm not sure they'd want to take that risk. Brynna and I had a very casual conversation on the subject, and Brynna read more into it than she probably should have. Entirely my fault—I should have been more prudent in my choice of words."

That dovetailed with my earlier suspicions, which made me feel a bit smug. It also reinforced my assessment that Brynna was too much of a loose cannon for Linus to trust her to fulfill Gena's valuable contract, though it seemed like Brynna had other opinions on the subject.

We finished the dishes in companionable silence. I was ready to say my goodbyes when Linus spoke: "You want to stay for a drink? Entertaining always gets me wound up, and it's very comfortable and relaxing chatting with you."

There was a decent chance this was an invitation to hook up, and I wasn't sure whether I was up for that, but it wasn't like I had anywhere better to be. "That sounds nice."

He poured splashes of tequila from a bottle with a parrot hand-painted on it into short tumblers. In lieu of ice cubes he used chilled granite spheres, the kind high-end retailers sell for fifty bucks even though they're quite literally rocks. We sat on his suede couch and clinked glasses.

"To Serge and Gena," he said. We sipped. The tequila was grassy and peppery and very, very good.

"I think dinner went well," I said. "I'm still processing everything I learned from it, but it was useful to hear everyone's perspectives on Gena. I know this must have been a little rough on you, though."

"You're kind to say so. Tonight was a mess." Linus shook his head. "I hope Gena emerges soon from wherever she's hiding, because everything seems to be falling apart without her."

I set down my glass to stare at him. "That sounds like you're pretty sure she's alive," I said. "Is that anything more than a hunch?"

"She has to be alive, right? The police know she returned to her home after Serge was killed. I think she saw something, something bad, and she got spooked."

Boots had suggested that theory as well. At the time, I found it improbable and wrote it off as the product of Boots's unwillingness to believe something awful had happened to her friend. It didn't seem any likelier now. "It could have been anyone driving her car, though. And she left behind her wallet. Besides, she's in the middle of treatment for cancer. You think she'd skip her medical appointments?"

"She might have access to money and resources we don't know about. She could be seeing another doctor. It wouldn't surprise me if Gena had made some kind of contingency plan a long time ago. Gena always thought ahead." Linus looked at me. "There's something I was thinking about today, some way we can help her out. Between you and me, we might be able to lure Gena out into the open."

"Yeah?" I said. There was a tingle at the back of my neck. I wish I could say it was latent psychic energy, but it was just my brain warning me something was afoot.

"I don't think I believe in psychics, though I mean no offense. I believe you operate from a place of honesty; I just have reservations about the idea in general." His smile was conciliatory, as though he was worried about insulting me. "But I guess I'd describe myself as spiritual, in a way. I believe things happen for a reason, and you showing up right now, looking exactly like Gena, when her disappearance has caused so much trouble for so many people, well . . . that seems like it must mean something, right?"

"Sure." It meant someone noticed I was the spitting image of a high-profile missing person and reported me to the authorities.

"So here's what I'm thinking." He stared into his tequila, swirling it around the sphere of granite in his glass. He was silent for a long time, like he was mulling over his next words carefully, then he looked up at me, his expression very focused and earnest. "What would happen if Gena reappeared now? And what if she made it clear she wasn't involved with Serge's death in any way—let's say she left Serge's place in the evening and went home, and then saw a news report in the morning about his murder and realized she might be a suspect. Let's say she panicked and hid. What would happen then?"

"You think that's how it played out?"

Linus shook his head, frowning. "I have no idea. And that's not the point. The point is that with you here, that's how it *could* play out."

I stared at him. "Wow. You mean I should pose as Gena? Why on earth would I do that?"

"Because it would draw Gena out. As soon as she realized someone was pretending to be her, she'd reveal herself. You and I would explain to the police why we did it. They might be annoyed about the interference in an investigation, but if Gena returned, they'd forgive everything."

I couldn't speak. Linus's face appeared open and sincere, and it was alarming to realize he was serious about this. "I can think of so many ways that would backfire," I said.

"I don't think it would, Jenny. If the cops got mad, I could explain it to them. I'm good at explaining things. If there were any consequences, I'd shield you from them. I promise. All responsibility would fall on me."

I tried to pinpoint exactly why the warning siren was going off in my brain, and then I had it. "Is this about the contract?"

"Hmm?" Linus raised his brows in what I was pretty sure was feigned surprise.

"If Gena comes out of hiding, and if it turns out she's not

involved in Serge's death, the contract goes through as planned. That's good news for you." I followed the thread of thought through the winding corridors of my brain. "As long as everyone thinks I'm Gena, the client won't nullify the contract. Eight figures, right? What's your cut of that? Fifteen percent?"

"Twenty. You can see why I've been anxious about it." Linus didn't look anxious. He was as calm as ever, which under the circumstances was a bit alarming. "I'm pragmatic enough to realize Gena might never return, and this mess might never be solved, and that's two million dollars I might be out if the Elliott Thwaite folks decide Gena could be a killer. I already received half of that up front; I'd have to give it back."

He set his empty glass down on the coffee table, then shifted on the sofa to face me. He braced his hands on his thighs and leaned forward. "Look, I don't want to be presumptuous, but I'm probably not too far out of line if I suggest a nice chunk of cash might be welcome, right? I did some quick research into your business today, and nothing I found suggests you're thriving right now. I bet if I did some digging, I'd find your financial situation is a bit precarious. Am I right?"

My secondhand jersey dress felt especially shabby at the moment. The hair dye that came out of a box, the at-home manicure, the earrings from Target . . . "What's the proposal?"

"Ten grand up front. You'll want that in cash, and I don't have it on me, but I can go to the bank tomorrow. We'll work out the details together, and we'll give you a makeover to look exactly like Gena, and I'll train you on everything you need to know, and then you'll step into her life. You're an actress, aren't you? This will be easy for you." Linus smiled at me, and while he still seemed relaxed, there was a new tension in the corners of his eyes. "Once it's all sorted out, and once Elliott Thwaite agrees the terms of the contract are fulfilled, you'll get another fifty grand."

Part of my lizard brain immediately demanded I ask for more. Sixty grand was a tiny slice of two million dollars, considering the risk I'd be taking and considering how crucial my role in his scheme would be. A separate part of my brain pointed out that sixty grand might not be a fortune, but it would be life-changing for someone in my position. The remainder of my brain found the whole concept foolhardy and dangerous, not to mention grotesquely unethical.

Linus looked expectant. I cleared my throat. "I'd have to think it over."

"Sure, of course." If he was disappointed or annoyed by my hedging, he showed no sign of it. "The sooner you decide the better, obviously, but take some time to mull it over. And ask me any questions you like; I've been thinking about this all day, and honestly, I think this could work out well for both of us."

"Okay, I will," I said. "I'll call you." I got to my feet and started looking around for my purse. "I should get going."

"You want to stay?" The offer was made very casually, and the intent was unmistakable.

Under other circumstances, I might have stayed. I found Linus attractive. It might be fun. His apartment had air conditioning; I might get the first pleasant night of sleep I'd had since the start of the heat wave.

But I needed to think about this, and I needed distance from Linus to do that, so I shook my head. "I've got an early day tomorrow," I said, which was a lie; my day would involve making sure I rolled off my mattress at nine forty-five and brewed a pot of coffee so my head could be clear enough to flip the CLOSED sign to OPEN at ten. "But thank you."

He took another stab or two at getting me to stay, and while it was more friendly than pushy, I felt a splash of irritation. At a guess, his offer was made not out of a longing to spend more time in my company or even a passionate desire to explore my body, but simply because he wanted another chance to convince me to go along with his plan.

I had the sneaky suspicion he *could* convince me if he worked at it, and some rational corner of my brain knew that would be a terrible thing. So I fled.

CHAPTER 10

Nonspecifically French

A pain that wouldn't go away, localized in my right temple, bright white and tasting of copper pennies, and that was going to make filming unbearable today. The set was a painted backdrop of Gena's murky, stylized cornfield, but Serge assured me it would look exactly like a real field on camera. "Movie magic," he told me, before placing his arm around my shoulders and squeezing me against him. We were on a sound stage, yet Serge had arranged for it to rain inside the building, a pounding downpour that made beautiful, stupid Ronnie howl like a coyote and rip off his shirt and lean his head back while standing amidst the stalks of rotting corn, letting his shaggy blond mane get drenched to the roots. I was worried, because the rain was falling in sheets on the cameras and the lights, and surely that wasn't good, surely we were all in danger of being electrocuted, but Serge laughed at me and told me not to worry, to go in and do my thing, except I didn't want to go into that cornfield, not now, because I could hear a distant rumble of thunder, could smell the gathering ozone that told me lightning was about to strike, and it was dangerous in there, too dangerous. I had enemies in there waiting for me, and there was something else, something in the cornfield that I'd forgotten, and I knew it needed to stay forgotten, that if I went in there right now, I might remember it, and that might destroy me. Serge laughed again and told me it was fine, I wasn't in this scene anyway, and he called over Gena, who, I now realized, was me, only wiser, braver, tougher, better. Gena stepped into the cornfield and I yelled at her to stop, but she couldn't hear me over the bang of thunder, which sounded just like someone pounding on a door . . .

I was awake, bolt upright on my mattress in the windowless dark room, heart hammering in my chest. The dream was an illusion; the pounding on the door was real.

My back door faced an alley. Over the summer, a small community had sprung up there, four or five tents dotted amongst the dumpsters. The inhabitants kept it clean and were mostly friendly, but even still, when I would lie on my mattress in the back of my clinic, trying to sleep in the sweltering summer heat, I'd overhear loud conversations that would blossom into shouting matches, and occasionally I could hear someone crying. They'd been rousted by the city after a few months, and it had been pretty quiet back there ever since. But now someone was in the alley, and they wanted my attention.

That didn't mean I had to give it to them. Whoever it was could be ignored. After a startled moment, I lay back on my mattress and tried to relax, though my heart still pounded. It was hard to break the hold the dream had on me; when I closed my eyes, I could sense the cornfield lurking somewhere in the darkness.

The cornfield. The cornfield that Gena had painted, like she knew all about it, understood it much better than I did. I didn't know how that could be possible, because I'd buried it inside some part of my soul that didn't exist anymore, a part that had disappeared around the time Sheila Bunn completed her transformation into rising star Jenny St. John. But my dream had dislodged that part, nudging the cornfield back into existence, making it flicker on the edge of my conscious brain. Curled into a protective ball on my mattress, my back soaked with cooling sweat, I realized I was terrified.

More pounding, louder this time. I groped around the floor for my phone and saw it was just after eight.

A rattling noise. Was someone trying to turn the back doorknob? It was worse than that, I realized; it was the sound of a key being slid into a lock. I climbed off the mattress and turned on the overhead light just as the back door opened.

And there was Kenneth. I didn't know Kenneth's last name; I'd met him in person only a couple of times. He was a representative of the company that owned my building, and mostly I dealt with him whenever I needed repairs, which happened infrequently. I didn't like reminding the owners of my existence in case they got it into their heads to raise my rent.

"What the hell, Kenneth?" I embraced the anger that replaced the icy fear. Barring an emergency, Kenneth didn't have any business coming in here without my permission. I was presentable in the tank top and boxer shorts that I sleep in during hot weather, but barely.

He looked at me, implacable, then down at the mattress and tangled sheets. "You're living here," he said.

Kenneth was what I would categorize as a weasel. He was probably in his late twenties, blandly attractive with no distinguishing features, and he clearly considered himself on the way up to whatever level he viewed as his entitlement. He wore a white button-down shirt, sleeves rolled, and he dangled a large zippered vinyl pouch by his side.

"Just for tonight," I said. "My apartment is having some plumbing problems, so I crashed here instead of staying at a hotel. What's up?"

"You've been living here for a while," Kenneth said. He glanced around the back area, taking in the rolling rack of clothing, the sagging boxes of books and personal stuff. "This is a violation of your lease. You're not allowed to use this as a residence."

"It's just been a couple of days. What's the big deal?" It had been forty-seven months, actually, but that wasn't something he needed to know.

"I know you've been here a long time. Months. The office got a report about it."

I went blank at that, because no one knew where I was living. I hadn't invited anyone over, and I didn't allow clients to use the back area for any reason, with the exception of Dora McKinley, one of my few regulars, who was eighty-nine and diabetic and walked up to my clinic from her Park La Brea apartment on the first day of every month, because it would be stupidly cruel to deny her the use of my bathroom.

Oh. Fuckballs. Detective Moreau, damn her cold, prickly exterior and her crackerjack observational skills. "Did the police talk to you about me?" I asked Kenneth, which of course was an absolutely brilliant thing to say.

Kenneth wrestled with the zipper on his pouch, which looked like a larger version of the kind I'd used to store my charcoal pencils and vinyl erasers for Rooney's art class in high school. He extracted a stapled sheaf of papers and handed them to me. "Notice to vacate. You have three days. On Tuesday we'll be changing the locks."

I stared at him. "That's ridiculous. What about the sixty-day notice?"

He shrugged, his face impassive, though I had a dark suspicion he was enjoying this. Probably considered this the best part of his job, the rush of power that came from scuttling lives into chaos. "Doesn't apply here. Improper use of the premises. We're terminating the rental agreement for cause."

I leafed through the papers, which seemed to be just a short eviction notice stapled to a copy of my original lease. "What if I fight it?"

"Go for it. Get a lawyer. Go to court. Newsflash: You'll lose. You have no case," he said. "You've had a sweet deal on this place, and you know it. Properties in this neighborhood are going for five or six times what you're paying for this."

"Those properties are five or six times better than this place," I said. "This building is a teardown. Good luck finding another tenant who'll put up with it."

"We'll take our chances. Tuesday morning, nine on the dot. Make sure you have everything out before that, or it goes in the dumpster."

He left through the back door. I closed it behind him with the greatest of care, my hands trembling. A lawyer could buy me more time, probably, but the fees would be more than my rent, and in any case, I *had* been violating my lease. No wiggle room that I could see.

Detective Moreau had left me her card. It took me a couple tries to dial her number; my fingers were shaky from anger and worry and shame. I heard her cold, snappish tone: "Moreau."

"This is Jenny St. John. You talked to me about the Serge Grumet murder, remember?"

"I remember."

"Why did you tell the people who own my building I was living in my clinic? You had to go out of your way to do that, and now I'm being evicted, and I don't have anywhere else to go." I sounded angry, whiny, weak. I took a shaky breath. "That was an unnecessarily cruel thing to do. I just want you to know that."

"I didn't . . . It wasn't . . ." Moreau sounded unnerved. There was a long pause on the line. When she spoke again, she sounded as coldly collected as she'd been during her visit to my clinic. "I did contact the building owner to confirm you'd been operating out of that location for as long as you said you had."

Moreau had been investigating me. Apparently flashing my boobs at her hadn't ruled me out as a suspect. That sudden realization unsettled me, made me feel even shakier than I had before. "Okay, but why did you mention I was living here?"

"It came up. It was germane to the conversation," Moreau said. "You know you're not allowed to live in a rental space designated for commercial use. This is on you, not me." She paused. "I'm in the middle of a lot of things this morning, and I don't have time for this. If you don't have a place to stay, I can connect you with the Department of Public Social Services. They can get you into a shelter."

"Thanks, I can google," I said. "I hope you've managed to take me off your suspect list, at least."

"You're not Genevieve Santos. That's all we've ruled out." Moreau was starting to sound irritated. "You got a place to stay?"

"Nope. Thanks so much for that."

She started to say something else, but I'd already disconnected the call.

I was wide awake, wired. This was bad. This was very bad. Still in my tank top and shorts, I spooned too many grounds into a fresh coffee filter and started brewing a pot. I paced around the small space, endless loops into the front of the clinic and through the doorway into the back room. My workplace for six years, my home for most of that.

It was Saturday, and weekends tended to be busier than weekdays, so I had two clients booked for the day, one newcomer and one regular. I could tell the regular I'd be switching to video consultations again, which is what I'd done exclusively during the long and arid months of the pandemic, while my savings dwindled right along with my ambitions. Maybe I could change my tactics. I could offer in-home visits, try to sell it as some kind of luxurious private experience, though I wasn't sure I could pull that off. Many of my clients viewed consulting a psychic as something embarrassing, a shameful habit to hide from their loved ones. Nothing they'd want to bring into their homes.

Where could I go? Boots owed me a bit of money to cover

my time at Linus's party and the visit with MMP, and maybe I could get her to pay me today. Combined with what I had in my account, I could afford a cheap hotel room for a bit. Maybe video consultations would keep me afloat until I figured out a better plan.

Or . . . I could call Linus and tell him I'd considered his offer. Move into Gena's life as best I could.

I thought for a long, long while. He'd put his number in my phone last night and urged me to call him as soon as I had reached a decision. I stared at it.

I sent a text to Boots: Want to meet to discuss last night's party?

I didn't get a reply until two hours later, after I'd already opened the clinic for the day, time I mostly spent staring at Linus's number on the screen of my phone until it was seared into my memory. I mulled over the logistics of replacing Gena. Tricky, very tricky, especially since a bunch of Gena's friends knew about me. It'd be much, much easier for "Gena" to waltz back into her life with a great cover story to explain her absence if her closest circle of friends weren't aware of the existence of a look-alike.

With Linus vouching for my identity and protecting me from bad consequences, it was *maaaaaaybe* possible. But it was also ridiculously reckless. No matter how much Gena and I looked like each other, there were physical differences that couldn't be disguised, starting with our fingerprints and ending with Gena's recent partial mastectomy. Despite Linus's calm assurances, there seemed every chance I'd wind up in jail.

But sixty thousand dollars . . .

My phone buzzed. A reply from Boots: D'Artagnan @ 8.

I went through my day as usual, though my mind wandered off on anxious tangents during my two consultations; the new customer wasn't shy about telling me she thought I gave her a lousy return on her fifty bucks. She was right, and I almost handed her money back, but I needed it more than she did.

D'Artagnan was a cocktail lounge with what seemed like a

nonspecifically French theme in one of the strange corners of the Grove. I arrived right at eight, and I expected Boots to be late, but she was already there, nestled in a corner table with a martini in front of her. She inclined her chin slightly when I walked in, which was probably the celebrity version of calling me over; she wouldn't want to draw unnecessary attention to herself in a public place.

She wasn't the only celebrity there. On my way to her table I passed a cluster of three beautiful young women, their arms tanned and shimmering in sleeveless tops, their hair glossy, their faces painted with multiple soft layers of cosmetics. I didn't know their names, couldn't even say if they were on the same television show or in the same music group or had starred in the same film franchise, but I knew them in the hazy way older people sometimes know young celebrities. I'd seen their faces while scrolling through various websites on my phone often enough to become vaguely aware of their existence, but I hadn't been interested enough to learn anything about them. They might not be actresses or singers at all, for that matter; they could be reality stars, or social media personalities like MMP. Not long ago we would have referred to that sort as famous for being famous, which was glib and probably unfair; it suggested there was no hard work involved, and yet I suspected that lifestyle was all hard work, all hustle, all planning and fretting and maneuvering, a tremendous outburst of effort to manufacture an unassailable display of effortlessness.

The three celebrities had a prominent table in the center of the restaurant beneath a three-tiered chandelier of smoky glass that enveloped them in an angelic glow, whereas Boots was in a darkened corner. I didn't know how the Hollywood hierarchy worked anymore. Back when I first came out here, Boots's position would be the preferred one: it would show that the restaurant understood and respected her level of celebrity and would work to keep her hidden from prying eyes so she could enjoy her evening in relative privacy.

But now . . . I suspected the three young celebrities were the bigger catch for the restaurant. They were on display, so other diners could look at them and know D'Artagnan was the kind of place that attracted beautiful and famous young people.

I slid into a purple velvet barrel chair opposite Boots. "Hi. I hope I didn't keep you waiting."

Boots didn't answer, just raised a hand to signal for the server. I ordered a glass of the house white. As soon as it was placed on the table in front of me, as soon as our server had moved out of earshot, Boots leaned forward. "So?"

"So I'd really like it if Brynna was Serge's killer. I think she's a brat, and I think she could benefit a great deal if the police—and more importantly, the people at Elliott Thwaite—think Gena killed Serge." I took a sip of my wine. It tasted like the bottle had been sitting in a refrigerator, open and uncorked, for several days. I hadn't seen a menu, but in this place it probably cost something like eighteen bucks a glass. "But I didn't get any sense that she did it. She's opportunistic, and she wants Gena's contract more than she's ever wanted anything in her life, and she's certain she deserves to have it. But if she killed Serge to frame Gena for his murder to make her lose the contract, she's got more foresight than I think she does. She's a creature of impulse, not strategy."

Boots lifted the olive out of her martini and scraped it off the toothpick with her perfect front teeth. "Brynna is Gena's protégée," she said around a mouthful of olive. "You think they didn't get along?"

"I think Brynna admires Gena, maybe sort of worships her. But she wants that contract more. If she could cheat Gena out of that contract, she would. I think she'd stop short of killing her for it, though."

"Malis?" I had to admire Boots for saying it so casually, like my assessment of Malis didn't matter.

"Wasn't passionately in love with her husband, but didn't hate him, either. I think Malis and Serge probably got along well, but Malis is a realist. She knew Serge was cheating on her, but she was okay with that; she's no fool, and she went into the marriage with open eyes." I took another drink of the wine. It hadn't improved. "But I could see how she could get fed up after a while. And Malis is the primary beneficiary of Serge's will, which certainly gives her a motive to kill him. Still, she told me at the party that money doesn't mean much to her. For what it's worth, I believe her."

"I don't know why you would. Serge was a multimillionaire and a philanderer when Malis married him. The only way she'd excuse the latter was because she'd benefit from the former." Boots sounded cross. "You've been thinking too much about this. I don't want you to investigate, I want you to *know*. Just by looking at her and talking to her, can't you tell whether she's a killer?"

"Investigating and using my psychic ability are pretty much the same thing. I'd guess detectives, at least the good ones, are psychic, whether or not they know it or acknowledge it. They can talk to a suspect and *know* things. That's what I do. But it helps to have a framework of knowledge to understand how those things fit into the greater picture. I can't look at Malis and know she killed Serge. I can look at Malis and know that she was frustrated with Serge, or that she was looking forward to spending Serge's money, and then I can fit that into the overall framework. But I need to spend more time with her. I thought I'd drop by her studio this week and talk to her there."

"Okay, so we're in agreement that Malis is our pick," Boots said, even though I hadn't exactly said that. "Anything about the others? I can't imagine Antoinette being a murderer."

"Me either, though it's worth keeping in mind that she will very certainly profit if Gena turns up dead. Gena's artwork will spike in value."

There was a new light in Boots's eyes, which were leonine and ferociously beautiful. The three young celebrities at the front table might be close to thirty years younger than Boots, but they seemed inconsequential in comparison, a cluster of handmaidens in the court of a queen. "Good point. You think Antoinette has that on her mind?"

"Not really, no. She and Gena are close, she doesn't seem like the homicidal type, and she strikes me as being smarter than that. You know the story about killing the goose that laid the golden egg? There are a lot of people who'd kill the goose, but there are some who'd wait patiently for as many eggs as the goose chooses to lay. I think that's Antoinette."

"What about Linus?" Boots asked.

Ah. Linus. "No motive that I can see. I don't know why Linus would murder Serge; they're old friends. And he'll suffer a direct negative financial impact if it turns out Gena was responsible for Serge's death. Possibly reputational too; I gather Linus takes great pride in his work, and it wounds him that Gena's deal might be collapsing around him. So I'd say he's out of it, although . . ." I paused, uncertain how I wanted to broach this with Boots.

"Although . . . ?"

"Linus is a bit shifty. In his business, 'shifty' is probably a positive trait. But it makes me wonder about that friendly and laid-back exterior of his, just a bit. He's always *thinking*."

"Shifty how?" Boots asked.

"Just a sense I have." I shrugged, super casual. "Hey, look, another reason I wanted to see you today . . ." My face grew warm. "I wondered how I was going to get paid from you. It'd be a big help if we could take care of that soonerish rather than laterish." It sounded nonchalant, which was good, because that was not at all how I was feeling on the subject.

"Invoice me. My assistant will cut you a check. Every two weeks sounds about right, right? You've only been doing this for a couple of days."

"Ordinarily that would be fine, but . . ." I'd started speaking a bit faster. I stopped to take another drink of my wine, which tasted a little more like drain cleaner with every swallow. I took a deep breath before speaking again. "I was served with an eviction notice today, because I've been living in my clinic, which was against the terms of my lease. I could use some quick cash to stabilize myself."

Boots stared at me. "You were living in that place?"

"I lost my apartment," I said. "I thought it was temporary, but . . ." I shrugged. "It wasn't. Business has been scarce lately."

Boots looked confused, like what I just told her was forcing her to change her entire perception of me. I could follow the path of her thoughts pretty well: she'd been proceeding on the assumption that I was successful, at least modestly so, because my clinic address was in a good area of the city, and because I'd managed with some effort to look at least somewhat polished. She'd been taken in by my outer presentation, and now she was forced to consider that maybe it was all an illusion, that she'd allied herself with a person she'd ordinarily overlook. Not a posh intuitive counselor like Della DeLaurenti, just someone broke and a little bit sketchy.

When she spoke, though, I detected only compassionate concern. "Wow. That's rough. I'm sorry."

"Thanks. It will work out okay, but right now I'm feeling a little anxious about the immediate future." I sipped the wine. As long as it was eating into my limited cash supply, I was going to drink every last sour drop. "If I invoice you today for the work I've done thus far, how long would it be before your assistant could cut a check?"

"It'd be fast. Don't worry about that." Boots stared at me, her mouth slightly open, copper-glossed lips parted, like there was a thought in her brain that was threatening to spill off her tongue at any moment. "When do you have to be out of your shop?"

"Tuesday. Three days."

"You know where you're going to go?"

"A hotel if I can afford one," I said. "You have any suggestions?" I didn't want to look like I was angling for a favor, but if Boots could pull any strings for me, whether in the form of getting me work or finding me a cheap place to stay, that could save me.

Boots nodded, slowly and so imperceptibly that it was hard to confirm it was a nod at all. "Yeah. Yeah, I might. Yeah, this could work out well."

"What could?"

"MMP." Her eyes flashed in triumph. "Crash with MMP. Gena's house has enough room, and that would put you right in the thick of things."

I stared at her. "Why would he go along with that?"

She rolled her eyes. "Because he would. Kids today, they're like that, they have people crash with them all the time. He's got a generous soul."

"He doesn't even know me. And with the police investigation—"

"Do you want a place to stay or not?" Boots sounded exasperated. "This is a good plan. MMP isn't going to care. You heard him when we visited him the other day, he said he's been lonely without Gena around. And even if he minds, he'll say yes if I present it as a favor to me. What do you say?"

"If he genuinely doesn't mind, it'd be awesome. And yeah, you're right, it'd be ideal for our purposes. Great idea. Thank you." A knot of tension between my shoulder blades began to ease. I felt a lightening of my spirit, a sense of gratitude toward Boots for swooping in and solving my housing problem, albeit temporarily; yes, her motives were complicated, but all the same, it'd been a long time since anyone had gone out of their way to do a favor for me.

Boots was already typing on her phone. "I'm telling him we're coming over now." She signaled to our server for the check. "Honestly, I think this is going to work out great for you. This could be the best idea I've ever had."

CHAPTER 11

Free Please Take

As Boots had predicted, MMP was shockingly chill about having a stranger move into the home of his missing-and-presumed-dead-or-a-murderer girlfriend, which was the sort of thing that made me realize once again that I was growing increasingly out of touch with modern-day twentysomethings. "Sure, yeah," he said, nodding vigorously as soon as the suggestion was out of Boots's mouth. "You've been evicted? Oh, man, that sucks. I was locked out of my apartment by my roommates in Seoul when I was seventeen, and I ended up couch-surfing at my manager's place for a couple of months." He beamed happily at the memory.

"Thanks. I really appreciate it. It won't be long, just a couple of days until I can find a new place."

"No worries. Stay as long as you need." The three of us sat in the living room, drinking hard kombucha in cans. MMP wore a tattered Joy Division T-shirt with the sleeves hacked off and jeans that were ripped down both sides of his thighs along the seams, and he looked leggy and beautiful.

Innocent face aside, there was always the possibility he was a murderer, not that I could picture him ringing Serge's doorbell and coldly gunning him down. From a logistics standpoint, though, he was an obvious suspect: He could have driven Gena's car back to Silver Lake, probably after killing her as well and dumping her body somewhere. He could have parked in the garage, left her purse and phone in the foyer, and gone up to bed. Tidy. As for motive, who knows? Maybe Gena was going to kick him out for sleeping with Boots and/or Kira, maybe he was jealous of the time she'd been spending with her ex-husband, maybe there was some factor I hadn't considered. Like maybe he was a psychopath.

If so, he hid it well. It seemed more likely MMP was exactly what he appeared to be on the surface: open and guileless, careless but generous, aware of his own appeal without being too overtly narcissistic.

"Have you heard anything new about . . . any of this?" I asked MMP.

He winced, contorting his perfect features into an exaggerated mask of anguish. "I don't know. A detective came and talked to me again yesterday, and I'm pretty sure she hates my guts, but there wasn't anything about her questions that made me think I'm likely to get arrested. I asked her if there were any developments, and she told me it was none of my business. Which . . . I mean, it seems like it very much *is* my business, but I wasn't in a position to argue about it." He slouched back on the sofa like a carelessly discarded doll, looking overwhelmed, the kombucha can propped between his long thighs right at his crotch. "I hope they have a lead on where Gena is. It's so weird and lonely being in this place without her."

"Maybe Jenny being here will help you forget," Boots said. She sounded friendly, but I wondered if she felt a trace of possessiveness toward MMP, maybe a hint of regret for placing me in such close proximity to her onetime lover.

"I doubt it," he said, as innocent and affectless as ever. "But

I think it'll be great having you around, Jenny. I could use some company. I've never lived on my own before."

"Great!" Boots grabbed her purse and stood up. "I'm going to leave you two here to sort out the details. Jenny, I'm glad I could arrange this for you."

"Thanks a lot, Boots. This was a great suggestion," I said.

"No problem. Glad to help." Boots pressed her cheek against mine in a brusque yet affable farewell, and it seemed like she viewed me as not quite a friend, but at least as someone who'd been granted a temporary pass into her inner circle.

MMP and I exchanged phone numbers, and he assured me he'd be home on Monday when I was ready to move in. He gave me a spare key to the front door along with the code to the front gate, which was a level of trust in a relative stranger that startled and scared me.

I spent the next couple of days trashing the remains of my old life. I sent emails to all clients with standing appointments explaining that I'd be canceling in-person consultations for the time being but would be happy to meet via video. I hauled all my cheap or scavenged furniture and furnishings—the mattress, the table and chairs I used for my psychic readings, the spray-painted statue of Kali—out to the back alley, where I taped hand-printed signs saying FREE PLEASE TAKE to everything and left it all beside the dumpster. I lugged a couple bags of books and clothes and bedding and kitchen utensils to Goodwill, then trashed the junk that was beyond donation. When I was done, I'd whittled my life down to a large suitcase, a smallish shoulder bag, and a lidded cardboard box. That seemed like a reasonable amount of stuff to take to MMP's place without making him worry I was planning on staying forever.

MMP insisted on carrying my suitcase and the box of possessions up to a guest room on the second floor. It featured a big picture window, through which I could see the downtown Los Angeles skyline, shadowy behind a brownish-gray haze.

The guest room was papered in pink jacquard in a faint pattern of fleur-de-lis; it had a low platform bed topped with a navy linen duvet, four overstuffed pillows, and sheets in that blinding shade of white I only ever see in good hotels, and it looked so clean and inviting I wanted to climb into it immediately, curl up like a child under the covers, and never leave.

I took a quick tour of the place, following at MMP's heels as he carried on a stream of energetic chatter. He reminded me of a little kid, excited about having a brand-new school friend over for a sleepover. He opened cupboards in the kitchen to show me his stacks of ramen packets and his boxes of organic bone broth and his plastic jugs of protein powder and his multiple economy-sized bags of Swedish Fish, all of which he insisted were mine as well.

On the tour, I didn't see what I was looking for: that poster of *The Divide* that I'd glimpsed in one of his early videos. I'd thought it would be in the master suite that Gena shared with MMP, but the black walls in there were adorned with multiple lacquered wood panels from an antique Chinese screen that formed a long golden dragon that stretched the length of the room. If I'd remembered the details of the video correctly, the poster had hung against a deep blue wall, and I hadn't seen a room to match anywhere in the house.

MMP cleared up the mystery over pint glasses of a milky, fizzy fermented rice liquor that he told me was called makgeolli. We were sitting out back on the patio chairs on the redwood deck; the sun had gone down, and a near-chilly breeze had blown in, sweeping out the last punishing traces of the heat wave and making me feel like fall might have arrived at last. The air smelled good, like freshly dug earth laced with some kind of heavy floral perfume. Jasmine, maybe. It was quiet here, quieter than anyplace I'd ever lived in Los Angeles. I felt peaceful and comfortable and insulated from all the troubles of the world.

"Yeah, we moved here a couple years ago. Gena had a small house in Venice, and it was nice but a little cramped, and she wanted someplace bigger and quieter so she could paint in peace. And it worked out really well for me, too; I got to have my studio here." He beamed and gulped down a mouthful of his makgeolli.

"You and Gena seem to have a really good relationship," I said. I was fishing, but I thought I knew MMP well enough by now to know he would view it as supportive instead of intrusive.

He nodded while taking another long drink. "Yeah. Gena's really cool. I wish you could meet her. I hope you can someday. She'd be fascinated by you." He beamed at me.

"I hope I get to meet her, too." I stared out at the view beyond the wrought iron fence at the end of the property. There were homes dotting the hillside, some above us, some below us, but not many, and in this twilight hour, they faded into the surrounding landscape. "Where is she?"

I put it as bluntly as I could, because it had dawned on me there was every chance MMP knew exactly where she was. If she'd returned here that night, either fresh from murdering Serge or freaked out from having witnessed his death, her first impulse might be to wake MMP up, and between the two of them, maybe they'd work out a plan for her to go into hiding.

"I wish I knew." It sounded simple and sincere. "I keep thinking about it. For a while, I thought maybe Antoinette knew. Gena and Antoinette are like sisters, and Antoinette would step in without question if Gena asked her for help. But after all this time . . ." He looked intense and grim. "Antoinette knows how frantic I am. She'd convince Gena to get a message to me."

"What about Boots? Could she be hiding Gena?"

He shook his head. "I don't think so. Boots is awesome, you've met her. She's great, isn't she?" He looked at me and waited until I'd made some murmur of affirmation that yes, Boots was certainly both awesome and great. "I love Boots, and I know Gena does too, but they're not *close*, if you know what I mean. Gena wouldn't tell Boots her darkest secrets."

"That seems logical," I said, keeping my tone bland and

nonjudgmental. "I mean, Boots and Serge had an affair behind Gena's back, right? Isn't that why Gena and Serge divorced?"

"It's probably part of it," MMP said. "I think Gena and Serge probably had a pretty open relationship. Neither of them seem—seemed—like they'd make a big deal about things like affairs. But from what Gena has told me, Boots and Serge hid their affair from her, which made it worse when she found out."

"Sure. Even in an open relationship, if they felt the need to hide it from her, it's a betrayal."

"Yeah, that's exactly it." MMP nodded at me. "So I don't think Boots would be Gena's first pick to turn to for help."

He refilled his glass from the plastic liter bottle of makgeolli that he kept beside his chair. "You probably know from what Boots was saying at Linus's place the other night . . . Gena and I are open."

"I gathered that. None of my business." I held up my hands to show my lack of interference. "I don't want to pry, so please shoot me down if I'm overstepping, but were she and Serge still involved with each other?"

"Oh, wow, no. No way." MMP laughed, and it seemed very natural. "No, Gena says it took them a long time to be friends again after the divorce, and while they're cool—were cool—Gena still didn't trust Serge enough to get involved with him again."

"Yeah, but they were working pretty closely on Gena's new project, right? The documentary? It sounds like she was spending a lot of time at his place."

"That's different. That's their art, for both of them, and that exists somewhere entirely outside their personal feelings about each other." MMP laughed again. "I asked Gena about that documentary, and she told me I'd hate it, but she wouldn't tell me what it's about. She thinks what I do is stupid, my videos and stuff, so I suspect it's about that. She interviewed me for it, and she asked me all kinds of questions about how I feel about my work."

"Gena and Serge were making a documentary about how your videos are stupid?"

MMP shook his head. "It wouldn't be about me specifically; that would be weird and mean. But I think it's about influencers and the hustle to find followers and get partnerships with brands. That's the aspect of what I do that fascinates Gena the most, but not in a good way."

We sat in silence for a moment. When MMP finally spoke, there was something almost unbearably wistful about his question. "Hey, if you're actually Gena, you'd tell me, right?"

I turned to stare at him, but he was looking straight ahead at the darkening horizon, his face expressionless. "Do you really think that's a possibility?" I asked.

He shrugged. "I would say there's no way you could be her, but I keep thinking about that movie. *The Divide.* You played like five different characters in that."

"It was all the same character," I said. "She was the same person, only from five separate parallel universes."

"But every version of that character was different, really different. One was crazy, one was slutty, one was super smart, and so on. And you were so good at playing each of them, like you could have been five totally different actresses. So I was thinking just now, Gena could be another character that you've been playing for years at the same time you've been doing your psychic thing. Not that I really think that's the case, but . . ." He gave his head a small shake, still staring straight ahead at nothing in particular. "I mean, that's what the police suspected, right? That Gena was posing as you?"

There was one surefire way to resolve the matter, but I hadn't had nearly enough makgeolli to think flashing my breasts at MMP was a smart move. "The police ruled that out," I said. "They're one hundred percent certain Gena and I are two different people. And look, nothing I've heard anyone say about Gena suggests she's a cruel person. Deceiving you in that way would be cruel."

He turned to me at last. His face looked very young and open and sad. "That's what I'd say, too, but she lied to me about being in *The Divide*. We watched it together, and she let me believe it was her in your role. And if she lied to me about that . . ." He let out a weak breathy noise, like he was making an exhausted attempt at laughing. "I think watching that movie really messed me up."

"Because of Gena?"

He shook his head. "No, not that. Just the whole movie in general. You know Serge wrote the script?"

"Yep. I did know that."

"It was made so long ago, back when I was just a baby, and yet it was so far ahead of its time. Like, the science in it turned out to be really solid, you know?"

For a moment I was too jolted by the cold reminder of how very many years I had on MMP to focus on his main point. "Science? The parallel universes?"

He nodded. "Yeah. I mean, nowadays, scientists have proven that the multiverse is a real thing. Quantum physics, right? Everything we do, every decision we make, every big life event, it branches us off into another separate universe within the multiverse. Serge was way ahead of the curve on that. It's like he could predict the future."

The reminders that MMP was very, very young kept flooding in, one after another. "None of that has been proven," I said carefully. "It's just a theory."

"Gravity is a theory," MMP said, his tone very clear and emphatic. "Scientists can't prove gravity, either, but that doesn't mean they don't know for certain it exists. And there's lots of evidence of parallel universes. What about all those people with memories of historical events that never happened? There's a whole name for that. The Mandela effect, right? People get stuck in the wrong universe sometimes, and things that had happened in their home universe never happened here, so they get confused, like they have the wrong memories."

I wasn't entirely sure where he was going with this, but at least it was a better line of conversation than his paranoid yet sort of heartbreaking suspicion that I might be his girlfriend in disguise. "I suppose anything's possible," I said.

"That could explain doppelgängers, couldn't it? Maybe you and Gena are the same person, but you're supposed to exist in different universes. Only you somehow both got stuck in the same one."

I snorted. "If that's the case, she got the better end of the bargain," I said.

"Maybe not," MMP replied, his expression serious. "It depends on where she is right now."

I didn't have an answer to that, because of course he was right, and as much as I envied Gena's easy life and her comfortable home and her eight-figure contract, none of that seemed to be doing her much good right now.

CHAPTER 12

Red Catuai Beans

Since Boots saw Malis as the most likely suspect in Serge's death, I figured it would be a good idea to spend some time with her. That would necessitate a chat with Linus, but I owed him a call anyway. I dialed from the guest bedroom, keeping the door closed and my voice down to avoid disturbing MMP. It was almost ten, and I hadn't seen any sign of my host. After waking, I'd gone down to the kitchen to fix myself black coffee and toast; MMP had some kind of gluten-free bread loaded with ancient grains and used organic ghee from a jar instead of butter, but it worked out well enough for breakfast.

I detected the steady hum of Los Angeles traffic noises in the background of the call. "Jenny! Good to hear from you. What's up?"

"Not too much. I'd promised you a call. Is this a bad time?" I sipped my coffee, Red Catuai beans harvested on Moloka'i and sold in elegant black-and-gold bags by a small-batch roaster, and it was a hell of an upgrade from the supermarket-brand stuff I'd buy in jumbo-sized cans.

"I'm about two minutes from the office, so I don't have a ton of time, but this is good." Linus paused. "Did you think about my proposition?"

"Yeah, having mulled it over, I'm not sure your suggestion would work." I found myself reluctant to be specific, because impersonating Gena was surely a crime, and discussing illegal activities on the phone generally wasn't considered a smooth move. "I think there's a risk we'd make things worse."

"That makes sense to me. I've had some thoughts along those lines, too." I couldn't detect any disappointment in his voice. Probably after the party he'd thought about it and realized how bananas his suggestion really was. "Gena's going to show up any day, right? It's best to keep things uncomplicated."

"Any change in the situation with Elliott Thwaite?" I asked.

"None." Linus cleared his throat. "I'm keeping the lines of communication open, but they've made it clear they're not moving forward until there's some progress in the investigation."

"I'm sorry about that. I know it must be frustrating for you, on top of the worry about Gena."

"If the deal gets killed, it gets killed. It's a disappointment, considering all the work Gena put into those designs, but it's not the end of the world." Linus sounded pretty plucky for a man staring down the potential loss of a life-changing chunk of money. "But thanks for getting back to me."

"No problem. While I have you on the phone, I wanted to ask a quick favor. When I talked with Malis at your party, she'd invited me to drop by her studio sometime, but I forgot to ask her for a way to contact her."

"Oh, cool. You and Malis must've really hit it off. She usually doesn't encourage visitors." Linus didn't sound like he thought I was lying, which I absolutely was. "She's got a loft downtown. Hang on a second, I'm pulling into the parking garage." There was a lengthy span of dangling silence before he returned to the line. "I'm parked. I'm going to text you her number. She's in her studio seven days a week, so you'll probably catch her there."

"Thanks, Linus."

"Do you want to meet for dinner this week? I've been feeling weird and glum about Serge's death, and it might be nice to discuss it with someone who also knew him back when."

I didn't know whether to take that at face value. It could be the truth, or he could want another shot at talking me into posing as Gena. I'd prefer the former, but if it turned out to be the latter, I'd still probably get a nice meal out of it. "Dinner would be great. My schedule's mostly open," I said.

"Great. Tomorrow? I could pick you up around eight."

"Sure. Let's meet at the restaurant, though; it'll be easier than picking me up."

"Perfect. I'll call you." Linus ended the call, and a few seconds later I had an incoming text from him: Malis's phone number followed by a smiley-face emoji.

Malis picked up on the first ring. "Yes?" Brusque but not unfriendly.

"Malis. Hi. This is Jenny St. John. We met at Linus's party."

"Of course. Hello, Jenny." She didn't seem surprised to hear from me. At a guess, it was probably difficult to surprise Malis. "What can I do for you?"

"May I stop by your studio today?"

"Why?"

"I'm curious about your work. I'm curious about anyone who's skilled at anything, and I'd love to observe your process."

There was a long pause. "And?"

Malis wasn't dumb, and I didn't want to insult her by playing dumb myself. "And I think you know something about Serge's murder. I know it's presumptuous, but I was hoping you'd tell me whatever it is."

There was another long pause. "*Know* is too strong. But I have my suspicions." The silence dragged out on the line. I resisted the urge to fill it with chatter. "I'm in the Parker Building downtown. On Olive. You know where that is?"

"I can find it."

"I'll be here all day. Tell the guard at the desk you're here for me."

The Parker Building was an old textile factory in a decayed section of downtown that was in the process of being revitalized, thanks to an influx of wealthy young people determined to simulate the traditional experience of big-city downtown living in a place as sprawling and fragmented as Los Angeles. Like many of its neighbors, it had been meticulously restored to its former glory in recent years. The intricate stonework, a detailed carved façade involving tall columns adorned with creeping vines and flower garlands, gleamed a soft white; on the ground floor, an upscale wine bar took up one front corner, while a neon-lit restaurant with the faintly absurd name of Bánh Mì and My Shadow occupied the other.

The brass front doors were huge and heavy, embossed with more garlands and vines; the lobby beyond was all polished green marble. The guard on duty at the security desk nodded when I told him my name and who I was there to see, then picked up a phone and exchanged a few words with Malis. "Tenth floor," he said to me, gesturing to the elevator.

After the turn-of-the-century splendor of the exterior and lobby, the loft floors themselves were disappointing. The elevator opened into an unfinished hallway with bare boards lining the floors and exposed metal ducts crisscrossing the ceiling. The security guard hadn't given me a loft number, but I saw a small printed tag above a buzzer beside the door closest to the elevator: MALIS SAO. I buzzed.

Malis opened the door. "Jenny. Hello," she said. She held the door open wider so I could enter.

She was barefoot, dressed in a roomy beet-colored smock made from what looked like burlap. Her hair was twisted up in a messy topknot. "I'd shake hands, but I've been working in plaster." She held up her arms. Her skin from her hands to her elbows was streaked and smudged with a pale chalky substance. "Would you like to see my sculptures?"

I kicked off my sandals by the door. "I would love to. Thank you." I glanced around the studio. Like the hallway, it was largely unfinished, with pipes lining the exposed ceiling. Her floors were covered in pale laminate, protected by overlapping drop cloths. "I looked you up online after Linus's party. I really like your work, though my opinion on art isn't worth much."

Malis smiled back at me as she led me into her loft. "The art world isn't quite as elitist as all that," she said. "Of course your opinion is worthwhile. Why would you think it isn't?"

"I was really into my art class in high school," I said as I followed her inside. "It was pretty much the only part of school that I loved. I thought I was hot stuff, but as it turns out, I wasn't very good. My ego outpaced my abilities. I have the feeling I was pretty insufferable at the time."

"You didn't stick with it?" Malis asked.

I shook my head. "No point. And now every time I'm around art, genuinely good art, I immediately start to feel like an idiot, because I love it, but I don't understand it."

"Art isn't calculus. There's not one single correct way to understand it," Malis said. "Look around, if you want. See what it makes you think or feel. Don't worry about coming up with the right interpretation."

Malis worked in a wide variety of materials, I'd learned from her professional website, though her specialty was plaster. She operated on a large scale; the studio was filled with towering humanoid figures. I stared at one of her sculptures, which was constructed from what looked like stiff dried vines, twisted and knotted into the rough shape of an impossibly tall, slender female form. Her head was tilted toward the ceiling; her arms flowed all the way to the ground, her long fingers spreading out across the floorboards like a tangle of capillaries splitting off from an artery. Vines knotted to look like chains encircled her wrists and ankles and kept her anchored to the floor. She was featureless, but I could detect a quality of defiance in the way she raised her chin, the graceful curve of her wrists as she lifted them against the chains. Boots had said Malis's works were political; I felt certain the piece, this embodiment of dignified resistance, had some deeper meaning behind it, if only I were knowledgeable enough to understand it. Despite Malis's reassuring words, I felt uncultured and foolish. I found myself wishing I'd studied this kind of thing, had devoted my life to it, instead of spending all those years fruitlessly chasing stardom.

"Can I get you anything to drink?" Malis gestured at a jelly glass half filled with red wine resting on a stool beside her. "The jug is in the kitchen area, if you want to help yourself," she said. She tilted her head toward a curtained-off alcove in a far corner of the big space.

It was early, but wine might make the conversation flow smoother. I wandered my way through a maze of half-completed sculptures and ducked behind the curtains, great lengths of dusty black velvet draped over a long metal rod that dangled from chains attached to the high ceiling. Behind them, I discovered a refrigerator, plus a microwave and a coffeemaker nestled next to each other on sturdy wire shelving.

I found a clean jelly glass and poured myself a healthy splash from the gallon jug of red wine that rested on the top shelf. It tasted like pinecones that had been marinating in pickle juice. I'd had worse.

Malis was hands-deep in plaster by the time I rejoined her. I had no idea what her current sculpture would turn out to be; right now it was a towering frame of balled-up chicken wire that branched out in all directions. An angel with spread wings, maybe, or possibly a Gundam. The base was wrapped with layers of wet plaster-soaked newspapers. Malis smoothed and pulled and tugged them into place, her hands moving deftly and without hesitation.

"This is a great space," I said. "Seems perfect for your kind of work."

"It's not bad, is it." Malis looked up at the high ceilings. "I've been here for eight years. When Serge and I met, I was living here. There's enough room in our home for me to keep a studio there, which would be more convenient, but I work best in my own space."

I looked around at her sculptures. The ones built using the same technique as her current work would be hollow, or primarily hollow. She could wrap chicken wire around a dead body—Gena's body, specifically—and build a sculpture up around it.

No. Terrible idea. A corpse would decompose and stink beneath the layers of newspapers and plaster. "I hope I'm not distracting you from your work," I said.

"I can sculpt while I talk." Malis stepped back and examined her work. She brought a hand up to scratch the side of her nose, leaving a streak of plaster on her cheek. "Though I have a hard time concentrating while you're hovering. Why don't you work on something?"

"Work on what?"

"Art. Play around. It doesn't have to be good. Just sit down and keep occupied." She gestured at a sheet of plywood set up on two sawhorses, which she was using as a workbench. "That white tub on the table contains polymer clay. It's easy to manipulate. Tear off a hunk and drag that stool over here."

Eccentric, but it sounded like a decent idea, so I followed her instructions. The clay was a damp white block; I tore off a softball-sized chunk and positioned myself on a stool a few feet away from Malis, close enough to converse easily but leaving her enough room to maneuver around her sculpture.

The tactile feeling of clay in my hands triggered memories of high school. Rooney's art class, the smell of oil paints and modeling paste. I'd loved everything about that class. Art was an elective, and it was never popular, so it was just me and a scant handful of other students, and Rooney mostly gave us free rein to work on whatever projects we chose. She'd seemed old and faded at the time, with frizzy hair and shapeless beige sweaters worn over print skirts that fell almost to the floor, though she must have been younger then than I was now.

I fondled the clay, pushed and pulled at it, warmed it between my palms. What had I done for Rooney's class? Oil paintings and acrylics, mostly. By graduation, I'd developed a distinct abstract style; I'd enjoyed the process of translating familiar shapes into strange and nearly unrecognizable objects that nonetheless retained something of the essence of their original forms. I'd hung the canvases on my bedroom wall and felt a swell of pride.

I pulled the clay into various shapes. I started making a human form, doll-sized, pulling out the limbs, shaping the head. I'd forgotten what it felt like to create something, create *art*, taking a hazy idea that had sprouted in my mind and bringing it into the world via my hands. The process relaxed me and rejuvenated me, long-dormant neurons in my brain flickering back into life. Why had I ever stopped doing this? Yeah, okay, a fancy art school had rejected me; so what? I loved this process. Why had I voluntarily deprived myself of the sheer pleasure of creating?

Because I'd given up on that dream, rejected that part of myself. I'd pushed it away from me, along with so much more, in the depths of my pain and fear and misery, during that ugly summer night in the cornfield . . .

No. Don't think about that. Think about Malis, think about whether I saw her as a potential murderer.

I considered grilling Malis, launching into an interrogation about who she thought might have murdered her husband, but letting her guide the discussion seemed like a smarter move. I worked in silence, making little tweaks to my clay doll.

At last, Malis spoke. "We'll start with an observation. Everyone seems to assume Serge was the target and Gena was either the culprit or an unfortunate bystander."

"You think Gena was the target instead?"

"I think it's possible. If so, though, I doubt she was the only one. If someone meant to kill her, and only her, surely they could find better opportunities than ambushing her at my home." She crouched down and made some minute adjustments to the plaster at the base of her statue.

"That makes sense," I said. "But is there anyone who would want both Serge and Gena dead?"

I didn't think she was going to answer me. Then: "Gena's documentary is interesting," Malis said slowly. "The one she was working on with Serge. Has anyone told you about it?"

"I talked about it a bit with MMP. He thought it might be about him, in some way," I said. "It didn't seem like he was overly interested in it. In any case, I don't see him as a killer."

"Neither do I. The documentary isn't about him. At least not specifically, though it's possible he was the impetus for it." Malis wiped her plaster-covered hands on her smock. "I could describe it, but I think your impressions might be more valuable if you viewed it without too much foreknowledge."

"Is that possible?" I asked. I felt the prickling of interest at the back of my neck. "Viewing it?"

"The police have Serge's laptop, which contains copies of all the video footage he and Gena were editing the night of his murder. Gena's phone, which the police also have, has the original footage." Malis stood up and stepped a few feet back from her sculpture, looking it over critically. "But Serge backed up everything. He'd lost some valuable footage through carelessness during one of his early productions, and he took that lesson to heart. So he'd dumped all the video Gena shot onto a portable drive. There's nothing on it the police don't already have, so I didn't bother handing it over to them."

"Will you let me see it?" I asked.

"Yes." She nodded at her sculpture. "I'll be here all day. If you come out to Malibu tonight, I can show it to you."

"Thank you."

She looked at the hunk of clay in my hands. I'd been shaping it into a nude woman while she talked, my attention divided, pinching and pulling the clay to form features and musculature. She frowned. "You've captured Gena very well," she said, a note of surprise in her voice.

I looked at her in confusion, then down at the clay in my hands. "Oh. No, it's me."

Malis shook her head. "You modeled Gena," she said, her tone firm. "Look."

I looked. I could see what she meant, sort of. It had been unintentional, but the figure in my hands wasn't my own. The shoulders were bony, the breasts were small, the hair was tangled.

"I don't know Gena," I said. "I tried to model myself, but I guess I didn't do a very good job."

"You modeled your impression of yourself. Without being able to refer to an image for comparison, your hands captured your mental idea of who you are." She smiled at me. "Apparently you picture yourself as Gena."

CHAPTER 13

Ethically Sourced

Heavy fog rolled in off the ocean as evening fell, and there weren't many streetlights along the road leading to Serge's Malibu home; I had the sensation of moving across the surface of an alien planet, its atmosphere dense with toxic vapors. The road curved along the cliffs above the water. When I rolled down my window, I could hear the roar of the ocean somewhere to my left. It sounded like television static, radio waves from deep space traveling billions of miles to earth, the universe speaking to me in an untranslatable language.

The otherworldly environment seemed right for my present mood, which had been unsettled and distracted since leaving Malis's studio. Malis had tried to give me the little clay sculpture I'd made, and I'd refused to take it, because it had unnerved me. It hadn't seemed to come from my hands at all, or if it had, it was the product of some long-slumbering part of myself that I'd thought would never be awakened.

I'd sculpted myself as Gena, and I had no idea why I'd done that. Maybe hanging around Gena's creative friends had made me think of myself as an artist again, for the first time in a long while. Or maybe I'd spent so much time thinking about Gena and envying her life that I found myself fixating on her, even when I tried to focus on other things. Either way, I disliked the feeling of having no control over my actions. I found it downright creepy.

The front of Serge's home was lined with an overgrown bamboo hedge that ran the full length of the property, interrupted in the middle by a tall cedar gate. I searched and searched for a call box; eventually I had to get out of my car and hunt it down on foot before finding it buried within the bamboo. I pressed the button. After a moment, I heard Malis's voice, muffled through the intercom. "Yes?"

"It's Jenny," I replied.

The gate slid open, and I got back in my car and drove through. I parked in the front courtyard, which was bursting with tropical foliage, leafy banana plants and chubby blue palms and exuberant birds of paradise. Serge's home, boxy and contemporary, was painted a light gray that disappeared in the fog.

Malis stood in the open doorway. She'd changed from her paint-stained smock into a shrunken black T-shirt and wide-legged pajama pants in washed silk. "Come in," she said.

She glanced past me into the fog to confirm the gate had rolled shut and no one had followed me onto the property before closing the door and bolting it shut.

"This is where Serge was shot?" I asked.

She shook her head. "We rarely use this door. Our friends know to come to the patio entrance. There's a footpath leading around the side."

She led me through a shadowy foyer and formal dining room into the living room at the back of the home, where I found myself trapped in a fabulous 1970s drug den. I followed her across thick shag carpeting in a shade somewhere between burnt orange and brick red. The walls were paneled in dark wood; the furniture was black leather in a texture so glossy it looked like it dripped with oil. The living room was sunken, a square shag-trimmed pit bordered on all sides with those dripping leather sofas, which surrounded a blocky coffee table made of smoky green glass.

"This is a great place," I said. "It's very . . . I want to say groovy?"

"It is, in fact, groovy." Malis wrinkled her nose. "This house was built in 1972, and apparently no owner since then has wanted to remove the conversation pit. I loathe it, but Serge was entertained by the retro appeal when he bought this place and designed the interior to match. I'm looking forward to never having to see it again."

"You're going to sell the house?"

"As soon as I can. I can't stand being here. The first few nights after he died, I slept on the floor of my studio. I was miserable and frightened, and everything about this house reminded me of what had happened. Of course it isn't lost on me that his killer is still out there." The back wall of the house was all glass, floor to ceiling, with sliding doors leading out onto a patio; I couldn't see much through the darkness and fog, but in the daytime, it probably boasted spectacular ocean views.

She moved over to the patio doors and stared out into the darkness. "It happened here," she said.

A lamp mounted somewhere above the doors provided a soft white cone of light that permeated a narrow slice of fog; I could make out the silhouettes of lounge chairs, heating lamps, an enormous gas grill. "If the patio light was on that evening, Serge could see who was at the door," I said. "And whoever it was knew enough about your habits to skip the front and come around to this side of your house."

"The light is automatic. It stays on all night." In the dim interior, Malis seemed insubstantial beside me, only a shadow. "Serge was killed by someone he knew."

Malis turned away from the sliding doors. I trailed her to the conversation pit, where we descended a short flight of shaggy stairs. "Serge and Gena were working here that night. There's a professional editing suite upstairs, but this was a small project, so he and Gena preferred to edit the footage on Serge's laptop." She gestured for me to take a seat on one of the sofas. It felt disconcertingly warm and fleshy, like I'd just plopped down on someone's well-cushioned lap.

She sat beside me and pulled out a small laptop from a low shelf beneath the smoky glass table. She booted it up and navigated to a video file. "This is the raw footage."

The video began to play, and I saw Boots, seated on what looked like a high-backed stool against a brick wall somewhere in a light-filled room. She looked great, clad in an electric blue dress that reached to midthigh, showing off her muscular legs, which were crossed at the knee, a gold slide sandal dangling from the toes of one foot. She had a large glass of white wine in her hand, and she was very animated. "Animated" is a euphemism polite women sometimes use to describe a friend, if that friend is drunk off her ass.

It wasn't like she was slurring her words, but her voice was a little too loud, her eyes a little too bright and shiny. If she'd been planning to drive somewhere in that state, I would have gently commandeered her phone to summon the rideshare service of her preference.

Malis and I sat next to each other on the fleshy leather, leaning close to the small laptop screen, listening.

"There's an art to it," Boots was saying. "I don't know if most people know that, but there's an art to it. And it's a lot of work. A *lot* of work. Kids today, the Gen Zers or whatever they're called, they get it, they know. My generation is lost. We were so stuck up our own asses for so long, so afraid to 'sell out' . . . " Boots tried to make finger quotes on that, but she was still holding her wineglass in one hand, and when she raised it up, the wine sloshed precariously close to the rim. "We missed all those chances, and now we wonder why we're miserable. It's because we got in our own way, you know?" Boots widened her eyes in an exaggerated manner, staring at the unseen person behind the camera—Gena, no doubt—as though waiting for her to voice her agreement.

If Gena responded, it wasn't in any kind of verbal way. After a moment of hanging silence, Boots nodded and continued. "So these kids today, they know that the entire concept of selling out is a crock, and bless them for that. If there's money to be had, who cares where it came from, right? But they're also dumb, because they're kids, and they get worked up over the weirdest stuff, like trying to figure out which soap brand to buy to save the world, and I want to shout at them to get a clue, none of them will. We're all screwed, so we might as well do whatever we can for ourselves."

"And that's what you do?" The voice came from off-camera. Female, calm, composed. That was Gena. She didn't sound much like me. We both had roughly the same vocal tone—relatively low, relatively well modulated—but Gena's voice sounded silvery and light.

"That's what I do." On-screen, Boots nodded emphatically. She kept nodding as she spoke. "I take the money, no matter who's offering it. All the skin care in my company is ethically sourced, right? It's clean, no bad chemicals in it, nothing that can poison you or poison the world. It all has carbon-offset credits. I mean, that's what they tell me. I'm not making this stuff myself; I just sell it and take the money."

Malis turned to look at me, the corner of her mouth forming a curve that wasn't quite a smile. "There's three hours of this."

"She's had too much to drink," I said.

"She has. It's not as though she's revealing state secrets, but Boots has a reputation for maintaining high standards, for being in constant control. This makes her look sloppy and greedy." She nodded at the screen. "Gena knows it. Gena is coaxing this performance out of her, fueling her with wine and leading her down this path."

Gena hadn't exactly poured wine down Boots's throat and

forced her to answer questions, but I saw Malis's point. "This would embarrass Boots, if the public saw this. I can see this demolishing their friendship. But I don't see it as anything close to enough motive to kill Gena. And why would she kill Serge?"

"Boots despised Serge. Didn't you know that?"

"I didn't, actually." I couldn't remember if Boots had said anything specific about their current dynamic, but I'd been left with the impression that Boots and Serge were okay with each other, that they'd remained friendly. "Why? Was it a messy breakup?"

"Serge left her. I don't think they were ever a great match, but after their affair destroyed his marriage to Gena, Boots felt determined to make it work. That way she could frame it as a sweeping romance instead of something a bit tawdry." Again that curving half smile. "It didn't work, of course, because Serge sleeps around. Slept around. Which runs counter to Boots's need to be the epicenter of everyone's universe."

Malis flushed a light pink, and while she looked unruffled, I realized she was in the grip of some strong emotion. She looked straight ahead, toward the patio doors, toward the place where she'd found her husband's body just over a week ago. "So when I found Serge dead, my very first thought, before thinking of Gena or Ronald or anyone else, was *Where the hell was Boots?*"

I tried to wrap my thoughts around the possibility of Boots as a killer, but I was sidetracked as soon as Malis's words sank in. Ronald. To the best of my recollection, no one I'd talked to about Serge or Gena had mentioned anyone named Ronald. "Who's Ronald?" I asked.

"A friend of Serge's. He's staying in our cottage. He was asleep the night Serge was killed." Malis gestured with her head toward the glass wall. I'd seen no sign of a cottage out there in the fog.

"Boots mentioned something about that. She said he's an ex-con?"

"He has a criminal record, a serious one, though Serge always maintained he was just stupid, not dangerous," Malis said. She frowned. "I wouldn't say I've been entirely comfortable with him living so close, but Serge had known him for years and insisted he was a good man at heart. In any case, Ronald has been a well-behaved tenant. He was involved in an armed robbery five years ago. He was halfway through a ten-year sentence at Men's Central, but to mitigate overcrowding, they're letting him serve the remainder under house arrest. One of the conditions of his release is a stable place to stay, so Serge gave him our cottage."

Someone with a history of armed robbery seemed like a pretty likely candidate for murder. "He's got to be a suspect, right?"

"He wears a monitoring bracelet. He can't leave our property. He can go up to our house—he'd have dinner with Serge at least once a week—but there's a constant electronic record of his movements. It shows he was asleep in bed all night." She stared through the glass, thoughtful. "Detectives have questioned him, of course. He's adamant that whatever happened here, he slept through it. None of our neighbors heard anything, either; it's assumed the gun was silenced."

Serge had been shot in the doorway, probably when he opened it, which meant he hadn't had time to shout. However . . . "So Gena didn't scream, or make any noise that would wake Ronald?"

Malis shook her head. "It's hard to imagine Gena staying silent while Serge was killed in front of her, isn't it?"

"Maybe the killer thought Serge was alone." I spoke slowly, feeling my way around a new idea. "Maybe he didn't see Gena. Gena might have hidden inside the house until she was certain he was gone." I tried to think that one through. Gena, in a panic, could have driven back to her home in Silver Lake before going into hiding. Hiding from what? Or from whom? I hadn't thought much of the theory that Gena was hiding from Serge's killer when either Boots or Linus had suggested it, but now, talking to Malis, I could almost see how it could happen.

The theory still had some crucial flaws. "But why wouldn't Gena call the police, once she knew she was safe?"

"It suggests the killer was known to Gena as well as to Serge, doesn't it? Boots fits that description," Malis said. "Maybe there was something about the situation that made Gena think telling the police Boots killed Serge was a bad option. Maybe Gena wanted to protect Boots; they're close, after all." She motioned at the laptop. The video was paused; Boots's face was frozen on the screen, her eyes closed and her mouth partially open, somehow managing to look radiant even while caught at a wildly unflattering moment. "Do you want to watch more of this? I'd like to go to sleep, but you can stay if you want."

"Yeah, if you don't mind. Thank you. How do I lock up when I leave?"

"The patio door will lock behind you if it's closed all the way. Press the green button on the security alarm keypad before you open it; it'll give you ten seconds to open and close the door without activating the alarm." She rubbed the side of her neck with one hand. "Do you need anything else?"

"No, thank you. I appreciate this, Malis." I paused. "Why are you doing all this for me?"

She gave the question some thought. "I don't know if I trust the sheriff's department to be doing as thorough a job as they should. Serge was famous and wealthy, and he had famous and wealthy friends, and thus the investigators are being . . . cautious. I've aired my concerns, but it's clear they don't view Boots as a suspect." She smiled at me. "You're not cautious. You have the potential to be extremely disruptive, and that might be what this investigation needs. At least, I don't see how you can hurt it."

"Thank you," I said. It wasn't entirely a compliment, but I liked the idea of being disruptive. Being someone who gets noticed, which is something that hadn't happened to me in a very long time. Malis smiled again and headed down a hallway into darkness, leaving me on my own in the sunken living room.

I watched the rest of the video, all three hours of it, just because I thought I should. By the end, I was no wiser than when I started. Boots grew increasingly sloppy and arrogant the more the video dragged on, as she engaged in a one-sided conversation about her acting career, her Oscar win, her pivot into selling skin care and products designed to combat aging and promote wellness. Off-camera, Gena would periodically lean in to refill Boots's wineglass from a slim green bottle of Riesling.

Gena might end up with a pretty juicy documentary on her hands, though it would come at a cost to Boots, and maybe when Boots sobered up, she'd realized that. Maybe she'd come over to have it out with Gena and Serge. Maybe she'd brought a gun.

I shut down the laptop. The house was dark and still. I exited through the sliding patio doors, making sure I heard the click of the door lock sliding into place behind me. The alarm should be engaged; Malis should be safe from intruders.

Outside, it was still hard to see beyond the far edge of the patio, but I could hear and smell the ocean. I found myself struck by a desire to see it, so I climbed down the patio stairs.

The grass was wet and cold beneath my sandaled feet. Through the fog, I saw a faint impression of the cottage, which looked like a miniature version of the main house, down to the small wooden patio that surrounded it. I moved past it silently. No lights were on, but of course the sole resident—Ronald—would be home. House arrest made that a certainty.

Beyond the border of the patio light, it grew even darker, the fog close to impermeable. I took out my phone and used it as a flashlight to make sure I wouldn't tumble off the cliff into the ocean.

There I was, standing on the edge. No fence or other barrier separated the property from the cliff edge; someone really could fall over the side, if they were careless. I shone my phone down and spotted a slim strip of rocky beach below, black waves licking close to the base of the cliffs.

I detected a faint smell under the pleasant brine-and-sulfur scent of the ocean. Someone had smoked a cigarette here, not too long ago. I turned back to the cottage.

My flashlight, aimed low so it wouldn't shine through the windows, caught a glimpse of bare hairy legs under baggy shorts. Someone was sitting in a deck chair in the total darkness, probably listening to the sound of the sea.

A long, frozen moment, and then that someone spoke. "Jenny?"

CHAPTER 14

The Next Keanu

I felt the world slow down to a stop, the moment preserved in amber, as I tried to make sense of what had just happened. The hairy legs shifted and moved, and then a porch light switched on.

He stood in the open door to the guest home, hand presumably on the light switch inside the doorway, and stared at me. He had shaggy bleached hair that reached his shoulders, darker at the roots. A couple days of dark stubble covered his cheeks and chin. He wore an unbuttoned blue shirt, which showed off a flash of well-defined abs. Thick dark brows were drawn together in confusion, and it was those brows, plus the big brown puppy-dog eyes, plus the strong, straight nose that jutted out from between them, that made the connection for me. "Ronnie?" I asked.

"Jenny St. John." He walked toward me, eyes wide, mouth hanging open in shock. "I saw your profile when you turned to the water, and I knew you weren't Gena."

He opened his arms, and without any hesitation I stepped

forward and hugged him. Strong arms closed around me. He twisted his upper body, rocking me back and forth. He smelled of stale cigarette smoke layered with cheap drugstore body spray, but it wasn't unpleasant. He felt warm and comfortable.

"Ronnie!" I broke the hug first and stepped back. "Malis told me a friend of Serge's was staying here, but I didn't guess it was you. She called you Ronald, so . . . How long has it been?"

"Damned if I know. How long ago was that film?" He grinned down at me, and the years melted off him. Ronnie Kostan. *Entertainment Weekly* had done a little feature on him to promote the first film he'd made after *The Divide*, a half-page piece complete with a photo in which he'd posed shirtless, in profile with one of his surfboards, looking soulfully out at the Santa Monica sunset. I'd cut out that article and kept it for several years before it finally got lost in the shuffle during one of my many moves.

His smile was so wide it threatened to break his face in two. His shock had turned into sheer delight, a happiness that seemed to make him vibrate all over with uncontrolled energy, and I was astonished to realize someone could be that overjoyed to see me. "I knew Gena wasn't you. I felt like I was going crazy, the way everyone kept telling me I'd made a film with her." His surfer drawl, always prominent, had only grown stronger over the years. There'd been a fleeting moment when he'd been touted by the press as "the next Keanu," at a time when the current Keanu was in ascendancy and thus had no immediate plans of being supplanted by an up-and-comer.

"I'm so glad to hear you say that," I said. I felt breathless, like my lungs weren't taking in enough oxygen, like I was going to become giddy at this unexpected reunion. "Ever since I found out about the existence of Gena, I've felt like I've been going crazy, too. I know we look alike—"

"You don't." It was immediate and forceful. "You don't. I mean, physically you do, sure, but Gena was nothing like you. She didn't sound like you, she didn't act like you. Serge and

Gena and I would get together sometimes and talk about *The Divide*, and I'd sit there and think I was losing my damn mind. People change over the years, but not that much."

"Did Serge know?" I asked. "He was married to her. He knew she wasn't me, right?"

Ronnie shrugged, loose and jangly. "You got me. Offhand, I'd say he didn't know. I'd say he thought Gena was you from the start, and it never occurred to him to think differently."

"That doesn't reflect too well on me," I said. "I couldn't have been that memorable."

Ronnie was shaking his head before I'd finished speaking. "No, it doesn't reflect that well on Serge." He thought for a moment, his forehead creased with the effort of putting his thoughts together, entering that surfer-philosopher mode that had so charmed me, way back when we were young and ridiculous. "I loved the hell out of Serge, but you know how he was with women. You had to know. He treated the women in his life like goddesses, but he loved women as an undifferentiated concept, the way some people love, I don't know, kittens. I don't think I'm explaining this well."

"No, I get it. That makes sense." I exhaled. I felt wobbly; my legs felt boneless. I wished Ronnie's arms were still wrapped around me, because I felt I might collapse at any moment. "Ronnie, it's good talking to you."

"You too. This is crazy. Are you and Gena sisters or something?"

"No, no relation. I found out last week that Gena had been pretending to be me, so I've been curious about her life. I was just over at the house, talking to Malis about Serge and Gena." A breeze rolled in off the water, clammy like a wet hug, and I wrapped my arms around myself to keep from shivering.

"You're freezing." He gestured at the cottage. "You want to come in? My place is a little gross right now, but at least we won't be standing around in the fog."

I followed him indoors. The cottage was a single room, but

it was spacious enough and expensively furnished. A kitchenette took up the back corner, and the rest was a combination living space and bedroom. The bed was unmade, and no one would consider the place tidy, but Ronnie hadn't been expecting guests, so I wasn't going to give him a hard time about the overflowing ashtray or the empty seltzer cans on the coffee table next to a largely uneaten microwavable dinner, something with lots of noodles and cauliflower in a sticky brown sauce.

"Grab a seat. Sorry about the mess. I'm not allowed to keep alcohol on the premises, but I can get you some OJ or seltzer?" He looked at me with those puppy-dog eyes, anxious to be a good host and embarrassed about being out of practice.

I sat down on a leather couch that seemed to be a match for the ones in the conversation pit in the main house. Again I felt that warm, fleshy sensation as I sank deeply into the cushions. "I don't need anything. I just want to get caught up." My eyes drifted to his bare leg. A chunky black monitoring device was wrapped around his right ankle. "House arrest, huh? How's that going?"

"It sucks." Ronnie plopped down next to me. "I can't really complain, it's better than being in the pen. But I can't go anywhere, except up to the house, and now that Serge is dead I don't have any reason to do that."

"You don't get along with Malis?"

He shrugged. "Malis is okay. She doesn't like me much, but if I were in her position, I wouldn't like me much either." He exhaled. "She wants to sell the house, which means I'm going to go back into gen pop. They won't let me stay out unless I have a stable living situation."

"That stinks," I said. "Ronnie, I'm sorry."

He waved that away. "It's not the end of the world. I did five years in there, and I survived. If I have to do the rest behind bars, I'll get through it."

He leaned back into the couch. The lighting in his cottage was dim enough to fade most of the signs of age from his face, the creases and the darkened patches from sun damage, and he more or less looked like the smoking-hot, sweet-natured guy on whom I'd nursed a secret crush during those two months of filming. He smiled at me, and I wondered if he was experiencing the same effect, the years draining from my face via the powers of flatteringly low light.

"They think I could've killed Serge," he said. "I hope you know me well enough to know that it's bullshit, but with my record and with being right on the premises, I can't blame them for being suspicious."

"Malis said your ankle bracelet proves you were asleep," I said.

He nodded, hair flopping forward into his eyes. He shoved it back, raking one large hand through his messy mane in a failed attempt to get it under control. "That's a big point in my favor, but ankle bracelets can be tampered with, and they know it. They took my laptop away, probably to check if I'd been googling 'how to remove an ankle monitor' or whatever."

"I didn't know anything about your arrest," I said. "I hadn't heard anything at all. It was, what, armed robbery?"

"Yeah." He winced. "I was hanging out with this guy, Marco, who I know from the beach. Cool guy, owns a board rental shop. Pretty laid-back, but with a wild streak. And he needed some quick cash from this producer who owed him money, and he was willing to cut me in if I helped out, and . . . we brought guns." He shrugged. "Guy handed over the cash, no argument. We wore masks, but the guy figured it was Marco, and I got picked up by the cops later that week. No one was hurt, but I got ten years." He fell silent, contemplating his life choices. "I can't honestly say I didn't deserve it. I wasn't in the right headspace then. Prison was probably the right place for me."

I was a little horrified by Ronnie's blasé account of his foray into violent crime, but I kind of got it. All of us go down pathways we never expected, and often those pathways wind up being fantastically stupid and shady. "No one got hurt, at least. That's good," I said, mostly to be saying something.

"Yeah. The guns weren't even loaded. I felt sick and miserable afterward. It was sort of a relief when I got arrested," Ronnie said. "Hey, what about you? What are you doing? You're not acting anymore, right?"

"Right. As it turns out, *The Divide* was both the beginning and end of my career." I cleared my throat. "I tried, I really did. After my agent dropped me, I kept showing up for cattle calls, trying to grab whatever I could, and it was like there was this glass wall separating me from everyone who was actually making it." Ronnie nodded as I spoke, and it struck me how nice it was to talk to someone who understood that my lack of success maybe wasn't due to me being a lousy actor, but simply because success in Hollywood is a lottery with bad odds. As long as you hit certain levels of looks, talent, contextual intelligence, and determination—and believe me, there are thousands upon thousands of aspiring actors in Los Angeles who tick off all those boxes—luck is the only factor that makes a difference.

I continued my tale of woe. "I needed some way to make money, and I wasn't good at waiting tables, so I took a bunch of classes at this beauty college on Fairfax, and then I did hair on movie sets for a while. All that time, I kept thinking maybe being so close to the film industry would help me get roles. And of course that was dumb; with the massive talent pool to draw upon, no director is going to be desperate enough to pull a hairdresser in front of the camera."

"They should've, though," Ronnie said. "You're gorgeous, Jenny. Always have been."

"Thanks." I smiled at him. "I got old, though. I aged out of that window where I could reasonably start a film career. After a while, it stung too much, being around beautiful young people who were so successful at what I'd failed to do."

Ronnie nodded. "I felt the same way when the acting roles

dried up. I'd look at Serge and Linus just getting more and more successful the older they got, and I'd wonder why that couldn't be me. I used to have magazine articles written about me, and now no one knows who I am. When I got arrested, the news reports barely even mentioned that I was an actor."

"I've seen Linus," I said. "I had dinner at his place last week. It seems like he's doing great. You've kept in touch with him?"

"Sure. Serge and Linus and I used to hang out a lot together, back when Serge was still married to Gena. And we've stayed close after all this." He gestured at his ankle bracelet. "They both had my back when a lot of people gave up on me. Serge let me stay here, and Linus found me a better lawyer when it looked like the fuckwit the court assigned me was messing up my defense."

I wished Ronnie had been allowed to keep alcohol on hand, because I felt like I needed a drink while we were spilling our hearts and souls out like this, and I didn't think seltzer would do the trick. I cleared my throat. "After I figured out I was never going to have a film career, I tried to set myself up as a real hairstylist, rent a chair in a salon, but I didn't have a strong client base. So I tried something new."

"Yeah?" Ronnie seemed interested in my life, though unsurprised by the turns it had taken, because stories of failure like mine were commonplace in the industry. He had more screen credits than I did, but he'd also reached the point where he'd seen armed robbery as a viable career change, so he wasn't likely to view me with much judgment or condescension.

"I became a psychic." I felt a stab of embarrassment, even shame, upon saying it. Funny. Ever since making that strange career move, I'd often thought I'd made a bad decision, but I hadn't actually felt ashamed. Lately, though, surrounded by Gena's world and all her successful friends, I felt an acid pit in my stomach at the thought of what I'd done. I'd become a grifter. "I set up a clinic on Beverly and gave psychic readings to people."

Ronnie just nodded. "Oh, yeah, I remember, your grandma was psychic, right? I thought that was really cool. You told me it hadn't been passed down to you, but it seemed like maybe it had. You always seemed to just *know* things about me. It made you so easy to talk to."

"It was my aunt. I'm surprised you remember. And thanks." I paused. "But, Ronnie, that's the thing. I'm not psychic. I'm a good listener, and I'm smart enough to figure out what people want to hear about themselves, and that combination can fool people into handing over money to me. But it's a fraud. I spent six years swindling people out of money."

Ronnie just shrugged. "You didn't actually hurt anyone, did you? I mean, you didn't give them advice that would lead them to ruin their lives, right?"

"I don't think so. I never got too specific with my psychic readings. I'd just try to nudge people in the direction they wanted to go. Like if someone was unhappy with her job, I'd poke around and find out what she genuinely liked to do, and then I'd tell her I saw a happy career in her future in whatever field that was. I wouldn't tell her to quit her job, but maybe I'd encourage her to start exploring other options. I don't think that's a bad thing, necessarily, but there's probably someone out there whose life I made worse by giving them false hope."

"Maybe, but you probably also made someone's life better. It all balances out." Ronnie seemed unconcerned about my transgressions, which was comforting. While listening to his easy acceptance of my sordid existence, I wished I'd stayed in his life all these years since *The Divide*. Maybe we could have helped each other stay on better paths. At least we could have commiserated with each other about the ways our career trajectories had disappointed us. I could have used a friend in the depths of my flailing misery. "Are you still doing that? The psychic stuff?"

"Don't know. I just got evicted from my place of business, so everything is on hold." I looked over at Ronnie. "I'm so sorry about Serge. When I heard the news, I couldn't believe it at first."

"Yeah, me too. Serge was my brother. I don't say that lightly. I have a real brother; he lives in Fullerton. After my arrest, he cut off all contact with me, and honestly, I don't even care." Ronnie exhaled. His shoulders slumped. "When the LASD knocked on my door to tell me Serge was dead, I sobbed like a baby. I couldn't stop bawling until they'd hauled me into the station to talk to me there."

I nodded in sympathy. "You didn't hear anything at all that night?"

"I was sound asleep the whole time." He shuffled his bare feet on the floor and hunched his body over, forearms braced on his bare thighs as though he were trying to form a protective shell. "I'm not allowed to keep alcohol on hand, or drugs, or anything like that. They drug test me weekly, and my probation officer does periodic inspections to make sure I'm not hiding any contraband. But I can have over-the-counter medicines, within reason. I take a lot of pills to help me sleep. Just drugstore stuff. Nights are hard here; I start kicking myself for getting to this stage, and I just want to make it all stop." He must have seen something in my face, because he reached over and patted me on the knee. "Don't start thinking I'm suicidal or anything like that, because I'm not. But sleeping pills help quiet my brain down when I get like that. And so . . . yeah. Serge got shot twenty yards away from me, and I didn't hear a thing."

"They think the killer used a silencer," I said.

"I don't think it matters whether he did or not. I might not have heard anything anyway. Living on the ocean is noisier than you think. You and I, we've been talking a lot louder than we would if the water wasn't right there."

He was right, of course; both of us had raised our volume to compensate for the background roar of the ocean. "You said *he*," I said. "That it doesn't matter whether *he* did or not. Do you have a suspect in mind?"

Ronnie shook his head. "No. I mean, honestly, it seems more

likely Serge was gunned down by some guy, right? Women don't go around shooting people nearly as much as men do."

"Not in random attacks, no, but if some woman had some reason to want Serge dead . . ." I let it trail off.

"Sure, but who? I'm not saying Serge didn't have enemies, because he had a long career in Hollywood, and that doesn't happen without pissing off people along the way. But women always got along fine with Serge. I know he had a lot of partners, but he made it seem uncomplicated, just two people having a good time, no strings attached. It seems more likely this was random," Ronnie said. "If I were the cops, I'd be aiming my attention that way. Maybe a bum knocked on the door wanting a handout and got mad when Serge refused."

The idea of anyone wandering through Serge's multimillion-dollar neighborhood and knocking on random doors without being stopped by private security or a patrolling deputy seemed absurd. It occurred to me that Ronnie was maybe a little too dead set against the idea of Serge being murdered by someone personally known to him. "If Serge was killed by someone he knew, who do you think it would be?"

He was shaking his head before I finished the question. "That's the thing, he wasn't killed by anyone close to him. No one hated Serge like that. I'm going to swear to you right now, cross my heart and hope to die, I don't know why anyone would murder Serge." He looked very open and honest, and my instinct was to believe him.

Then again, Ronnie was always a better actor than reviewers gave him credit for.

Viewed without the warm, fuzzy, comforting haze of old friendship and nostalgia, I knew Ronnie couldn't be counted out as a co-conspirator, if not the culprit. While the evidence of his tracking bracelet might show he couldn't have killed Serge, it didn't mean he was entirely innocent. He could have used his criminal connections to help someone—Boots? Malis?

Gena?—hire a hit man. Or he could've provided the gun that killed Serge.

It felt disloyal to entertain those thoughts. I liked Ronnie, and he liked me. His misery over Serge's death seemed deep and genuine. Seeing Ronnie had transported me back to the best time of my life, and for a few minutes at least, the emotional turmoil of the past few days seemed less overwhelming. But I couldn't be naïve. I doubted Ronnie was a killer, but there was a lot of gray area between innocence and guilt, and I couldn't be certain where Ronnie fell on that spectrum.

I got to my feet. "It's the middle of the night, and I've got a long drive back into Los Angeles," I said. I hesitated. "Would it be okay if I stopped by again sometime?"

"Oh, yeah, absolutely. Anytime. Let me give you my number." He rose and extended a hand. I unlocked my phone and passed it to him, then watched as he added his number to my contacts. "Honestly, though, you can just drop in whenever. You don't need to call first. It's not like I won't be here."

He grinned, but something about the idea of him spending his days alone as a prisoner in this small cottage tore at my heart. I busied myself with putting my phone back in my purse so he wouldn't interpret my expression as pity. "I'm so glad I crossed paths with you again," I said.

"Me, too." He spread his arms wide. I leaned in and let him hug me. He buried his face in my hair and murmured near my ear, "I knew she wasn't you. I always knew she wasn't you."

I melted into that hug, my body as light as a helium balloon. It was amazing how much better his words made me feel.

CHAPTER 15

Been Here Forever

I met Linus for dinner at Lloyd & Lewis, which sounded like a law firm but turned out to be a posh steakhouse in Hollywood. After he'd told me the name over the phone that afternoon, I'd googled it, looked at the prices on the menu, and mentally replayed my conversation with him to make sure all indications suggested he would be picking up the check. It looked like it was a degree more formal than most restaurants in Los Angeles, so I'd dressed appropriately, I hoped, in a stretchy black jersey dress with a draped neckline. I felt matronly; twenty years earlier, I would have worn something tight, short, and sparkly. As I moved into my forties, it became harder to figure out how to dress for social occasions. I still had the same body I'd had in my twenties—maybe a slight thickening around the waist, maybe some sagging skin beneath my upper arms—and when I looked in the mirror, I thought I still looked pretty much the same as I did back then. But I'd read somewhere that that was an illusion, that our mental picture of ourselves gets locked in our minds at some point in our midthirties, and beyond that we fail to see the ravages of age. Our friends and acquaintances get older, but to our own eyes, we ourselves don't.

Linus met me at the bar. After exchanging greetings, he signaled for the bartender, and we settled in with drinks—gimlet for me, dirty martini with extra olives for him—while waiting for our table to become available.

"Cheers," he said. He raised his glass to clink it against mine. He looked expensive, dressed in a charcoal three-piece suit in a windowpane plaid. In his office, framed by the bright Los Angeles sun streaming in through his window, Linus's eyes had been that sun-faded blue common to people who spend a lot of time outdoors. Here in the bar, which was lit with low-hanging lamps with frosted glass shades, they deepened into gold-flecked azure, perfect twin circles of lapis lazuli. "Thanks for meeting me. You look fabulous."

"Thank you. And thanks for inviting me." We drank. "This is a nice place."

"You haven't been here before? It's a classic. It's been here forever." "Forever," in Los Angeles terms, usually meant a decade or so. I knew quite well this place hadn't been here when I'd first moved out from Iowa. There used to be an IHOP on this spot; I'd gone there multiple times to drink endless cups of coffee to kill time and psych myself up before auditioning at one of the many casting agencies in the area. Los Angeles likes to rebuild and rewrite its past in an endless cycle, tearing down landmarks and putting up new ones in their place, then forgetting the former ever existed.

The hostess led us to our booth, which was roomy, with green leather seats that were raised so high my feet barely touched the ground. We perused our menus. I liked steak and didn't run into nearly enough opportunities to eat it, so I ordered the bone-in ribeye, rare, with a green peppercorn sauce; Linus ordered the same, plus grilled asparagus to share and, after a short and productive consultation with a black-suited sommelier, a smooth purple Malbec that tasted of cherries.

Our food arrived, and it was magnificent. Linus grinned at me. "This is a splurge. I'm trying not to eat much beef. Carbon footprint, you know. And I'm normally a super healthy guy. CrossFit five mornings a week, four Ironmans a year. Most of my diet consists of whey powder and steel-cut oats, so I'm very, very happy about this right now."

"I can't remember the last time I had a steak. This was a great idea, Linus."

"How's the psychic business? It seems like the kind of thing where your income would fluctuate wildly from month to month. Or do you have a lot of steady customers?"

"Mostly it's the same people. I do get clients wandering in off the street who've never been to a psychic before and just want to see what it's like." I chewed a bite of steak and swallowed before continuing. "I should be speaking in the past tense, though. I don't really have my business anymore. I got evicted from my workplace."

He stared at me. "Yikes. I'm sorry to hear that." He took a long swallow of the Malbec. "If it's any consolation, if Gena doesn't show up soon, I might be joining you on the street."

"The Elliott Thwaite deal?"

"Yep. I'd been counting on that commission for a while. My business took a hit when everyone shifted to working from home. Corporations weren't too interested in spending tons of cash on artwork for unoccupied buildings. The Thwaite deal was a great opportunity for me to finally make up some lost ground." His tongue was stained purple from the wine, which meant mine certainly was as well. "I hope Gena's found safe, and I hope she's not a murderer. Mostly because I love Gena, but also, I do need this deal to go through. That first half of my commission from Gena's advance, that's already spent. If the client asks for it back, it'll get tricky."

"I'm sorry. That's got to be rough." I didn't know how much sympathy needed to be spent on Linus. He owned a cushy condo in one of the best areas of the city and had enough disposable income to drop a few hundred dollars on a Wednesday-night dinner with a passing acquaintance. Still, everyone has a different definition of poverty, and I had no doubt Linus was feeling the squeeze. “Let’s hope she turns up soon.”

“Amen to that.” Linus raised his glass and clinked it against mine. “So I assume you’re looking for a new business site? Any luck with that?”

“I haven’t been able to think that far ahead. I’d been staying at my place of business for a while, so my first priority is finding a stable place to live.” I tried to make it sound loose and bright, but to my ears I sounded strangled, like the mounting desperation that lay coiled in my stomach was now trying to slither its way out through my esophagus and throat.

“Are you staying with friends?”

“In a manner of speaking,” I said. “MMP offered to let me crash at his place for a while until I find something more permanent, which was generous of him. It was Boots’s idea.”

He stared at me. “You’re living in Gena’s house right now?”

It was clear the news alarmed him, which made sense; I’d wormed my way into Gena’s life both swiftly and deeply. “I’ve just been there a couple of days. My goal is to clear out by the end of the week.” I had no such goal, but it sounded good, like I had a firm plan in place for correcting the bumpy trajectory my life was on. Just a brief spell of turbulence that would soon pass, nothing to get worried about.

“I’m not sure that’s a great idea,” he said. He held his fork raised above his plate, frozen in midair, as though learning about my living situation had shorted out his motor functions. “For your own safety, I mean.”

I stared at him, unable to follow his line of thought. “What does safety have to do with it? You don’t think Serge’s killer is going to mistake me for Gena, do you?”

“No, but . . .” He frowned and seemed to search for words. “You don’t know MMP very well. Hell, I don’t know MMP very well, even though I’ve met him a few times. He seems like a great kid, don't misinterpret what I'm saying. But you never really know people, right?"

I put it together, slowly. "Do you think MMP . . . ?" I didn't need to finish it.

"No. No. Of course not." Linus shook his head to emphasize his point. "Like I said, my impression is that he's a nice guy." He thought over what he was going to say. "In my office last week, you know how Boots thinks it's Malis? That's only because Malis was Serge's wife, and when in doubt you look to the spouse, or the girlfriend, or the boyfriend, or whoever's closest to the victim. Whether you're looking at financial gain or a crime of passion, that person is probably going to have the best motive. And if we're thinking Serge is the victim, that person is Malis."

"But Gena is missing, and this might be about Gena, not Serge?" I nodded. "Yeah, I see what you mean. Does MMP have a financial motive, though? He has his own money from his online stuff, and nobody seems to think Gena would've left him her estate in her will. And if he's the culprit, wouldn't Gena's body have been found along with Serge's?"

"I don't have answers, but it might not be about money. Maybe Gena and Serge were getting back together, or maybe MMP suspected they were and got angry about it."

I pictured MMP, lovely and carefree. "It's hard to think of him as any kind of diabolical criminal."

"Because he's so affable? I know." Involved in his line of thought, Linus had abandoned the rest of his steak. "But here's the thing, and I don't mean to slander the kid, because like I said, he seems nice. I like him. But he's a void. You talk to him, and there doesn't seem to be much there other than an upbeat pleasantness, and that makes me suspicious. You know his background? When he was just a teen, he underwent training in South Korea to become a pop star. That life is pretty rigorous, from what I gather. Lots of discipline, living together with a bunch of other boys, not allowed to visit their families, not allowed any kind of social life. Just long days of studying, and dancing, and singing, and watching what they eat, and learning how to be bright and cheerful and always *on*. I don't say that's inherently bad; I think learning how to work hard toward a specific goal is a valuable skill for any kid. But I'm saying MMP has that background, and that background doesn't really mesh with what we know of him."

"I'm not sure I follow that," I said. "It seems exactly like what we know of him. Have you seen his videos? He's putting that background to good use. He knows how to charm the camera."

Linus shook his head in impatience. "Sure, there's that. I'm not explaining this well. I guess what I mean is, we don't know what's under that fun-loving exterior. What does he feel passionate about? He has a goofy childlike fondness for everything, and I do mean everything. One time I went out to lunch with Gena and MMP, and he spent twenty minutes telling me everything he likes about bubble tea. And the whole time he was talking to me, I thought to myself, *This is fake, this is unreal, he's hiding who he is beneath this hyped-up rising-star façade.* And that scared me, just a little."

Nothing about MMP had ever scared me, though Linus might have a point: MMP's smooth, appealing blankness was almost certainly cultivated. His personality lacked all rough edges; he seemed to like everything and everybody. He was generous to a fault; that he was letting me stay with him surely proved that. All of which seemed to suggest he couldn't possibly be a murderer, and yet . . .

Anyone who was that good, that polished, that much of an expert at hiding any negative emotions, like anger or irritation or disappointment or jealousy—surely a person like that had something going on beneath the surface. Jealousy over his lover's closeness to her ex-husband, maybe.

I took a sip of wine. "In any case, I won't be staying at Gena's home any more than another day or so. If I haven't found a new place by the weekend, I'll move into a hotel."

"I'd feel better about that," he said. "I don't want to scare you, but there's a killer out there somewhere, and as much as I think it's overwhelmingly likely it's no one Serge knew, we can't rule out the possibility it was someone close to Serge, or to Gena, or to both."

My thoughts kept returning to Serge's patio door. When I'd arrived at his home, I'd headed straight for the front, as any first-time visitor would. But Serge's killer had gone to the back of the house, to the entrance Serge and Malis and their friends used regularly, and Serge had willingly slid the glass door open to greet his murderer. As much as Ronnie and Linus might prefer to think their friend had been gunned down by a stranger, I was certain Serge had been killed by someone he knew and trusted.

As we resumed our steaks, I mulled over Linus's warning, which seemed sincere and well-intentioned. Even still, at my core, I found it difficult to believe MMP was a killer, if only because it would be unfathomably reckless to let me move into Gena's house with him if he was hiding a damaging secret. I reminded myself to keep my eyes wide open, though, just in case Linus turned out to be right.

The rest of dinner passed uneventfully. Linus expressed curiosity about my history as a psychic. I still had the strong sense he thought psychics were bullshit artists, but he was polite and seemed genuinely interested, and I was in a mood to talk.

So I found myself telling him about my aunt Connie, about how she'd known since she was a small girl in rural Iowa that she had the ability to see into people's thoughts. How she'd done psychic readings to entertain her friends before deciding to make a living at it. How my mom and Aunt Connie were never close during my childhood, and yet when I'd discovered my own psychic abilities when I was six or seven, I'd recognized it as a mysterious gift that ran in the family. How I'd let that gift fall by the wayside to pursue my dream of acting, only to turn to it once again later in life.

The story was an awkward blend of truth and fabrication, since those psychic abilities had never existed, but Linus displayed a flattering interest, asking all the right questions, and if he noticed that I dodged his inquiries into my family members apart from Aunt Connie, he took the hint and let the matter slide. When we finished the first bottle of wine, we mulled over the possibility of ordering a second, and then Linus suggested, as I thought he probably would, that we should just go back to his place and explore the options on his wine rack.

At the start of the evening I'd been undecided on the issue of whether I'd go to bed with Linus. I felt an easy chemistry with him; I enjoyed his company, and I felt confident he enjoyed mine. As with Ronnie, he made me feel connected to a time of my life that I dearly missed. Over the years, my circle of friends had grown increasingly smaller as my circumstances had grown more and more meager, leaving me feeling isolated and lonely; sex with Linus could help neutralize those feelings.

But I felt a hint of wariness, too. Just a small prickle in the back of my head, but nothing I should disregard. I'd gone into this date half suspicious Linus would try once more to steer me into agreeing to pose as Gena, and while it had become increasingly clear he'd abandoned that idea, his earlier enthusiasm for his plan hinted at a reckless streak beneath that low-key exterior. He was closely tied to both Serge and Gena; was it possible he was also tied to the violent tragedy at Serge's home?

No matter how I looked at it, though, I couldn't see how he'd have any motive for harming either Gena or Serge. Unless Linus turned out to be a deranged monster, I was probably safe with him. After half a bottle of very good wine, after an excellent steak dinner, after some good conversation with a sympathetic listener, spending the night with Linus seemed like an ideal way to cap off the evening.

CHAPTER 16

Selling Out

I made it back to Gena's place before eight the next morning. Linus was an early riser and liked to get to the gym before heading to the office, and while he told me it was cool if I stayed in bed a while longer, I got up when he did and sipped coffee with him at his kitchen counter before bidding farewell with a quick snuggle and a promise to call.

It had been a nice night. Linus was good in bed, dutiful and conscientious, and he made sure I was enjoying myself. His daily workouts had done his body a world of good; he was flexible and strong and confident in his movements. I hadn't slept with anyone in years, and I'd felt awkward at first, a prom-night virgin worried about disappointing her chosen swain with her lack of savvy. Linus said all the right things about my body, my face, my mouth, my prowess in the sack. His bed was a California king, all the space in the world, with soft, clean bedding that smelled of lemons and thyme. In the morning, driving back to Silver Lake, I'd felt relaxed and more optimistic than I had for a while, like Linus had given me a glimpse of a better, cleaner, less marginal world than the one I'd been living in.

None of this was permanent. I had to remind myself of that.

I had a message on my phone from someone who worked for Boots, a woman named Kimberly with the voice of a worried child, who was wondering if she should mail me a check for the invoice I had emailed to Boots, or would I rather pick it up? Back at Gena's home, after I'd showered and changed, I called back to say I'd pick it up now, if she told me where to go.

The address turned out to be Boots's home in Hancock Park. It was a brick Tudor house that looked like a pretty little castle on a spacious corner lot, with steeply pitched roofs and a small turret in front. The windows had diamond-shaped leaded panes; flower boxes overflowing with paperwhite narcissi in full bloom perched on every windowsill.

I parked on the street. Kimberly, who turned out to be Boots's personal assistant, came out to the gate to meet me when I texted that I'd arrived. She seemed to regard me with suspicion, and for a moment I thought she was going to ask to see some identification. Kimberly was young and extremely pretty, with an enormous puff of natural hair that she flattened back away from her face with a series of pearled barrettes. She wore a baby-blue cardigan twinset and matching pencil skirt. She frowned when I asked if I could come in and talk to Boots.

"I'll see if she's here," she replied, which was a weird way of putting it, but I understood the dodge. Of course she knew whether Boots was home; of course Boots *was* home, but Kimberly didn't know whether she would see me.

In the past week of spending time with Boots, I had never lost track of the idea that Boots was a public figure whom I'd known by reputation for the past thirty years, but my mind had kind of blurred over how famous she really was. Gena and MMP each had a high degree of niche fame in their respective fields, but Boots was an Oscar winner, and that put her on another level entirely, particularly in this town. So I tried not to feel miffed when Kimberly left me standing outside the locked gate while she went back inside the house, closing the door behind her.

In about five minutes, she was back. She gestured for me to follow her. "You'll need to take your shoes off," she said as soon as we were inside the front door. I thought I detected a bit of unhappiness in her expression at my sneakers, which were clean and presentable yet clearly budget priced, but maybe I was feeling overly sensitive. It had seemed like Boots and I were on the path leading in the direction of at least a casual friendship, but Kimberly's silent dissatisfaction with my presence in her boss's house made me keenly aware of the imbalance between us.

Boots furnished her home with good-quality antiques. The focal point of her living room was a huge bronze multitiered chandelier that dangled on a thick chain from the ceiling between the exposed beams; her curtains were heavy brocade, intricate patterns embroidered in gold on dusty violet fabric. Her house looked like a refuge for a medieval queen in exile.

I liked her decor, but I was disappointed by her art choices. Boots favored muted landscapes, well composed and tasteful, done in colors clearly chosen by her interior decorator to match her furniture, like the pleasantly inoffensive paintings found on the walls of nice hotel rooms. Despite counting a world-class painter among her closest friends, Boots had no use for fine art. I'd created more interesting works in Rooney's class, all those years ago.

The more I exposed myself to Gena's world, the more I thought Rooney might not have been entirely wrong about me: maybe I did have a gift for art, if only a small one, one I could have cultivated over the years instead of chopping it down before it had a chance to take root. At the very least, I'd been grievously shortsighted for letting one single art-school rejection dissuade me from embarking upon a career as a fine artist.

But it's more complicated than that, isn't it? Some shadowy corner of my brain tried to seize my attention, tried to alert me to something hidden in a cornfield halfway across the country, something bizarre and incomprehensible and shrouded in layers of violence and terror. Boots's living room was warm, but the sweat that had suddenly broken out along the length of my spine was cold, so cold that I desperately wanted a sweater.

It was a relief when Boots appeared at last, descending a dark wood staircase with an ornate carved banister, dressed in a wide-legged halter-top jumpsuit in teal velvet. "Hi, Jenny. I'm in the middle of eight million crises today, but I wanted to touch base with you. Did Kimberly give you your money?"

Kimberly appeared at my elbow, thrusting a long cream envelope at me. I accepted it with thanks and stuffed it in my purse. "I don't want to bother you if you're busy. Maybe we could meet for drinks later."

Boots shook her head. "This week is a mess. I have a new product line launching behind schedule, and too many people I trust have dropped too many balls already." She pointed a teal fingernail at a lavender jacquard love seat. "Grab a seat. I can give you five minutes."

"Sure." I perched on the edge of the love seat, which felt like it was stuffed with compacted sand; Boots took a high-backed armchair upholstered in gold corduroy for herself. "I had a good talk with Malis on Tuesday. I spent some time at her studio and then visited her in Malibu in the evening."

"Yeah?" That finally broke through Boots's aura of impatient inattention. Her gaze sharpened as she fixed her beautiful eyes on me. "Did she kill Serge?"

"I don't get that sense from her at all. Maybe she's very good at hiding her thoughts and her motives, but my impression is that she felt a good deal of affection for Serge, though she was clear-eyed about his flaws. She's unhappy about Serge's death and the idea that someone got away with murder; she'd like to see the culprit caught and punished, though she's not mired in deep grief."

"Of course she's not. She's going to get all his money. You said it earlier, that gives her one hell of a compelling motive."

"True. But I also mentioned that Malis isn't concerned with money," I said. I might not be a real psychic, but I felt certain that was true. "She loves her downtown studio and couldn't care less about the Malibu home or the rest of his estate. She's content with doing her art and living her life on her own."

This wasn't what Boots was paying me to tell her, and since Boots was my employer, that was probably dangerous to admit, but it was the truth, or at least the truth as I interpreted it.

On the one hand, I was a fraud anyway, so I didn't know why I wasn't drawing out the fraud to its expected conclusion. In my psychic readings, I was always careful to make sure I told my clients exactly what they wanted to hear, disguised beneath a veneer of real-sense tough talk: *You've been letting your need-to-please personality push you too far into the background; if you put yourself first for once and go after this opportunity, I see lasting positive benefits for you down the road.* To be a fake psychic is to be a motivational speaker.

But I'd been approaching a fork in the road for a while: keep taking Boots's money while making sure to stay in her good graces, or do my genuine best to solve Serge's murder. I'd hoped I could do both, but that no longer seemed possible.

"Okay, fine," Boots said. "If it's not Malis, though, who is it? You're not going to tell me it was some random stranger."

I shook my head. "Malis told me about Gena's documentary," I said.

"Yeah? What about it?" It was challenging, and Boots seemed to sense immediately that was the wrong tack to take, at least before she knew where I was going with this. She softened her tone to one of disinterest. "That's what Serge and Gena were working on the night Serge was killed, sure, but it doesn't factor into any of this."

"She said you were unhappy with how you might be portrayed in the documentary."

The veneer of bored irritation didn't change. "I don't know why she'd say that. Malis and I aren't friends; we don't exactly share our feelings with each other. And in any case, why would I be unhappy about it? The documentary isn't about me; I just donated an evening to talk with Gena about my business and my philosophy." Her eyebrows drew together. "What are you getting at? Did Malis tell you she suspects me? Because that's messed up, if that's the case."

"Do you know what the documentary is about?" I asked. "Malis tried to explain it, but I don't think she really knew. Something about the various pathways to success?"

Boots waved a slim hand in a gesture of impatience, like she was batting an annoying flying insect away from her face. "Something like that, I guess. I don't even think Gena knew. I think she was just getting a bunch of successful people on camera to talk about what makes them tick. She talked to MMP, too. She's always been interested in the division between the perception of success and the perception of failure, that kind of thing." Gena and I had that in common.

"From what I gather, the focus was on selling out," I said. "You know how when we were young, none of us knew exactly what it meant to sell out, but we all knew it was the worst thing you could do? Like it was on the same level as selling your soul to the devil. And now that whole concept has been flipped inside out; everyone keeps actively trying to partner with as many corporations and brands as they can, because that seems like the only remaining viable path to success. I think Gena was exploring that idea in her documentary, trying to figure out where she stood."

"I hope she wasn't trying to claim any moral high ground on the issue. Look at her Elliott Thwaite collab. If that's not the definition of selling out, I don't know what is," Boots said. "If you already knew what the documentary was about, why are you asking me?"

I paused. "Malis showed me your interview with Gena," I said.

It hung in the air. Boots looked blank at first, and then she frowned. "Are you serious about this?" she asked. "You think I killed my ex-lover and my good friend because they acted shady to get me on camera?"

"You didn't consent to the interview?" I asked.

Boots wrinkled her nose in distaste at the question. "I'm a big girl. I knew what I was doing. But we'd split two bottles of wine over an evening of what I thought was just going to be girl talk, and then Gena sprang the idea of the interview on me when I'd had just enough to drink to view it as a good idea, which it most certainly wasn't. I was pissed off at her afterward, but I was willing to give her a lot of leeway." She shook her head. "Hell, she'd been diagnosed with cancer a couple of weeks earlier. Dealing with her own mortality suddenly made her very concerned about the state of the world, and that concern extended to me and my business practices. I didn't find her judgmental attitude appropriate, but I knew she was working through some issues. And I also knew I could talk her out of using that interview, if necessary."

She sat up straighter and put her hands on her thighs, knees tightly together, leaning forward to make sure I knew she was deadly serious about this. "I haven't seen the footage, but I know what I said. I probably come off like an asshole, right?"

"Pretty much," I said.

"Yeah, that's what I figured. I'm not thrilled about it. If that interview goes public, I might be in for some bad press. But I'm not naïve. I know how to spin things. If that documentary comes out—came out, I should say; I'm pretty sure it's dead in the water now—it would be embarrassing, but at the end of the day, I could get public sympathy on my side."

I didn't know whether she was right about that, but she made a good case, and I'd swear she believed what she was saying. "Okay. That sounds reasonable," I said. "I went about this clumsily, and I'm sorry about that. But I sensed you were hiding things from me."

"For fuck's sake." It came out with the force of a gunshot. "I wasn't hiding anything from you. I didn't mention the documentary because it has nothing to do with anything. Answer me this: Do you think I killed Serge and Gena because of that interview?"

"I don't think you killed Serge and Gena at all. I'm sure you didn't."

Boots blinked her long lashes, startled at my sudden capitulation. "Great!" she said. "Then why are you wasting my time with this?"

"I had to eliminate you as a suspect. That's done now."

"If you were psychic, you would've known I had nothing to do with any of this." Boots shook her head, slow and unforgiving. "I should've realized you were a fraud just by looking at your Yelp reviews. And I called Della DeLaurenti to see what she thought of you, and she hadn't even heard of you, which was another big warning flag right there. But you seemed cool, and I felt sorry for you, since you'd obviously fallen on hard times. I was trying to help you out, and you picked a weird way to repay me."

The dig at my Yelp reviews, which, for the record, were perfectly fine if not outstanding—a tiny smattering of one-star reviews mixed in with a majority of fours and the occasional ego-stroking five—didn't bother me, and there was no earthly reason why Della DeLaurenti should know who I was. But the idea that Boots felt sorry for me stung. It was meant to wound, and it did. It burrowed its way under my skin like a scabies mite, made me realize Boots could see straight through my outer semi-polished exterior and into my shabby, mediocre core. I had wanted Boots to like me, to view me as a peer and possibly a friend, and now I realized that was wishful thinking. I wasn't friend material; I was a charity case.

I smiled, keeping my eyes especially wide and bright. I got to my feet. "I'm sorry I insulted you," I said. "It wasn't my intention."

Boots didn't reply. Kimberly materialized at my shoulder and gestured wordlessly in the direction of the front door. I flashed her a sunny smile and let her walk me to the curb.

CHAPTER 17

Young and Cool

It was hard to feel good about the way that turned out. In my car, I allowed myself a pang of worry that Boots would call MMP to tell him I wasn't to be trusted and that he should kick me out of Gena's home. Then I realized she wouldn't care enough to go to that kind of effort. This whole situation sucked, but it wasn't catastrophic. I still had a place to crash.

When I pulled through the gate of Gena's home in the early afternoon, I saw a strange car parked in the courtyard, an electric-blue Prius that seemed to sparkle with thousands of points of glittery light in the direct sun. As I approached the front door, Linus and Brynna came around the side of the house along the path leading to the back patio, deep in conversation. When Linus glanced up and spotted me, his face burst into a sunny grin. Brynna looked murderous.

"Jenny! Fantastic. I thought about texting to see if you wanted to grab some lunch, but I should get back to the office. Maybe dinner tonight?" He was dressed for work in a dark suit; Brynna wore cutoffs, her legs long and bare, feet shoved into dirty checkerboard Vans. She glared at Linus as he talked to me.

"Dinner would be great."

"Nine-ish? Maybe a hair later? I have a meeting that might go long, but I can pick you up here when I'm done."

"Perfect. I'll see you then." I was prepared to leave our goodbyes at that, but Linus stepped forward and gave me a quick peck on the lips, passionless yet affectionate. He pulled back and smiled at me. "I know the circumstances are weird, but seeing you transports me right back to *The Divide*. You and me and Serge hanging out on the set, laughing and having a great time, back when we were all young and cool."

I started to smile back at him, and then it glitched on my face.

A memory from the set. We were filming outdoors in an alley somewhere east of downtown in the dead of night after a long, long day, all of us exhausted and punchy. I'd had too much coffee in an attempt to keep up my energy, and I felt increasingly ragged and humorless as morning approached. Serge wasn't happy with the way Ronnie kept delivering a line, and he ordered him to do it over and over and over, a truly preposterous number of takes. At some point Ronnie, uncharacteristically bitchy from getting sucked into some kind of weird pissing match with Serge, asked Serge why he wasn't nearly as tough on me. Serge settled into his canvas-backed folding chair, tilted his head to the side, grinned, and said, "Because Jenny gives a *great* blowjob."

And there'd been a stunned moment, and then we'd all burst out laughing, because we were all young and cool and raunchy and irreverent, and Ronnie shook off the tantrum that had been brewing and nailed his delivery within the next few takes, and we'd all been able to go home. And I was just glad the focus had been on Ronnie, because I could feel the heat of my skin burning beneath my heavy layers of makeup, like I was going to erupt into flames under the white-hot lights. Because of course I was sleeping with Serge, and I *did* give a great blowjob, and everyone sort of knew that, just like they sort of figured that was how I snagged this big, meaty part as my film debut, but it was okay, because I was doing a good job, I was inhabiting this tricky, multilayered role like I was placed on earth for just that purpose, and anyway, it was nobody's business except mine and Serge's. Except now there was no *sort of* about it; it was out in the open, taking up valuable real estate in the front of everyone's brain, and I felt embarrassed and kind of trashy. I couldn't complain about it to anyone, even to Serge, because that wouldn't fit with the young, cool, raunchy, irreverent vibe we'd all gone to great pains to cultivate on the set.

I thought about pretty young Kira, brokenhearted over Serge's death because her dream of stardom had been snatched from her. If Serge had lived, and if Kira had starred in his film, at some point during production he would have tried to coax her into his bed, because that was what Serge did.

I had no idea how Kira would have responded; I didn't know her well enough. I knew Serge, though. I knew he wouldn't have been pushy or overtly creepy. If she turned down his advances, he wouldn't have threatened to whisk the role away, he wouldn't have deliberately made life on set difficult for her, he would have assured her he respected her choices. Serge was a fun guy to be around, and he was always decent to me; he and I genuinely had a good time together, during that brief, giddy period when our trajectories had intersected.

But . . .

I had slept with Serge—dated him, if I'm being euphemistic—because I really did enjoy his company, but also because I didn't want to give him any excuse to dismiss me from the film. When he'd initiated a sexual encounter up in the Hollywood Hills after my audition, I hadn't known whether I could refuse and still be considered for the role. That he turned out to be an okay guy was beside the point; he had power while I was nobody, and I desperately wanted to hang on to the big, juicy part that was so improbably mine. Now, all these years later, I felt resentment toward Serge for putting me in that position, and frustration with myself for my unquestioning acceptance of the situation. Maybe today's starlets were braver than I had been; maybe Kira would have felt she could blithely turn Serge down, confident in her own worth and unafraid of repercussions. I hoped so.

But Serge had made a lot of films, and if reports were true, he'd slept with a lot of his stars along the way. I'd felt snubbed when Serge hadn't responded to my attempt to reestablish contact. My ego had been too bruised to try again, but another actress might have responded differently to finding herself discarded by someone who'd once held such power over her. Maybe one of Serge's past leading ladies had reacted to his rejection with anger, even violence.

Linus turned to Brynna. "Brynna, thanks so much for bringing this to my attention. Hang in there, kiddo. I'm around if you ever need to call."

Brynna didn't say a word. Her stare drifted from me to Linus and back again, her bushy brows mashed together like warring baby muskrats. Linus hesitated, like he wasn't sure whether to call attention to her obvious unhappiness, then settled for smiling brightly at us both before getting into the Prius.

As soon as he was gone, I fished my house key out of my purse and turned my attention to the door. I expected Brynna to slump back around in the direction of Gena's studio. Instead, I heard her behind me. "Hey!"

I turned from the door with unbothered slowness. "Hi, Brynna. What's up?" I asked.

"What are you meeting Linus for?" she asked.

"Just dinner." I managed to let a note of surprise into my voice, like I couldn't fathom why she was asking the question. Indeed, I wasn't entirely sure what Brynna's specific objection was this time, though socializing with Linus undoubtedly fell under the blanket umbrella of things Brynna disliked about me. Fair enough. Everything Brynna did fell under the blanket umbrella of things I disliked about her, so that made sense. "Why do you ask?"

"Why are you seeing him?" She took a step closer, paint-streaked legs pale and glowing in the sunlight.

"What possible business is it of yours?"

"Linus is my manager. He's nothing to you," she said. "Why are you seeing Linus? What are you telling him?"

What are you telling him? "I don't know. What should I be telling him?"

"Are you talking about the Thwaite deal? Are you telling him not to give it to me?" Brynna asked. "Because if you're interfering with that in any way, I will fuck you up, do you understand that?"

I stared at her. Then I laughed. That sole physical fight I'd been in, many years ago, had been terrifying and violent, and it had gone very poorly for me. Compared to what I'd been through back then, Brynna seemed about as menacing as an agitated squirrel. "You'll fuck me up? You'll *fuck me up*? Do you realize how utterly ridiculous you sound?"

Her cheeks and nose reddened. "You don't get to insult me," she said. She moved even closer, her stance aggressive, her hands balling into fists.

"Sure I do," I said. "Hostility is a two-way street. You insult me, and I'm going to insult you right back. And if you move any closer to me, I'm going to punch you in the face. Got it?"

The front door opened, and MMP, clad in boxers printed with cartoon frogs locked in various carnal vignettes, squinted at us. He yawned through his words. "Guys, it's a little early."

"She started it," Brynna said, as I could have predicted she would. I'd never had a sibling, and I used to think I would have given a great deal for a younger sister, someone I could protect and befriend and educate about the world. Brynna's relentless brattiness made me reconsider. "She threatened me. Did you hear her? She said she was going to punch me in the face."

"I don't care," MMP said. "I *so* don't care. I just care that I had a late night, and you two are being super, super loud out here."

"I'm sorry, MMP," I said. "I lost my temper. It shouldn't have happened."

"It's cool." MMP flashed me a smile, a sleepy imitation of his usual megawatt grin. "Just keep it down, okay?"

Brynna didn't answer. She glowered at me, and then she turned and stormed down the pathway to the backyard. MMP looked after her, confusion on his sleep-dazed face. "Where's she going?" he asked me.

"Gena's studio, I assume," I said. "You didn't know she was here?"

He wrapped his arms around his bare chest and shook his head. "Gena lets her use the studio, but only on a schedule. Gena needs a lot of creative time to herself." He smiled at me, and it seemed more genuine this time. "She'd yell at me if I visited her while she was working. It wasn't like she'd actually be mad, but she had certain hours where she wouldn't let me or Brynna or anyone else come over. I guess since she's . . . gone, Brynna figures those rules no longer apply."

He yawned again. "I'm going back to bed before I fall asleep talking to you. Are you coming in?"

"Sure," I said. I followed him inside the house.

He paused in the foyer, and when he spoke, his voice had an air of artful casualness. "Hey, any luck finding an apartment? There's absolutely no hurry, of course."

"I'm looking at places this afternoon," I lied. "I'll be out of your hair by the weekend."

"Cool. No big deal, obvs." MMP smiled at me, though it seemed a little wary, like maybe he was used to people promising to do things for him but never following through. *Give me your number; I'll call you this week about that audition. Let me check my schedule and see if this weekend would work for dinner. I promise I'll bring up your name the next time I talk to my agent.*

The next film I make, I'm going to give you a call, I promise. Serge had said that to me at the wrap party for *The Divide*, or to be more specific, the private party Serge and I had thrown for ourselves at the Chateau Marmont following the wrap party. He was booked on a morning flight back to New York, where he was paying what seemed like an exorbitant monthly amount for what he described as a mouse-infested studio apartment in the Meatpacking District, but it was okay, because he'd be back in Los Angeles soon enough to meet with the producers and to oversee the eight million things that needed to be done before the film could make it into theaters. I'd probably see him then, and I'd definitely see him at the premiere and on the pre-release publicity circuit.

There was no premiere and no publicity, and Serge didn't call me when he made his next film, or the one after that, and I never saw him again.

By the time I'd emailed Serge and received no response, five years after completing *The Divide*, he was already an A-list director, linked to big-name stars. Whether or not he'd ever received my note, his silence sent the message loud and clear: I was no longer in his league. Even still, I held on to a stubborn dream of working my way back up to his level for far too long. As the years moved on, that dream seemed increasingly unlikely; now, with his death, it was an impossibility. If I uncovered his killer, though, I might end up as important to the overall narrative of Serge's life as he was to mine, and maybe that would bring me some comfort.

Thoughts of Serge consumed me during a long and frustrating afternoon spent searching for a new place to live. I set up an appointment with a woman on Craigslist who was looking for someone to share her Koreatown place, but she ghosted on me. I toured a basement studio in Inglewood and asked the building manager so many carefully phrased questions about the necessity of a credit check and whether the deposit amount was negotiable that she finally told me she didn't think the place was right for me. I inquired about weekly rates at a couple of beachfront hotels that looked dodgy yet not outright dangerous. I walked along the beach in Venice and sat on the sand and looked out at the ocean, chin resting on my knees, watching the sun sink down the horizon while trying not to cry.

I hated everything I'd become. While filming *The Divide*, I'd been certain I was doing exactly the right thing for my career. Now, twenty-five years later, I realized how much I'd let that film in general—and Serge in specific—dominate my life, and how little those twin obsessions had given back to me in return.

I considered walking away from all of it. Maybe I'd drive up the coast and search for whatever work I could find in random seaside towns; maybe I'd head back to Iowa and ask Aunt Connie if I could crash with her for a while until I sorted myself out. I didn't owe Serge or Gena anything. Serge's murder could go unsolved; Gena could remain missing. It was nothing to me.

No. Like it or not, Gena and I were forever linked, just as Serge and I were linked. I'd embarked upon this endeavor with the original goal of confronting Gena over her theft of *The Divide*. Now, though, I felt a bit foolish for feeling such self-righteous fury over what was probably nothing more than a silly lie that had spun out of control, a lie that was no worse or more destructive than all the ones I'd told to my clients. Somewhere out there, Gena was either dead or in the worst trouble of her life, and I felt a connection to her now; I wouldn't be able to let this go until I knew the truth behind what had happened to her. As the sun set, I headed back to Silver Lake.

Gena's home was silent and still when I returned in the early evening. The lights were off in the living room; when I climbed upstairs to the guest room, the door to the master suite was open all the way, and I could see that it was empty. MMP's bed was unmade, the sheets in a tangle, the comforter spilling to the floor. I moved down to my end of the hall and opened the door to the guest room.

Brynna was lying on my bed, which gave me a jolt. The jolt shifted into sick dread when I realized her neck was at an angle necks couldn't achieve without something being terribly, horribly wrong.

She was face down, lying in a boneless heap like a rag doll a child had flung to the ground. Her ear was smashed against her shoulder. Minutes passed, years, decades as I stood in the doorway, frozen, before I could force myself to walk into the room.

Blood roaring in my ears, I checked for a pulse, even though it was a useless gesture. Her skin was rubber. With two fingers, I pushed her thick mass of hair away from her face. Her right eye was partially open and sightless, nothing but a slit of milky, filmy white.

I backed out of the room. My brain immediately offered up a primal, foolish, chickenshit plan of action: grab my suitcase and my box of stuff, drive away from here, keep driving until I was far out of the state, never come back to Los Angeles. I'd be the main suspect; Brynna was dead in my room, and we'd fought just that morning, loudly enough to wake MMP. He'd overheard me threatening to punch her in the face. The owner of this house was missing and presumably involved in a violent homicide; I was a near-exact duplicate of her, and my presence in her home would be difficult to explain to the satisfaction of the police.

I had to close the guest room door, inhale deeply, count to ten, and release the breath. I repeated that five or six times before I was able to take my phone out of my purse. I stood in the dark hallway and called 911 to report a murder.

CHAPTER 18

Legal Match

They didn't arrest me, but it was close. They questioned me at the house for four hours before transporting me in an LAPD squad car to the downtown headquarters, an imposing glass-and-concrete structure, nothing but flat planes and sharp angles that stabbed at the sky. I spent the night in a boxy, barren, blindingly bright interrogation room that smelled of corn chips and ball sweat, seated in a molded plastic chair that wobbled with my every movement, being intermittently questioned by two detectives between long stretches of isolation. One detective was named Jones and one was named Svoboda, and they were both absolute dickheads. Jones was young and unsettlingly handsome in an aggressively clean-cut and plastic way that made me think of killer cyborgs from the future, and Svoboda had a hairy neck and a bald head, and neither of them liked me very much. It was mutual.

While waiting for the cops to arrive, I'd called MMP to tell him what was going on, and he'd hurried back home from Kira's apartment, where he'd been spending the evening. The police separated us from each other immediately; it was possible MMP was here at headquarters as well, maybe being questioned in a different room, but I hadn't seen or heard anything from him. I'd also called Linus and left him a shaky voicemail briefing him on the situation. He'd called back several times, but the police wouldn't let me answer my phone at the house, and it had been taken from me before we went into the interrogation room.

The detectives asked for permission to take a DNA test, and I was too scared to say no, so a somber young technician with cystic acne came into the room and stabbed a long cotton swab around my inner cheek. At first I thought they might suspect I was Gena in disguise, but after thinking it over, it seemed more likely they would be looking for my DNA at the crime scene. I thought I'd probably be okay; my DNA would be all over the guest room, of course, but I'd never touched Brynna, other than to make sure she was dead, and I didn't think there'd be any of my DNA lurking on her corpse.

They questioned me in bursts, first both of them together, then Jones alone, then Svoboda alone, then back to Jones, then together again. They asked me who I was, why I had been at the house, why I had a key, what my relationship was to the late Brynna Shanley, to MMP, to Gena. They made me account for my every movement for the past several days and yelled at me when I got confused and contradicted myself. They left me by myself for long stretches of time, sitting underneath grim fluorescent lights, one wall taken up entirely by a mirror, which was, of course, one-way glass. I spent much of that multi-hour stretch needing to pee but not wanting to ask. They brought me black coffee, which smelled like armpits and which I didn't touch, and a bologna sandwich on sticky white bread, which I ate because I thought having something in my stomach might help me feel more stable. It didn't; I felt nauseous for a couple of hours afterward, my guts nothing but battery acid and bile, and found myself hoping I wouldn't vomit during questioning.

Detective Moreau arrived very late in the proceedings, probably early morning by that point, and I was frankly glad to see her. Jones and Svoboda ignored her when she entered the interrogation room; there were only three chairs, all occupied, the two detectives and me facing off across a stainless-steel table, so Moreau stood back by the door, leaning against the wall. She hadn't said a word to me, hadn't even really looked at me apart from a quick glance to assess the situation when she'd first entered the room. She held a file folder close to her chest with both arms wrapped protectively around it, the way some people would carry a baby, and stayed quiet as Jones and Svoboda pounded me with questions. At a lull in their questioning, she spoke at last. "I'm going to need the room to talk to Jenny alone."

"Absolutely not," Svoboda said. He didn't turn his head to look at her. "This is our case. You're here as a courtesy."

"My case before yours. The killing of this girl has got to be linked to the Grumet murder. LASD has priority here."

"Yeah? It's not our problem if you haven't been able to solve your cases. In this building, the Grumet murder takes a back seat. The Shanley girl is the focus."

"No shit. But Jenny is mine. I talked to her first, and I need to talk to her now." Moreau rolled her head from side to side like she was working out a crick in her neck. She wore a well-cut suit, maybe the same one she'd been wearing during our first encounter, over a pale blue shirt buttoned to the throat. "Give me the room. You can have her back when I'm done."

They didn't like it, and I thought they were going to refuse. Jones opened his mouth, but stopped when Svoboda reached over and poked his wrist. They exchanged a look, then got up and left the room.

After the door closed behind them, Moreau settled into the chair Svoboda had vacated. She placed her file folder on the table, lining it up carefully with the edge. She waited for a long moment before speaking, which would give Jones and Svoboda plenty of time to situate themselves behind the one-way mirror to observe the proceedings, and it dawned on me that their little disagreement had been staged for my benefit. They wanted me to think the police department and the sheriff's department could be pitted against each other, that I could look to Moreau as an ally who would protect me from the mean, bullying cops. That was dangerous, because I desperately wanted to believe I had an ally right now.

Moreau spoke first. "What the hell were you doing at Santos's house, Jenny?"

"Boots Pontifex asked MMP, Matthew Mark Park, if I could stay there," I said. "She hired me to talk to Gena's friends and see if I could find out what happened to her."

"Using your psychic powers." To Moreau's credit, only very faint traces of withering scorn seeped into her tone.

"Right, using my psychic powers," I said. "Mostly, though, I just needed a place to stay. MMP offered to let me sleep at Gena's house for a few days until I found something else."

"Nice of him."

"Yeah. He's a nice guy."

"You fucking him?"

She wanted to provoke a reaction. I was careful not to give her one. "He's eighteen years younger than I am, so no, I'm not. The guest room that I found the body in, Brynna's body, that's where I was sleeping."

"Something against younger men? Genevieve Santos didn't seem to mind the age gap," Moreau said.

"I'm not Gena," I said.

She just nodded, slowly. "Something you haven't been telling us, Jenny? Something you've been holding back?"

"I've been talking for hours. I've told them everything," I said. I gestured toward the one-way mirror. I tried to think of some magic words that would explain everything, that would let Moreau and the two dickheads know I was telling the truth. I came up with nothing I hadn't already said many times and in many different ways, so I just stayed quiet.

Moreau let the silence expand until it sucked all the oxygen from the room and threatened to suffocate me. She was motionless, unblinking; it didn't seem like she was breathing. Using one finger, she slid the file folder across the table to me.

"Have a look at that," she said. "It was just faxed up from the lab. It's technical, but I can help you with it."

I opened the folder, which was unlabeled and contained a stapled sheaf of papers. I flipped through the sheaf and saw mostly a bunch of numbers and abbreviations. At a glance, it meant nothing to me. "You guys are still using fax machines?" I asked.

"LAPD is." There was a wry undertone to her voice. I looked up quickly, but her expression was as humorless as before. "You know what this is?"

"Can't say I do."

"It's your DNA test result. Crime lab rushed it through."

I looked at her, the papers still in my hand. "Yeah, so? If it shows that I was in the room where Brynna's body was found, I already told you I was staying there."

Moreau shook her head. Her face was still sphinxlike, composed and perfect. "Your DNA is a legal match for Genevieve Santos's."

My brain emptied, like Moreau had yanked out a plug, forcing all my thoughts to gush out of me and drain down to the tile floor, which was dirty and sticky with what I hoped was something innocuous, like a spilled soda. "I'm not Gena," I said.

"Test says you've got her DNA," Moreau said.

"Then it's the wrong test." I looked around the room, looked at the one-way mirror behind which the LAPD detectives were almost certainly sitting, observing my reaction to this news. "Or you're trying to get me to confess to something I didn't do. That DNA test couldn't match. Gena and I are two different people." I could hear my voice getting higher and louder.

Moreau nodded slowly. "Yeah. I know you are."

Her calm cut through my mounting panic. "But what—?"

"I said it's a legal match." Her dark eyes bored into my soul.

"But there's more than enough non-DNA evidence out there to prove beyond any kind of doubt that Genevieve Santos and Jenny St. John are two different people."

It was a relief to hear her say that, because for a wild stretch it had seemed like we were heading into some kind of bizarre territory where Gena and I were the same person, and I didn't think I could handle that right now. "Then why does it match? Just a coincidence?"

Moreau shook her head, just once. "You and Santos have to be related. Identical twins."

I stared at her. "I don't have a twin."

"Clearly you do." Moreau almost sounded amused, like she was finding some entertainment value in my confusion. "DNA doesn't lie."

I had no response to that. Neither of us spoke. This time the silence wasn't suffocating. It was lonely and distant and disorienting. I placed the sheaf of papers back in the folder and slid the folder across the table to Moreau. It seemed very difficult to do simple tasks. My fingers were thick and clumsy.

Moreau waited, then finally broke the silence. "Jenny, think. Is it possible your mother gave birth to twins and never told you?"

I shook my head. Moreau tried again. "You were born in Iowa? That place you mentioned in our first interview, Hayes?"

"Miami," I said. I looked up at Moreau. "I was born in Miami. That's where my mom was living at the time. She grew up in Iowa, though, outside Sioux City, and she moved back there with me when I was only a couple of months old."

"And your father?"

I shook my head again. "Never knew him. My mom said he wasn't worth remembering."

"So your mother could have had twins and never mentioned it. Maybe your daddy raised the other baby, maybe she gave him Santos and raised you on her own."

I didn't answer. I stared at the far wall, which was painted the color of scrambled eggs. There was a footprint at eye level, a perfect dark impression of the sole of a cleated boot.

I guess I zoned out, because the next thing I knew Moreau was snapping her fingers in front of my face to get my attention. "Jenny? You still with me?"

I focused on her. I cleared my throat. "Yeah. I am. I just . . ." I shook my head. "It's some kind of mistake. It has to be."

"Deep breaths, Jenny. You're okay." She leaned forward across the table. "Here's the straight truth, okay? Nobody in this building has much of a hard-on for the idea of you as Brynna Shanley's killer. Tracks on the floor suggest she was dragged by her arms up the stairs and down the hall. Besides the obvious that it'd be a weird move for you to kill her somewhere else, drag her body to your bed, and then call the cops, you might not have the physical strength. She was hit on the side of the head with a heavy object with enough force to shatter her skull and break her neck. Could be a lucky blow, but I don't see you being strong enough to pull that off."

I knew I shouldn't cling to shreds of hope offered by someone who might be telling me whatever she thought I wanted to hear in order to trap me into saying something I shouldn't, but I did anyway, grabbing to this information like a shipwreck survivor paddling out to reach some small bit of flotsam. "I'm not a suspect?"

"Didn't say that. Just saying it doesn't seem as though you're likely to have done it." Moreau settled back in her chair and considered me. "But it's impossible to think the Shanley girl's murder isn't directly connected to the Santos disappearance, and let's face it, you are one hundred percent beyond a doubt directly linked to Santos."

I tried not to feel too much relief; there was still danger here. "Even if that DNA test is right, it's a coincidence. I've never met Genevieve Santos."

"And yet here you are, living in her house. You've got to admit, Jenny, it looks bad."

"I'm living in her house because of you." It came out louder than it should. "You know that. I'd never heard of Gena until you came to question me. You were the one who told me I had a doppelgänger, and you were the one who got me evicted, which is how I ended up staying at Gena's. If I'm under any suspicion, it's all because of things you've done."

From Moreau's face, I could tell none of this was any surprise to her. "I might have unintentionally set things in motion that got you evicted. That wasn't what I set out to do, but you were living in that place illegally, so I'm not going to shed any tears that you got caught. But you had a reason for staying at Santos's house out of all the places you could have gone, and I just want to make sure we're all clear on that reason."

"I've been through this," I said. Weariness poured out of me, spilling over the metal table, puddling underneath the stark fluorescent light. "I've been through this so many times. I just wanted to find out who killed Serge. Boots Pontifex offered to pay me for my time, because she thought my psychic abilities might help me find out what happened to Gena and Serge. I needed money, and I needed a place to stay. That's all."

Moreau huffed out a burst of air, a gesture of either frustration or finality. She shook her head and picked up the folder. She got to her feet and pushed in her chair, holding on to the back of it for a moment so she could look at me from across the table. "Hang tight, Jenny," she said before leaving the room.

CHAPTER 19

This Isn't Good

Jones and Svoboda questioned me for a while longer, and I think there probably were some behind-the-scenes conversations about whether to place me under arrest, but just before five in the morning, they returned my phone and said I could go.

The sun wasn't up yet. My car was parked at Gena's house. My stuff was there as well, but it would have to stay there for the time being; the guest room was an active crime scene. Nothing was open, and I had no place to go, so I sat on a bench in the little park outside City Hall in the darkness, dazed and empty and with the beginnings of what would probably end up being a monster headache, and checked my messages, mostly to give my hands something to do. I had three voicemails from Linus, the concern in his voice growing closer to naked worry with each message. One text from MMP: "U OK?" with a frowny-face emoji.

I wasn't okay. Finding Brynna's corpse had been a shock; Detective Moreau's revelation about my DNA results had been an electrical fire that consumed me from within, leaving only a charred husk. All along, I'd assumed my physical similarity to

Gena was just a coincidence, one of those freakishly improbable things that happen every once in a great while. Under no circumstances had I thought it possible I had a long-lost twin.

If I tried to phone my mother to ask her questions about my birth, she would refuse to take my call. But she would know, of course, why there was someone out there who shared my DNA, and if she refused to tell me, which seemed entirely likely, Aunt Connie might be able to help.

The detectives had ordered me to be available if they needed me, but nobody had explicitly told me not to leave town, though that was undoubtedly what they meant. I didn't want to go to Iowa, but I needed answers, and that was where I'd find them.

I spent a long time on my phone working out the logistics, then booked myself a round-trip ticket on a budget carrier to Sioux City via Denver, leaving in two hours. I'd arrive in the late afternoon; my return trip would be early tomorrow morning. It ate up dangerously close to all the money in my checking account, and I'd have to rent a car on top of that, but it was necessary.

I caught a city bus to the airport. I don't remember anything about the ride, or about arriving at LAX and making my way through the security checkpoint and finding my gate. I felt numb and disconnected, like I was watching a long and confusing film while drunk and half asleep. Every once in a while, a panicked thought would try to emerge through the fog in my head, and my brain would shut it down, like some mental defense mechanism was trying to keep me safe from additional trauma.

I had no luggage apart from my purse; I was still wearing the jeans and sneakers I'd thrown on to pick up my check from Boots after returning home from Linus's place the previous morning, and I had grabbed one of MMP's oversized hoodies from the coat closet before going downtown with the police, thinking I might need a bit of warmth in case I ended up in a holding cell. A hoodie wouldn't offer much protection in November in Iowa.

As the sun started to rise, I began to feel a bit more like myself. I texted MMP from the terminal to tell him I was staying with a friend and would be back to pick up my car the following day. During my layover in Denver, I called Linus. It went to voicemail, so I left him a message telling him I was fine, that I was horrified about Brynna, that I was spending the day recovering from a long police interrogation but would be available to talk more tomorrow.

At the Sioux City airport, I rented the cheapest car available, an ancient hatchback with a permanent smell of french fries and a strange pull to the right that took me a while to figure out how to overcome. I turned the heater up as high as it would go so I wouldn't freeze along the way and drove straight to Aunt Connie's shop.

Unlike me, Aunt Connie didn't put on airs by calling her shop a clinic. It was located outside the city in a wide, flat area next to a golf course, wedged into a strip mall between a Christian bookstore and a Thai restaurant. Winter was fast approaching the Midwest; I didn't see any snow on the ground, even along the long, open stretches of road leading from the airport, but there were patches of frosty ice on the asphalt in the parking lot.

The door to Aunt Connie's place was unlocked, though her reception area was empty; a laminated sign on the door leading to the back room informed me that Constance Bunn was with a client at the moment and to take a seat and wait.

Aunt Connie's shop was cuter than mine, and cozier. I sank down onto an overstuffed love seat covered in teddy-bear fleece and basked in the warmth radiating from the baseboard heaters running along the wall. I leafed through the stack of lifestyle and gossip magazines on her coffee table and settled in to read.

Twenty minutes passed, and I was all caught up on the romantic complications of various dewy young celebrities I'd never heard of before, when the door to the back room opened. A sweet-faced woman with soft gray curls slipped past Aunt

Connie, who held the door for her. "Thank you so much, Connie. That was exactly what I needed to hear today," she said.

I set aside my magazine and rose to my feet; Aunt Connie caught my eye and gave me a quick smile, utterly unsurprised to see me there. "I'll be with you in a moment, Sheila," she said.

The gray-haired woman pulled a puffy blue ski jacket off of a coatrack near the door and struggled to zip herself into it. Padded pink mittens dangled from strings attached to the jacket cuffs. She smiled at me as she maneuvered the mittens onto her hands.

"Hi, hon," she said, exactly as though she'd known me all her life. "I'm sorry if we ran into your appointment time. I just started gabbing to Connie and couldn't stop." She beamed at my aunt. "I don't know what I'd do without her. I always feel a million times better after a consultation with her."

"That's what I'm hoping for," I said.

The woman departed, sending a gust of chilly air into the shop. Aunt Connie closed the door behind her, then spread her arms wide. I let myself be folded into a soft, warm hug. She smelled like wintergreen breath mints and floral shampoo. "It's good to see you," I said.

"You too, Sheila." She patted me on the back of my head and squeezed me against her. "I'm glad you could make it, sweetheart."

I pulled back. "That sounds like you were expecting me."

She smiled. "I was." Her face was a near-perfect circle, though her jawline was beginning to droop into jowls as she moved into her seventh decade. Her hair was light brown with gray tufts around the ears, cut into an unfussy shape shorter than a bob but not quite a pixie cut. She wore a fleece tunic and black polyester slacks paired with sensible black boots with thick rubber soles. She looked kind and pragmatic, like an elementary school principal, or an office manager for a family-owned business.

If I hadn't known her so well, if someone gave me a notebook and told me to list all the possible jobs I thought she could have just from looking at her, I would reach the last line on the last page before I'd come up with "professional psychic."

"Did the police contact you?" I asked, trying not to feel alarmed. That would be very bad. I'd checked my phone after my flight landed and I had no new voicemails, but if they knew I'd left town . . .

"Oh, no. Nothing like that." Aunt Connie waved the police away. "But I knew you were heading here. I know you're in some trouble right now, aren't you?"

Under the circumstances, I wasn't in much of a mood for Aunt Connie's psychic visions, but I smiled at her and tried to look relaxed. "A little bit, yeah. Something strange came up back in Los Angeles, and I wanted to talk to Mom about it. You, too."

She nodded and looked solemn, as she often did when discussing anything to do with her sister. "Have a seat. I have a fresh pot of coffee brewing in the back, and Alicia dropped off some snickerdoodles."

"No, thank you. I'm fine." I sank down into the warm fluff of the love seat. Aunt Connie perched beside me. She rested her hands on her thighs and looked at me, her expression kind but searching.

"About two weeks ago, I thought you were in danger," Aunt Connie said. "I woke up in the middle of the night absolutely certain you were in need of help. I almost called you. And then I got out of bed and made some coffee, and I realized you were fine."

Two weeks ago, I really *had* been fine, or mostly fine. That was before Detective Moreau had contacted me, before I'd ever heard of Genevieve Santos, and while I'd been racked with constant anxiety about my crumbling financial state, I hadn't been a suspect in a homicide. Two homicides. Possibly three.

Aunt Connie pursed her lips. "But I've had a nagging worry about you in the back of my mind ever since. What's this about the police?"

"I don't even know where to start. Before I get into the whole messy story, I have a question I hope you can answer. Do I have a twin sister?"

Aunt Connie's psychic abilities had failed her. Whatever she expected me to ask, that wasn't it. She blinked at me. "A twin?"

"Did mom give birth to twins in Florida? And then maybe gave one up for adoption?"

Aunt Connie was shaking her head before I finished the sentence. "Absolutely not. She never mentioned anything like that to me, and she wouldn't have kept it a secret."

"Is it possible, though? Maybe my father raised the other baby?"

"Whoever he was." There was a faint touch of acid to that, disguised under layers of cheerful midwestern friendliness. "He was out of the picture by the time you were born, sweetheart. Shelley tried tracking him down to get him to help her out with some child support. The name he gave her was a fake, so that never worked out to anything. No, Sheila, you are one of a kind."

Legally changing my name was the first thing I did upon moving to Los Angeles. "Sheila" no longer appeared anywhere except on my birth certificate and in some old high school yearbooks, but I talked to Aunt Connie so infrequently the name change hadn't stuck with her. I used to correct her, but now it was easier to let it slide. "But it's physically possible, right? You weren't with her when she gave birth, were you?"

"I didn't know she was pregnant." Aunt Connie frowned and wrinkled her nose. "She called me about two months after you were born to say she was moving back to Iowa. It'd been years since I'd heard from her. She said she'd introduce me to my niece, which was the first I knew of your existence. You two stayed with me for a couple of weeks, and then she found a place in Hayes." She looked at me. "Why are you asking all this? Did someone tell you you have a twin?"

"I do have a twin. Identical," I said. "Only she's missing now, and she might be dead, and people have been killed, and I'm mixed up in it because I look exactly like her." I'd felt pretty calm and composed going into this conversation, lulled by Aunt Connie's soothing kindness and stability, but I could hear a note of hysteria creep into my tone. I was speaking too loudly for the small, cozy room. I lowered my volume and continued.

"There's an artist in Los Angeles, Genevieve Santos, Gena, and she looks like me. The police say her DNA is a match for mine, close enough that we have to be identical twins. Her ex-husband, Serge Grumet, he was murdered a couple of weeks ago, and Gena disappeared that same night. At first the police thought I might be Gena in disguise. I don't think they do now, but they're suspicious of me. So I need to check with Mom to see if she knows who Gena might be."

Aunt Connie's expression didn't give anything away, but I had a weird sensation that something I'd said had triggered a sudden unwanted thought. When she spoke, though, it wasn't anything I expected. "She's an artist?"

"A successful one. Her work is in a gallery in Beverly Hills," I said. "And it seems like she occasionally pretended to be me, which makes this really complicated."

"She pretended to be you?" Aunt Connie's brow creased.

"Not exactly, but you remember that film I did when I first moved to Los Angeles, *The Divide*? Her ex-husband, the one who got killed, he directed that. She told everyone she'd been in the film, that she was me. And it seems like everyone, including Serge, believed her."

The cozy room was plenty warm, but it seemed like Aunt Connie shivered a little. She sat beside me, staring straight ahead at the far wall, her expression distant, like she was listening to voices I couldn't hear.

When she spoke at last, her words were filled with a cold resounding dread that I couldn't quite understand.

"Oh, Sheila," she said. "Sheila. This isn't good."

CHAPTER 20

Assisted Living

My mom had been in the nursing home for six years, just as long as I'd had my psychic business, and this was the first time I'd visited her. The home was about four miles from Aunt Connie's shop, located in the heart of what looked like an upmarket suburban neighborhood. It was nice. When Aunt Connie first told me Mom was entering an assisted living facility, I'd feared the worst. My grandmother had been in a retirement home in Cedar Rapids for the last decade of her life, and Mom had taken me there every year at Christmas until I was eleven. The corridors smelled like urine and gravy, everything was dirty white or sickly yellow, and all the residents looked defeated.

Mom's place wasn't like that at all. When I'd looked at photos on the facility's website six years ago, I'd felt a sense of relief at the sight of the château-style estate with the tidy green front lawn and the beds of spring flowers lining the walkway. Aunt Connie emailed me photos of my mom's comfortable living space. She had her own room, and it was spacious enough to include a small round dining table and a seating area with an armchair near a window with gauzy white curtains.

Thankfully, reality measured up to those photographs. The front yard was touched with frost and the flower beds had been replaced with hardy juniper shrubs, but even still, pains had been taken to keep the exterior well maintained. Inside, the front lobby smelled like clean laundry.

I checked in with the smiling receptionist, a young man wearing a crisp white smock over a button-down shirt and tie, who gave me directions to my mom's room after calling someone to confirm she was up to receiving visitors. Aunt Connie had insisted on loaning me a long, roomy wool coat before she'd let me leave the warmth of her shop, and while it probably looked a little silly with my canvas sneakers, I had been grateful for the extra protection. But the interior of the facility was pleasantly warm without being stuffy, so I shrugged out of the coat and draped it over my arm while approaching my mother's room.

Her door was open. Mom sat at a small table, sipping tea out of a mug. In front of her was a book of crosswords open to a half-completed puzzle, pen uncapped and resting in the book's spine. She looked deep in thought, as though she was mulling over a particularly tricky clue. She glanced up at me when I knocked softly on the doorframe, no recognition on her face.

She looked . . . okay. My first thought was that she'd gotten old, but hell, she *was* old. It had been years since I'd seen her, and time had not reversed itself for any of us. She was old and sick. She looked frail, and some petty and spiteful part of me thought she probably was happy about that. She'd been locked in an endless war with her weight all my childhood, probably all her life. Small and curvy, she'd obsessed over a tiny roll of fat that spilled over the front of her bikini bottom, the extra bits of creamy white flesh on her thighs, her upper arms. Franklin, the guy she'd married when I was twelve and whom I never could bring myself to think of as my stepfather, called her chubby at least as often as he called her beautiful, which was daily.

She'd told me she'd been a beauty queen in Florida, just a month or two before she became pregnant. She'd won some beachfront competition there, Miss Coconut Grove or something. I'd seen photos of her as a teenager, and she'd been lovely, a small face dominated by huge blue eyes and a tiny pink kitten mouth, her golden blond hair falling in perfect waves to her shoulders.

The blue eyes were lighter than I remembered. Her eyelashes had faded to white, or maybe it was my first time seeing her without a full face of makeup. Her hair was now a very pale brown, and it had been cut recently into a chin-length shag.

The walls of her room were unadorned. Well, that made sense; my mother thought art was puerile. Or she thought my art was puerile, at least. That was her favorite word for it, "puerile," and she used it frequently. "It barely looks like a person," she'd say while staring at one of my abstract portraits, during a prolonged phase where I worshipped Elaine de Kooning and mimicked her style as best I could. "It's just a bunch of smears. It's puerile, like those messy bits of paper you'd paint with your fingers in kindergarten." And then she'd chuckle, low and sultry, and she'd shake her head gently from side to side while sipping her gin and Squirt, scornfully entertained by the artistic pretensions of her underwhelming daughter.

I cleared my throat. I realized I was trembling. "Hi, Mom," I said.

There was still no recognition in her face, but no curiosity either; my presence wasn't confusing her. If I'd been asked to do a psychic reading of her, I would have been screwed. I detected no interest in me of any sort. She blinked once, very slowly.

When she finally spoke, I felt a flood of remembrance at that low, rich voice, which had always surprised me. She looked like she should have a baby-doll squeak, like a fifties gangster's moll, instead of sounding like the chancellor of an elite university for women. "Sheila. How was your trip?"

"It was good," I said. I tried to smile and felt confused when I couldn't make it work, and then I realized I was clenching my jaw muscles too tightly. "I'm not dressed right for this weather, though. Aunt Connie had to loan me a coat." I held up my arm with the coat draped over it.

"This time of year, it must be even colder in New York," she said.

I stepped into the room, keeping my movements slow and deliberate. I pulled out the other chair at the table. My mother stared at my hand from across the rim of her tea mug, and I froze. She didn't say anything, so I went ahead and sat, arranging the coat over the back of the chair. I folded my hands on the table like a good girl waiting politely for her teacher to call on her. "I flew in from Los Angeles," I said. "It hit ninety-six degrees there earlier this month."

She looked at me, her mouth pulled in a tight line like she was ready to argue the point with me, and then her shoulders relaxed. She nodded. "I forgot," she said. "I forgot you're in Los Angeles now."

I'd never lived in New York. My mom had frontotemporal dementia. She'd probably developed it in her late thirties, while I was still living at home; she'd been erratic, mercurial, hurtful during my teen years. It had taken me time and distance to realize her cruelty was a progressive disease, not a whimsical personality quirk. Franklin had stuck it out with her for years, though I knew from Aunt Connie the topic of divorce was raised by each party on a regular basis. In any case, I assumed Franklin was footing the bill for this place, probably with Aunt Connie's help, and it probably wasn't cheap. No one had ever asked me to chip in, not that I'd be able to contribute much.

After all this time, I expected her to have deteriorated, physically and mentally. But the blue eyes were sharp, and I felt wary. Illness ravaged her brain, making her see things that weren't there and remember things that had never happened, but that core intelligence was still intact.

Even here and now, I felt the power imbalance between us. Asking for a favor was a terrible mistake, I knew that just by looking at her. I'd be forced to surrender whatever was left of my dignity, and I'd leave with nothing but more confusion and heartache.

She examined me, her expression searching. "I'm not sure blond hair suits you."

I touched my hair. "I've grown used to it."

"The dark brown wasn't much better. And that stringy perm made you look like you were trying to be Latin."

I'd never had dark brown hair. I'd never had curls. I cleared my throat. "This is a nice place," I said, looking around the room. "It's good that you've got a lot of space."

She flattened me with a glance, cold and knowing. "Don't go fishing for compliments. A smaller place would have been fine."

I hadn't been fishing for compliments; that she was living in a nice place was no credit to anything I'd done. She'd turned my words over in her head to come up with some way to put me in my place, but her brain pathways didn't work as they should, and this was what she'd landed on, something that didn't apply to me in any way and yet, incredibly, still made me feel rebuked.

"Still, I'm glad you have all this room," I said. It sounded feeble. A corner of her mouth turned up in a tiny smile, like she was satisfied she'd scored a point against me. She picked up her pen and looked down at her crossword puzzle.

"Hey, do I have a twin sister?" I asked. I'd meant to work the conversation around to the subject gracefully, maybe by bringing up a funny story about running into someone who looked just like me. Here, though, in front of her, I knew that was the wrong approach. Better to throw her off guard, if I could, and see if anything interesting happened.

"Do you have a twin sister?" My mom looked up, her eyes cold, her tone scathing. "Did you grow up with a little girl who looked just like you? Did I buy all your clothes in duplicate, fix you twice as many school lunches, send you off on the school bus with two pats on the head? No? Then don't ask stupid questions."

"Did you give birth to twins, though?" I asked. "Maybe you

left my baby sister with my father, maybe you gave her up for adoption, maybe the hospital told you she died at birth?"

"There was no *hospital*." My mom sounded contemptuous, though I wasn't sure why that part of my line of questioning should be the bit that annoyed her. "Hospitals were for rich and respectable girls, and I was neither. There was a girl, Dolores, who worked at my hotel. She'd been a midwife in Havana. She delivered you, and I gave her thirty dollars and a hat with a pretty scarf tied around it. It was mine; she'd admired it."

My auspicious start in life. "Did you give Dolores my twin sister along with the hat?"

"Twins." The single syllable was laden with scorn. "No, Sheila, you weren't twins." The sharp eyes met mine, searching and penetrating. "Don't make up stories about your past to feel special."

"There's a woman out there with my DNA," I said. My voice quavered, and I realized I was terrified of making my mom angry by contradicting her. "And she looks exactly like me. The only explanation is that she's my identical twin, and the only person who could confirm that is you. So you're lying to me."

My mom sat up straighter. Her hand tightened around the handle of her mug. Her brow creased dangerously, and even though I was a grown-ass adult who hadn't lived under her thumb for decades, I felt a wave of panic; she'd hurled her highball glass at me in a fit of pique more than once when I was a teen. "Get out," she said, her voice rich and glowing with anger. "If you're going to call your mother a liar, I don't have any use for you."

I left the room without another word. Some fragile part of me hoped she'd call out and ask me to stay. Maybe she'd give me some small indication she was glad I'd visited.

She didn't, because of course she wasn't. Without turning around, I knew by the time I'd reached the door that she was deeply immersed in her crossword puzzle.

In the hallway, a pretty nurse in clean aqua scrubs smiled

at me with an expression of interest, probably because I was a brand-new visitor to a long-term resident. "Are you Sheila?" she asked.

I paused. She had an amazing amount of strawberry-blond hair, worn off her face in thick braids. She looked like she was barely out of her teens, but I'd reached the age where everyone under thirty blurred together into an undifferentiated pool of youth and vitality. "I used to be," I said. "But I changed my name years ago. I'm Jenny, Shelley's daughter."

This confused her, though I didn't know why. "Oh! The payments all come from . . ." She stopped whatever she was going to say and shook her head. "I just wanted to say it's nice to finally meet you. And to thank you for the painting. We keep it in our break room."

I stared at her. Her cheeks reddened into shiny round apples. "Shelley told us you'd meant for the staff to have it. That was right, wasn't it?"

Somewhere inside of my soul, a star exploded into a burst of white-hot fragments of light before collapsing into a sucking black hole that threatened to yank me inside it. I fought my way out and found myself answering. My voice sounded friendly and natural. "Of course. I'm so glad you like it. Would it be possible to see where you put it?"

"No one but staff is allowed in the break room." She pulled her pink lower lip between her small white teeth and glanced around. "But if no one else is in there right now . . ." I followed her down a corridor.

She peeked inside a room, then gestured for me to come in, closing the door behind us. The break room was cozy. The walls were lavender trimmed with cream; I saw a cluster of round lunch tables and chairs, a wheat-colored sofa against the wall, a matching armchair. A clean white bookcase was filled with trade paperbacks and a shelf of DVDs; on the countertop next to the microwave rested a single-cup coffeemaker with a basket filled with individual pods of coffee and tea beside it.

All of that flew out of my head as soon as I saw the painting, which hung high on the wall above the sofa. It consisted of multiple layers of soft color, each piled on top of the others in a way that seemed nebulous at first, and yet formed familiar shapes after I'd looked at it for a while. I could see shades of biscuit and coffee and ash punctuated with splashes of saturated green beneath a white-blue wash of sky. Standing back near the doorway, staring at it while deliberately letting my eyes grow sleepy and unfocused, I knew what she'd painted. This was Gena's view from her backyard. She could have painted this in her studio, standing at an easel and staring out a window at the hills and homes and canyons, the cluster of downtown skyscrapers rising up in the distance.

And here my mother had been indignant when I called her a liar. Some weird emotion was undoubtedly visible in my expression, because the young nurse sounded newly worried. "Is it okay there? Your mother said you didn't want it displayed in a more public area."

"It's perfect, thank you." Gena's painting. Genevieve Santos, my heretofore unknown twin sister, who apparently sometimes used my birth name, Sheila. Gena, who had sent my mom—our mom—one of her paintings with instructions to give it to the staff at her nursing home.

Well, no, that probably wasn't what happened. I knew my mom better than that; she didn't want the damn painting for herself, so she passed it off on others and let them deal with the burden of owning it.

"I think it's really nice," the young nurse said. "Some of the other nurses don't like it because you can't really tell what it is, but I love looking at it. I grew up near the Badlands, and it makes me think of my old home." She stood beside me near the door, then folded her arms over her chest and observed the painting from a distance, like we were in a museum. She nodded her head. "It's good. You could do this professionally, probably. Have you ever sold a painting?"

"It's just a hobby," I said. I smiled at her. "Thank you for showing it to me. I shouldn't take up any more of your time."

"Oh, it's no problem at all. It was nice to meet you at last. You live in New York City, right?"

"I moved to Los Angeles a while ago," I said. I wanted to contradict her about New York, but it seemed easiest to go with the flow right now. I didn't feel capable of coming up with any words of explanation; forming complete sentences was a struggle.

That my mother had lied to my face wasn't all that startling, but the scope of the secret she'd hidden from me made me dizzy. My mom hadn't simply given up a baby at birth and moved on with her life. She had reconnected with Gena at some point and had learned about her life, and now, due to my mom's decaying mental condition, she'd grown confused as to which twin was which, or whether there were two of us at all. In her fractured mind, Gena and I had merged into one being: her mediocre daughter, the artist and actress, who lived in New York and Los Angeles, who was successful enough to pay for this nice facility to keep her in relative comfort in her waning years, yet who nonetheless was a crushing disappointment.

And Gena . . . Gena must've known all of this, or at least most of it. She'd known she had a twin, and instead of making any effort to meet me, she'd simply claimed ownership of the only part of my life that could benefit her.

I couldn't even feel angry about that right now. I felt too drained and hollow, as though my mom had siphoned all energy from me, a vampire feeding on my shallow reserves of vitality. I wanted to be alone, to slip away and hide somewhere to give myself time to process what I'd learned, but the shadows outside were growing longer, and there was still one more chore I had to tackle. After bidding a distracted farewell to the young nurse, I left the facility, got in the rental car, and headed to Hayes.

CHAPTER 21

Barnburger

Franklin had never been my favorite person, much like I'd never been at the top of his list, but it wasn't as though we'd constantly fought. We just didn't have much common ground; he was the guy who had married my mom when I was still a kid. He disapproved of me and my friends; he thought art school sounded like a one-way ticket to poverty and unspecified depraved behavior; he groused about how if I wanted to go to college I'd have to pay for it myself, because he'd get better value for his hard-earned money if he scooped it into a pile and set fire to it. He wanted me to get a job in town, maybe as a bank teller or a receptionist, get married, move somewhere else with my husband, get out of his hair entirely.

But Franklin, for his flaws, was a straightforward guy, and he had no patience for other people's games or schemes. If he knew his wife was in touch with my heretofore unknown twin sister, he wouldn't withhold that knowledge from me just for the thrill of keeping secrets. If Franklin had any useful information, he'd probably tell me, provided I didn't annoy him too much in the asking.

Hayes was just over an hour outside of Sioux City. It was dark, but we were still within business hours, so I drove straight along the highway to Franklin Ford, close to the center of town. A fresh-scrubbed young man with a blond crew cut gave my rental hatchback a once-over as I parked in the lot, then tried to interest me in a new Explorer. When I asked if Franklin was around, he led me through the dealership to the back office.

I hadn't seen Franklin in twenty-five years, but unlike my mother, he looked about the same. He seemed fixed in time somewhere in his late forties, even though he must be past retirement age by now. Probably approaching seventy, if he hadn't passed it by now. Tall and balding, he wore a long-sleeved yellow polo shirt with the Ford insignia on the pocket and khaki pants belted very high across his long torso. While my mom had shriveled with age, he'd remained robust, like he ate three squares a day but kept active enough to prevent it from going straight to his gut. As I hovered in the doorway, he pushed his eyeglasses farther up his nose, stared at me for a bit, and got to his feet, the corners of his mouth turned down. For a moment, I thought he was going to order me off of his property, and then he stuck out a hand and shook mine in his firm, dry grasp.

"You see your mom already?" he asked.

"I just came from there." He gestured for me to take the client chair across from his desk. It was warm in his office, but I kept my coat on; I didn't want to stay any longer than absolutely necessary, and I had a hunch it might alarm him if it looked like I planned to hang out for a while. "She looks good."

He grunted in response. When he and my mom got hitched, I hadn't expected the pairing to last out the year; he was marrying her for her looks, and she was marrying him for his stability, and they pretty obviously couldn't stand each other. "What can I do for you, Sheila?"

"I go by Jenny now," I said. I checked his reaction to see if this caused him any confusion, but he only grunted again. "I just wanted to pop in. I don't mean to keep you from your work."

"You need any coffee? Been on a while, but at least it's hot." The coffee, four inky inches at the bottom of the pot on the ledge behind him, smelled acrid, so I shook my head at the offer.

"I'm good, thank you. My mom said some things that were kind of weird, so I wanted to check with you and see how she's doing."

"You know your mom is crazy. Crazier now than she was." Franklin shook his head. "She tells me all kinds of nutty things, and I don't pay any attention."

"You visit her a lot?"

"I call her. More often than I should. Every Sunday afternoon, like clockwork." He fixed me with a stern stare. Behind the amber lenses of his glasses, his eyes were small and swollen. "She doesn't want me visiting. I used to, maybe once or twice a month, and she'd snap at me that I was keeping her from her activities. Lord knows what she has to do at that place, but I guess it's more important than seeing me."

I cleared my throat. "Hey, this is weird, but when I was talking to her, she seemed to think I'd been to visit recently. Except she thought I had brown hair and lived in New York. Obviously she's confusing me with someone, but she seemed pretty definite. I wondered if you knew of any visitors who might fit that description." Until I had sounded out Franklin's ideas on the matter, I didn't want to tip my hand about my knowledge of Gena.

"I don't know your mom's friends. I don't care. The ones I met have been a gaggle of nitwits." He looked around his desk and picked up a file folder. He leafed through the contents without looking at them, just to give his hands something to do before setting it back down. "Can't imagine she has any friends your age, anyway."

"I guess I got a little worried that someone might have befriended her under false pretenses."

Franklin stared at me. "The hell are you talking about?"

"Probably nothing. But she seemed pretty definite I'd seen her recently. I thought it was a little spooky."

"This isn't any of that psychic doo-doo, is it? Ghosts or something?"

"That wasn't what I meant," I said. Discussing my mom with Franklin made my stomach feel tight and sore, like I'd been punched in the gut. "I might have the wrong idea. It just seemed weird that my mom was so certain she'd seen me. I felt like I had a twin or something." I gave a small laugh at that, just making a little joke, but I kept a close eye on Franklin.

He had no reaction at all to the mention of a twin. He looked bored and a little contemptuous. "Your mom's brain is made of Swiss cheese. You know that. It's littered with holes." Franklin doodled little circles in the air with an index finger. "It's getting worse. Harder and harder to talk with her. Next time you visit, she'll probably say John Travolta asked her to marry him."

"Okay. Cool. So she never said anything about me visiting her? Or sending her some artwork, or anything like that?"

"Artwork, sure. That painting you sent to her for her birthday." Franklin rolled his eyes toward the ceiling. He didn't say anything more than that, but I could guess what he thought of my art.

Gena's art. Damn it. Weird that my impulse had been to assume credit for Gena's work. Was I starting to feel proprietary about Gena's paintings because I felt I could have done them if given the right opportunities? Was this how Gena felt when she took credit for *The Divide*, like that role could have been hers, if only the circumstances were different? "Yeah, I saw it. She gave it to the nurses, and they hung it in their break room."

"Well, that makes sense. She's particular about her possessions. You should've asked me what to send her. She always needs slippers, or warm socks. That would have been a better gift."

"Sure. But I didn't send her that painting. That's the thing. Someone else did, and she thinks it was from me. I don't paint."

Franklin stared at me. "You trying to tell me you didn't ruin my basement floor with a gallon of spilled green latex?"

"That was when I was a kid. I used to paint, but I gave it up when I didn't get into art school. I haven't picked up a brush in more than twenty years."

When I said it out loud like that, the words seemed foreign and wrong. Sheila Bunn was an artist, dead set on a life as a painter. Everyone in Hayes, Iowa, had known that. Even Franklin, who had never cared much about me one way or another, knew that. A confused, anxious fragment of a thought flickered through my brain that maybe I *had* sent that painting to Mom and simply didn't remember.

I was being stupid. I hadn't slept since I'd stayed over at Linus's place, the night before last. I hadn't eaten since I'd choked down that gruesome sandwich in the interrogation room. I was exhausted and overwhelmed by recent events, and it was fair to say my mental processes were not operating at peak capacity.

Franklin's stare hardened. "Then who's that painting from?"

"I'm asking you."

We were locked in a full-fledged staring contest now. Franklin broke it off first. "That don't make no sense," he said. I didn't know much about Franklin's origins, never cared enough to ask, but whenever he got angry, which was fairly often, something rustic and homespun would creep into his grammar, undermining the worldly businessman persona he tried hard to cultivate. "Who'd be sending your mom a painting and saying it's from you?"

"That's why I'm here. Someone has been letting Mom think they're me. I wanted to see if you knew anything about it."

Franklin was quiet. Then he spoke, and he sounded calm, but I could hear the struggle beneath his words to keep from snapping. "I'm in the middle of work here. Don't really have time to chat."

He was spooked, and for a moment I wondered if he knew more than he was letting on, and then I realized he just suspected I might be crazy. Crazy in the way his wife was crazy, crazy in a way that was confusing and exhausting and unnerving to be around. "Sure, no problem." I got to my feet, relieved the visit was over. "Good seeing you."

He stood as well and walked me out of the dealership. Probably a polite gesture, but maybe he wanted to make absolutely sure I left the premises. At the door, he paused.

"Don't be like her," he said. It came out gruff. "Men don't want that in a woman. When I met your mom, I liked that about her, that she wasn't like other girls, that she didn't see things the same way. But it's just gotten damn tiresome over the years. Men want a girl who's just like all the other girls."

"I'll keep that in mind," I said.

I got back in the car. I'd wasted valuable time with this detour. Franklin had known nothing about Gena, and I wanted to get out of Hayes as soon as I could. I was beginning to feel dizzy from hunger, though, and I figured I was on the verge of becoming unfit to drive. A short hop down the road from the dealership, I pulled into the Barnburger parking lot.

I'd worked here for one summer, right after I'd graduated from high school, and while the exterior was still shaped like a red-painted barn with cheery white trim, and while the interior still featured brick-patterned linoleum floors and booths made of molded brown plastic, it had been overhauled in ways I couldn't pinpoint. Inside and out, it looked both identical and entirely different at the same time, and I had the bizarre thought that at some point it had been torn down and rebuilt with new materials to look exactly the same as it had before. I stood at the counter and placed my order for a plain hamburger and a small Coke and felt a sense of displacement.

I'd intended to ask for it to go so I could sit and eat in the parking lot, but it was a lot warmer in the restaurant than it was in the car, so I took my little red plastic tray and headed for a seat near the door, so I could wolf down my food and make a quick getaway.

"Sheila?" The name was said so tentatively that I at first assumed it was in my head. I looked up. A woman, thin and unnaturally tan, her white-blond hair winched back into a tight ponytail, hovered beside my table. She wore a silver puffy coat with a fleece-trimmed collar. She'd just walked in; her car keys were still in her hand. "Sheila Bunn?"

I stared at her, my mind completely empty. At first I assumed this had something to do with Gena's shenanigans, that Gena had gone to Hayes and made new friends while pretending to be me. Then I saw the bright blue eyes, the pale lashes and brows, the pert ski-jump nose, and I knew, with a sense of mounting horror, exactly who this was.

The last time I'd seen Aimee, she'd been screaming expletives while doing her best to beat the ever-loving snot out of me. In the warm, stuffy restaurant, I felt a deep, fundamental chill in my core.

I opened my mouth to say something, but no words came out. After a moment, I closed it again and fought down a sudden wave of nausea.

Aimee smiled. It was strained, and her eyes were worried. She looked like a frightened doe, ready to bolt if I made any sudden moves or loud noises. "I thought that was you. You haven't aged at all. How have you been?"

"I've been fine." I sounded defensive, even angry. I swallowed and took a deep breath to stabilize myself. I *wasn't* fine, clearly, but I could make it through this encounter. It'd been years. Decades, actually. Aimee and I were both different people now, grown adults; surely we'd moved past the stupid overblown drama of our teen years. Surely I could hold a civil conversation with her. "Hi, Aimee. It's . . . nice to see you."

Her shoulders sagged in clear relief. Her smile finally touched her eyes. "You too. I don't want to bother you if you're busy . . ."

I shook my head. "I was just getting something to eat on my way out of town." I considered, then made the offer. "Grab a seat. If you want."

She paused, then smiled again, deeper and more genuine. "Let me place my order first. I'm on my way to pick up my oldest from hockey practice, and he's always famished."

It took her a few minutes at the counter as she chatted with the teen manning the register, who seemed to be a friend of the family. She took long enough for me to finish my burger and strongly consider slipping out the door and driving off.

After her order was successfully underway, she sank into the seat across from me. Her smile was warm, but the set of her neck and shoulders was stiff. "It's good to see you, Sheila. I didn't know if you'd want to talk to me, after . . ." She let it dangle.

"It's been decades. The statute of limitations for high school grudges has expired. We both behaved badly." The sentiment sounded very reasonable and mature, and I was proud of myself for expressing it, but that didn't mean I meant it. Twenty-five years ago, I think I would have murdered Aimee if I'd thought I could get away with it. "Do you still live in town?"

"I moved back here. I went to Marquette for college, I don't know if you knew that?"

I shook my head. I'd known that had been her plan, but after Aimee had left me bleeding in a rain-soaked cornfield, I'd done my best to forget she existed. She continued her narrative: "Anyway, Travis stayed here. You remember Travis." This was said as a statement of fact, not a question. "We fell out of touch until I moved back to take care of my dad when he got cancer. We've been married for sixteen years."

"Congratulations," I said. It sounded a bit snotty, so I took a sip of my Coke to cover for it. The sugar and caffeine might do me some good; I could feel a crippling wave of sick exhaustion creeping in. "It sounds like everything has worked out for you."

"We're happy. Two boys, both of them at St. Matthew's.

Money's always tight, because I quit working to be home with the kids when the schools closed, and we still haven't built our savings back up, but . . ." She shrugged. "Everything considered, we're doing okay."

"That's good to hear." It sounded more sincere. "I'm glad you're doing well."

"What about you, though?" she asked. "Your name comes up at reunions. We all know you're an actress in Los Angeles, but Matt Crawford—you remember Matt, right?—swears you became a famous artist in New York."

"I'm in Los Angeles," I said. "I was in a film directed by Serge Grumet. *The Divide*."

"He's the one who was recently murdered, right? Wow." Aimee looked genuinely impressed. "I didn't realize he'd directed that. He was kind of a big deal, wasn't he? Were you close to him?"

"At the time, yeah. *The Divide* was his first film. We'd been out of touch for years, though." I cleared my throat. "Acting work dried up after that, so I've been styling hair on film sets for a while." Here in Barnburger, faced with my high school nemesis, the idea of mentioning that I'd been a failed psychic was inconceivable.

"So you're not an artist now?" She sounded curious, maybe a little confused, and I wondered about our classmate Matt and where he'd gotten his information about my purported art career. Maybe he'd seen something about Gena and assumed she was me.

"Not at all. I didn't pursue that beyond high school," I said.

"That's a shame. I remember you were always so talented. You did that mural on the back wall our senior year, remember? I thought that was really cool."

My sole high school claim to fame. I'd almost forgotten about it. The school board asked students to submit proposals for a mural to adorn an ugly concrete wall that ran along the back of the student parking lot. Mine had won. I'd painted the main downtown stretch of the town, complete with dozens of blurry, translucent figures in motion, going about their daily activities. I'd deliberately made the figures smudgy and stylized, but my fellow students were certain they could identify themselves in the tableau. It became a popular activity for a couple of weeks, looking for yourself in the mural. I'd received compliments from students and more than a few congratulations from teachers, even ones I didn't know, who were probably just pleased I didn't sneak in any awkward political statements or references to songs with inappropriate lyrics.

I'd been proud of my work, disproportionately so, and Rooney had been thrilled as well. She'd contacted the arts desk at the *Sioux City Journal*, which had sent out a reporter to photograph the mural and interview me for a short, fluffy piece in their Sunday supplement. She'd driven me into the city on a Saturday afternoon, where we'd toured the Art Center before heading to the downtown studio of an oil painter of some note, who was a distant cousin of Rooney's college roommate. A Pratt graduate who taught painting at Morningside, he'd invited us in for tea and egg salad sandwiches while he looked over the works in my portfolio, carefully examining each photo or sketch in turn before agreeing to write me a letter of recommendation. With his endorsement, I'd felt confident and almost cocky, certain I was on the right course. I chalked it up to my psychic abilities: I could see the future, and it involved an art school acceptance.

The rejection letter, received in the mail in a very thin envelope, caused a physical reaction, turning my guts and bowels to acid. I'd locked myself in the bathroom, pants around my ankles, bent over while clutching my stomach, hoping I wouldn't have to projectile vomit while I was still very much involved with the business of projectile shitting, while Franklin pounded on the door and yelled at me to stop hogging the house's sole bathroom.

"I liked that mural," I said to Aimee. "But I don't think I

felt all that passionate about art. I always wanted to live in Los Angeles."

Aimee looked at me with confused sympathy, like she knew I was lying about something painful but couldn't guess what and was too polite to press for details. "Travis and I watched *The Divide* together just last year. Your name had come up in conversation, and we were curious, and it turned out we could stream it online. It was great. The story confused me a lot, all those different universes, but you were so cool in it. You really inhabited all those versions of your character. I think you probably could have become a big star."

"I thought so too, at the time," I said. "But I guess everything worked out for the best."

"That night in the cornfield . . ." Aimee trailed off. Her eyes met mine, sincere and guilty. "Kids do dumb and cruel stuff all the time, I know that really well now as a mom, but even so, I'm shocked by what we did to you. I thought I might have killed you. You were unconscious, and your head was bleeding so much, and we just left you there. I spent the weekend hiding in my bedroom, absolutely certain I was going to be arrested for murder."

I had to suppress the urge to touch my forehead. I'd had the scar removed years ago, right around the time I'd had my breasts done, after a casting director had mentioned it during a sitcom audition. The scar had been in place, shiny and pinkish white, when I'd filmed *The Divide;* it was hidden by my hair. Serge had asked about it, of course, and I'd told him the truth, that I'd been clocked in the head with an empty bottle of Zima by a classmate who was irate that I'd fucked her boyfriend. Serge found that hilarious.

Serge's reaction had anesthetized me against the pain of the memory, at least temporarily. With his encouragement, I'd transformed my shameful, humiliating violation into a cheeky anecdote, a story he'd encourage me to recount in public while he basked in the amused/horrified reactions of my audience.

He'd done his best to persuade me that my trauma was slight and silly, that I'd been foolish to feel so emotionally destroyed that I'd strongly considered fleeing town immediately, getting on a bus with only the clothes on my back and the cash in my pocket, leaving Hayes and never returning.

I'd left Hayes, of course, but it had been several months later. And here I was, back again, facing down my teen archenemy, who seemed like a nice, mildly exhausted middle-aged mom who still carried around a lot of guilt about her actions.

I smiled at her. It probably looked insincere, but it was the best I could manage. "I survived," I said. "I did something terrible to you first. We all behaved like little assholes back then. It's all good."

"Really?" Aimee exhaled. "You're not just saying that?"

"Aimee, it's been twenty-five years." I felt the gooey elastic stretch of time, like Aimee and I were caught in a wet, sticky web that extended back through the years, anchoring us to our shared past, and I felt sick and spent. I was a possible murder suspect. I'd fled Los Angeles one step ahead of the cops—okay, that last part was too dramatic; I had no reason to think a frenetic manhunt was going on during my absence. But I hadn't done well for myself in life. I had none of the benchmarks of success, no career, no stable relationship, no kids, no extensive network of friends, no nest egg. No home. No accomplishments, save one, and the world now thought that belonged to someone else.

Talking to Aimee, it felt like I could rewind time, go back to that cornfield, where I woke up bloody and in pain and soaked to the bone from the pouring rain, spooked by the flashes of lightning that came closer and closer and the continuous rolling roar of thunder. I could run down the road, where the bus stop was located.

The stop was marked with only a small sign atop a tall post. A bus arrived once a day, every evening, en route from Sioux

City, heading east to Chicago. I'd never taken that bus, but I knew the schedule. I knew which bus I'd need to transfer to when I reached Chicago to get to New York. I'd copied down the information from schedules kept at the reference desk at the public library. I'd had it planned.

Running through the cornfield to the road, seeing the big headlights coming down the road in the darkness, vision blurry with rain, knowing it had to be the bus, my only way out of this place. I had some money on me, enough cash to buy a ticket from the driver. I was soaked and bloody and distraught, but the driver had seen worse, and when I got on board, he didn't even blink at my appearance.

Wait. Where was that memory coming from? None of that had happened. I'd stayed in the cornfield for a long time, sitting on the wet earth, knees drawn to my chin, arms wrapped around my legs, shuddering convulsively from the shock of the attack. I eventually pulled myself together enough to limp my way home, my head exploding with fiery pain, like hot knives had been pulled from a glowing forge and stabbed through my skull. I'd crawled in through the cellar window and snuck upstairs with my sneakers in my hand to avoid waking my mom and Franklin, and then I'd sat in the bathtub and cried as quietly as I could while taking inventory of my injuries.

But maybe I'd also been on that bus, leaning my head against the window, shivering and in pain but filled with overwhelming relief that I was on my way to New York at last, that I was leaving Hayes behind for good.

Not me. That hadn't been me. *Her.* Here in Barnburger, with Aimee sitting across from me, for the first time in twenty-five years, I remembered the other girl.

A product of my concussed brain, maybe an out-of-body experience, similar to the one I thought I might be slipping into right now, as Aimee's flow of chatter about her life grew more and more distant and distorted, like I was underwater and she was speaking to me from the surface. I couldn't focus on what she was saying, because my thoughts were consumed with the other girl.

It had been the other girl who'd run for the bus, the one who'd stared at me for a long, long moment, her eyes wide, blood streaking down her face and trickling alongside her nose. She'd stared at me, and I'd stared at her, and then she'd turned and bolted toward the road.

Aimee was still talking, and at some point she must have gone up to the counter to pick up her order, an enormous white paper bag of food, surely enough to feed an entire team of adolescent hockey players, but I didn't remember any of that. I had zoned out, unable to hear anything over the sudden roar of blood in my ears. I could hear my heartbeat thumping, pushing the blood around with more force than it should, and suddenly, in the middle of Barnburger, I could smell the clean metallic scent of ozone.

"Sheila?" Aimee leaned forward and frowned, one thin hand clutching the bag. Her short nails were done in a French manicure, not recent, the tips chipping. I smiled at her and felt the roar of the blood subside to a low murmur.

"Sorry. Lost in memories of the past, I guess." I folded my hamburger wrapper into a precise square, aware my hands were trembling. I focused on this small task, making it as compact and as neat a square as I could, like I was getting ready to create an origami masterpiece, because if I tried to pick up my half-full soda now, I would drop it and spill it all over the clean plastic table. Or I would throw it in Aimee's face, or I would scream or cry or vomit or have a heart attack, right here in this bright, clean fast-food joint. I didn't know what I'd do, really. No course of action seemed any more or less likely than any other, because I didn't know who I was anymore, and I had no idea what this strange person inhabiting my body would think was the right thing to do under the circumstances.

"Yeah, I hear you." Aimee smiled, but it was tight, and purple shadows appeared under her eyes. She thought my sudden spaciness was about her, that I was still holding grudges from the past, and I couldn't reassure her that it went far deeper and weirder than that.

"It's been great running into you. I'm glad you saw me." I sounded cheerful. Good. I got to my feet. My hand didn't shake at all when I picked up the cup; I turned around and trashed it in the bin without feeling even the slightest temptation to throw it at Aimee.

I almost said "Give my love to Travis" without thinking, because in Los Angeles I was always giving my love to everyone, but under the circumstances that would be bizarre, so I left it at that.

Aimee stood as well, and for a moment I thought she was going to hug me. Must've been a habit she'd picked up at Marquette; Hayes was not a hugging kind of town. She reconsidered at the last moment and just wrapped her arms around her enormous sack of burgers and smiled at me. "I'm so happy you're doing well," she said.

We walked out together. Aimee had an SUV, a big beige Ford, probably bought from Franklin's dealership; I looked into the back seat and saw a battered pair of ice skates and a padded goalie's chest protector. Seemed like an okay life, probably; Aimee and Travis almost certainly owned a home, and even though money was a little tighter than they'd like, they were probably happy enough, living here in their hometown, taking their kids to school and hockey practice, planning for the holidays, maybe Thanksgiving at Grandma's house, maybe skiing at Mount Crescent after Christmas.

Did I want that for myself? Owning a home sounded pretty good right now, but other than that, no; this was why I'd left Hayes behind to set off for New York.

Los Angeles. I'd set off for Los Angeles. That hadn't been me running through the cornfield in the pouring rain, desperate to catch that bus. That had been the other girl, the girl who'd appeared in the field when I'd come to my senses after the attack, my head pounding, blood from the gash on my forehead blurring my vision. A girl who looked exactly like me.

Who was dressed like me who'd worn the same sleeveless white shirt now soaked in the rain so you could see the same pink pushup bra from Sears underneath it the same cutoff jean shorts and white sneakers the same three-dollar Keds knockoffs that I fished out of a wire bin at the discount store . . .

Aimee parted from me with a cheerful wave goodbye. I had to wait until she had pulled out of the lot before I could get my rental car started. My hands were too thick and clumsy on the controls, my sweaty palms slipping around on the steering wheel when I tried to grip it. I drove slowly, timidly, like a driver's ed student hitting the road for the first time, annoying a car full of teens who had to wait for me to exit before they could turn into Barnburger's drive-through lane. I flinched at the angry blast of their horn, my heartbeat jackhammering in a frenetic rhythm. It seemed like years before I managed to leave the parking lot and started driving down the road, heading in the direction of the cornfield.

CHAPTER 22

In the Cornfield

The cornfield was about four miles outside the town limits, but Hayes was tiny, so it only took me a few minutes to get there. The bus stop no longer existed. Was Hayes no longer accessible by bus, or was there a bigger, better stop somewhere down the road? I'd always thought Hayes would expand with time; the hospital, huge and well equipped, had opened a couple of years before I moved, and the assumption had been that it would bring hundreds of jobs to town, even thousands if it had time to flourish. But maybe Hayes was withering instead, the older generations dying off, their children moving to bigger places. I'd assumed Aimee's trajectory—see a bit of the world, then return home to raise a family—was the default, but perhaps Hayes had been filled with young Sheilas, all of us chomping at the bit to leave and never come back.

But here I was, back and more confused and miserable than I'd ever been.

This time of year, the cornfield was dormant, the stalks dead and dry, the ground white with frost. I parked on the shoulder and got out of the rental car. The frozen night air stung my face, little prickles of cold fire across my nose and cheeks. Nothing looked familiar. I tried to orient myself, closing my eyes and sliding back through the years to that muggy summer evening.

We'd all crammed into Aimee's tiny white Suzuki Samurai, the four of us, me and Aimee and Tessa, who'd been my lab partner in bio and had always seemed quiet but sweet, and Jeanne, who held the district record for the fifty-yard dash and who'd won a full-ride track scholarship to Kansas State. I didn't know any of these girls well—Aimee and I were friendly but not precisely friends—and after tonight, I knew I might never see any of them again. This cornfield excursion could be my farewell to Hayes. That thought gave me a feeling of impossible lightness that started in my guts and spread out to my entire body. I was happy, almost giddy. I laughed a lot that evening, at least at the start of it.

We parked on the side of the road before entering the field. The cornstalks, tall and healthy under the August sky, swallowed us up. A six-pack of Zima dangled from each of Aimee's hands: her brother Mark, home for the summer from Iowa State, had hooked up his kid sister with illicit libations for our impromptu end-of-summer celebration. Tessa and Jeanne had made an emergency stop at the Hy-Vee for assorted snacks; my contribution was a bag of Franklin's Doritos that I'd swiped from the pantry and would have to make sure to replace before he noticed its absence.

I hadn't quite made my peace with the Pratt rejection, and I never really would, but I'd had most of the summer for that initial tidal wave of devastation to recede. Now, I felt a growing optimism about my future, which rolled out in front of me, unwritten but filled with promise. I'd saved up some cash at my Barnburger job, and it wasn't much, but it could get me to New York on the bus. I could find an apartment, probably something tiny and glamorously horrible, which I'd undoubtedly share with multiple roommates, and I could get a job answering phones at an art gallery or something while practicing my craft.

I didn't need the validation of art school to become a painter, I just needed to paint. It was a shaky, risky, half-assed plan, and I hadn't yet committed to it, but it was always in the forefront of my mind, growing more real to me with each passing day. As we moved deeper into the field, I felt carefree and reckless, and maybe a tad smug at the prospect of leaving all this behind.

Goddamn, I'd been young then. Now, standing on the side of the road on a frozen Iowa evening, I felt the weight of those unsatisfactory intervening years pressing on my shoulders, pushing me down into the frozen earth.

The field was separated from the road by a low fence, nothing more than wire stretched between stakes in the ground, low enough to step over. It didn't serve any practical purpose apart from marking the territory, letting people know they were trespassing.

I trespassed anyway, like I had all those years ago. The ground was hard, the chill bleeding through the rubber soles of my cheap canvas sneakers. My breath formed an opaque white cloud with every exhale. If I inhaled too deeply, the cold air tickled my lungs and bronchial tubes, leaving me perpetually on the brink of a coughing fit. I walked through the rows of dead stalks until I figured I must be right at the spot where we'd held our informal cornfield party.

It had been a setup, of course. Aimee knew what had happened the previous weekend at the barbecue Marlene had thrown in the yard of her split-level ranch home while her parents and younger siblings were at their lake cabin.

For the record: I hadn't gone to the barbecue with any intention of trying to seduce Travis. Travis had been the power forward on the varsity basketball team, but he'd also been in Rooney's art class with me for a single semester, where he churned out desultory line drawings of empty courts and vacant bleachers while Rooney urged him to dig a little deeper inside himself. Travis and I had gone to homecoming together the previous fall, our first and only date, and we'd had a fine old time at first, ditching the dance floor in favor of hanging out in the student parking lot, right in front of my hand-painted mural. I'd nursed a fierce crush on sunny, uncomplicated Travis since sophomore year, so I was perfectly happy to engage in some light groping in his Trans Am until Mrs. Scott, the chemistry teacher, had knocked on the window and told us to cut it out, that we'd either have to go inside and dance, or drive off and find some other place to neck.

We'd gone inside, and at some point that night I'd found Aimee in the girls' room, vomiting up a shocking amount of Hawaiian Punch and vodka while sobbing about how Nate Deacon had left in a huff because she'd been too drunk to stand upright. I'd calmed her down and cleaned her up, and Travis had offered to drive her home in his two-seater while I stayed at the dance chatting with friends, and the next day Travis had called me to confess that he liked me as a friend, but hadn't felt any sparks. He'd saved all his sparks for Aimee; by the time the winter formal rolled around, they were inseparable.

It stung, sure, but Marlene's barbecue wasn't about vengeance against Aimee for unwittingly stealing my crush. It was just about being a dumb, drunk, horny teenager.

That barbecue. Damn it all. At some point late in the evening, Travis had been manning the keg when I'd gone for yet another refill. He looked good, floppy hair falling in his eyes, and he threw me a sweet, wobbly smile as he filled my Solo cup with Miller High Life, more foam than beer, maybe my fifth or eighth or twelfth beer of the night. "Good to see you're still here, Sheila," he said. "Everyone in our whole damn class is leaving, and I feel like I'm the only one staying behind. Hayes is going to get awfully lonely pretty soon."

I took a sip, and if Travis saw that I accidentally splashed half of it down the front of my blouse, he was too polite to point it out. Probably he was too drunk to notice. I glanced about the backyard while discreetly wiping off my chin. "Is Aimee around?" I asked.

A moody crease appeared between his brows. "Milwaukee."

"She's already gone?"

He shook his head, the ends of his mouth pulling down. "Her mom is helping her find an apartment near campus. Two weeks. We have two weeks before her semester starts."

There was something uncharacteristically morose about his tone. "You two are going to stay together, aren't you? Even though she'll be at . . ." I trailed off, my beer-addled brain unable to come up with "Marquette." "Even though she'll be in Milwaukee?"

He exhaled deeply and looked at me with big, wobbly, soulful eyes. "I don't see how we can. Long-distance relationships never work. Right? They *never* work." He pitched his voice low, almost a mutter, and I had to lean in close to make out his words. "I said I'd come live with her, find a job in Milwaukee, but she said no, she has to do this on her own. She's going to forget all about me. All those college boys. By Christmas break, she won't remember I exist."

Nothing in his words should have led me to assume they'd already broken up, but the beer had messed with my thought processes, so that was precisely my interpretation. I made some noise of sympathy while mentally making a set of assumptions that would prove to be only halfway accurate: Travis was in need of some comforting, and Travis was now unattached.

Travis managed a brave smile. "Hey, what about you? You're leaving for New York soon, right? Going to that place, that school. That art school?" That piece on the mural in the *Sioux City Journal* had mentioned my Pratt ambitions, and all my classmates believed that was my future. I hadn't corrected their assumptions. Somewhere deep inside, I harbored a belief that the rejection had been a mistake, one that would be soon fixed. Someone in the admissions office would take another look at my portfolio and realize their grievous error, and I'd receive a phone call any day now reversing their decision.

Here, though, drunk off my ass and faced with Travis's

mournfulness about his cratering relationship with Aimee, I embraced honesty. "I didn't get in."

His face crumpled in distress. "Oh, fuck. Fuck. Sheila, I'm sorry."

I shook my head. "It's okay. It's fine! No big deal. I'll go to New York anyway. I mean, if I can." I tried to smile, but the alcohol suddenly decided to swing my mood from optimistic to devastated, and I burst into tears.

"Fuck," Travis said again, instilling the syllable with all the despair and pathos of the universe. "Sheila, that's ridiculous. I'm so sorry. You're the greatest artist I've ever known." It was a kind sentiment, and he clearly meant it with his entire drunken heart, so I didn't bother pointing out that his firsthand experience with artists was probably limited to our smattering of peers in Rooney's art class. I wanted to thank him, but I was crying too hard to get the words out. I tried to wipe my nose, but my hand-eye coordination had taken a hit, and I ended up splashing more beer on myself, which only led me to sob harder.

Travis stepped away from the keg and put a protective arm around my shoulders. "Come on. It's going to be okay. Come on."

When I couldn't stop crying, he gave me a gentle shake. "Hey. Come on. Let's go somewhere and talk about it, okay?"

We ended up in Marlene's younger brother's bedroom, where we sat on a bedspread patterned with *Scooby-Doo* characters, and Travis patted me on the back while I sobbed, and then he wrapped his arms around me and rocked me back and forth, and at some point I kissed him, because I was drunk and it was nice being held by someone who smelled good and had well-defined arm muscles, and I remember him saying, "We really shouldn't do this," but then he kissed me back anyway, his tongue entering my mouth, and he was good at kissing, an absolute A-plus kisser, I'd remembered that from the night in his Trans Am, and then his hand slid up my thigh, under my denim skirt, under the hem of my bikini underwear, and I found myself on my back, lying amongst a field of Scooby-Doos, and my hands were in his shorts, and I felt warm and loved and *super* horny, and I figured this was okay because Travis and Aimee had broken up, or had practically broken up, and anyway, it's not as though anybody would ever find out about this, right?

Right?

We rejoined the party shortly after the grand finale of our brief, messy, sticky tussle, both of us far from sober yet much less euphoric, as it started to dawn on us that we'd acted like a pair of tacky and monstrously self-absorbed idiots. Travis had gone beet red and was unwilling to look me in the eye, while I felt that special brand of sharp-pronged mortification that springs from realizing you've done a bunch of dumb shit while plastered. I was ferociously worried it'd been obvious what we'd been up to, but it was fine; no one looked at us suspiciously or even asked where we'd been. The next day, as I nursed a gargantuan headache and fought the urge to puke during my long shift manning the grease pits at Barnburger, I felt profoundly guilty and foolish, but relieved. We'd gotten away with it.

And of course I was too dumb to realize that just because no one had confronted us in the moment, it didn't mean our actions had gone unnoticed.

Word got back to Aimee, as of course it would, but her reaction took me unaware. When she dropped by Barnburger the following week and, in the middle of ordering cheese-topped tater tots, suggested I join her for a casual Friday night out with her best friends to celebrate her last weekend in town—not a formal invitation, just an idea that had occurred to her right that second, because she hadn't even known I was working there and certainly hadn't stopped by just to see me—I didn't suspect she meant me ill.

Standing in the cornfield on a cold November day, winter drawing closer like a horde of visiting relatives the week before a big family wedding, I closed my eyes and returned to that evening.

Ozone. That smell of ozone. The rain started, the lightning

split the sky. The four of us shrieked and jumped at the first boom of thunder. I bent down to gather up our detritus, the Doritos bag, the spilled cookies, the wadded-up paper towels we were using as napkins, and Aimee whacked me across the temple with an empty Zima bottle.

My entire skull felt like it exploded, and in that moment, I thought maybe I'd been shot in the head, or that a meteor had fallen from the sky and smashed my brain into glittery pieces of broken glass. Everything went a blinding white, unearthly, the color of heaven or the color of nothingness; I assumed I was dead. Aimee kicked me, the toe of her Reebok-clad foot hitting me in my unprotected stomach, over and over and over, and she shrieked words at me, but I was too confused to make out what she was saying, and by now the nonstop thunder and pouring rain were drowning out all sound, like a bombastic rock opera played at full volume, but it didn't *really* matter, because it wasn't like I didn't know why she was so monumentally pissed at me.

You slut. I remember hearing that, shouted directly in my ear, probably by Aimee, maybe by one of her cronies. Or maybe that was my conscience, verbalizing the sentiments I felt in my soul. *You sneak. You traitor.*

My brains were oozing out of the side of my head, or I assumed they were, because there was no way my skull could hurt that much while its contents still remained intact. I squeezed my eyes shut as tightly as I could and listened to the booms of the thunder, felt the ground shaking beneath me, waiting for the moment when everything would fade away.

And indeed, at some point, everything faded away.

When I opened my eyes at last, I was alone, and I was curled into a ball in a muddy puddle, broken glass and soggy Doritos pressed beneath my cheek. My head felt like an overinflated balloon, ready to burst at any moment. I struggled to sit up.

I saw a flash of headlights, big ones, blurred into blobby orbs by the pouring rain, heading down the road, and I knew it could only be the bus. If I ran now, I could catch it. I could leave town forever, start over in New York, leave all this misery behind me. It was a huge risk, an irreversible decision, but it might be worth everything. I poised in a crouch, legs twitching, indecisive.

The cornfield went blue white at the same instant the loud, hollow bang echoed through me, starting in my ears and rattling through my rib cage and spine, bringing with it a ripple of fiery agony that caused every muscle in my body to seize up violently. I thought I could see the skeleton beneath my flesh, my bones lighting up like an X-ray; I thought I could smell burning metal. In that first wave of uncomprehending panic, I assumed a nuclear bomb had been dropped on the cornfield. As my muscles unlocked and I realized I hadn't been obliterated into a smear of grease, I amended my conclusion: I'd been struck by lightning.

Or . . . maybe the lightning had struck the other girl, the one with the dishwater blond hair that turned brown in the downpour, plastered with rain to the sides of her face. Her forehead was bleeding, and her white tank top was soaked, her pink bra showing through.

She had my face, and she was me, but she wasn't, because I was here as well.

We stared at each other, crouched a few inches apart, so close we could touch our foreheads together if we leaned forward just the tiniest amount.

We were frozen in place, our poses identical, and then she stood, turned, and fled.

She was heading to the road, to the bus stop, racing to make it there before the bus arrived. She was going to New York, and I was going to remain behind in Hayes. I was going to continue working at Barnburger, keeping my head down, avoiding all the classmates who remained in town, avoiding Travis most of all. On a lark, I was going to apply for a part-time position as a junior reporter at one of the local stations in Sioux City, and I'd feel astonished when they asked me in for an interview, which would turn into an on-camera audition, which would turn into a provisional job offer. I'd sleep on Aunt Connie's couch for eight weeks, bonding with her and basking in her unconditional kindness and support while giving the job my best effort. I'd try to learn from the seasoned reporters who wanted nothing much to do with the dumb teen from Hayes who'd been hired to cover local interest stories designed to appeal to the youth of Sioux City: a free concert series, the grand opening of a water park, new shops at the mall. I'd make mistakes, lots of them, but at least I looked good on camera.

It wouldn't be enough: at the conclusion of my trial period, no full-time job offer would be forthcoming. I wouldn't feel much like going home and living with Mom and Franklin, so I'd kiss Aunt Connie goodbye, clear out my savings account, and catch the bus. Not to New York, but to Los Angeles. The starving-artist dream was dead, but the starving-actor one was sparkling and new.

By the time I reached Los Angeles, Sheila Bunn had vanished, replaced by aspiring starlet Jenny St. John. On the other side of the country, Genevieve Santos blossomed into existence, scraping to get by in New York while living the bohemian life of an artist. The art was crucial to this, somehow; maybe her paintings had enabled Gena to reconcile the two halves of herself, to accept everything that happened here in the cornfield, to accept that Jenny/Gena were both different and the same. When she'd seen me on the movie screen after she'd stumbled into that art house screening with Antoinette, she must have understood who I was, and understood that my performance in *The Divide* was, on a subconscious level, telling the story of our creation. When she'd taken credit for my role, she hadn't viewed it as a theft.

I'd buried my memories of the cornfield, only to have them forcibly unearthed when my life intersected with Gena's. Here, now, in the present, my feet numb with cold, I wished with all my soul that I'd been able to keep them hidden.

In the freezing night air, the cornfield looked tired and gray.

I *felt* tired and gray. I thought about staying right here, lying down in the field, curling up on my side, falling asleep and never waking, letting the cold take me.

I walked back to the rental car. I sat behind the wheel for a long, long time, until a nice young couple in a pickup truck pulled up alongside me and asked if I needed help. I couldn't speak, but I managed to shake my head, and eventually they drove away. I finally got the car in gear and headed toward Sioux City. I couldn't stand the way unwanted thoughts kept jostling their way to the forefront of my mind, so I fiddled with the radio, turning the volume up and blasting an oldies station. I tried my best to sing along with the songs of my youth, hoping this would distract my brain, at least for a bit. It didn't work, though, and after a few miles I had to switch off the radio and drive in silence, leaving myself alone with my dark, strange thoughts about whatever might or might not have happened in that cornfield all those years ago.

CHAPTER 23

The Dead Sea Dazzler

Aunt Connie could tell I didn't want to talk when I arrived at her home. Instead of pushing, she simply microwaved a bowl of homemade beef-and-barley stew, even though I told her I'd already eaten at Barnburger, and sat beside me on the sofa while I ate it. She silently reached over to give me a pat on the knee.

She had to be consumed with curiosity about why my visit with her sister had sent me into a near-catatonic state, but she asked no questions, speaking up only to tell me she'd put fresh sheets on her bed. That would leave the sofa for herself, and I noticed she walked with an awkward hitch to her step, like she might have a problematic back, so I insisted she keep her bedroom.

"It'll be easier for me to leave without waking you if I sleep out here," I told her. The soup tasted of nothing, no flavor at all, like my taste buds were locked into the same state of shock as the rest of my body, but by the time I finished the bowl, I felt steadier, more stable. "My flight's at seven."

"You could always stay longer, you know. As long as you wanted." She looked very serious, and I had no doubt she meant every word. "I'd love the company, Sheila. I'm not sure how many good jobs are available right now, but you could help out in my shop. In the holiday season, I always end up with more people wanting appointments than I can handle on my own."

While I mentally recoiled at the idea of going back to bluffing my way through psychic readings, the kindness behind the offer made my eyes fill with tears. I couldn't reply. Still holding on to my empty bowl, I leaned against her, pressing my shoulder against hers. She pulled me into a hug, soft and warm and filled with uncomplicated affection.

I caught my flight to Denver the next morning, then killed time waiting for my connecting flight to Los Angeles. At some point, as I sat on the floor in the crowded terminal—a cute guy with dreadlocks offered me his seat, but I had the glum suspicion it was because he thought I looked like somebody's mother, not because he thought I was hot—I grew paranoid that the LAPD or the LASD or possibly both had issued a warrant for my arrest and I'd be grabbed as soon as I stepped off the plane at LAX.

I checked my phone and saw I had no ominous messages from the authorities, which soothed me a bit. Linus had texted; Boots had called, but hadn't left a voicemail. Even though my savings account was down to fumes and it was early in the day, I downed three glasses of wine at the airport bar before boarding. I felt better after that, more stable, happy to put some distance between myself and Iowa.

A small part of me, though, wished I'd stayed behind. I could have spilled out the whole messy, weird story to Aunt Connie. She would have listened to me, and she would have believed me. If there was any validity to her psychic gifts, any at all, maybe she could have used them to help me sort through whatever had happened during the lightning storm. And even if her abilities were as fraudulent as my own, she still understood me and loved me, and she'd do her best to fix everything that was wrong with me.

Assuming, of course, that I could be fixed.

At some point during the flight, I drifted off, only to find myself in the cornfield with Gena sitting cross-legged in front of me as rain poured down on us. Her dark curls were plastered to either side of her face, and she was telling me that her art career was fine, the multimillion-dollar Elliott Thwaite collaboration was very nice, but what she really wanted to do was act, and could I refer her to my agent?

There could be a rational explanation for the cornfield, of course. I'd almost certainly been concussed by the Zima bottle in that field all those years ago, and perhaps that plus the lightning strike had scrambled my brain enough to make me hallucinate another version of myself who was following a path I would never take. That theory made sense, sort of, though it didn't explain the DNA test results. Maybe I'd subconsciously known all along that I had a twin out there somewhere; maybe my mom had dropped enigmatic hints to that effect at some point during my childhood. Maybe I'd forgotten or ignored that bit of knowledge, chalking it up to one of her unstable flights of fancy, only to later summon it up in the cornfield.

Maybe MMP had been correct, back on that night when we were sitting on Gena's patio. Maybe his makgeolli-fueled babbling about parallel universes had been right on the money. Maybe at the moment of the lightning strike, when the bus was heading down the road and a life-changing decision needed to be made, two Sheila Bunns had branched off from the original, meant to exist in separate worlds but somehow stuck in the same one.

Maybe it's not a great idea to drink three glasses of wine on an empty stomach while emotionally exhausted and under a surreal amount of personal stress.

Whoever she was, Gena had known about me, but had made no effort to meet me. She'd eventually moved to Los Angeles, but only after my career was long dead; she must've figured the risk of encountering me was low, as our social circles didn't overlap. Was she curious about my life? Did she keep tabs on me? I felt certain she did; she wouldn't have been able to resist, because *I* wouldn't have been able to resist. Maybe she'd sometimes drive by my clinic and wonder how I was doing. Maybe she'd feel a sense of pity, maybe mixed with a little guilt, over my marginal existence. Sitting in my cramped economy seat, unable to find a comfortable position, exhausted and sore and overwhelmed by recent events, I tried to feel angry with Gena. Instead, I felt almost unbearably lonely. As impossible as it would have been to explain, I wished she'd revealed herself to me.

I made it back to Los Angeles in the afternoon. I'd been gone for just over thirty hours. Barely counted as leaving town at all. I texted MMP from the airport to ask if it was an okay time to drop by and pick up my car and my stuff. I still had a key, but under the circumstances, I couldn't presume I was still welcome to enter the house whenever I chose. A reply came back within seconds: Im home. U OK?

It occurred to me that reaching Gena's home from LAX would be problematic. I could try a rideshare service, but at this point I doubted I had enough in my bank account to cover it; I could get downtown on a bus, but from there I didn't have any idea how to get to Silver Lake, how to navigate those twisty roads around the reservoir on either public transit or on foot. I sat on a hard plastic chair in baggage claim and mulled over my options.

I'd just made up my mind to call Linus—if he wasn't available to pick me up, he'd probably be game for sending me the cash for a ride—when my phone buzzed. It was Boots. She started speaking as soon as I picked up. "MMP told me about Brynna. Holy shit. Are you okay?"

"Yeah. I think so." I wasn't okay. I was *so* not okay. "The police questioned me almost all night, and they're really suspicious about who I am and what I was doing at Gena's house, but I swear to you, I had nothing to do with it." My voice sounded a little high and thin, like I wasn't getting enough oxygen in my lungs.

"Calm down, Jenny." Boots sounded brusque yet compassionate, like she didn't have time for me to go to pieces on her right now but understood why I might be feeling a little shattered. "MMP said he didn't know where you were. Are you safe?"

"Sort of? I guess?" I could feel my throat tighten. "I'm at the airport right now. I don't have any business asking you for a favor, but I've had a bad couple of days, and I'm trying to get to Gena's house so I can pick up my car, and I don't have any money . . ." I let it trail off.

There was a long pause. "LAX or Burbank?"

"LAX."

"I'll be there in half an hour. I'll text when I'm close. See you soon." She disconnected the call before I had finished thanking her. That was probably for the best; I was only a few seconds away from bursting into messy, embarrassing tears at the idea of Boots coming to my rescue.

It was closer to an hour before I spotted her SUV navigating through the endlessly circling traffic on the arrivals level, but I was so pathetically grateful for her help that I would have been willing to wait all night if necessary. As she pulled in to the curb, I grabbed my shoulder bag and climbed into the passenger seat.

She glanced over at me. "No luggage, so I guess you weren't trying to skip town. What's going on?"

"It's a long story. Thanks so much for picking me up, I really appreciate it. I know it's a hassle, but I didn't know what else to do."

Boots raised a hand from the steering wheel and flapped it in my direction to halt the flood of grateful babble. "Lucky for you I've been moonlighting as an Uber driver." She grinned. "Nah, it's all good. I wanted to talk to you anyway. I've been feeling lousy about putting you on blast for asking me about the documentary. I brought you into this and asked you to find out what you could, and then I bit your head off when you did exactly that."

"I messed up, though. I offended you, and I didn't mean to." I cleared my throat. "I never really thought you were involved in Serge's death. Not seriously, at least. If you were, you wouldn't have hired me to find out what happened to Gena, and you wouldn't have mistaken me for Gena at Antoinette's gallery. But the documentary footage shook me up, and I had to look into it."

She was silent as she guided her vehicle onto La Cienega and began the trek north into the city. "I'm sorry I said you were a fraud," she said at last.

"I am a fraud, though," I said. I stared out the window at the passing scenery, sun-drenched and dazzling, tall spindly palm trees swaying in a light breeze, a million light-years away from the frozen cornfields of Iowa. "I'm not psychic. I don't even believe they exist. I tell lies for money. If that's not fraud, I don't know what is."

I allowed myself a small glance over at Boots. She looked composed. She nodded, mulling this over, still staring at the road. After a long while, she spoke. "You know my company, Eternality?"

"Sure."

"We have this new skin-care product. We introduced it early this fall, and it's already one of our top sellers. The Dead Sea Dazzler." She smiled. "It's made with synthetic allabogdanite. You know what that is?"

"Some kind of mineral, I'm guessing." I couldn't tell where Boots was going with this. My skin in the airport bathroom had looked gray and dull from stress, and I could probably benefit from any product called a Dazzler, but surely Boots knew I didn't fall in the right tax bracket to buy anything sold by Eternality.

"Yep. It's a mineral. Super rare. The real stuff is, at least. It's a form of phosphorus found only in space; meteorites sometimes carry it to earth. We synthesized it in a lab and combined it with salts from the Dead Sea to form a nice, smooth, perfectly round rock. It's a pretty pink color; it's scented with rose water and coriander. Get the rock wet and rub it over your skin twice a day, and clinical tests conducted by scientists on the Eternality payroll have shown that it reduces wrinkles and fine lines by twenty percent over ninety days. It retails on our website for two hundred and eighty dollars."

She smiled. "I use it myself. And my skin looks pretty good, right?"

"You have amazing skin," I said.

"Yep. I do. Thank you," she said, nodding. "And who knows, maybe it's the three-hundred-dollar rock, or maybe it's all the injectables and peels and serums and everything else that goes on or into my face to make it look like this. You know? And I tell myself it's no big deal, that the kind of woman who can spend three hundred bucks on a salty rock probably suspects it's not a miracle cure. Maybe it makes her feel fancy and special whenever she uses it, and maybe that's enough."

I thought about this. "Is your point that I shouldn't feel bad about scamming my clients?"

"No, my point is that we're both terrible people." Boots cracked herself up at this. "I mean, we're actors, right? We're all a bunch of con artists at heart."

I laughed along with her, even though it wasn't all that funny, just because it was nice to have a moment of feeling silly and carefree. "I guess you're right."

"I don't love that you lied to me, or that you've been lying to everyone. You know that's not great. But on the other hand . . ." Boots shrugged. "My accountant tells me I gave twelve thousand of my hard-earned dollars to Della DeLaurenti last year for her psychic readings. He seems to regard this as money poorly spent. And sure, Della could be a fraud. Who knows? But talking to her always makes me feel better about myself, more confident about the choices I'm making. Maybe you have that same effect on your clients."

"It's nice of you to say that," I said. I cleared my throat. "But

I think that part of my life is over now. I'm ashamed of it. I can't see myself ever going back."

"I don't know that I'd blame you for that. It sure brought you more trouble than good lately," Boots said. "Are you still staying with MMP?"

I shook my head. "I can't. Not under the circumstances. I'm just going to pick up my car and my stuff. He's not going to want me there, and I don't want to be there. I found Brynna, you know. Someone left her on the bed in the room where I was staying."

"Wow. That's awful." Boots glanced over at me, her eyes wide with shock. "I keep thinking about Brynna. I didn't like her much, but she didn't deserve what happened to her. But you don't think MMP had anything to do with it, do you? Why on earth would he target Brynna?"

I thought it over. "I don't know. No reason I can see. But I keep going back to that Elliott Thwaite deal. All that money. Maybe if MMP thought that money would go to him if Gena was dead, maybe if he was afraid Brynna would get the contract instead . . . It seems taken for granted that Gena wouldn't leave her estate to MMP, but do we know that for a fact? Has anyone seen her will?"

Boots shrugged. "Who knows? Something to look into, sure. But MMP can't be a killer. He's too *nice*."

Nice people often did terrible things when money was at stake.

Boots dropped me off outside Gena's house, waving off my attempts to thank her for coming to my rescue and urging me to call if I needed anything else. MMP came to the door shirtless and disheveled, the wide elastic waistband of his underwear sticking out of the top of his striped flannel pajama bottoms. He looked like I'd woken him up, even though it was late in the day. "Hey, come in." He held the door open all the way. "How are you? I thought you might still be in jail."

"They just talked to me. They didn't place me under arrest," I said. I trailed him inside. The house smelled of scented candles and top-quality weed, like a dormitory at an expensive private college.

We stood in the foyer, awkward. I didn't know how best to raise the subject, so I went with the direct approach. "I didn't kill Brynna."

"I know. Neither did I," he said. He shrugged. "I mean, we'd both say that even if it wasn't true, right? But it *is* true. You're not a killer. Me either."

I thought I might believe him. "Someone with a key to the house must have done it, though. How many spare keys are out there?"

"The detectives think the killer could have used Gena's set. They weren't in her purse when it was left here the night Serge was killed. The detectives asked me about that a bunch of times. I told them I didn't know of anyone else who had a key, but Gena could have given a spare to someone. Boots, maybe." He frowned. "They asked me a lot of questions about you. They said . . . I mean, they *didn't* say, they're really good at not saying anything, but it sounds like they think you're Gena's sister?"

I felt exhausted. "They tested my DNA. It matches hers. We're probably twins."

"Whoa." MMP stared at me, his eyes wide and unblinking. "And you didn't know?"

"My mom was young and unmarried. She gave birth in a hotel room in Miami with a local midwife to help her. My best guess is that she gave up Gena for adoption." That wasn't my best guess, not at all, but my actual best guess had the disadvantage of sounding absolutely batshit.

Then again, MMP was probably the perfect audience for my unhinged tale. He'd nod agreeably and tell me he always knew parallel universes were real, and maybe it'd be reassuring to have a confederate in this madness. But I couldn't tell him, couldn't say any of this out loud, because it was much too frightening and overwhelming to put into words.

I cleared my throat. "Are the police done with the guest room? Can I grab my stuff out of there?"

"Yeah. They were here last night and took more fingerprints and stuff, but they removed the police tape when they left and said it was okay to go in."

He accompanied me upstairs, but left me alone to enter the guest room. I couldn't blame him. I found I intensely disliked being back in that room after the shock of finding Brynna's corpse there. The bed was stripped down to the mattress. My box of belongings was open and had clearly been searched, and the contents of my suitcase were dumped in a pile beside it. I repacked everything as quickly as I could.

I hovered in the doorway for a second, box resting precariously on my hip, shoulder bag slung around my neck, suitcase dangling from one hand. "I'm sorry, Brynna," I said at last, out loud. I hadn't liked Brynna. Finding her corpse had been a horrifying jolt, but in my anxiety about the police interrogation followed by the world-upending reveal of my DNA test results, I had barely spared a thought for her. She was rude and spoiled, but she'd met a violent end, she'd been far too young, and she was undoubtedly loved by someone who would mourn her loss.

MMP insisted on carrying the box to my car. I tried to give him his borrowed hoodie back, but he told me to keep it. He hugged me farewell, pressing me against his bare chest, and I snuck in one final intoxicating sniff of his fantastic cologne.

"You have a place to stay tonight?" MMP asked. "I mean, I get that you wouldn't want to stay in that room, but you can still crash here. You can sleep on the couch, or there's always Gena's den."

"Gena has a den?" Gena's home didn't have many rooms. The living room, dining room, kitchen, and foyer took up the first floor, and the second floor only contained the master suite plus the guest bedroom and MMP's office, where he edited his videos and kept his elaborate gaming setup. "Do you mean her studio?"

He shook his head. "Downstairs. Beneath her studio. It's nice. It has its own bathroom and everything."

The back of my head tingled, neurons activating at this intriguing new snippet of data. A room in Gena's home I hadn't seen, hadn't ever heard about . . .

I didn't want to stay another night in that house. A murderer had a key, a key that apparently he or she was using with impunity. MMP himself could be a killer, as improbable as that seemed. But MMP had just dropped a valuable tidbit of information, one I thought might be the puzzle piece I'd been missing all along, and I'd be foolish not to follow up on it.

"Thank you," I said. "I'd love to stay in Gena's den."

CHAPTER 24

Fire Exit

My shoulder bag with my essential toiletries in hand, I followed MMP out the patio doors to the studio. The sun was setting, and the sky had turned a deep violet blue. There was a chill in the air by Los Angeles standards, but after Iowa, it felt balmy.

At the studio door, he stopped and waggled his phone at me. "You'll need the code to get in and out, so I'm going to text it to you." He did, and then observed me as I entered it into the keypad. The electronic lock slid open, allowing us entrance. In the past handful of days, I'd seen him give that code to Boots and now me; he'd given me a house key as well. With his lackadaisical attitude toward security, it seemed likely many unknown parties had access to the property.

I followed MMP across the paint-stained tarps thrown down over the floorboards, not having the faintest idea where we were heading. When I'd been in here with Boots, I'd been pretty certain the studio was just a single room.

MMP stopped. He stared at the back wall. "That's clever," he said. "I didn't know Gena did that."

He was looking in the direction of the tall canvas that hung on the back wall next to the closet door, the one I'd noticed during my first visit, the painting of the blobby white figure under attack. Stupid young Sheila Bunn in the cornfield, getting the crap kicked out of her by Aimee and her friends. "You mean the painting?"

He shook his head. "No, I mean she did the painting, obviously, but . . ." He walked up to it and scrutinized it for a moment, then gripped the right edge of the unframed canvas and pulled at it. His motions were delicate, like he thought he shouldn't touch Gena's work.

The painting swung forward, revealing a dark entryway, and I saw the illusion. The canvas had been mounted to a frameless door, the left edge flush with the hinges, the doorknob removed so the canvas could lie flat.

MMP reached into darkness and yanked on a dangling chain. An overhead bulb switched on, revealing unfinished wood stairs leading into a basement. "Come on," he said.

He started down the stairs. I hesitated, frozen by some fragmented concern for my own safety. MMP could be a killer, and if so, I should probably not willingly accompany him into a hidey-hole.

No. I trusted my gut instincts on this one. In no universe could MMP have shot Serge; it simply wasn't in his nature. I followed him down the stairs.

At the bottom, he flicked on a light switch, then turned to grin at me. "Gena's den," he said.

The first thing I saw was a gigantic framed poster for *The Divide*. I'd seen that before. I'd seen this room in MMP's lamp-repairing video.

Gena's den was dark and lush. In the windowless space, the deep blue paper covering the walls seemed to glow in the warm overhead light; the overstuffed sofa was upholstered in thick bottle-green velvet.

I spotted signs of recent habitation. A pair of black fur blankets were balled up on the sofa; on top of a brass coffee table sat an oversized leather duffel bag, expensive but in disrepair, its zipper open, clothing spilling out of it. In the tangle of clothes, I could see a terry-cloth romper, smeared with paint.

"This is Brynna's," I said. "Apparently she'd been staying here."

MMP looked startled. He stared at the duffel bag. "Gena said Brynna argued with her dad a lot. She still lived at home. Last summer, she told Gena she'd been staying in a hotel after a fight with her folks. Maybe they kicked her out again, and she'd been crashing here."

MMP moved around the room, switching on a gold table lamp, the one I'd seen him repair in his video. "Thermostat is on the wall, and the bathroom is through there. I don't think the sofa is a sleeper, but it's long enough to stretch out on."

He stopped in the middle of the room and stared at me, and I realized some kind of response was required. My brain was going in too many directions, because there was something about this room, something important, something to do with the fact that Brynna had been staying here, but I couldn't pinpoint what it was.

"Is this okay?" he asked. He sounded concerned.

"This is great. Thank you." I cleared my throat. "Do I need to use the code whenever I leave?"

"Yeah. Don't go in or out unless the light is solid green. And you have to make sure you close the door within ten seconds or it alerts the security company. It's a pain in the ass, but for insurance reasons it can't be turned off. Whenever Gena needs extra time to move her canvases out of here, she has to call the company to let them know to ignore the alarm," MMP said. "You also have to use the code for the fire exit, but there's no reason to go out that door. It just leads into the hillside."

"Okay, cool." *Fire exit.* A fluttering in my stomach, a sudden feeling of giddiness. My clothes felt hot and prickly, like my body had suddenly broken out in a rash at MMP's words. It took some effort to look composed and collected. "Thanks so much. I think I'm all set here."

"Text me if you need anything from the house, toothpaste or whatever, and I can run it out to you." MMP grinned at me.

"Hey, do you know if the police knew about this place?" I asked before he could reach the stairs. "Did they search here?"

He paused and turned. "After Gena's disappearance, or after Brynna's murder?" he asked.

"Either. Both."

"Sure, I assume so." MMP looked frozen in thought. "But now that I'm thinking about it, they could have missed it. They entered the studio, but they didn't let me go in with them, and I didn't think to specifically mention the den when I gave them the door code. I didn't know Gena had hidden the entrance. They would have spotted it while they were in here, right?"

"Maybe. Unless they didn't want to mess with Gena's paintings too much. They would have known they were valuable." After Serge's murder, the sheriff's department would have searched the house for Gena, but there'd be no reason to think Gena's studio had a basement; like the majority of homes in Los Angeles, the main house didn't have one. After Brynna's murder, the LAPD probably would have included the studio in their search for clues, but I thought there was a good chance they wouldn't disturb Gena's artwork more than necessary.

A crease appeared between MMP's well-groomed eyebrows, and for the first time I could see traces of age in that beautiful face. This whole experience had weathered him a bit, taken away some of the gloss of youth. "Do you think it's important?"

I did. I really, really did. But I wasn't entirely sure how, and I didn't want MMP around while I tried to figure it out. I was so close now to uncovering the secret of Gena's disappearance that I could feel my scalp start to prickle with excitement, but I had to think carefully about the best way to proceed, and MMP, as sweetly well-meaning as he was, could only distract me. Maybe it was arrogance, or possessiveness over my strange kinship with Gena, but I felt, very strongly and deeply, that finding her was something only I could do. "It doesn't matter. Next time the detectives talk to you, you can bring it up."

"Okay. Good night." I watched him closely as he went up the stairs. Out of a sense of faint paranoia, I crept to the top of the flight and listened until I heard the beep of the keypad and the electronic click of the security door closing behind him.

Fire exit. It took me under a minute to find it. The bathroom was located down a short concrete corridor, and right beside it was a sturdy metal door to match the one upstairs. The security keypad mounted to the wall glowed red in the darkness. I got out my phone and entered the six-digit code, hands trembling the entire time, and the light switched to green.

I ventured outside. The darkness was instantly disorienting, so I used my phone as a flashlight to get my bearings. I found myself standing at the far edge of the windowless concrete base of the cottage, which was built perpendicular to and flush with the concrete retaining wall protecting Gena's property from the hillside. I didn't know much about architecture or building codes, but I would bet that retaining wall was the reason the cottage had needed a basement. Directly above me was the edge of Gena's backyard.

The ground was uneven and steep. I could head down the hill on foot, charging through the low bushes, but that would be reckless without knowing where I was going. To the north, though . . . I shone the flashlight around. If I headed up the hill instead, past the edge of the wall, the incline was modest, and there was a worn path in the dry grass.

I started climbing, following the path, moving cautiously. There were rattlesnakes in this area, and while I wasn't sure they'd be around in November, I wasn't sure they wouldn't, either, so I kept the light fixed on the ground and stepped with care.

It wasn't steep, but it was a workout; I could feel it in the back of my thighs. I paused once, staring out over the long sprawl of city lights while trying to catch my breath before continuing.

By walking straight up the hill and crossing through an

undeveloped lot between two houses, I made it to a residential street in just a few minutes. I stood on a quiet road in the darkness and thought about what I'd just learned.

Someone could leave Gena's home the way I had and disappear without being noticed. What did that mean?

The night of Serge's murder, Gena had apparently returned to the house and vanished. She could have left her purse and phone in the foyer, then gone to her studio, descended into her den, left through the fire door, and climbed up here. If she'd planned it in advance, she could have arranged to have a car waiting, money, somewhere to hide.

But there was no proof it had been Gena who'd returned from Serge's home that night. Someone, presumably whoever had shot Serge, could have driven to her home to make it look as though she'd returned. Someone who'd known about the back exit, and someone who'd known the security code.

Brynna had been living in Gena's den, or crashing there on occasion to work on her paintings whenever she wanted, and she hadn't been parking in either the courtyard or the garage. She'd been using this back entrance. She'd probably parked somewhere up here and used the fire door to get in and out without anyone seeing her.

Probably Gena had known about Brynna's use of her den, but it seemed likely no one else did, if MMP's surprise was genuine. So if someone had known about this exit and used it the night of Serge's murder, they would unexpectedly encounter Brynna. Which meant Brynna had known who'd killed Serge. Which was probably why Brynna had ended up dead.

I jumped when my phone rang, loud in this quiet neighborhood, and I rushed to silence it. I glanced at the display screen. Linus. I owed him a phone call, but I didn't want to chat out in the open on this dark street, so I sent it to voicemail.

I retraced my path back down the hill. I used the code to reenter the studio, made absolutely certain I was alone in Gena's den, and called Linus back.

"Jenny," he said. He sounded relieved to hear from me, which was gratifying. "How are you? What's been going on? Were you arrested?"

"No, they just talked to me all night. It's been a little overwhelming, so I had to take some time to myself," I said. Telling him about the DNA test seemed beyond me at the moment; that could wait until later. "I'm really sorry about Brynna."

"Yeah. Goddamn, what a shock. I think I'm still trying to process the news." He paused. "I'd like to see you. I have dinner plans, but it shouldn't be a late evening. Could I pick you up later? Where are you staying?"

"At a hotel," I said, the lie coming immediately to my lips. He wouldn't approve of me staying here, especially not after Brynna's murder, and I didn't feel like a lecture just now. "Could we meet tomorrow? I thought I'd get an early bedtime tonight."

"Sure, yeah, that's a good idea. You've been through a lot lately. Give me a call tomorrow when you're up, and we'll make a plan."

We exchanged good-nights and ended the call. If I stayed with Linus tomorrow, that would give me an extra day to figure out a living situation. That could be a good solution.

Unless Linus was the murderer, of course. He managed both Gena's and Brynna's careers, and he was an old friend of Serge's, so obviously he had strong connections to all concerned parties. In terms of motive, though, I still couldn't make it fit; his life had been upended for the worse by Gena's disappearance and the subsequent loss of the Elliott Thwaite deal.

I stared at the screen of my phone, lost in thought. Linus. I was looking right at Linus's phone number, saved in my contacts list, and I was feeling an acute sense of déjà vu, coupled with a growing feeling of unease.

Because I'd just typed that number, or the great majority of it, into the keypad of the security alarm. I double-checked the text MMP had sent me to confirm: Gena's door code was the first six digits of Linus's phone number.

The security doors had been installed because of the Thwaite contract. As Gena's manager and the person responsible for that deal, Linus would have overseen their installation to make absolutely certain Gena's security was in compliance with the strict terms of that very important, very valuable contract. Out of convenience, when asked to set the code, he simply used his own phone number.

Did that change anything? Had Linus killed Serge? And Gena and Brynna? If so, why? Gena's absence damaged him financially; even now, he was still in danger of losing that enormous Elliott Thwaite commission.

I sank down onto the overstuffed velvet sofa, barely noticing the way the soft cushions surrounded me, like they were welcoming me back to the womb, where I was safe and protected on all sides. I wasn't safe here, not at all. I was willing to bet Brynna had been murdered here. She would have been hit over the head with something—probably that heavy gold lamp, the one MMP had dissected in his video—before being carried into the main house and left in the guest bedroom to cast suspicion on me, the convenient stranger with the weird connection to Gena. Linus would have entered the house with the key he'd taken from Gena's purse after killing Serge. And, almost beyond a doubt, after killing Gena.

But, again, why would Linus kill Serge and Gena? The Elliott Thwaite contract was completed, the designs delivered. All that remained was settling the final payment, which would give Linus that much-needed second half of his commission. Because Gena's body hadn't shown up, because it was still unknown whether Gena was a victim or a murderer, that payment had been withheld, and Linus was in a financial crunch. It didn't make sense.

If Gena's body showed up, though . . .

Serge's Malibu home, those cliffs out back. Something Boots had said, that she thought Malis might have dumped Gena's body into the water. If Gena had fallen into the sea, if she hadn't ended up on the rocks below, her body might have been swept away, never to resurface. If Linus was the killer, he wouldn't have wanted that, but it could have happened somehow. It could have been an accident.

The cottage was right at the cliff's edge, and even if Ronnie was asleep as he claimed, he almost certainly would have heard a scuffle. But Ronnie and Linus knew each other back from the days of *The Divide*. They were close. Maybe Ronnie was keeping Linus's secret.

I stared at the poster of *The Divide*. It was huge, sized to display at a bus stop, though the film hadn't been advertised anywhere, not after the planned theatrical release was scrapped. Posters might have been made already, though, and maybe Serge had been given one, or maybe Gena had bought this one from someone's dead stock. None of her own artwork was displayed on the walls; for Gena, this den was about the life she could have led, but didn't.

The poster dominated the wall. The thick gold frame must have been a custom job. If it hadn't been for Gena's canvas concealing the door to the den, I might not have thought of it, but it struck me then that, with the way the frame jutted into the room by a couple of inches, there'd be a gap between the back of the poster and the wall. I rose from the couch and gently tilted the base of the frame up toward me.

The frame covered an electrical outlet near the base of the wall. Something was plugged into it, something small that had been resting on the inside bottom ledge of the frame; I heard a muted thump as it dropped to the blue Persian rug covering the floor. I crouched down and picked it up.

I held a glossy black object, cold to the touch, flat and slim. Gena stored a tablet, fully charged and ready for use, behind the poster of *The Divide* in her secret sanctum. I didn't have any idea what was on it, but I knew it was something she didn't want anyone else to see.

CHAPTER 25

Health and Welfare

The home screen on Gena's hidden tablet looked unremarkable. Gena mostly stuck to default apps: a web browser, news headlines, the weather report. She hadn't linked an email account to the tablet, and when I checked her calendar, it was empty and unused. Her browser history was empty. It was possible she cleared it after every use, but it was more likely she never used this tablet for web surfing.

Then what did she use it for? The only app I couldn't identify was something called OKMood. I clicked it open.

It brought me to a welcome screen. The app was tastefully designed, with soothing fonts on a neutral background and a header image of daffodils in a field. The introductory text advised me that OKMood brought the knowledge and services of licensed psychologists into the privacy of my home, available around the clock to fit my busy schedule. A small bell icon in the corner notified me that Gena had some messages. I clicked.

Gena had missed two appointments on the past two Mondays, both with one Doctor Hilde Sauer. Along with the automatic notifications, Gena's inbox included two personal messages from Doctor Sauer. The first, the Monday after Serge's murder, was short and simple: Gena, please contact me at your earliest convenience. Thank you. The second, a few days later, was a bit longer: Gena, I'm concerned about your health and welfare. Please reach out if you're able. Day or night.

It was a Saturday night, and it was just after seven in the evening, and while OKMood promised around-the-clock support, that didn't mean Doctor Sauer would be on hand right now. Nonetheless, I spent a few minutes fiddling around with the app, trying to figure out how to set an appointment. It wouldn't let me schedule anything with Sauer until the following week, but there was an option to send her a message. I paused, then decided to embrace recklessness.

I typed a quick message: Hello, Dr. Sauer. I'd like to talk to you, now if possible. I had no idea what Gena's communication style was like, and I mulled over the wording of the brief message for far too long before concluding it with a simple Thank you, Gena. I sent it off.

And then I waited, sitting on the terribly soft, terribly comfortable velvet sofa, tablet in my hands, a fur blanket over my legs for extra protection and warmth, because I couldn't seem to stop trembling. After a handful of agonizing minutes, I saw Gena had a message in the OKMood notification center informing her of a new appointment with Doctor Sauer, set for 7:15. Hands trembling against the glossy touch screen of the tablet, I accepted.

At 7:15 on the dot, I clicked on a link embedded in the appointment notification, and after a hazy moment of uncertainty, the tablet screen filled with the lined and weary face of a middle-aged woman. The angle was unflattering, her chin jutting too close to her camera; I had the sense she was viewing this on a laptop while she sat in what looked like a high-backed armchair. She frowned at the screen and made some adjustment to the angle.

I'd caught her at home. Probably she'd already been in bed;

she wore what could be a striped blouse, but was more likely a pajama top. She wore no makeup; her graying hair was pushed back behind her ears.

"I have no picture," she said. "Before we go any further, I'll need you to turn your camera on." Her voice sounded tinny but loud over the tablet's built-in speaker, and I was glad I was alone in Gena's den.

It took me a minute to figure out how to unmute the microphone and turn the camera on. The woman's brow creased as my face presumably filled her screen.

"Gena," she said at last. "Good evening. Under the circumstances, I was surprised to hear from you. Surprised but pleased."

"Hi, Doctor Sauer," I said. My voice sounded a little shaky. Her immediate acceptance that I was Gena startled me, but hell, I looked like Gena, and I was logged into her OKMood account while sitting in her den, so why on earth would this woman assume otherwise? "I'm sorry for disturbing you."

"Not at all. I was relieved to get your message. The news over these past two weeks has alarmed me greatly." Sauer had a low, soothing voice, pitched to calm agitated souls. It was difficult to imagine her being alarmed. I'd never met with a psychologist or any kind of therapist before, though for my clinic I'd deliberately tried to shape my professional persona after the coolly competent and well-spoken shrinks I'd seen in films and on TV shows. Sauer fit that mold; she radiated solemn intellect and unruffled compassion. "First I want to ask if you are safe."

"I don't know," I said. "But I'm fine for the moment."

"Sometimes the moment is enough. If you build up enough such moments, you might find you are, in a greater sense, fine." Doctor Sauer still sounded calm, but I had the sense my sudden presence had shaken her, and she was responding largely on autopilot, speaking meaningless words to fill the void until she'd managed to make sense of the situation. She cleared her throat. "I must make this clear before we talk. I won't ask you for details about your current situation, other than to confirm you are safe. I can't and won't tell anyone anything at all about your health, mental or physical, but patient privacy laws don't bar me from telling the authorities I've been contacted by you, if that seems like the correct course of action."

Which meant she was going to call the police as soon as I disconnected the call. Fair enough. "I understand. Do what you have to do. Can we talk for a while first?"

"Of course. I'd like you to feel free to tell me anything you think is relevant, though my earlier caution stands." She leaned closer to her screen, scrutinizing me. "You've changed your hair."

"I was in hiding," I said. "I was scared."

Sauer didn't answer at first. When she spoke, there was a new note to her voice, and I felt a flutter of sudden nerves. "You seem very different to me."

I forced myself to remain calm. "What I've been through has changed me."

She nodded once, slowly. She didn't say anything, and I decided it would be a good move to fill the silence before she had time to think too much about how I seemed very different. Like an entirely different person, in fact. "When we last spoke, I was worried about Linus."

This was a wild guess, and if Gena had never mentioned Linus to Sauer, I'd probably have to do some tap dancing to explain it. Sauer looked confused, and I figured I'd blown it. "You didn't convey much of that worry to me. You said you felt very confident in your decision."

I didn't know what decision that would be, so I just nodded. "I was. But I've had more time to think about it."

A decision. What decision had Gena made? What could she have told Linus that would have driven him to murder?

All of a sudden, I had it. I felt a musical chord resonate throughout my body, something in a jubilant major key, and I had to struggle to control my face so I wouldn't alarm poor

Doctor Sauer by grinning from ear to ear. I didn't have all the pieces yet, but this was it, this was the motive.

The contract. The Elliott Thwaite contract, the one Linus claimed Gena had completed in full. She'd decided to break it, and that decision would've hit Linus like an atomic blast.

I chose my words carefully. "It's a lot of money," I said. Keeping my tone neutral was a Herculean effort, the most difficult performance of my career.

"The last time we spoke, you mentioned things that were more important to you than money."

What was more important than money? Love? Gena was in love with MMP, maybe, or at least she liked him well enough to share her life with him. She didn't seem to have any grand passions in her life, apart from her art. What would cause Gena to break her contract?

Her cancer. Her recent surgery. Boots had said something along those lines when I'd asked her about the documentary, that Gena had become more judgmental after her diagnosis, as though her priorities had suddenly changed alignment. "Like my health?" I'd meant it to sound like a calm statement, but it came out as a question.

"You said your illness had changed your outlook."

"It did." I swallowed hard. "It has. Nothing like a brush with mortality to lend some perspective."

Sauer nodded. Her level of calm seemed inhuman, and for a wild moment I didn't know whether I was communicating with a real person at all. Maybe she was an advanced neural network, designed and programmed to give patients all the correct prompts and responses. "Tell me about your new perspective," she said.

That was tricky. Gena and Sauer had had this conversation before, and I hadn't the faintest idea what Gena had told her. If Gena's illness had made her reassess her old priorities, what new ones had risen in their place? What would be more important to Gena now than the money and prestige she'd earn from the Elliott Thwaite deal? What would be more important to me, if I were in Gena's situation?

Gena . . . Newly ill Gena, sickened with cancer, forced to come to terms with the fragility of human existence. Gena, who already had a good amount of fame and money and presumably was no longer desperate for more of either. Gena, who'd been working with her ex-husband on a documentary about artistic integrity and selling out, who'd been thinking an awful lot about such things lately. What would lead Gena to break the contract?

Ah. What Malis had talked about at the dinner party, the ethical problems inherent in the Elliott Thwaite contract. That was it, that was the key. "I don't want to make the world a worse place, that's all."

It sounded too open and heartfelt, and that made me cringe, because I didn't think Gena seemed like the open and heartfelt type. But Sauer just nodded. "The labor practices of the Elliott Thwaite factories overseas disturbed you greatly. As did the negative environmental impact of the fashion industry."

Thank you, Doctor Sauer, that was very helpful. Sweatshop labor, carbon emissions. I nodded, maybe too emphatically. "Yes, very much so. After thinking about it, I couldn't in good faith fulfill the contract."

"You mentioned that breaking the contract would disappoint your manager and deprive him of a large commission, but you didn't seem to feel that was an important consideration in making your decision. Has that changed?"

I thought about Linus in his beautiful Wilshire Corridor condo, the slight air of tension that wafted through his casually affable exterior as he talked about how Gena's disappearance was creating problems for him. "I think Linus needed that money more than I knew," I said. "He needed it very much. I didn't realize how much." I could see it now: Gena had told Linus she would renege on her end of the contract, even though she'd already completed the designs, even though she'd already delivered them to Linus, even though Linus had already spent the first half of his commission, which would now need to be returned to the client. Linus would have tried his best to talk her out of it, his exterior conveying nothing but deep concern for her well-being. And all the while, his clever brain would have been weighing all the possible ways he could make sure the contract remained unbroken.

"How did that make you feel?" Sauer asked.

I considered the question. "Not great," I said. "Guilty, I suppose. I don't like disappointing people or making their lives more difficult."

"Would you have made a different decision if you'd known?"

"No," I said. "My reasons were—are—good ones. Obviously if I'd known . . ." I stopped.

"Did your manager . . . ?" It burst out of Sauer against her will, and then she froze. For the first time, some emotion other than neutral compassion registered on her face. She looked startled and a bit ill, as though an awful thought had just dawned on her. She composed herself and shook her head. "Never mind. I won't ask that."

"I should go," I said quickly. We were on unsteady ground now, and I was in danger of dragging us both down together. "Thank you for talking to me."

"Please be careful, Gena. I don't know your full circumstances, but I urge you not to be alone tonight."

"I'll be fine." I cleared my throat. "Don't worry about me. Everything's okay."

"I'm glad to hear that." She'd call the police now, I was certain, and she'd tell them she'd spoken to Gena Santos, alive and well, at her home. The police would quickly figure out she'd really spoken to Jenny St. John, local Gena Santos impersonator and probable long-lost twin, and that was less than ideal, but it had to be done. It was worth it, wasn't it? I knew who'd killed Serge, and who had very likely killed Gena.

I wrapped up the call as swiftly as I could, feeling more unsettled than before.

CHAPTER 26

Surfer Boy

I thought there was a decent chance I'd receive a visit in the middle of the night from the LAPD or the LASD, depending upon whom Dr. Sauer thought to call. Sleep wasn't going to happen, and I decided I didn't want to be here, tamely waiting for the police to arrive. I slipped out of the studio, hopped into my car, drove away from Gena's house, and parked in the empty lot of a strip mall on Sunset to think.

I should contact the proper authorities myself. I should call my old friend Detective Moreau right now and tell her what I'd just learned, everything about Gena's den and the fire exit in back, and especially about Gena's decision to back out of the Elliott Thwaite contract. But she'd have questions, lots of questions, and the memory of my LAPD interrogation two nights ago was still too fresh. In any case, before I went to Moreau, there was someone I wanted to talk to first.

I texted Malis from the parking lot, asking if it would be okay if I dropped by her home for a visit. I waited for about twenty minutes, sitting in my car, before the answer came. Rain had started to fall, a dainty smattering of microscopic dots on my windshield, too faint to obscure my view. In another city, it wouldn't even count as rain; in Los Angeles, it could be the top story on the news tonight.

The response was short and to the point: Sorry, working at studio.

That was okay for my purposes. It was better, in fact, if Malis wasn't home. Ronnie would be home, because Ronnie couldn't leave, and I had the strong sense that I really, really needed to have a chat with him.

By the time I reached Malibu, the sky had turned from violet to black, and the rain had decided to stop playing around and get serious. I parked in front of the bamboo grove that lined the front of Serge's property and called Ronnie.

He picked up on the first ring. "Yeah?"

"Ronnie. Hi. It's Jenny," I said.

There was a moment of silence. Whoever he'd been expecting, it wasn't me. "Jenny! Good to hear from you. What's up?"

"I was in Malibu running errands, and I thought I'd stop by. I'm at the gate. Malis isn't around, but can you let me in?"

There was another silence. "You're here now?"

"Yeah, right outside. Sorry for the short notice, but I just found myself in the area. I hope that's okay."

"Sure, yeah, that's great. I'll be right there." I felt a pang of something nasty at the guileless cheer in his voice. I liked Ronnie, a lot. Tonight was probably going to be a bad night for him.

He came up to the gate shirtless, in jeans, his bare feet in flip-flops, a faded striped beach towel draped over his head and shoulders to shield him from the rain. He unlocked the gate from his side and ushered me in. "Hi, Jenny! Can you believe this rain? Come on, let's get inside."

We hurried along the paved path that ran beside the house, the rain spitting down on us with increased vigor. I glanced at the monitor bracelet affixed to his ankle, the damp leg of his jeans bunched up above it. "Thanks for letting me in. It dawned on me belatedly that your bracelet might not let you go all the way to the gate."

"Nah, as long as I don't step beyond the property boundary, I'm fine. I can walk out to the mailbox, even, but if I step onto the road, they send a patrol car here." He grinned at me, raindrops slithering down his bare torso. He still had a pretty great smile.

I followed him to his little cottage by the edge of the cliff. He'd cleaned up since my last visit: the empty bottles were gone, the dishes were done, and everything seemed fresher, neater. He closed the door behind us and smiled at me. "You want anything? I can fix some coffee, if you need to warm up."

"No, that's okay. I'm not going to stay long." I remained standing, sticking close to the door. Ronnie was a good guy, at least as good a guy as anyone under house arrest for armed robbery could be expected to be, but all the same, I was bringing him bad news, and I wanted to be able to leave quickly.

I came to the point. "It's Linus, right?"

I saw a flicker in his eyes, and for a moment I was optimistic we'd be able to skip through all the tedious denials and have an open conversation, but then I saw the barriers go up. A tight smile played on his lips, like I was making a joke he didn't quite follow. "What about Linus?"

"Linus shot Serge. He meant to kill Gena, too, and presumably did; I'm guessing whatever happened between Gena and Linus happened at the edge of those cliffs, right outside your door."

"What are you talking about, Jenny?"

"I know you told the investigators you slept through it all, but that explanation is going to break down when they bring you in for questioning again, which will happen right after they arrest Linus, if not before. I don't want to make things more difficult than necessary for you, so I wanted to give you time to think over how you need to play this."

"You've talked to the police?" Ronnie's eyes opened wide.

"I'm giving you a heads-up before I do, so you can figure out your story. I know you like Linus, and I know you feel you owe him, but not this much."

"Linus would never hurt Serge." Ronnie sounded emphatic, and his words dripped with what seemed like sincerity, but I'd worked with him closely enough while filming to recognize what this was: he was putting on a performance. "You know that. They were friends for decades."

"And both Linus and Serge were friends with you as well. I know. That's why I know you're involved in this." Ronnie's face was flushed with some strong emotion, or combination of emotions. Some anger, certainly, but mostly fear. Trapped animals could lash out, so I had to proceed with caution.

"Jenny, this is crazy. You know Linus. Does he seem like a killer?"

"I don't know, Ronnie, do you seem like an armed robber? We're all capable of doing bad things," I said. "I'm a fake psychic. I defraud people for money. On the surface, do I seem like that type?"

Ronnie shook his head, his damp hair sending droplets of rain flying. "Why would Linus kill Serge? Give me one good reason."

"I don't know his reason. But I know he killed Gena over money, and I bet he blamed Serge as much as he blamed Gena for the loss of income." Serge, I knew, was also a useful distraction: by killing both Serge and Gena at Serge's home, Linus had made it seem like Serge was the primary target, which had complicated the investigation. "And he killed another woman, this artist named Brynna who knew what he'd done. Two days ago, he hit her on the head hard enough to break her neck." I saw another flicker in Ronnie's eyes. My words shattered through his feigned veneer of righteous indignation, and I knew he hadn't known about Brynna. And I knew he believed me.

He stood near the door, close to me, frozen in place, and

all the life and vitality drained from him. In the low light, it'd been easy enough to still see the twentysomething rising star I once knew, the golden surfer boy who looked like an old-school movie star on film and acted like a goofy puppy in real life. Now, though, he looked haggard. He turned away from me, then sank down on the couch, elbows propped on his thighs, shaggy head buried in his hands.

I stayed where I was, watching him. After a long moment, he raised his eyes to meet mine. "Is that true?" he asked.

"Yeah. I'm sorry," I said. I felt an urge to sit beside him on the couch, to offer him some comfort and some commiseration, but there was too much danger here. I swallowed hard. "I liked Linus a lot, Ronnie. He seemed like a cool guy, and hanging out with him reminded me of all those great times we all had while filming *The Divide*. That was the best time of my life, by a huge margin. But I think you know he's a murderer, and I think you've been covering for him."

Ronnie's head dropped again, like his neck didn't have the strength to hold it upright. He spoke in barely more than a mumble, his words aimed at the floor. "I got him the gun," he said. "He comes over for dinner most Saturdays. Always has, ever since I was released. Serge would join us whenever he was free. Couple Saturdays ago, Linus told me someone had tried to break into his place at night, and he wanted to know where he could get a gun for his own protection."

"So you told him how he could get one?"

Ronnie shook his head. "Like I said, I got it for him." He looked at me, self-loathing plastered on his face. "Linus had showed me how I could remove the monitor. We've been taking it off regularly for several months now. He'd looked it up online on some shady website; he knew every step. He'd come over late at night, we'd slip it off and leave it in my bed so it would seem like I was asleep, and we'd go out together. The first time, we grabbed burgers in some neighborhood where no one was likely to know me. That seemed too risky, so after that, we'd just go to the beach. We'd sit on the sand in the darkness and look at the water and talk about the old days. Those have been the only times since my arrest where I've felt like a real human being, you know?"

"Yeah." I figured I did know. "So you got him a gun?"

"We went together. I know this guy, lives in Hawthorne, same guy Marco and I bought the guns from that we used when we robbed that producer. Linus drove me there. He insisted he needed a silencer as well, which I thought was weird if he just wanted a gun for his own protection, but whatever; I thought he just didn't know much about guns, like he maybe had seen a lot of movies and was asking for whatever he thought sounded cool. He stayed in the car while I made the deal. This was the Saturday before last." Ronnie shook his head. "I wasn't crazy about doing it. It kind of pissed me off, honestly. Sneaking out at night for a little bit of freedom, that was one thing, but I thought Linus understood I wasn't a criminal anymore. He assured me that he wouldn't ask if he didn't really need it, and I thought, okay, he's done a lot for me, I owe him this."

I did some mental calculation. "And the next day Serge was shot, right?" I asked. "What happened that night? Don't try to tell me you slept through it."

"I don't know." Ronnie sounded miserable. "Jenny, I swear on whatever you want me to swear on, I don't know. I want there to be any other explanation for it. Linus came over that night. I wasn't expecting him, he just called me from the gate, like you did, and I went up and met him and brought him back here. He was . . . weird. Jumpy, I guess; I wondered if he was on something, coke or whatever. He said he wanted to pay me back for getting the gun. So he removed the bracelet, and we went out to his car, and it turned out he'd brought me a board and a wet suit."

Ronnie shook his head. "I hadn't surfed since before my arrest. We headed to Zuma, and I went out on the waves. Just me, almost no one else around. The board he brought was this ridiculous foamie, because he didn't know what kind he should get, and I joked with him that he thought I needed training wheels, but it didn't matter. First time I went out on the waves, I almost cried, I felt so happy."

He was looking at me now, but he didn't see me. "It was like I pressed rewind and started all over from the beginning. I was young and pretty, no police record, a huge film career ahead of me. The next Keanu—you remember when everyone was calling me that?" He grinned at the memory. "At one point, I looked around the beach for Linus, and he was nowhere. I kind of panicked, because if he'd taken off, I wasn't sure I could walk back to the house without getting stopped. Malibu is crawling with private security. But I went back out on my board again, and the next time I looked for him, Linus was there, like he'd never left. He drove me back here, we got the bracelet back on my leg, and he took away the board and wet suit when he left. Best night of my life in years, and then in the morning, the cops pounded on my door, telling me Serge had been shot in the middle of the night."

"You figured it was Linus right away?" I asked.

"I still don't know it was him." Ronnie had snapped back to the present, knocked out of his nostalgic haze by the absolutely crappy set of circumstances in which he was currently mired. His eyes looked dark and murky in the low light. "I mean, goddamn, it has to be him, because I got him that gun. I'm not as stupid as all that. When he left me on the beach, he must've gone back here and killed Serge. I know that's how it must've gone down, but I still can't believe he'd do that." His voice broke. Ronnie had been through things in his life, and I'd never make the mistake of thinking of him as naïve, but in that moment he was a confused child, crushed by the betrayal of a trusted adult.

I exhaled. A knot had formed in my stomach during Ronnie's long, bad tale. "You've got some power here, Ronnie," I said. "It doesn't seem like it, but you do. You've got to talk to the police before they arrest Linus. Linus isn't going to keep you out of this, you know that. If you give him to them, it'll be better for you."

"I can't give them Linus," Ronnie said. "I won't. This is all a mistake, somehow."

"I really wish it was," I said, and I was amazed at how much I meant it.

Ronnie didn't answer. He kept his head down and turned away from me. He wiped his nose with the back of one hand.

"You want me to stay with you? We can call the police together. Or you can call your parole officer first. I can be here with you when they arrive."

He shook his head. "Just go away, okay? Leave me alone."

I was glad for the excuse to leave, because the knot in my guts had moved up through my chest, and it felt as though my heart were literally breaking. "Sorry about this, Ronnie," I said.

I left him sitting on the couch, drained and miserable. I looked back at him from the doorway, hoping I could still glimpse that magnetic young heartthrob who'd seemed poised for greatness, but all I could see was a broken middle-aged man with a criminal record and a life filled with bad luck, with even worse to come.

CHAPTER 27

Death by Misadventure

The rain came down harder. I pulled the damp hood of MMP's sweatshirt as low over my forehead as it could go. I should have hurried back to the car, but I was cold and wet already, and this would be my last chance to piece together what exactly had happened to Gena before Moreau and the other detectives took it out of my hands.

It was dark, but I didn't use my phone as a light, partially because I didn't want the rain to destroy my phone and partially because I wanted Ronnie to assume I'd left the property. He hadn't seemed dangerous; I'd never believe Ronnie would pose a threat to me. But I had to be smart about this: he was an accessory to murder, and his already marginal lifestyle was going to get crummier, and he could be feeling desperate to prevent that from happening.

I crept to the edge of the cliff, stepping carefully in the darkness. If I owned Serge's home, I would put up a fence here, just for peace of mind. Maybe Serge hadn't minded feeling like death by misadventure was just a poorly judged step away; maybe it reminded him that life was fleeting and dangerous. Or maybe he never spent much time here. Maybe he never stood at the edge to enjoy this view.

No. The Serge I knew would have loved this view, would have richly enjoyed this uniquely precarious backyard. He would have gone out here at night to sit on the edge, legs dangling over the void, maybe drinking a few beers while thinking about ideas for his next film.

Obviously Linus had meant to kill Gena. He'd wanted her body to be found with Serge's, but something had gone wrong. Maybe he'd planned for it to look like a violent home invasion; maybe he'd had some thoughts of rigging it to look like a murder-suicide. He'd left Ronnie surfing on the public beach and driven the short distance to the house. He was a frequent and welcome visitor to the home; it was reasonable to assume Serge had given him the code to the front gate at some point. He'd simply entered on his own, then headed around back to shoot Serge at the patio door.

But his plan had gone awry. Gena's body hadn't been found in the house, but since she'd vanished, it meant she was dead. She'd tried to escape, and Linus had shot her, and she'd gone over the cliff, her body swept out to sea instead of getting trapped on the rocks below.

Linus would have to think fast. He would have picked up Ronnie at the beach as planned and driven him back to the cottage, replacing the ankle monitor before returning to the main house. That would give him a little time to think it through: Gena's body was gone, so it had to seem like she disappeared voluntarily. He took Gena's phone and purse, being careful not to leave fresh fingerprints at the crime scene, then got into her car, drove to Silver Lake, went through her front gate, and parked in her garage. He used her keys to enter her home through the garage, then left her possessions in a heap in the foyer, keeping the keys. He went out the patio door, used the security code—his phone number—to get into the studio, went downstairs to the den, exited out the back, climbed up to the top of the hill, and arranged for a car service to pick him up and take him back to Malibu so he could retrieve his own car and drive back to his place.

Complicated and messy, but not a bad plan at the spur of the moment, and Gena's disappearance had the advantage of confusing the investigation almost beyond repair. Because it was complicated and messy, though, at least two things went immediately wrong. One, the people at Elliott Thwaite had brought up the morality clause in Gena's contract. If they thought Gena was a murderer, the contract, though completed, was null and void. No commission for Linus.

And two: Brynna had been sleeping in Gena's den, and she'd seen him. Linus might not even have noticed; I could imagine him slinking through the den in the darkness, heading for the fire door without realizing Brynna was curled up on the sofa. But she'd seen him and had wondered about it, and in the morning, when news broke of Serge's murder and Gena's disappearance, she had known. She'd tried to use the information to her advantage, tried to leverage Linus into giving her the Elliott Thwaite contract in exchange for her silence. Maybe that explained Brynna's deep hostility toward me, and why she'd been so angered and alarmed by my friendship with Linus. Maybe she'd thought Linus would use my resemblance to Gena to fulfill the terms of the contract while cutting her out of the equation. And indeed, that had been Linus's intention. He'd strung Brynna along, promising her the contract while waiting patiently to see if Gena's body would turn up, and waiting patiently for the right time to murder her.

But Gena's body hadn't surfaced. Was that unusual? If my hunch was right, and I felt it was, if Gena had gone over the side of the cliff, surely it was more likely that her body would get stuck on the jutting rocks below instead of drifting out to sea. Shielding the screen of my phone from the rain as much as I could, I shone a light down over the side.

It wasn't that steep, and it wasn't that far down. It was hard to gauge distances, but the slim rocky stretch of beach seemed only twelve, maybe fourteen feet below me. A fall would possibly be fatal, but not inevitably so; Gena could have survived. She could have crawled to safety, wounded yet alive.

It'd been two weeks since the night she disappeared. Could she still be alive, even now?

I crouched down. Maybe twenty years back, I'd dabbled in bouldering; on weekends, I'd scale the sandstone formations at Stoney Point, which was always a trendy spot for actors looking for alternate ways to keep fit. I hadn't forged any useful professional connections out on the rocks, but I'd discovered a knack for climbing: I knew my center of gravity, I had decent arm strength, and I had no fear of heights. This cliff looked like it might be manageable.

This was my last chance to investigate on my own. It was almost a compulsion now, this urge to find Gena, or at least some trace of her, probably stemming from my desperate, pathetic need for credit and praise. I'd solved Serge's murder, and Brynna's as well, but if I told Detective Moreau everything I knew or suspected, I wouldn't get much more out of it than a reprimand for meddling. But if I found Gena . . .

I knelt on the ground, wet mud oozing through the knees of my jeans. I faced Ronnie's cottage, staring at the light shining behind his closed curtains. I made sure my hands had a good grip on the rocky earth on the top of the cliff and lowered one leg, then the other.

The cliff wasn't sheer. It was much too steep to walk down, but if I took it slowly, moving backward bit by bit, there was little risk of dropping down to the rocks below. I felt around with my feet, testing each foothold carefully, making sure the rocky surface was stable and could support my weight before I began the descent.

Mud soaked through my clothes. Didn't care. One step down, then another, then two more, and my feet touched the relative security of a flat, narrow ledge. I stood on it, testing it with one leg before adding the other, all while clinging to the side of the cliff for added support.

The investigators would have searched here, surely, in the immediate aftermath of Serge's murder. Climbers would have swarmed the beach looking for traces of evidence, blood or clothing or footprints, and now, in the dark and the rain, two weeks after the incident, there was little chance I would find anything they hadn't. Still, I had to make certain.

I paused my descent and moved along the ledge, gripping the cliffside as tightly as I could. Moving to the side was easier than going down, and if Gena had made her way to this ledge, she would have realized that.

The ledge stretched on, narrowing in parts and widening in others. I continued along, trying not to think too much about how difficult it might be to climb back up to the top, especially with my hands growing cold and numb from the November rain and the chilly ocean air.

I would have missed the cave, were it not for the lightning. Los Angeles doesn't get dramatic electric storms, not like the midwestern ones of my childhood. No jagged bolt of electricity dividing the sky, this was just a pulse of white light that drained the color from everything it touched, like the flashbulb going off on a paparazzo's camera in a black-and-white movie. The thunder came a few seconds later, a low rumble that felt like it originated somewhere inside my belly. I barely noticed the sound, though, because I was still processing what I had seen in that flash of light: a dark raggedy crack in the side of the rocks, only a couple of feet from where I stood. It wasn't large, but a human could crawl through.

I moved to the crack, heart hammering in a way that seemed unhealthy, my mouth filling with the sour taste of bile. I expected to find Gena in the cave, either alive and wounded or dead and decaying. Up close, though, I heard nothing, and I could smell only the ocean and the rain.

I released my grip on the cliff with one hand and fished my

phone out of my back pocket. My hand was numb; my fingers were thick and clumsy, like twigs that had been submerged in a cold river until they'd softened and swelled up with water. When I tried to tap the flashlight icon with my useless fingers, my phone slipped out of my grip and hit the ledge. I grabbed for it, but it bounced over the side and fell to the rocks below.

Without any light to guide me, I tried to look into the cave. The interior was maybe the size of a shower stall, though half as tall. It was empty. I saw damp rocks; I smelled old moss. A small bundle of something lay among the rocks, gray and fuzzy; I thought it was a dead animal at first, but when I focused on it, I saw it wasn't fur, but textured fabric. Knitwear.

Didn't mean it was Gena's, but of course it was. It had to be.

I crawled into the cave, feeling reckless and unstable and yet absolutely certain this was what I needed to do. There was barely enough room to wriggle through the gap; I had to pivot my shoulders and contort into ungainly positions to make it work, but once I was through the narrow entrance, I found myself with more room to move.

I couldn't stand, but I could stay in a crouch, the roof of the cave a foot or two above the top of my head. I examined the gray thing. A sweater. A buttonless cardigan, the kind with a flowing hem that dangled to the thighs; I'd never been fond of that style, but from photos of Gena, it seemed like it could be her taste, coordinating well with her tangled dark hair and her sensible-artist persona.

I picked up the sweater and touched something stiff. As my eyes adjusted to the darkness, I could see a brown stain saturating one of the front lapels. Dried blood, which made the fabric clump together. I tugged on the fabric, the blood flaking off into featherlike chips that fell onto the muddy knees of my jeans, and saw the small, perfect hole an inch beneath the shoulder seam. The hole was located right at the epicenter of the brown stain.

Gena had been shot. I was no expert, but it seemed from the placement of the hole that her injury wouldn't have been fatal, if she'd been able to get treatment quickly enough. She wasn't here, but where had she gone?

"Gena?" I said out loud, which was dumb. The cave swallowed the sound of my voice. Gena wasn't here.

I left the sweater where I'd found it and wriggled out of the cave, extending my legs first, gripping the sides of the narrow gap and making sure my feet were securely placed on the ledge before trying to stand upright.

The ledge ended here. Beyond this point, the cliff wall curved sharply inward. The drop became sheer; I risked a glance down and saw I was standing above a small cove, not a rocky beach. If I fell from right here, I'd land in the water. My body could be swept out to sea and never be found.

Much like Gena's body hadn't been found . . .

Gena couldn't have gone any farther in this direction. Wherever Gena had gone, I wasn't going to find her tonight, and it was time to get the police involved.

I was preparing to climb back up when I heard Ronnie shout. Just once, an unintelligible cry of surprise or pain or both. He might have been saying a word, but it was lost in the sound of the pouring rain. Replaying it now in my mind, my memory fills in the sound of a pop, a single silenced gunshot, but I don't trust my recollections; I think I just heard Ronnie yell, and that was enough for me to know that Linus had shot him.

Because I'd been kind of dumb all along, and I hadn't put together what should have been blindingly obvious. Earlier this evening, Linus had told me he had dinner plans. Ronnie had tidied up the place. Linus came over for dinner with Ronnie once a week, on Saturdays. Today was Saturday. The whole time he was talking to me, Ronnie had been expecting Linus.

I stayed where I was, heart pounding in a dramatic and painful staccato that seemed like a prelude to a cardiac arrest. My car was parked out front; Linus would know I was here. He would have asked Ronnie about me, about what I knew, before killing him.

He surely wouldn't look for me over the side of the cliff. Going down here to search for Gena had been a reckless impulse. If I stayed exactly where I was until I was certain Linus had left, I'd be fine.

My fingers, which had grown white and swollen and sore from gripping jagged wet rocks, had lost all feeling. For the first time since embarking on tonight's adventure, I felt a burst of vertigo, the ground beneath my feet advancing and receding, pulsing up and down to match the rhythm of my heartbeat.

Then the light of a flashlight bobbed over the side of the cliff. I looked up just as it hit me in the face. I couldn't see anything beyond the bright white beam, but I could hear him, the ocean noise making it seem as though he was calling to me from very far away, even though he was right above my head: "Hi, Jenny."

CHAPTER 28

Cheap at Five

Linus moved the beam of his phone down from my face to my feet. I couldn't see much of him from where he stood at the top of the cliff, not far above my head, but I caught a glimpse of his other hand, and it was empty. I supposed that was good, but really, nothing about the situation could be classified as good.

Satisfied there'd be room for him, Linus lowered himself down to the ledge beside me. Of course I should have rushed at him immediately. One well-aimed push, and I could have sent him to the rocks below.

I missed my chance, my mind frozen and blank. Linus stuffed his phone into the front pocket of his nylon zippered jacket, which looked much warmer and snugger than my damp, dirty hoodie. He kept his hand in his pocket. His gun would be there, of course, and at some point he'd pull it out and shoot me, and that would be the end of that.

He was three feet away from me, maybe less. I gripped the cliffside with both hands, because my knees felt like they weren't planning on supporting me much longer. "I saw your car," he said. "What are you doing here?" He had to shout to be heard above the roar of the ocean, though he still managed to seem more curious than hostile.

"I was looking for Gena," I said. "They didn't find her body on the rocks below, so I was curious where she went."

"What makes you think she'd be here?" he asked.

I shrugged, the gesture lost in the folds of MMP's oversized hoodie. "She went over the side, didn't she?"

"You tell me." There was a small smile playing on Linus's lips, a smile I really didn't like. "Is this a psychic thing?"

"Sure, why not? Let's say it is." I didn't know where I was going with this. My mind spun in useless circles. I could go inside the cave, maybe, and the entrance might be too narrow for Linus to follow me, but even if I managed to wriggle through that gap before he shot me, I'd be trapped in there, and he could stand outside the opening and fire bullets in my general direction until he killed me. I could jump down the remaining distance and take my chances in the water.

Or I could push Linus off the ledge, somehow. That seemed like it would have the best shot at a positive outcome, but the highest degree of difficulty in execution. Linus probably outweighed me by a good fifty pounds, and he kept himself in great shape. If we grappled, I'd be the one to go over.

In any case, I had to keep him talking. "Gena tried to run for it after you shot Serge, right? You shot her while chasing her out here, and she went over the side."

Linus shook his head slowly, that amused smile still on his face. "Why would I shoot my friends?"

"You had to keep Gena from telling the client that she planned to break her contract. You needed that commission."

His brows went up immediately. My knowledge shocked him, and I felt an inappropriate sense of triumph. Maybe he'd genuinely think my psychic powers were real. Excellent. I could die knowing I'd fooled a murderer.

After an uncertain moment, the smile broadened. "And what about Serge?" he asked.

"Gena told him she was breaking the contract. Serge would have supported that, maybe even suggested it; from what Malis said during your dinner party, he'd been against the collaboration from the start. Gena had been thinking over some things in her life, and it seems like Serge had been helping her through that," I said. I didn't know this part of Linus's motivation, but I could make some good guesses. "You were furious with Gena for taking that money away from you, and you were furious with Serge for supporting her. Doing it here at Serge's home made it seem like Serge was the main target, and that suited your purposes."

His eyes locked with mine, Linus nodded as I spoke. "They'd changed, both of them," he said. "It's very nice that they had more important things in their lives than money, but they both had more money than they needed. My business was going under. My commission was spent before I received it. I was slipping behind on my mortgage, and it was looking like I could lose the condo. You might understand, Jenny. You know what it feels like to fall behind."

"Sure, absolutely," I said. My throat was beginning to feel raw. "I got kicked out of my place of business because I was living in it after getting kicked out of my apartment because I wasn't earning enough income to stay above the poverty line. That's pretty much exactly the same as losing my multimillion-dollar condo."

Linus frowned. He took a step closer to me, and I took one step back, trying to avoid any sudden actions that would alarm him while still staying out of shoving distance. "Don't be like that. You've always been cool," he said. "You know money is relative. You're poor compared to me, I'm poor compared to Serge. Serge was poor compared to, I don't know, Bezos or Musk or whoever. Compared to some orphan on the streets of Brazil, you might as well be Bezos. Don't start playing the poverty one-upmanship game with me. Let's both agree that having money makes things easier than not having money, and leave it at that."

I could argue the point, and indeed I wanted to, very much, but I had more important things on my mind at the moment. "Ronnie told you I figured it out, right?" I asked. "Did you shoot him for that, or were you planning on killing him anyway?"

Linus smiled again. "You seem to have a lot of thoughts about what I've been doing," he said. "You tell me."

"I'm guessing he was doomed. You came here to kill him. That's why you brought the gun tonight," I said. "You'd kill him with the gun he got for you, the same gun that killed Serge, and you'd leave it with him. Maybe investigators would assume he killed Serge and Gena before shooting himself. His ankle monitor record won't match that story, and it certainly wouldn't explain Brynna, but maybe they'd be able to come up with some theory to fit everything."

"Ronnie had to go," Linus said. He tilted his head to the side and seemed to consider the subject. "I'm sorry about that, I really am, but he was a danger to me."

"Like Brynna?" I asked. "I suppose sticking her corpse in my room instead of leaving her in the den was meant to draw suspicion to me, right?"

"No. No way. I knew nothing bad would come to you from that, other than giving you a nasty shock, which wasn't what I wanted. Out of everyone in Gena's circle, you were the one with no motive." Linus looked genuinely nice, and I was grimly reminded that I'd liked him. I'd slept with him. Jesus. "I couldn't leave her in the den. Her corpse would stink, and the longer the detectives kept out of that den, the better for me."

"Bodies are starting to pile up, Linus," I said. "You so sure you're not going to get caught?"

"Pretty sure, yeah," he said. "Ronnie will look like a suicide, which is a tidy enough solution to a messy problem; no one is going to look too hard for a more complicated explanation. The investigation will be closed, the client will be satisfied that Ronnie killed Serge and Gena, and I can collect the commission."

"But you don't know for certain that Gena's dead, do you?" I said. "Gena knew these cliffs. She'd lived in this house. She'd probably climbed down to reach the beach many times before. She was injured, but where's her body?"

"If she was alive, she would have turned up by now." I thought Linus looked worried, but he might have just been concentrating, thinking about how he was going to have to kill me soon. "Your psychic powers got one thing wrong, by the way: I shot her first. They answered the door together, and I hit her in the shoulder, and then I shot Serge in the face. She bolted past me and headed straight for the cliffs. Idiot move, not going to the street."

"She knew the backyard," I said. "Like I said, she knew these cliffs. Even injured, she knew she could escape from you here. And it sounds like she did."

"Yeah." Linus's mouth was an angry line. "I shone the flashlight around, and she wasn't anywhere I could see. Not clinging to the cliffs, not on the rocks below. I figure she slipped and fell into the water."

"Maybe that happened. Maybe she got swept out to sea instead of falling on the rocks," I said. "You think you're lucky enough to have the same thing happen to me? It's going to be tricky for you if they find me on that strip of land below us with a gunshot wound. Or is Ronnie going to get the blame for that as well?"

"I've been thinking about that. I'm going to have to push you over." It was said in a matter-of-fact way, like he was breaking a minor bit of bad news, like he was going to have to end our dinner date early. "It will look like you slipped. You've been mucking around this investigation so much already that the cops won't think too hard about what you were doing here."

Damn it all, he might be right. "You've killed four people, Linus. Was it worth it just for that commission?"

He smiled then, no trace of warmth anywhere on his face, and I felt a sense of mortal danger. "Cheap at five," he said.

I was moving before he lunged. I wanted to go up, but he would yank me down before I could get to the top of the cliff, so I had to head for the cave. I didn't hear him behind me, but I expected him to chase me.

Instead, he shot me in the back.

It was almost noiseless, and it didn't feel anything at all like what I always expected a bullet wound to feel like, which was something like an intense burning pain confined to a small area. This felt like a wrecking ball slamming into my right shoulder, and the force of it knocked me to my hands and knees. My left foot slid off the ledge and dangled in midair, and the rest of my body almost followed it.

It was only luck that kept me on the ledge. I felt a tug at the hood of my sweatshirt. He was going to grab me, and once he had me, he'd toss me over the side. I scrambled forward, still on hands and knees, yanking out of his grip. I got to my feet and dove for the opening of the cave, finding it by memory instead of sight.

Linus grabbed the waistband of my jeans and hauled me back. He said something that was lost in the roar of the ocean, and I gripped the sides of the jagged gap that served as the cave opening. I put one sneaker-clad foot on the bottom ledge of the cave, and I mule-kicked back with the other foot with as much force as I could manage. My foot connected with one of his kneecaps, hard and strong, and I heard his shout of surprise and alarm.

I wriggled through the gap, expecting at any moment to feel Linus's hands grabbing me again. I tumbled forward and landed on my hands and knees on the damp cave floor, the jolt sending a blast of pure agony into my wounded shoulder. My arms crumpled beneath my weight; I ended up flopping over onto my back, helpless, waiting for the end.

Inside the cave, everything was dark and quiet, and when I was able to raise my head enough to look toward the entrance, I saw no one on the ledge.

CHAPTER 29

Gena

I saw her then, in the cave. Gena.

No gunshot wound. She looked healthy and dry, crouched beside me, dressed in leggings and a loose black linen tank top that was far too lightweight for this rainy November evening. Her hair was uncombed, hanging in tangles around her shoulders.

I lay on my back and stared up at her; she looked down at me and smiled. She didn't show her teeth, just pulled her mouth into a small curve.

You're going to have to be tougher than I was, she said to me. Only she didn't say anything, anything at all, just stood there a few paces away. She spoke without moving her lips, and I wanted to ask her how she managed that trick, how she managed to transmit her thoughts directly into my brain. Maybe I was reading her mind, or maybe she was reading mine. Or maybe I was bleeding out, dying, hallucinating an image of Gena, the woman I'd been searching for and would never find.

Or maybe I was talking to a ghost.

I thought I could wait Linus out, then climb to safety. But I lost too much blood. I was dizzy. I still hadn't gained my strength back after my surgery, and my arms couldn't pull me up. I lost my grip trying to get to the top, and I fell. I missed the rocks and landed in the cove. I was too cold to swim, too weak to get to the surface. The undertow took me.

"That's what I thought had happened," I said. I spoke out loud, my voice muffled by the rush of noise of the water outside. "Not a psychic vision or anything, but it just sort of made sense to me." As soon as I said it, I felt a sense of shame, like I was bragging about how clever I was while Gena was telling me how she died. "Why'd you take *The Divide* from me?" I asked, because that was the thing I'd planned to ask Gena all along, the most important question, even though right now I couldn't remember why.

I wanted it to be mine. Gena frowned. *You were magical in it, so beautiful and brilliant. And I felt like that film was a part of me, something that belonged to me in the same way it belonged to you. That film was our shared experience; you understand that now, don't you? I'm sorry I took credit for it. But you're the one who gets to live, so I think it's all fair.*

"I guess so," I said, and when she put it like that, it did seem fair, so I couldn't argue the point any further. I tried to say something else, but then I started coughing, and it dawned on me that the feeling of being hit by a wrecking ball was evolving into something different, something white-hot, like my empty rib cage was filled with coals.

You're losing blood, Gena said. *Come on. Get your shit together, Jenny.*

"You're going to have to help me," I said. "I can't do it by myself." I reached out for her, feeling an agony of fire shoot through my chest at the movement. She extended her hand to take mine, but my fingers closed around nothing but air.

And she was gone, because of course she'd never been there.

My chest was growing hotter every moment even as my hands and legs were growing cold and numb, and I needed to move, or I would die here. It took me a million years to wriggle around onto my stomach and slither to the opening of the cave. I crawled out on my belly, rocks digging into my abdomen through MMP's sweatshirt. This was the perilous part. This was what had killed Gena; she'd lost her balance here, right where the ledge ended.

I don't have a clear memory of climbing up, though I suspect my ascent took another million years, and honestly, I'm just thankful I had the strength to haul my soaking-wet deadweight up the short distance to the surface with one shoulder out of commission. At the top of the cliff, I just wanted to lie on my belly, ankles and feet dangling over the edge, and take a quick nap.

I got to my feet, somehow, and made it to Ronnie's cottage. Linus had turned out the lights when he left, and it took me too long to find the switch.

Ronnie looked terrible in death, his skin gray white in the light of the ceiling lamp, his eyes open. He sat upright, head tilted against the back of the sofa. There was a small hole in his right temple and minimal blood. Linus would have come back here after killing me to leave the gun, probably after making sure to get the powder burns right; he would have wrapped Ronnie's hand around it and fired it, aiming out through the door and over the cliff where the bullet would never be found.

"I'm really sorry, Ronnie," I said, but it came out as a dusty croak, because my voice was shot after yelling my way through that whole conversation with Linus on the cliff.

Since I'd lost my own phone, I had to touch Ronnie's corpse to get his from his pocket. I couldn't unlock it, but that didn't matter, because at least I was able to dial 911.

CHAPTER 30

An Exception

My first visitor at the hospital was Detective Moreau, looking as unruffled and humorless as ever. When I woke from a nap, she was right at my bedside, seated in a hard plastic chair, staring at me. "How's it going, Jenny?" she asked.

I could remember fragmented bits and pieces of everything that had happened after I'd reached Ronnie's cottage: being loaded into the back of an ambulance in the pouring rain, sailing on a gurney down a long bright hallway, and waking up, head thick and foggy with anesthesia, to reassurances from a calm yet exhausted doctor that my surgery had gone as planned. That had been the previous night; I'd spent the day thus far alternating between sleeping in short bursts and wondering, through the addled haze of whatever painkillers they were keeping me on, what was happening in the outside world.

I tried to sit up, but that seemed beyond me. It didn't hurt to move, exactly, but it felt like it *should* hurt, like my brain was keenly aware that the painkillers were trying to gaslight it into thinking all was well. I felt stiff and numb, and like my body was three times the size it should be. "I think I'm okay, mostly,"

I said. “But nobody’s been able to tell me anything. Is Linus dead?”

“Not unless he’s gone into the great beyond since I last checked in. He’s at Cedars. He fractured his spine when he hit the water, but he managed to make it to the rocks along the shore, which is where we picked him up.” Moreau shrugged. She was dressed in a navy pantsuit. I couldn’t tell if it was the exact same one she’d worn both other times I’d seen her, but I thought it probably was. It looked great on her, so she was smart to wear it a lot. Maybe she had multiple identical navy pantsuits. “Might be paralyzed, too soon to tell.”

I couldn’t work up much emotion about that either way. “Is he under arrest?” I had a flash of memory of spilling out my guts to the sheriff’s deputy who arrived on the scene just after the ambulance, a nervous-looking kid who hovered by my side as I lay on a stretcher, the EMTs trying to get him to back off as I kept talking at him, telling him all about Linus and Brynna and Serge and Ronnie and Gena. Probably mostly about Gena, and it’d be good to know if anything I’d said had made any sense at all.

Moreau nodded. “He’s awake and angry and already lawyered up the wazoo, so he’s not saying anything to anyone.” She smiled, cool and sardonic. “Doesn’t matter. We’ve got him. Now that we know where to look, we’ll find plenty of evidence to nail his ass.”

She sounded confident, and I felt a flicker of triumph. Linus was alive, and he was under arrest, and that was almost entirely because of me.

Moreau leaned closer. “You fucked around in my investigation a lot,” she said.

“Yeah.” I nodded. I had to resist the urge to smile. Moreau sounded annoyed, but I had the strong suspicion it was mostly an act, that she respected what I’d accomplished, that she knew I’d done something remarkable.

“You posed as Gena to talk to her shrink about her private

life. You moved into Gena's goddamned house. You snooped around and questioned Halpern, Ronald Kostan, Matthew Mark Park, Malis Sao, Elizabeth Pontifex, everyone. You got everyone pissed off at you."

I didn't think that was true. Most of those people seemed to think I was okay. Some of them even liked me. Earlier, a health-care assistant had dropped off some deliveries, which now rested on a table beneath the room's sole window; I'd been too weak and groggy to investigate them in depth, but I figured the white orchid in an exquisite celadon pot was from Malis, while the Pokémon-themed balloon bouquet could only be MMP's contribution. Outshining those, however, was the open picnic hamper crammed with what I suspected was Eternality's entire fall product line, crowned with a glossy blue box emblazoned with gold letters. The box made me break into a loopy, stupid grin every time I saw it: Boots had given me a Dead Sea Dazzler.

"I found out who killed Serge and Gena. And Brynna," I told Moreau. I swallowed, my throat dry, my tongue thick and awkward. Talking seemed difficult and foreign; it felt like a dead toad was living in my mouth. "I might've gotten Ronnie killed. I don't feel good about that. But I stopped Linus. I did that."

Moreau made some kind of clicking noise that sounded almost, but not quite, maternal. I wondered if she had kids. Or nieces and nephews whom she yelled at a lot, but whom she secretly adored. "It's not worth your time feeling precious about Kostan. That guy was a criminal. Dumb as all hell, too. Seems like he was wrapped up in it about as deep as he can be. Halpern was the killer, but Kostan gave him a hand."

I wanted to tell her that Ronnie was okay, that he was just trying to be loyal to an old friend, but of course she was right. He'd been dumb, and he should have known better. He *did* know better, and he covered for Linus anyway, and that made it worse. I felt a sad urge to defend him, but couldn't find the words.

Moreau waited for me to say something further, then eventually shook her head. She picked up her shoulder bag. "I need a statement from you," she said. "Doesn't have to be right now, but as soon as you're able."

"It'll be a while," I said. "Not feeling too chatty at the moment."

"I don't doubt it. You look like hot garbage." Moreau rose to her feet. She turned toward the door, then paused and faced me again. She hesitated before speaking. "You told the deputy at the scene Gena went over the cliff into the water. You know that for a fact?"

"She's in the ocean," I said. "She went along the cliff and tried to climb up at the far edge of Serge's property, but she was injured, and she fell into this little cove. She'd been hiding from Linus in a cave on the cliff face. You missed it, or your people missed it when they were searching Serge's property."

"A cave?" Moreau's brows drew together, and her focus was laserlike.

"Yeah. It's hard to see. The opening blends into the rocks. I wouldn't have spotted it if lightning hadn't struck, making the entrance cast just the right shadow. I think I told the deputy about it, but I'm not sure I was making any sense, so don't blame him if he didn't pass the word along. But it's there." Carrying on a conversation was exhausting; I felt the urge to drift off into sleep again. "When you find it, you'll find Gena's sweater in there, with her blood on it. She slipped off the ledge when she was trying to climb up. There aren't any rocks beneath that spot. She fell into the water and went out with the undertow."

"Did Linus tell you this?"

"He didn't see it happen." I closed my eyes. "Gena told me."

Moreau's voice sounded like she was speaking from the end of a very long tunnel. "You said you didn't talk to the dead."

With an effort, I opened my eyes again. Moreau's face looked funny, like she was trying to maintain her usual composed and aloof exterior, but some kind of weird emotions were bleeding through the cracks. Spooked. Moreau was spooked.

"I made an exception," I said.

Acknowledgments

Boundless gratitude is due to my smart and tenacious agent, Kerry Sparks, for fishing my manuscript out of her slush pile and knowing exactly what should be done with it, and to my editor, Caitlin Landuyt, who deftly excavated new layers from my writing while helping me gain a deeper understanding of Jenny and her world. I'm also grateful to the entire team at Levine Greenberg Rostan, particularly Rebecca Rodd for her insightful notes, and to everyone at Knopf for drawing on their formidable skills and knowledge to guide this book through the publication process. Thank you as well to Kristina Moore and Jason Richman at UTA for their early enthusiasm, and for comparing *The Divide* to *Vertigo*, *Double Indemnity*, and *The Big Lebowski;* as a noir buff, I beam with happiness every time I think of it.

Some friends and loved ones who absolutely must be mentioned: Emiliana Dore read an early draft and gave me precise, useful feedback; Em, you are, as always, the best. Valerie Edwards provided pep talks and mimosas to put me back together whenever I started to unravel. My enigmatic and very cool friend

Francisco doled out crucial pieces of advice on too many occasions to count. Sincere thanks also go to Joe Richter and Elsbeth Monnett for their love and support; to Sarah Kurchak for her wry intelligence; to the fabulous David Orwick, who hopefully won't be disappointed by the lack of Duran Duran references anywhere in the book (I know, David, it surprised me too); to Ernest Cline for his boundlessly generous spirit throughout the years; to Ty Talbot and Julie Sponsler, who, along with Mark and Kara Odegard, are unbeatable dinner companions; and to Heather Stewart and Alex Albrecht, who serve as shining examples of how Los Angeles, contrary to its reputation, is a great place to find smart, funny, interesting people.

My experience working in Hollywood was considerably less fraught with angst than Jenny's, and with that in mind, I'd like to thank someone who ranks way, way up there on my list of all-time favorite people: the hilarious John Henson, who, along with the entire staff and crew of *Talk Soup*, made my first job in the entertainment industry a sheer delight.

Most of all, thank you to my brainy and witty sister, Ingrid, the only person in the world with whom I could share a tiny studio apartment during a global pandemic without coming to tears or blows. Ingrid has been ridiculously patient with me over the years, lending me support of all kinds and providing me with a safety net in uncertain times; she is wonderful, and she deserves all the best things life has to offer.

I wish my parents were around for this. They were brilliant and dazzling and awesome; I wish you all could have met them. Erich and Verna Richter, you are always loved and always missed, and everything I have accomplished or might someday accomplish is due to the foundation you built when you raised me. Thank you with all my heart.

A NOTE ABOUT THE AUTHOR

Morgan Richter is a graduate of the Filmic Writing Program at the University of Southern California's film school and has worked in production on several television shows, including ABC's *America's Funniest Home Videos* and E! Entertainment Television's Emmy-winning comedy series *Talk Soup*. An avid popular culture critic, she is the author of *Duranalysis: Essays on the Duran Duran Experience* and has amassed a cult following on her breakdown of classic Duran Duran videos. Morgan currently lives in Seattle.

A NOTE ON THE TYPE

This book was set in Minion, a typeface produced by the Adobe Corporation specifically for the Macintosh personal computer and released in 1990. Designed by Robert Slimbach, Minion combines the classic characteristics of old-style faces with the full complement of weights required for modern typesetting.

Composed by North Market Street Graphics
Lancaster, Pennsylvania

Printed and bound by Berryville Graphics
Berryville, Virginia

Designed by Nicholas Alguire